STAR

VULC
SO

BO

EXI

STAR TREK®
VULCAN'S SOUL
BOOK II
EXILES

JOSEPHA SHERMAN & SUSAN SHWARTZ

**BASED UPON *STAR TREK*
CREATED BY GENE RODDENBERRY**

POCKET BOOKS

New York   London   Toronto   Sydney   Triskelion

POCKET BOOKS, a division of Simon & Schuster, Inc.
1230 Avenue of the Americas, New York, NY 10020

STAR TREK is a Registered Trademark of Paramount Pictures.

This book is published by Pocket Books, a division of Simon & Schuster, Inc., under exclusive license from Paramount Pictures.

ISBN-13: 978-0-7434-6359-1
ISBN-10:   0-7434-6359-5

This Pocket Books hardcover edition June 2006

10 9 8 7 6 5 4 3 2 1

POCKET and colophon are registered trademarks of Simon & Schuster, Inc.

Manufactured in the United States of America

For information regarding special discounts for bulk purchases, please contact Simon & Schuster Special Sales at 1-800-456-6798 or business@simonandschuster.com.

For my godchildren,
Elly and Peter,
who are the future . . .
S.S.

Dedicated to the *Star Trek* fans
everywhere who are always
happy to "boldly go" with us!
J.S.

The authors would like to thank Diane Duane for paving the way, Geoff Landis for invaluable assistance, and Marco Palmieri and Keith R.A. DeCandido for taking over.

STAR TREK®

VULCAN'S SOUL

BOOK II

EXILES

ONE

MEMORY

*"We left Vulcan on the Fifth of Tasmeen. Since then, it
has been a day of remembrance on all the great ships
that survive."*

Before embracing exile, Karatek had been a physicist at the Vulcan Space Institute in a ShiKahr he would never see again. Now that Vulcan was receding fast, both in fact and in memory, the Fifth of Tasmeen had become a day of meditation and reflection. Thus, it was Karatek's duty to ask: Was it the fleet that needed the Fifth of Tasmeen, or Karatek himself?

He glanced out into the long night. Here were few stars. No planets; therefore no new home. Beside the viewscreen were hangings woven in traditional designs. His consort had hung them in his meditation chamber to soften the severity of the bulkheads. They fluttered constantly as air circulated through the ship like blood through a heart.

The air was cold. It smelled of chemicals, not the wild sweetness of the desert as the sun erupted up from the horizon, turning the cold into blazing heat and dazzling light, shimmering off the crimson sand.

Karatek focused on the gleaming crystals and bloodmetal circuits of his coronet.

Of all the tasks he performed as one of *Shavokh*'s leaders, Karatek thought the duty of remembrance was probably the most valuable. Certainly it was the one for which he was best suited. The thought, as it always did, brought some reassurance. He had reluctantly inherited the task of command, and it still came hard to him. Most of the people he would have preferred to follow were long dead.

He adjusted the coronet. His hair was brittle from the air, even more arid than that of Vulcan. It had begun to gray earlier than it would have done on the homeworld, assuming he had managed to survive the battles that had been the Mother World's daily lot.

From years of making this record, he knew that the great green gems that were the coronet's memory, created in an art banned by the adepts both of Gol and Mount Seleya, pulsed in time with the beat of the blood in his temples. Wrapped around the glowing crystals were fine-drawn unbreakable metal wires. Clad with bloodmetal, the wires formed intricate lattices that simultaneously ornamented the memory device and linked into his cerebral cortex through filaments almost too delicate to be felt.

The tiny wounds those wires inflicted every time he set the coronet on his head stung for a moment longer as they healed. They would reopen when he removed the crown. But the pain did not matter. As Surak said, there *was* no pain.

Certainly, there was not pain enough to interrupt the thoughts, memories, sensations, and even the emotions—for even after years of study of Surak's disciplines, Karatek's emotional control remained imperfect—that the memory device would capture and record for all the years of exile and afterward, when they finally found a new homeworld. If that day ever came in the long night of their exile.

It was Karatek's habit to combine meditation and memory. But the task that Surak had personally entrusted to him turned bitter every Fifth of Tasmeen when he recalled events from the past year and sealed them in the coronet's memory.

"I could make the calculation, if I chose, of today's date on the Mother World. At our current speed, while 3.9 years have passed on board this ship and its consorts, 25.86 years have passed on Vulcan. Obviously, today is not the Fifth of Tasmeen back on Vulcan. Although some who follow Surak deem hope to be illogical, I cannot agree: Surak might have been ruthless, but he was never cruel. Therefore, I believe it is not illogical to hope that the homeworld has survived and that finally—after all the bloodshed—it may live long and prosper, as Lady Mitrani wished us. She may still be alive. I hope she is well.

"On all the ships that have survived thus far, other memories occupy us today. It is with grief that I must record the loss of seven ships."

Karatek took a deep breath. He organized his thoughts, then marshaled all his courage before he made himself pour the memories of that loss into the coronet's glowing green gems. He recalled faces that, from now on, he would see only in memory, and knew the crown would preserve them for all times. Tears blurred his vision before the veils flicked across his eyes, preventing precious moisture from evaporating in the dry air of this chamber where art from home fluttered in a ceaseless artificial breeze.

Those ships that died had acted in error. They had paid for their error with their lives. And Karatek had failed to dissuade them. Their blood was on his hands.

In the last council among all the ships that traveled like a caravan across the Forge through this greater desert of stars, Karatek had heard a propulsion model advocated by an unlikely, possibly unholy, alliance of technocrat party functionaries with two of the adepts from Gol. Much to the council's not-well-concealed astonishment, they had even been joined by some of the te-Vikram who had found themselves trapped on board the great ships when they left at the start of what had to be, it just had to be, the last civil war on Vulcan.

The new propulsion model, admittedly, had at first been intriguing. It fused technology with the arts of the mind in a way that Gol adepts had once condemned as blasphemy. Those same scruples, Karatek recalled, had caused the priestess at the shrine atop Mount Seleya to hand over to Surak the crown of memory that Karatek now held.

But, ultimately, the new system was bad politics and worse science, Karatek had decided. He had refused to consider it for *Shavokh*. And he had argued against its implementation on any of the ships with all the authority of his training as a physicist and his experience as a propulsion engineer.

What had become of the logic of the adepts who advocated its use? For them to abandon their former scruples— Karatek shuddered. Seven ships went against the council's vote and installed the new propulsion system.

How triumphantly they must have raced ahead, Karatek imagined. *You see, the augmented drive works! When we return to the fleet, we shall tell Karatek how wrong he was! And then, we shall bring the ships home.*

Those ships had raced off like boys who dashed ahead of their friends on a dare, looking back to laugh or jeer, only to find that their mad dash forward had taken them to the *le-matya*'s den or to the edge of a precipice with no time to stop, no rock or root to grab to save themselves.

They had left themselves no margin for error and therefore no escape.

Karatek shook his head: how illogical it was of him to seek to deny his memory and the evidence of his own ship's sensors. But, in strict honesty, let the coronet record his denial too. Something hot trickled down his temple: he had jarred loose one of the filaments that bound him to the coronet.

In the most ancient rites, blood had been used as a sacrifice to appease the *katra*s of travelers lost in the desert, spirits blowing on the wind until they dissolved.

You, alone of all on board this ship, traveled with Surak. Though your journey now is greater, that is still no reason to lose control, he chided himself. The coronet would capture his self-recrimination as well as his mourning.

His memories would be preserved, but what of the thoughts and emotions, even the *katra*s of the people on board those lost ships? For the initial acceleration trial, the Gol adepts had been linked to brother and sister adepts on other ships. Some of those adepts had burned themselves out. Some had died as hearts and blood vessels burst from the strain.

Others survived, if one wished to call it life. Of the survivors, some howled, while others sat or lay soiled, mindless, and silent, a burden on family and healers who would tend them gently until their lives' ends, for there was no desert into which they could walk, had they been able to move. And it was thought blasphemy to assist them out into the Long Night.

As for the seven lost ships—Karatek hoped that gravitic strains would have made their engines explode. There had always been that possibility. The minute structural weaknesses he had distrusted would, at least, have given the people within a quick, merciful, and *sane* death before the black hole that had opened before them sucked them into a night devoid even of stars.

Perhaps if Karatek had argued more forcefully, if he had explained more clearly to Commissioner T'Partha how risky that drive was, the ships now lost to the exiles' fleet would still be traveling alongside *Shavokh* across this trackless forge of stars.

The catastrophe had caused some of the scientists who followed Surak to theorize that a chance—perhaps 1.3 percent, perhaps even less—existed that at least one of the ships might have survived a transit through the madness of space, light, and gravity into which they had plunged. Perhaps, if an exit were possible, such a ship might emerge in some other place, near some other star that might possess even one *Minshara*-class world and, in this second exile, finally find itself a home. The mathematics of that theory were dubious: cold comfort, if logic could be considered comfort. What was, was.

Karatek's eyes scalded. This much of his own disgrace he could spare future generations, he told himself.

He pulled the coronet off. A brief warmth, almost as hot as the tears he fought to suppress, spread at his temples as the filaments withdrew. His biocontrol healed the tiny wounds almost instantly. The pain of memory lingered.

The coronet glowed in his hands, the flicker in the crystals almost as subtle as the whisper of micrometeorites and dust as they brushed against the ship's hull. Useful finds of tritanium and duranium had enabled the surviving engineers to strengthen the ships' hulls in case they had to last well beyond initial estimates of one hundred years.

For all the emphasis on safety, the obsessive care the exiles took to strengthen their ships in case the journey lasted past even the most pessimistic estimates, they had made no advance that wasn't accompanied by accidents. A barrage of delta rays, two years ago, had taken out half of one ship's population and exposed the remainder to radiation that would, no doubt, shorten their lives, make their deaths more painful, and reap a deadly harvest among any children they dared to have.

Among the survivors had been a cadre of the fiercely independent te-Vikram, whose priest-kings had plunged Vulcan into at least three wars and constant border skirmishes in the past hundred years. A raid on the shuttles that carried the exiles to their ships had resulted in te-Vikram coming on board. They had never wanted to be there.

The surviving te-Vikram had seized the opportunity of catastrophic crew loss to stage a mutiny, wrest control of the ship from its surviving crew, and turn back. Karatek had watched that ship explode as its engineers, loyal to the fleet, staged a desperate, final rebellion. He himself had trained at least two of them. In physics, not in logic.

Karatek remembered the explosion as well as the pain of recalling it. The gems that were his coronet's eternal memory flickered, the rainbows buried in their depth shimmering, and he realized that his tears had fallen on them.

Where is your control?

Karatek tightened his hand on the artifact. Even though crystals and metal pressed into his skin, the coronet felt agreeably warm in his hands. At the last council, a vote had been taken to decrease some elements of life support. Vulcan's air had been thin; it was no sacrifice to reduce oxygen content. And a slightly lower gravity actually made them feel stronger than they were and gave them greater ease in manipulating heavy engine components or hull plating.

But Karatek had never quite accustomed himself to the cold. They could drape the bulkheads with weavings created here on the looms built for the workshops psychologists had deemed necessary to help ease the bleakness of the ship's environment. They could fill compartments with art: a geode found on a mining expedition; a ceramic representation, made by his adopted son Solor, of the *shavokh* for which this ship was named. They could wear warmer tunics and cloaks over their shipsuits. But the ship was still cold.

An incentive, of course, to find a new homeworld and find it soon. Illogical to have mixed feelings about that idea. Illogical to admit to feelings at all.

"If I forget thee, O Vulcan . . ." Karatek murmured. He squeezed his eyes shut, trying to form a mantra of control before resuming the coronet and the torment of memory.

Sunlight on the sands outside ShiKahr, where the flanged gate had stood for millennia, where he had watched for pilgrims and caravans ever since he was a boy. Where he had seen Surak and two of his disciples emerge from the desert, take his life into their hands, and weave it, like a thread of bloodmetal, into the tapestry of their hopes and dreams for their people.

A soft chime sounded. Karatek's lips softened in what would have been, in the days before he met Surak, a smile as his consort T'Vysse slipped into his study. On this Fifth of Tasmeen, she wore the dulled blood green of mourning. The color did not suit her. But she was always beautiful to him.

Karatek rose as T'Vysse entered the room. She pressed one hand to the small of her back. She was pregnant now with what would be the fourth child of her body.

8

With the door open, he could hear shouting in the corridor outside their quarters.

"Your pardon, my husband," she said, with the impeccable manners that had been hers since childhood: the formal training of a well-born Vulcan. Their eldest daughter, dead these many years, had had similar manners, as did Sarissa, their adopted child, who combined them with the control she too had learned from Surak.

By now, their grandson—stranded back on Vulcan with his parents in the last dreadful moments of violence before the final shuttles lifted off the Mother World—might well have children of his own.

Children I shall never see. Descendants of my House.

There was some satisfaction in knowing that his House, if nothing else, would continue. Assuming that Vulcan itself survived.

As if sensing his thoughts through their bond, T'Vysse stepped close to him. Karatek held out joined fingers to touch her free hand, then used their handclasp to ease her into his chair.

This child-to-be, however, this child of their exile, would have everything that Karatek could provide despite the healers' concerns about the health of a child born in the long, radiation-filled transit between star and star. Healers, like physicists, adepts, and warriors, had been wrong before. They could be wrong again.

With T'Vysse present, her fingers brushing his, the tiny chamber held all the warmth of home.

"Thee has word?" he asked her, gazing into her eyes.

"The shuttle awaits. Its pilot begs pardon if thy meditations were interrupted, but he asks that thee come swiftly. To avoid further controversy."

Karatek raised a brow at his wife's choice of words. T'Vysse was a mistress of understatement.

The decision taken at the last council to limit travel between ships and postpone transfers of people or families from one ship to another had been unpopular. But "limit" and "postpone" were words that the exiles, like the Vulcans left so far behind them, had grown to distrust. As a result, any time a shuttle took off from any one of the ships, Karatek heard protests and charges of favoritism.

If *Shavokh* was cold, the shuttles would be colder. Karatek had helped modify their design, diverting most of their energy to propulsion lest they fall behind the fleet and, lacking the power to catch up, be marooned alone in the night—another reason that councils were infrequent now.

But there was another reason still, one that was barely whispered. After te-Vikram rebels had commandeered one ship, the council had calculated a 47.1 percent chance that too-easy transfers could allow factions to concentrate themselves in individual ships and gain power again. Would a te-Vikram ship willingly keep company with one crewed by Surak's disciples or Seleyan adepts?

"I will come now," Karatek said.

He would finish the recording later, he promised himself. Assuming he survived this meeting. And if he did not, T'Vysse had informed him that she would take up the burden of memory. The crown had been given to him. Well enough, then: the task was his. But if he laid it down, she was a historian and logically the one to take it over—even if Karatek hated to see her further burdened. Logically, however, if T'Vysse inherited the burden of memory, he would not be alive to see anything at all.

Draping a heavy ceremonial cloak woven in shades of muted crimsons over the dulled green of his mourning clothes, Karatek entered the larger cabin where his family spent much of their time. Solor and Sarissa waited for him there. So did Commissioner T'Partha, wrapped in an even heavier cloak of her favorite bronze, along with two members of ship's security.

Karatek remembered them well: Streon, a slim, intense man who played the flute when he was off duty, and tall, foursquare T'Via. They had been handpicked as recruits and specially trained for the exile by Karatek's old friend Commander Ivek. If no one had assassinated Ivek, he was probably many times a great-great-grandfather by now. If he were dead, well, Karatek only hoped that someone had managed to convey his *katra* to the Halls of Ancient Thought. Ivek had had the integrity of a man who had studied no philosophy but his duty.

"An honor guard?" Karatek asked, raising his eyebrows at T'Partha. "Commissioner, I hardly think . . ."

She had never been a woman for superfluous formality. Karatek knew that if he played the role of leader aboard *Shavokh*, he did so only with her cooperation.

"There is a crowd forming," T'Partha confirmed his fears. "You can hear it in the corridor. And it would be unwise to allow any provocation."

"From security or from the crowd?" asked Solor.

T'Vysse and Sarissa fixed him with identical glares.

"My brother's manners may be atrocious," Sarissa announced, "but his question is appropriate. That is why we will accompany you to the shuttle. All of us."

T'Vysse raised her eyebrows at Karatek as if picking up one of the antique swords that some people brought on board, either smuggled or as part of their weight allowance. Karatek knew better than to argue with her. More: she was right. Even the most battle-hardened te-Vikram would not offer violence to women who were visibly pregnant, like T'Vysse, or old enough to take a mate, like Sarissa, who remained unbonded after her betrothed since childhood had been slain in the desert defending her.

T'Partha drew herself up, always her habit before she arrived at

11

what she considered the sense of the meeting. No one sensed how opinions flowed into a consensus better than she or channeled the information to the scientific, technical, and security staff more diplomatically. She had greater skill with the arts of the mind than anyone else he knew who was not an indweller on Seleya or at Gol. He would rely on her at the coming council.

But right now, he would have to rely on her, as well as security, to get to the shuttle that would take him there.

Before leaving, his guards put on their helms. The heavy cheekpieces made them look curiously faceless, symbolizing the fact that the law was no respecter of persons.

That some on Vulcan disagreed with this maxim had been one cause of the exile. The rule of law: many had already died back on the homeworld to defend it. Now, each year, more in exile died to preserve it.

Streon and T'Via formed up ahead and behind Karatek and T'Partha. T'Vysse and their children joined what Karatek began to think of as a procession. Lovar, their middle son—the eldest now remaining to him—was standing watch. He had inherited Karatek's gift for science and his mother's dislike of the politics in which Karatek regretted involving her.

("Am I an indweller, to be thus secluded?" she had demanded of him. "We all dwell within these ships; seclusion is not only illogical, it is impossible.")

Streon reviewed the small party. As always, Karatek felt a moment's surprise that a security guard had chosen to take an S-name in honor of Surak, now long dead. But he supposed that keeping order was, in itself, a logical activity.

"Ready," Streon announced through the com link built into his helm and opened the door.

Noise erupted in the thin air as they walked down the corridor.

The bleakness of its metal walls had been concealed, partly, by a mosaic of the land around Seleya, worked in cubes of glass that gleamed in the steady overhead lights.

"Let us pass, let us pass," Streon's and T'Via's voices were insistent monotones as they guided Karatek, T'Partha at his side, past people who pressed against the mosaics. Someone had chipped away some of the tesserae that had gone to form the image of the Gate of ShiKahr. Karatek saw Streon pause and quite obviously make a mental note for future investigation: casual disregard for public property was a hazard to the ship, even in so small a thing. Survival lay in detail.

He knew better than to turn to see how T'Vysse fared. For one thing, she had already rebuked him with "I am only pregnant, not helpless" three times just in the last day. For another, he knew well that their children had taken her arms and were guiding her. Besides, he knew T'Via had medical training.

As they edged through the gesturing, shouting crowd—no Surak followers there, to be sure—T'Partha kept up a far-from-casual flow of conversation. Duty rosters. The agenda of the conference they were to attend. It was meant to reassure, and it more or less succeeded.

The guards whisked them into the welcome silence of the nearest ship's lift.

"No doubt the crowd will be worse at the shuttlebay," Karatek observed.

Behind him, T'Vysse sighed.

Do you regret the decision to leave home, my wife? Karatek forbore to ask. He remembered their small, walled villa in ShiKahr. Every creak in the walkway leading to it, every splash of the fountain in the pebbled courtyard, every line of the Forge beyond its walls came to mind, long gone, yet instantly familiar and loved beyond all logic. *We have here all we need: the hope of Vulcan's safety and of a better life at journey's end. And our integrity,* he told himself.

You protest overmuch.

Streon and T'Via tilted their heads, listening to the communications links inset in their helms. Their shoulders stiffened.

"I agree. We face quite the sendoff," T'Partha remarked.

Streon awarded her a nod, tribute to the logic of her conclusion, if not her irony—although Surak too had been a master of the ironic reply. Karatek had taken more than one blow from it.

"Brace yourself," Solor told his sister. With a composure that had more to do with familiarity than with any control he had learned from Surak, he disregarded her hiss of rebuke.

Even though Solor had legally been an adult for decades, his elder sister still sometimes tried to correct him. The results would have frustrated her profoundly if her control—and her courtesy—had not become so strong.

"How is it out there?" Karatek asked Streon.

"Crowded," he replied.

In a Vulcan ship! In a ship intended only to wage peace and find a new home! Karatek felt his eyes heat.

He had already disgraced himself once today; he would not do so again. And when he returned from the council, he promised himself he would spend more time in meditation and less time recording events of what had already become a most painful Fifth of Tasmeen indeed.

The lift door hissed open. The cries of the crowd pushed at him like heavy gravity. Government on board *Shavokh* was more personal and therefore noisier than on Vulcan.

Karatek and T'Partha had expected to be met by people protesting various policies, people pleading for a chance to rejoin families, for lab space, for permission to demonstrate a new technique to the council. They had even expected protests such as had confronted them in the corridor outside Karatek's quarters.

What they did not expect was what they saw blocking their access to the shuttle, which had withdrawn its long boarding ramp: a party of male te-Vikram, all but snarling at the security that, thus far, held them in check. They wore the gemmed regalia that Karetek knew they brought out only for the most solemn occasions. At their hips, they wore the triangular ceremonial blades of te-Vikram warrior-priests. They each held a long bundle, wrapped in green, glittering fabric that they unwrapped to produce a *lirpa*, one end bladed, the other a blunt, deadly war-hammer. When they presented arms, three additional te-Vikram stepped forward. Two carried *systra*s. As they jangled the metal frames, the hundreds of bells strung on the instruments produced a painfully shrill chime that carried the message: *Pay attention. Here is danger.*

And there stood danger itself, unarmed, but potentially explosive.

The *systra* bearers flanked a man whose too-taut posture and blazing eyes were explained by the sash wound round his waist.

"How did *they* get in here?" T'Partha asked T'Via.

The guard murmured into the com built into her helm.

"Subterfuge," she replied. *"They claimed to have reserved a cargo hold for a religious rite. Under the circumstances"*—she gestured at the sashed man, clearly in the grips of the Blood Fires—*"that would only have been logical. A bonding ceremony would gain them access as well as the right to bring religious articles into the area. Once inside, they rushed the shuttlebay."*

"If there was to be a bonding," Solor asked, "where is this man's mate?"

It was a logical enough question. He edged his way out of the lift, moving toward his father.

"Observe the cloak on the deck," said Solor. "The color of pure water, running over silvery stone. A poor enough attempt at seclusion of the bondmate before the ceremony. Deceit is not quite honorable in the strictest tradition, but it allowed them to smuggle in one more warrior."

"Get back!" Streon's voice, raised to a most illogical pitch, echoed in the shuttlebay. After all, *Pon farr* was only an aspect of Vulcan biology, not a plague. As disciples of Surak, whose disciplines prescribed regular meditation, Solor and Streon were actually less likely to suffer from the deadliest aspects of the Fires.

That relative immunity to the Fires had also created some resentment on both sides: Surak's disciples considered the te-Vikram weak-willed, a judgment that the te-Vikram, understandably enough, resented, considering they deemed the people of the cities soft. And the question of mates had never been resolved to anyone's satisfaction.

T'Via's presence might be provocation, although she was a bonded woman. But the sight of Sarissa, unbonded and not even pledged, represented oil, ready to be poured upon a fire.

T'Partha directed a warning glance at Karatek. Seeing that no priestess or matriarch of the te-Vikram kin was present to conduct the rites—and no intended bride present—Karatek stepped forward.

"May one ask," he raised his voice, "what the problem is? Aside, of course, from the obvious," he added, with a glance toward the man in the grips of the Fires.

A cloaked te-Vikram pushed his way forward but was brought up short against Streon, who halted him. The cloaked man's hood fell back as he attempted to push past three more guards, who came up fast. Restrained, he stood there and simply glared. He was a man in late middle life, and though it had been many years since he, like the others of his clan, had walked the desert, his hair was still sun-reddened, his skin weathered.

"N'Keth!" Solor said. "Do you countenance this intrusion on my father's duties?"

The situation had just improved minutely, Karatek decided. N'Keth and Solor had a long history, since the time during Solor's rite of passage into legal adulthood when N'Keth had tried to kidnap the boy and take him back to his clan. Solor's counterattack, his escape, and their subsequent reunion on board the shuttle taking them all to the *Shavokh*, had made for a grudging, ironic respect over the years of the journey. And it hadn't hurt that Solor had interceded just when Rovalat, Solor's teacher for the *kahs-wan* ordeal, had been trying to pound N'Keth's head into a paste against a bulkhead.

"N'Veyan requires that shuttle," the te-Vikram elder told Solor. "His intended mate awaits him."

Karatek glanced quickly back at T'Partha. "The rule restricting travel was created to protect resources, not to cause madness and loss of life," he murmured. They could afford one shuttle trip if it would save N'Veyan's life and perhaps that of his intended mate. Many women could withstand the Fires without a mate, but there were always some who died.

T'Partha inclined her head. Her eyes were remote. "The law is the law. It is no respecter of persons."

"It is only a rule!" Sarissa said. "Surely, in this case, the needs of the one . . ."

Drawing a deep breath, T'Partha cast aside her cloak. She had aged during the journey, Karatek saw. There was a chance she might be considered a matriarch, venerable enough to mediate the ceremony of bonding, even one that still lacked a bride.

N'Veyan looked toward T'Partha like a pilgrim, lost in the desert, sighting water. He lurched forward as if he were going to attack, or fall. At the last moment, he steadied himself sufficiently to kneel at her feet.

T'Partha reached out with joined fingers to touch his temple. Her hand scarcely shook at all. Karatek revised upward his opinion of her yet again.

"My eyes are flame," N'Veyan whispered. "My blood is flame."

T'Partha's eyes filled with a cool pity. Perhaps this day of memory would not be marked by the loss of yet another life.

"The law was not intended to cause loss of life." T'Partha nodded as she spoke to Karatek, then turned back to N'Keth.

"Who is this man's intended mate?" she asked him.

Wrong question, Karatek realized as Solor stepped forward.

N'Keth's face went remote, and N'Veyan gathered himself as if to spring at T'Partha.

"You've just violated their customs," he hissed at T'Partha. "Te-Vikram seclude their mates before the ceremony and never mention women's names before strangers. Ask who her family is, instead." Louder, he cried, "Wait! If you tell me who her family is, I will bring her back to you."

"Unattended?" asked N'Keth. "Or would you send attendant *males* to guard her?"

He turned his back on T'Partha.

"I am the father of a family," Karatek said. "What use have I for another man's mate?"

N'Veyan looked wildly around. *Night and day*, Karatek thought. *The madness of blood fever makes him think I've challenged, and he is looking for a way of invoking* Kal-if-fee.

He touched T'Partha's shoulder.

"Kal-if-farr," she intoned.

"Where is the bride?" demanded N'Keth. The *systra* shook wildly. "The law is that if a bonding is forestalled, another bride must be provided."

N'Keth looked over at Sarissa. "You are my former captor's

18

sister. You are unbonded, though not of the order of unbonded. Need N'Veyan call challenge on your father and brother to win you? Or shall I add your bloodline to my family peacefully?"

T'Vysse stepped in front of her daughter.

Solor leapt between his old adversary and his elder sister. "When I was a child, I defeated you," he began.

"Which is why I rejoice at the opportunity to form a family relationship with you through N'Veyan," N'Keth replied. He glanced appreciatively at Sarissa. "She is fit to be the mother of heroes."

Sarissa looked down, in brief, obligatory modesty—and to hide the fact that her eyes were flame—the fire of pure rage, a loss of control for which she would not readily forgive herself. Then, she turned on her heel and walked back into the lift, escorted by T'Vysse.

"Come on," said Solor. "What are you going to do? Fight me again? Or will you have N'Veyan do it? He is younger than I, true, but he is weakened by the blood fever. Even in the *Plak-tow*, he is no match for me, or for Security here."

Karatek stepped forward, waving aside the attempts of Streon and three other members of his team to push him and T'Partha toward the lift. They were all one people: scientists, adepts, te-Vikram, even politicians. And if they were all one people, if they were all going to survive, he needed to attempt to resolve this problem.

"What do you think you are doing to our sacred customs? We have offered you a solution that will preserve life, and you spurn it. I submit that it is not logical to die and forget all you are."

"Some things are more important than life," N'Keth said.

"So they are, but this is about furthering life, carrying it to a next generation. So this, logically, is not one of those 'some things.'"

He strode forward. "Let me go and bring N'Veyan's betrothed back. Let us leave challenges behind as one more remnant of the Mother World that we left on her sands. Please."

"Let him challenge, Karatek," came a voice that still carried remnants of its former strength. It was old Rovalat, who had lost so many of his *kahs-wan* class the year the te-Vikram raided. *"T'Kehr* Karatek suggests we work together, and I concur. You do not? Well enough. Space yourself. Walk out those gates into the desert of stars as you would return to the Womb of Fire at your life's end. We can use the additional food and water. And we will make sure your names are forgotten."

N'Keth stepped forward, his eyes flashing.

"Look at him," Solor said again. "I have refused N'Veyan's challenge. My sister, who is *not* of the order of unbonded, has left this place. So, N'Veyan's only hope lies in finding his true mate. Give these elders her family's name, and they will bring her back. Refuse, and lose another member of your kin. Reject as you may the teachings of Surak, even you must logically conclude that you have lost enough kinsmen already."

N'Keth looked over at N'Veyan, who was trembling visibly. One of his attendants set down his *systra* with a final discordant chime of bells to kneel beside him and help him stay on his feet.

"Come," urged Karatek. "Let us help you!"

N'Keth's shoulders slumped, but only for an instant. "Seeing that she stands as matriarch here, I will tell *her."* He pointed with a stubborn chin at T'Partha.

"See you bring her back swiftly. Truly, I do not think he can last long," N'Keth added.

"My word on it," said Karatek.

Pulling his dagger, N'Keth drew its tip across his arm, letting three drops of blood fall onto the deck. Reversing the blade, he passed it to Karatek while Streon restrained himself from leaping forward to confiscate it.

Karatek drew his own blood, a sacrifice of life and water to match N'Keth's.

At Karatek's gesture, T'Partha came forward. N'Keth knelt. As T'Partha bent over him, he raised his head to whisper the name and clan of N'Veyan's promised mate. Karatek could not hear them.

"They will meet at the appointed place," T'Partha proclaimed.

She turned and swept forward toward the shuttle. Its crew, clearly, had been observing because, as she advanced, its boarding ramp slid forward. As Karatek followed, the *systras* sounded, impossibly shrill, until he and T'Partha were safely in the shuttle, its ramp retracted, and its doors sealed against the noise.

"Is the bay empty now?" asked the pilot.

"All personnel have withdrawn to safety."

"Prepare for takeoff." The pilot bent over the controls. The great hatch opened to space. A few stray canisters that had not been lashed down were sucked out into the dark.

"I require access to communications," said T'Partha as the great hatch opened.

True to her word, she would not betray the lady's name to males not related to her.

Karatek settled back in his chair as the shuttle left the *Shavokh* and set course for the nearest of the ships. He glanced out the viewport. The ships had drawn together in a formation like a spearhead. The gods grant they would hit their target.

It was the Fifth of Tasmeen. Karatek had much to remember— and much more to survive before he would be allowed to rest.

TWO

NOW

EARTH
STARDATE 54103.7

Ambassador Spock stood with hands behind his back, looking calmly over the room in the Palais de la Concorde in Paris. It was large, rectangular, and soothingly, simply furnished in warm reddish wood paneling and deep blue carpeting. The curtains that half covered the tall windows were a slightly lighter blue— Federation blue, the color was officially named. It was the same shade of blue as the beautifully enameled Federation logo on the far wall. The seat of the Federation government, with the Federation Council chambers on the first floor and the president's office on the top, this building was constructed on the site of the signing of the Traité d'Unification that united Earth's governments into one in the twenty-second century. This was one of the larger meeting rooms in the building's middle floors. The room's main

22

furnishing was one long, rectangular table of the same reddish wood as the paneling, with terminals placed in front of every seat.

It was a room that had been deliberately designed to seem tranquil to many species, but, Spock thought, it certainly wasn't doing its job just now. The restlessly milling crowd of Federation dignitaries—human, Bolian, Zanri, and others—were definitely not interested in anything soothing. Nor were any of them anything even remotely approaching calm.

The reason for their impatience was that the whole purpose of this meeting that had brought them here from so many different worlds concerned one non-Federation species, one that was unaccountably missing.

There were no Romulans present.

Ambassador Dara Mellon, who, Spock mused, had the ill fortune to be the head of this particular mission, brushed back a stray wisp of her pure white hair, which was caught up in an elegant corona of braids. She gave Spock one of her charming political smiles, the sort that involved her mouth only. Her clear blue eyes remained, as ever, coolly calculating, almost as unreadable in their deceptive clarity as the eyes of a Vulcan.

"Ambassador Spock, you know the Romulans far better than any of us." Her tone was almost sweet. "Do you believe that they'll show?"

Since her career had been in diplomacy almost from the start, Ambassador Mellon had seen many more ambassadorial missions than he. But one of the reasons for her success was her ability to accept that others might know more about specific subjects.

"They have no logical reason not to appear," he replied without hesitation.

She sighed. "Then they are deliberately keeping us waiting."

"That does seem likely."

"How childish of them."

Spock raised an eyebrow. "Such stalling is, we both know, hardly a new tactic, and one that is used not only by the Romulans."

"That is true," Mellon said flatly. "Ah well, you will excuse me, Ambassador Spock. I must speak with Dr. Ikata."

He dipped his head slightly in courtesy. "Of course."

Self-control might be Ambassador Mellon's forte, Spock thought, watching her walk away, *but impatience is definitely a general Federation trait, regardless of species.* Any successful diplomat or ambassador soon became far too well acquainted with the wide application of that ancient military rule, "Hurry up and wait." But that didn't mean that they had to like it.

No one seemed about to do anything as calming as sit down. Instead, they continued to mill around the large, rectangular table, little groups of two and three forming and breaking up again.

This agitated behavior is hardly likely to inspire the Romulans to arrive any sooner, Spock thought. *Far easier for them all to accept what cannot be changed and simply relax.*

By now, of course, he was thoroughly familiar with the ways of many Federation species, including the more emotional ones. But the not-quite-suppressed wave of this group's concerted uneasiness was beginning to be more than a touch . . . disconcerting. Comfortable enough in his dark, heavy ambassadorial robes despite what was to a Vulcan a rather chilly room, he moved away from the others to stand alone by one of the large windows, quietly enjoying the view since he could hardly slip into full meditation here and now.

The curtains had been drawn back enough to let in the clear Parisian light of an early winter morning, and sunlight glanced brightly off the windows of buildings on the far side of the Champs-Elysées, sparking Spock's insignia and House sigils into small rainbows. There was no snow yet, and the street two stories below where he stood was crowded with a mix of busy officials and eager shoppers.

The vista was quite agreeable. Paris was as much a city of the past as it was of the future, and structures that had stood for a thousand years were crowded in between ultramodern buildings constructed since the end of the Dominion War one year, two months, and seven days earlier. Just barely visible in the far distance were the tops of the structures of the Paris Spaceport, and the sun turned one thin contrail into bright silver. The complex was also known, Spock thought, by a form of its ancient name, the Paris Roissy-Charles de Gaulle Airport and Spaceport.

Tradition is important here, he thought, understanding.

Closer, Spock could see the now charmingly archaic structure of the five-hundred-year-old Tour Eiffel, the Eiffel Tower that, he'd learned, few people had liked when it was built back in the nineteenth century.

Change is a constant. A fact that our sundered cousins do not always accept.

But his hopes for unification rested on what would happen in this room.

"Well, Spock, what do you think?" a voice asked suddenly, bringing him abruptly back to the present. "Is anything positive actually going to come out of this meeting?"

Spock raised an eyebrow once again, recognizing the man without having to turn. Dr. Eric Nagata, a short, stocky, and earnest human, was an excellent diplomat in his own way, but he lacked patience, and his brusque manner could be quite disconcerting to a Vulcan.

I believe it was a human, Will Rogers, who might have described his technique: "Diplomacy is the art of saying 'Nice doggie!' until you can find a rock."

"Extrapolation without sufficient data is illogical, Dr. Nagata, as we both know. However, it would also be illogical for the Romulans to have come as far as Earth for no purpose."

"Well, yes, there is that, of course. But it's been two months of this cursed stalemate, two months without any progress," Nagata insisted. "Oh, other than agreeing on a proper tariff on Romulan ale," he added wryly.

"It has been one month, twenty-nine days, and 8.25 standard Earth hours, to be precise," Spock corrected gravely. *Not quite two months since the encounter with the Watraii. And,* he added with a sharp little pang of sorrow, *the death of Pavel Chekov.* But nothing of what he was feeling showed on his face or in his stance. Spock merely continued calmly, "That is, you must surely admit, not a very long span of time, especially when compared to the centuries of noncommunication. It should not be surprising to anyone that Federation–Romulan relations have not yet advanced very much."

Even, he thought, *with all of what these people might call my "behind-the-scenes" work.*

"Good point," Nagata conceded with a wry grin. "Sorry. We humans just can't be as patient as you Vulcans."

"Patience is not only a Vulcan trait. And at any rate," Spock added, turning from the window at the sound of the doors opening, "there is no need to wait any longer."

"Uh-oh," Nagata muttered, tensing. "Here we go."

Into the chamber stalked—there was no other word for it—the Romulan ambassador, T'Kala. She was a slim, cold-eyed, straight-backed woman who would be—and presumably often was—not out of place on the deck of a warbird. Although Spock had never chanced to meet her either on Romulus or elsewhere, he was well aware of her reputation as an ambassador. T'Kala was as strong-willed as she was undeniably beautiful, even in her unornamented, steel-gray diplomatic garb.

The ambassador's entourage followed her closely, their glares constantly sweeping the room. All six of them were grim-faced, muscular Romulan men and women who carried themselves more like warriors than diplomatic aides—hardly a surprise, Spock thought, since they probably were her bodyguard first and her aides only second.

"Ambassador T'Kala," Ambassador Mellon greeted her just as warmly as if the Romulans hadn't kept everyone waiting. "Pray be seated."

But T'Kala remained standing. "I have studied your terms," she told them all without preamble, "and they are not acceptable."

And you, Spock retorted silently, *are quite predictable. If you could have hurled down a scroll onto the table, you would have done so.* "No insult is meant to you or to your people, Ambassador T'Kala," he said smoothly, "but we all know that it would not be logical for you to have come all the way to Earth merely to tell us that."

He sat. Sure enough, the Romulans took the hint and sat as well. So did the Federation diplomats. Ambassador Mellon shot a glance at Spock that mingled humor and gratitude.

"Now, Madam Ambassador," she said charmingly to T'Kala, "let us begin anew."

"Indeed," the Romulan woman snapped. "First, I wish proof and guarantees that the Federation will make no further incursions into what you call the Neutral Zone."

"Ah, but surely you agree, Ambassador T'Kala, that the Romulan Star Empire must issue similar proof and guarantees."

T'Kala raised an eyebrow. "Do you claim that we are the offenders?"

"Surely," Spock commented mildly, "both sides have been equal offenders over the centuries. But I agree that both sides must, indeed, issue similar guarantees—even as we agreed to do one month and 4.5 days ago. I believe, Ambassador T'Kala, that we may now safely move on from there and discuss other matters."

"Indeed we may," she agreed as firmly as though she'd been the one to suggest it. "And there are many other matters that need to be settled. Let us begin with reparations to the Romulan Star Empire."

Murmurs shot up and down the row of diplomats.

"Your pardon, Madam Ambassador." Ambassador Mellon's voice was sweet and gentle. "I wouldn't deign to insult you by defining terms. But since the Romulan Star Empire fought as part of the allied forces against the Dominion, and was not defeated by the Federation, surely reparations are neither possible nor, in fact, legal."

The Romulan ambassador gave a sharp little laugh of contempt. "How typical of the Federation—and how predictable! We have helped them win a war, we have sacrificed the lives of countless numbers of our brave warriors for the cause, and now the Federation rewards us with *semantics*."

Dr. Nagata leaned forward, both arms on the table. "Perhaps the ambassador forgets that we have already offered your people Federation help in the rebuilding of the empire's damaged defenses."

"Oh yes," T'Kala snapped, "I am certain that the Federation would enjoy learning all the details of our defenses!"

"Please," Ambassador Mellon said, hands raised, "let us not quarrel."

"Romulans do not quarrel," T'Kala retorted coldly, sitting back in her chair. "We fight, and we win. And we do not tolerate being considered a secondary power."

"We don't—"

"No?" T'Kala cut in. "Then what of the behavior of our sector of the Cardassian Union as opposed to that in the other powers' sectors? Is it mere coincidence that we should have so very generously been given the most unstable of regions?"

"Oh dear," Ambassador Mellon returned, "has the Romulan Star Empire, then, become so weak that it cannot control its sector?"

"Ah, and now you mock us. Is it the custom of the Federation to attack those who fought as its ally?"

Spock, face absolutely unreadable, watched the diplomatic battle. Words, he knew, were being carefully chosen by both sides and were meant to sound more dangerous than they were. This would, he knew from personal ambassadorial experience, go on for hours. Both sides knew exactly what they wanted, and what they would not consider worthy of argument. But they would continue to argue over exactly what the Federation was willing to cede to Romulus, and what Romulus was willing to accept.

No matter, Spock told himself. They would come to terms eventually. This was not a matter in which Vulcan needed to intervene—not yet, at any rate.

". . . war crimes on the part of the Dominion," T'Kala was continuing, eyes fierce.

"The Federation is already looking into that issue," Ambassador Mellon returned.

"Ah yes, of course, just as the Federation is already looking into the exploitation of the Gamma Quadrant!"

"As is the Romulan Star Empire."

"That is a lie!" T'Kala all but shouted. "We do not look to exploit others—not as the Federation does!"

Ah yes, this was still predictable. Romulan pride was guaranteed to make this meeting more difficult, since it was all but impossible for Romulans to be totally open about their military or private affairs—particularly not when they were speaking to the Federation.

But then Spock straightened ever so slightly, suddenly aware of the faintest change in T'Kala's tone, listening to what was all at once hidden behind the practiced words.

This is more than an example of Romulan pride, he thought. *Something is wrong, and the Federation is not meant to know it.*

Bit by delicate bit, Spock put together the small scraps of data, logically working out that yes, there must have been another attack on the Romulans. By the Watraii? Was there something more to it, something even worse than that?

But before he could ask any leading questions, the meeting suddenly broke up in confusion. "I have had enough of this nonsense!" T'Kala declared, springing to her feet and storming off, closely followed by her warrior-aides.

Again, quite predictable, Spock thought. *But hardly logical, or desirable.*

Spock got to his feet with seeming indifference. If he went after her, perhaps he could convince T'Kala to abandon theatrics and return. Yes, and perhaps be more forthcoming about Romulan problems, difficult though she would find that.

But before Spock could get more than a few strides down the hallway, an urgent beeping from his small message unit stopped him in his tracks. He looked down at it in genuine surprise: The coded signal was from none other than Admiral Uhura.

"Admiral?" he asked.

"Sorry to be so abrupt, Spock, but I need to see you, and Ruanek with you. And Spock, I know that this isn't the best time for either of you. I'm sorry to interrupt your meetings, but I mean now!"

It was an open secret—at least to some, most of them Vulcan—
that Ruanek, who was apparently a Vulcan, was actually a Romulan living in exile on Vulcan. It was a relatively contented exile by
this point since he had a Vulcan wife and had served for years as
an aide to Spock's late father, Ambassador Sarek, and as a lecturer
at the Vulcan Science Academy.

Spock wasn't surprised that Uhura knew that Ruanek was on
Earth just now. She would know that he was here both as a member of the Interplanetary Linguistics Conference and as someone
with a vested interest in Romulan–Federation peace. Uhura was,
after all, head of Intelligence for Starfleet Command, and it would
have surprised him only if she hadn't known.

But that she should ask for them both was fascinating . . .

Logically, it could only be a matter concerning private Romulan affairs. Security affairs, perhaps, to do with the renewed attacks he'd just postulated—and possibly concerning Federation
security as well.

There was an ancient saying on Earth, a cleverly worded curse.
There was little logic in the idea of a curse, but the words were
wise: *May you live in interesting times.*

We most certainly do, Spock thought.

THREE

MEMORY

As Karatek found himself part of a wedge of people thrusting themselves on board the shuttle that would take them away from *Shavokh*, memory struck again, almost making him reel.

This was a waking dream. He was still on Vulcan, and the news was grim. The light from Vulcan Station—all those lives snuffed out, those *katras* lost!—still smoldered in the sky. The dust, sand, and grit stirred up by the explosion had rendered it the violent crimsons and violet-black of sand and rock in the Womb of Fire, and the wind was fierce. Over the wind's howl came shouts as raiders broke through the perimeter of the launch site. Security had pressed close, pushing strangers among family, thrusting them onto shuttles to take anyone they could into what seemed like the greater safety of the great ships.

My eldest son, his wife, my grandchild, Karatek recalled with the anguish a lifetime of meditation had never been able to control. They had been separated: Karatek knew himself fortunate that T'Vysse had not managed to rush away to search for them.

And there they were, thrust onto shuttles with no regard for family, clan, or nation-state.

When had N'Veyan found time to seek a bondmate on board one of the ships? Some city people, Karatek knew, maintained contact with the desert-mad te-Vikram. They said it linked them to Vulcan's most ancient traditions and kept them strong.

He shook his head. He took a deep breath. *Control,* he told himself. He would need it when he boarded *Rea's Helm,* the flagship commanded by S'lovan. Already, he knew some of the subjects that would, once again, be debated. He could assign a 100 percent certainty to the appearance by a deputation of physicians and healers demanding a systematic collection and storage procedure for reproductive material. He knew, too, that some on the council would condemn their petition as indecorous at best, and impious and corrupt at worst.

Control.

Even on the shuttle from *Shavokh* to *Rea's Helm,* it was not as if Karatek had no work to do. First, he needed to review *Shavokh's* status reports with T'Partha, a final check before the meeting. Then, he could review his latest research project. The last time they had stopped to mine duranium, he had received a gift from the head of mining operations—a peculiar sort of crystal that had the property of directing power in such a way that ships could be propelled nearer and nearer to the speed of light. It should be possible, Karatek thought, to refine these crystals, to modulate them, perhaps adjust their refraction so that, one day, the ships' engines might be adapted to his great dream of faster-than-light travel. Provided that they could withstand matter–antimatter collisions without cracking and producing catastrophic explosions.

Admittedly, Karatek's ability to experiment with these crystals had been extremely limited due to the need to preserve his ship's physical integrity. But the next time they made planetfall for any length of time, he intended to request the opportunity of the council to test his theories in the safety of a world.

"You realize," T'Partha's voice, wry and a little wistful in his ears, brought him back to the here and now, "they will never get around to discussing pure research today."

Karatek allowed himself to sigh.

He glanced away from the temptation of his report, staring instead out the shuttle's viewscreens. They were filled with blackness, lit only by the dim lights within the ships and the faraway stars. The shuttle felt small, much more precarious than *Shavokh*, adrift in a prodigious emptiness. He might have felt more in control if he could have piloted. As he told himself every time he had to take one of the wretched things, it was illogical to dislike an entire class of ship, and even more so to resent those ships for their function—but there it was. Karatek did not like shuttles.

Therefore, he was one of the few who did not resent the fact that their use was now restricted to official business: transportation to councils, mining, or surveillance of the very few planets they had found in this sector of the galaxy. Nevertheless, Karatek would order that a shuttle be prepared to unite N'Veyan and his intended bondmate once T'Partha found her.

Something about the incident troubled Karatek. Why hadn't N'Veyan entered the Fires earlier? If Karatek were not *Shavokh*'s commander, that would have been a vastly improper, almost obscene question for anyone except family members and healers. Perhaps he could make discreet inquiries at this council about how other ship commanders had handled this situation.

Perhaps, as the great ships' engines strained closer and closer to the still-unbreakable barrier of light speed, the rhythm in their blood that told fertile males when it was the time of mating was delayed. Even back on Vulcan, necessity did not come regularly every seven years.

Perhaps the blood fever truly did take longer to kindle here in the darkness and the cold. Perhaps that meant that their biological cycles would be delayed or permanently deranged.

None of that mattered: what would be, would be, and must be endured. For now, what mattered was that N'Veyan suffered, which meant that his betrothed suffered too. Lacking an adept's control, N'Veyan would die, although his pledged mate might not.

That death must be prevented. They could not risk further limitations on their genetic pool. Even if N'Veyan was te-Vikram.

So. Karatek had made his decision now, and he knew it. It would take some few tedious hours of argument, plus additional time to ready the shuttle, but if all went as intended, N'Veyan would meet his betrothed at whatever the appointed place was, here, where there were no circles of *Koon-ut-kal-if-fee.*

And that would be one positive thing accomplished on this Fifth of Tasmeen.

"Preparing to match course with Rea's Helm," the pilot's voice echoed over the communications system.

Finally.

Karatek drew his first unfettered breath of the day, then another and another until his breathing was as focused, as centered in his body as when he meditated. Soon, he would be able to escape the shuttle for what was, to him, the far greater security of one of the great ships. With S'task present, Karatek could lay down the burden of command, at least for the duration of the council, in favor of aiding S'task to judge wisely.

Like *Shavokh, Rea's Helm* was on envirosave. Karatek promised himself that he would learn how this ship's engineers had managed to keep the docking bay warm, relatively speaking. He could recall one evening during his *kahs-wan* as particularly cold. As the Forge had blackened into night, he had dug into the sand. Heated all day, it had warmed the chill from his hands and feet and preserved him until dawn.

Rea's Helm possessed no drifts of reddish sand, no scarps and glints of obsidian, but the ship's light was the right color, and their weight felt right. The officers who received them led them to S'task's consort, who blessed them, then offered water and fire in the old ways that had almost disappeared from shipboard use.

Karatek was glad to kneel and inhale the incense from the burners she had had set up in the reception bay. The blue-gray smoke spiraled up from replicas of the ancient flanged bronzes that weight restrictions had caused many in his ship's company to leave behind. Someone had painted murals of Seleya's ablutions pools, with their stand of *kylin'the* blossoms, on the wall behind the lady's chair. The sight of them, as well as the memory of that wealth of water below the mountains of awe, eased his soul.

The journey had left Karatek's mouth dry. He drank deeply, as was proper for a guest, politely ignoring the taste of the chemicals *Rea's Helm* used to purify the recycled water. For good or ill, the taste was different from the recycled water on board *Shavokh*. But the cups in which the water was presented were ancient, much like the set carved from fossilized wood that T'Vysse had once used to welcome Surak. He drank to absent friends, and the grave courtesy with which the lady received back the cup made him think that his sorrow was shared.

The conference room to which courteous, helmed guards led him and T'Partha reminded Karatek poignantly of the seminar rooms at the Vulcan Space Institute. Even the badge check for radiation, toxins, or disease possessed a welcome familiarity.

This room, like the VSI's halls, contained a conference table, glowing screens set in at every place. But there was no acerbic Torin to raise a white, sardonic eyebrow in silent reprimand that Karatek was late *again,* and what excuse for it could he possibly have this time?

Torin would have taken the seat at the head of the table. Here, indeed, there stood a chair, but it was occupied only by a great sword. Karatek had seen the bared blade before in this room. As always, he wondered what in the way of vital supplies someone had sacrificed in order to bring that thing on board.

Today, however, was the Fifth of Tasmeen, and for the first time, the blade's presence on board made sense to him. It looked ancient, priceless, the sort of thing that should have been preserved in a family shrine or the Vulcan Science Academy. It reminded him of one of his journeys to the artisans near the Forge. He started toward it, hoping to see the master's mark stamped somewhere along the sword's length.

"Karatek," T'Partha warned as the ship's officers tensed.

Fascinating. When had a sword, even a great heirloom, been transformed into some sort of talisman? Most illogical.

Would you let just anyone handle the coronet Surak gave you? he asked himself.

Karatek turned his gesture into a nod of respect, and hastened toward the seat marked with his name.

T'Partha seated herself quietly next to him. "The sword is an heirloom of Surak's House," she whispered.

Trust T'Partha to know, and to produce that information at need.

Rea's Helm's commander walked in, accompanied by S'task. A quiet man with thoughtful, poet's eyes, he had disclaimed responsibility for the entire fleet. Nevertheless, the fleet, or at least most of it, looked to him for leadership. How thin he was, as if his responsibilities had fed on him!

Feeling far younger than he had a right to be, and untutored, Karatek began to rise, eager to show respect. S'task raised an eyebrow, in a gesture so like *T'Kehr* Torin's that Karatek's heart twisted in his side as he remembered.

He nodded at S'lovan, the ship's commander, realizing that the structure of his name revealed a kinship with the older man. Old loyalties persisted even this far from Vulcan, mingling with philosophy and even politics. Karatek had chosen what he considered exile for the good of the homeworld he renounced. In that, if little else, he shared some commonality of thought with the te-Vikram, many of whom had never intended to leave the desert at all. He knew, however, that S'task and those of his House and extended clan considered their journey not exile, but a quest for a new home. As for the technocrats, for all Karatek knew, they probably saw it as an opportunity—a prejudiced observation, but one he could not shake off. Surak had been the only man he ever knew totally without factional loyalties, and yet, he had split the Mother World as no other philosopher or prophet had ever done.

"We have a long agenda today," S'lovan said, activating his screen.

Karatek could see it: everything from crop blight to techniques for strengthening ships' hulls to a debate on whether they should even continue with the journey.

If the meeting went on as long as it would have to in order to deal with all those topics as thoroughly as they deserved, he should have been told, so he and T'Partha could pack food and water in order not to be a drain on the resources of *Rea's Helm.*

Could the tradition of guest-friendship extend this far into the darkness? Karatek wondered, and knew it for an illogical question. The years of wandering had tested his resolve. Surak should have tried deep space, rather than the mere desert, Karatek thought to himself, and knew, as he thought, how absurd the notion was.

S'task raised a hand so pallid that only the ship's lights, reddish like the sunlight of the Mother World, lent it any semblance of health.

"Your pardon," S'lovan interrupted. Taking up the water flask at his place, he walked around the table and poured for each person seated there, even if they had already been formally welcomed on board.

By the time he finished, only drops remained in the flask. Nevertheless, he poured them into his own cup and raised it in silent remembrance not just of the people lost in exile, but of the world lost to them forever. Then he sat again and looked toward T'Vria, seated to his left.

"Your report on hydroponics?"

T'Vria rose. She was still quite young. Karatek recalled that her earliest training at the VSI had been overseen by T'Raya, who had not managed to scramble on board any of the shuttles bound for one of the great ships. The loss of her teacher must have come as a blow, but the botanist's voice was sure as she explained new procedures for containment of hydroponics areas. They could not afford another crop failure, she said into an ominous silence.

Avarin, from off the Forge, rose next. He nodded respect at S'task, then smiled faintly. "As most of you have heard, far too often, I spent several years in the Guard. One of the habits of the Guard—those deemed fit to mention in public—is debriefing, specifically what we called 'lessons learned.' We have learned, once again, the lesson of redundancies. Where there are no people, there must be machines. Where resources are scarce, the machines, like their masters, must be more efficient. Where neither is possible, we must do without or devise new machines."

He gestured, and schematics of generators came online, followed by computer systems that Karatek saw instantly were smaller and more efficient than anything he had ever imagined. And to think he still called himself a scientist! He was no scientist now, but an administrator with an absorbing hobby. But self-recriminations and regret were unproductive in the face of Avarin's excellence. The other man was speaking once again.

"Before the exile began, the Vulcan Science Academy had begun a study of artificial intelligence. It occurs to me that we might use this as a sort of force multiplier, to extend the capacity of surviving crew members—"

"How?" Iria rose to her feet. If not for the authority that emanated from her, and the robes of a Seleyan underpriestess that she wore, she might still have been mistaken for a girl. Even standing, she was only as tall as the men and women still seated, but her eyes blazed even more brightly than the gem that glowed on her brow.

"I know you, Avarin. I know you have been speaking with Vortal about cybernetics. You know that technology is proscribed," she said. "You would do better to work with those new crystals."

With what felt like a flicker of Karatek's inner eyelids, he remembered the high priestess in the Halls of Ancient Thought, holding out the coronet Karatek now treasured to Surak himself.

"Before thee departs or the world we have known ends, may I present thee with a gift? It was taken from thine enemy, a product of the arts of their hands and their mind. To us, it restrains the mind from its final destiny and is therefore abomination."

"But I may wish to study it?" Surak lifted both his slanted eyebrows. "And, incidentally, serve thee by removing blasphemy from thy presence? What can I do but obey?"

One of the unbonded had brought Surak the coronet. It resembled the headpiece the high priestess wore, far more elaborate than Iria's bloodmetal headband with its beaklike white gem that blazed at Avarin like a third eye able to pierce his soul.

Avarin coughed delicately. Iria's brows came up, as if she studied him for signs of illness. S'lovan turned in his chair, clearly alarmed for S'task.

The cough had the additional advantage of drawing people's attention back to Avarin from whatever trails of memory they had wandered.

The man held up a hand. "The physicians—secular physicians, not healers of your order, Priestess"—he bowed respect at her—"are concerned not with fusing man and machine, which I agree is blasphemy, but with preserving our people's genetic heritage by establishing a bank of . . . reproductive material."

He glanced politely away and down, deliberately not meeting the eyes of a woman not bound to him when speaking of such a matter. T'Partha stirred in the way Karatek knew meant she had observed something worthwhile and wanted him to pay attention. In this case, she showed him a critical truth about Avarin: he might be able and urbane, but he was ultimately evasive. Although averting his gaze from an unbonded female, or even a bonded one who was not his mate, was simple courtesy when speaking of the Time of Mating or any reproductive matters at all, it was characteristic of the man. Avarin never looked into people's eyes, making his own thoughts harder to discern.

He spoke of lessons learned. Evasions, Karatek told himself. But then Avarin had never concealed his political ties to the technocrats. What was it he had said once? *I build tools. I build bridges between groups. Those too are tools.*

Once, Karatek had seen water spilled, wasted, on the deck near *Shavokh*'s hull, where the cold was greatest. The water had solidified. Although he knew that ice existed at Seleya's peak, and that some of the richest, rashest houses on the Mother World had occasionally consumed water in that fashion, it seemed extravagant, wasteful. Someone had stepped on the water and fallen. The man had managed to stand up and made light of the mishap. The water had been chipped from the deck into a container, then reintroduced into the ship's water supply. And Karatek had forgotten the episode until now.

Slippery. That was the word defining the quality of that solidified water, the ice, on his ship's deck. Avarin was slippery.

Karatek forbore making a note. Who knew what Avarin's eyes might be taking in as he flicked them about the room, never meeting anyone's gaze like a man of honor? It would be better to allow the man to underestimate him as a scientist past his prime, his mind in his memories, or his circuits.

Now, Avarin was looking around the table. After the barrage of delta waves that had killed half of one ship's population, physicians—what Avarin had called secular physicians—had suggested creating a bank of sperm and eggs, in case the population on board the ships fell below critical levels. Then, the suggestion was greeted with such outrage as un-Vulcan that it was abandoned. Now, Avarin repeated it, as he did every time council met. Still, he kept his eyes down. It concerned Karatek that he could not read whether the man expected his resolution to be passed this time, next time, or not at all.

"I might ask whether my team could receive daily transmissions about ship's radiation levels," Avarin spoke directly to S'lovan.

"You might indeed," said S'lovan. The man was no fool. He knew that Avarin had just moved a *le-matya* on the game board, taking a warrior and placing the priestess in jeopardy. He would not let go of this idea, and everyone on the council knew it.

T'Partha stirred in her seat. "Surely," she said, attempting to draw the consensus about her like a warm cloak, "it would be more logical to adjust the ships' present course to avoid concentrations—forgive my imprecision; I am no scientist, but only an administrator—of radiation?"

S'lovan rose. "If we shift course, we will be forced to travel through regions less densely populated with stars of sufficient age that they might have viable planetary systems." He might regret it, but he spoke the truth.

"Viable!" a tall man with hair still scorched from Vulcan's sun scoffed, drawing a reproving glance from S'task. "After all, we have done so well in finding systems that can support life," he added with quiet but bitter sarcasm. Intriguing to see one of the te-Vikram adopt the controlled hostility that Surak's followers could wield with such great effect.

"Is it the wish of the ships' commanders that we consider turning back?" Avarin asked.

S'lovan again turned toward his kinsman. S'task barely raised a brow.

Who knew if Vulcan remained whole? If the fleet returned and found only radioactive fragments, they would have exceeded the ships' maximum projected life expectancy by so much that it was likely that the Mother Sun's light would touch only derelicts, their crews long dead and mummified in the dry, frigid air, assuming any air at all remained.

S'task pushed himself to his feet. Instantly, the priestess raced to his side. "The knowledge of how to return to Vulcan is gone." He labored for further breath, his head down. Karatek was horrified at how thready his voice had become.

43

If any of the people seated around the table had even used their copies of Surak's *Analects* to do more than collect dust, Karatek would not have been able to tell from the way most of them leapt to their feet.

With the exception of the priestess Iria at S'task's side, her small fingers testing his pulse, most were outraged, shouting things like "wanton neglect!" and "criminal negligence!"

Avarin was in the lead. Karatek lowered his eyes, watching T'Partha watch the younger man. Would he challenge S'task for leadership?

The old leader pulled away from Iria, then raised an eyebrow at S'lovan, who shrugged.

"Computer error?" T'Partha whispered to Karatek.

"The last time the computers went down, there was a great deal of consultation back and forth among the ships' navigators," Karatek replied. "We know that information was lost. This specific datum could easily have vanished with the rest."

T'Partha raised a hand over her lips, either to conceal a smile or mask her words.

"I expunged it myself from the navigational databases," S'task said, prompting another eruption. "Since the data no longer exist, this dispute is pointless."

He sank back into his seat, accepting the cup Iria offered him with a hand that quite visibly shook.

T'Partha was nodding approval. Karatek wondered how much of that tremor she thought was natural.

"S'task is nobody's fool," the woman said. "In fact, I think the only man who could ever argue him to a standstill was—"

Surak, Karatek thought.

S'task had pushed himself back onto his feet, supported now by S'lovan.

"May I have your attention?" S'lovan was asking politely. "Counselors, healers . . ."

S'lovan drew a deep breath. *"Kroykah!"* he shouted.

When the echoes of his command subsided, he escorted S'task to stand by the chair that held the ancient sword. S'task extended a hand to touch the back of the chair. His fingers trembled, then were stilled by a clear effort of will.

"Recriminations are illogical," the old man rasped. "I acted as I did because I believed my actions were indeed logical. The question that remains is this: Have we the resolution to see the task through, or have we become less than we thought? If so, then I submit that we do not wait for mischance or metal fatigue to take us, but die with what honor we still possess. If that is your decision, then I give you my word that I will lead the way, as I led the way into exile."

He slipped his hand down from the back of the chair and brushed his fingers against the hilt of the ancient sword.

"I swear it," he whispered.

Then the old man swayed, and Iria joined S'lovan in easing him back down. *Another outburst like that, and they could lose S'task here and now,* Karatek thought.

T'Partha rose. "I would like to propose a short recess," she began. Her voice was warm, and smooth with long practice, and she drew consensus about her like a ceremonial cloak. "Perhaps a brief interval of meditation or refresh—"

"Commander!" A young man who looked enough like S'lovan to be his close kin raced into the room, drew himself up, and bowed his head: deference to a commanding officer or to a Head of House.

"A message has just come through for *T'Kehr* Karatek and Commissioner T'Partha of the *Shavokh,*" he said.

"What is it?" T'Partha asked, while Karatek, feeling immensely old and colder than even envirosave could account for, sank back into his chair.

"You're required to return immediately," the young crewman said. "*Shavokh* is under attack."

FOUR

NOW

EARTH
STARDATE 54104.1

Ruanek, once of Romulus but now of Vulcan, waited, a tall, lean, dark-haired figure in a simple white tunic and trousers, poised on the balls of his feet, crouching slightly.

Ah yes, the other was giving away exactly what he was going to do by the quick flicker of his gaze and the tensing of his muscles—

Ha, yes, here he came. Ruanek timed the rush with practiced skill, and then, at the last moment, twisted sharply to the left. His opponent hurtled helplessly past him, and Ruanek calmly turned and hurried the man on his way with a shoe to his rump. The man landed flat on the exercise mat with a loud *"oof!"*

Refusing to reveal so much as the slightest trace of a grin, since he was, after all, supposed to be Vulcan, Ruanek turned to face the row of academics watching them and gave them all the smallest of

Vulcan bows. His students were an unlikely lot, some of them overweight, some of them definitely not in the proper fitness for their species. But they all stood voluntarily out here in the early morning on the lawn behind the white bulk of the conference center, watching him as earnestly as a group of awed children.

If you'd had early morning drills as often as I did back on Romulus, you wouldn't be so eager, he thought wryly. All these years on Vulcan, and he still hadn't forgotten what those cursed drills had been like.

Ah well, give these folks credit for wanting to learn. "And so," Ruanek told them all, "as you have just witnessed, if you keep yourself calm and wait for the attack, you can use your enemy's strength against him." Still fighting that inconvenient grin, he gave a hand to the man who was sprawled on the mat and pulled him back to his feet. "Are you undamaged? Yes? Good." Ruanek turned back to the others. "This is true even if your enemy outweighs you or is twice your size."

With that, he snatched up a towel from one of the piles on the workout table and pretended to be busy wiping his face dry, but now actually allowing himself a full Romulan warrior's grin into the towel's shelter. All these years away from the empire, all these years on Vulcan as a scholar—and yes, admittedly, as a martial arts trainer as well, since the Vulcans found unarmed self-defense quite logical to learn—and he was still a warrior underneath it all.

But training anyone in warrior skills had been the furthest thing from Ruanek's mind when he had accepted the invitation to the linguistics conference. He'd been genuinely surprised once he'd gotten here to find that they'd scheduled him to lead something like this. Without, of course—academics being what they were—bothering to ask or even tell him. Still, Ruanek supposed that even academics, like this willing but definitely out-of-condition group of humans and Zarins, might find self-defense techniques useful.

As an exercise regime if nothing else, Ruanek thought.

Of course, the lovely coincidence that Romulan–Federation negotiations happened to be going on at the same time in the same region here on Earth had also been part of the reason for his quick acceptance . . .

Which fascinating fact, of course, my wife figured out almost before I did! That was one of the prices one paid for marrying a Vulcan—along with the illogical happiness that came with mutual love, one also married into a life of relentless, flawless logic and extrapolation. *Not that I regret anything about T'Selis,* Ruanek thought with an inner smile of complete contentment. *Except that her medical duties kept her on Vulcan rather than coming here, visiting Earth with me. I would have enjoyed sharing San Francisco with her.*

Ah well, I'll admit that I still wonder what she saw in me— though I'm glad that she saw it!

Just then a warning bell sounded, signaling the end of the session. "Gentlebeings," Ruanek said formally, "you are dismissed."

As they left, Ruanek headed in the direction of his room, meaning to change into more suitable academic garb and then attend the session on "Folkloric Interchanges in Bogati and Vulcan Transmissions." Since none of the scholars in that session were actually either Bogati or Vulcan, their talks promised to be interesting, at the very least, and—

Just then his small personal communicator beeped at him. With the faintest of frowns at the unexpected interruption, Ruanek glanced down at it. What session had been canceled this time?

"Ruanek," a familiar voice said.

Josepha Sherman & Susan Shwartz

"Spock." Ruanek stiffened. "What is it? Is something wrong?" That had come out sounding far too emotional for a Vulcan or, for that matter, a Romulan. Fighting to keep his voice properly Vulcan-calm, Ruanek asked, "Has something happened at the meeting?"

"No. The two sides are as far apart as before."

"Then why—"

"We must discuss something else, Ruanek: I have just received a rather mysterious and quite urgent message from Admiral Uhura."

"Uhura!"

"She wishes to see both of us as quickly as possible."

One of Ruanek's eyebrows quirked up, a gesture he'd picked up from Spock over the years. "Shall I hazard a guess?"

"Guesses are illogical."

"Of course they are. But I'll wager—yes, yes, I know, illogic again; blame my background—I'll wager that this has something to do with Romulan security. What else could it be, with the meetings taking place, or not taking place? Are we to meet in Admiral Uhura's office?"

"Indeed." Spock quickly transmitted the location of that office, since Ruanek wanted to be certain of it. His last visit there had been over two years ago. *"Meet me there as swiftly as possible."*

"Believe me," Ruanek said, "I will."

"Excellent. Spock out."

Ah well, Ruanek thought wryly, *I probably wouldn't have found anything useful in that Bogati–Vulcan session, anyhow.*

Uhura's office was as quietly sophisticated as ever. The room was not overly large; it could more accurately be described as a comfortable space, one that was pleasantly furnished in warm golds and browns that set the mind at ease. A Vulcan calligraphic scroll, tranquil in its brushstrokes, hung on one wall, and a

50

Ghanaian kente cloth worked in an intricate geometric design of brown and sand hung on another.

It had never looked like the office of anyone with any real power. But then, Spock mused, Uhura had never liked anything ostentatious, even back in her career as communications officer of the *Enterprise*. In her opinion, he knew, nothing more than this agreeably casual office was needed, even by someone who was head of Starfleet Intelligence and had been so for quite a few Federation-standard years.

Admiral Uhura, who had been thoughtfully studying a monitor, turned in her *partha*-leather chair to face Spock and Ruanek as they entered. In the two months since Spock had last seen her, she had not changed at all but remained an elegant, deceptively tranquil, fiercely competent woman. Her dark skin, somewhat weathered by time and stress, was beautifully set off by her crown of silver hair, and her eyes were those of someone who was well used to calibrating chances, analyzing data, and making the necessary conclusions work.

It was Uhura who, two months ago, had sent Spock, his wife Saavik—Captain Saavik of the *U.S.S. Alliance*—Ruanek, and Admiral Pavel Chekov on a secret mission to aid the Romulans. At the time, the Romulans had been under attack by a mysterious, ritually masked alien race, the Watraii. The Watraii had made the incredible claim that the Romulans had usurped their worlds of Romulus and Remus. That issue, Spock thought, had never been settled. But the mission had been counted a success, with the theft of a vital piece of Watraii military equipment that put the Watraii at a strong disadvantage. They had been turned back from what might well have been a massacre.

But in the process, Pavel Chekov, once one of the crew of the original *Starship Enterprise,* had been killed.

A Pyrrhic victory, as the humans call it, Spock thought. *And where have the Watraii been in these many weeks? What have they been planning? Why have we not heard from them?*

Uhura smiled at them both. "Spock, Ruanek. Welcome, gentlemen. I'm sorry to pull you away from your respective business, but this matter simply can't wait. You see, it's about Chekov."

Both Spock and Ruanek straightened in shock.

"But Admiral Chekov is dead!" Ruanek protested. "We both saw him die, torn apart in that transporter accident!"

But Spock, picking up the odd note in Uhura's voice, raised a thoughtful eyebrow, studying her, carefully revealing nothing of the sudden, utterly illogical inner rush of mingled hope and guilt that was sweeping through him.

"Did we?" he wondered aloud.

In all the years that he had known her, back to the days when they'd both served aboard Jim Kirk's *Enterprise,* Uhura had never been given to inaccurate outbursts. Could it be that Ruanek and he had somehow been mistaken? Did that mean . . . Could it have been the Watraii warrior, not Chekov, who'd died? Had they actually abandoned Chekov to the Watraii?

"There was, after all, no visible proof of his death," Spock continued.

"There was that cry of agony during the transporter malfunction," Ruanek countered.

"Which need not have come from Admiral Chekov," Spock replied. "The Watraii warrior who was with him as the beam took them both might have been the one to utter it, and might have been the one who took the worst damage in the malfunctioning transporter beam. The only evidence that we have, other than that cry, is merely the knowledge that the Watraii beam was incompatible with our transporter equipment."

"Surely that is sufficient in itself," Ruanek returned.

"Circumstantial evidence alone is hardly logical."

"No, it's not," Uhura cut in. "But, gentlemen, I must interrupt this Vulcan logical debate. I can assure you both that Pavel Chekov is, indeed, very much alive. And from all that my . . . shall we say . . . certain sources tell me, he is very much in need of a rescue."

Spock nodded. He knew that Uhura had a series of "listeners" who served as her eyes and ears throughout the galaxy. He was not aware that she had any such listeners in the small area of space controlled by the Watraii, but she would not have made him aware of such operatives until he needed to know, either.

"That brave man in the hands of the Watraii," Ruanek exclaimed. "Of course he shall have that rescue."

"He shall," Spock vowed, "and swiftly."

For now it is clear that we are partly to blame. We were so certain that he had been slain, and so eager to avoid further confrontations with the Watraii . . .

Yes, we should have waited and investigated further. And Chekov is not a young man. He could not endure long captivity.

But regret for the past was illogical.

Hope was also illogical. But hope would not be denied.

Uhura held up a warning hand. "Unfortunately, gentlemen, the situation is even more complicated than that. My sources all agree on one thing: Chekov is being held not on a ship or a station, which would be relatively easy to take, but on what we believe to be the Watraii homeworld itself."

There was silence for a few moments. Then Spock began thoughtfully, "That is, indeed, a complication."

"Oh, indeed." Uhura gave them both a slight, wry smile. "You understand, I'm sure, that no matter how reliable my sources may be, I can't risk revealing them. And even if I could, they can hardly be put before the Federation Council for a declaration of war."

"Even if they could," Spock continued, "Starfleet cannot very well invade a sovereign world, not without being instantly labeled an aggressor by all its enemies and most of its allies. Nor can it risk a war at this time, or the potential unraveling of new alliances."

Uhura folded her arms on her desk. "And the Federation has no treaty with the Watraii, so there's no hope for diplomatic action."

Ruanek glanced from Spock to Uhura and back again. "Well, then it must be a covert mission."

Uhura leaned forward on her folded arms, not quite frowning at him. "You say that so lightly."

"Your pardon, but no," Ruanek countered, "I don't say it lightly at all. Believe me, I know what's at stake for everyone: You *know* my background, and I know the military mind. But if it can't be an official mission, a secret one is the only logical alternative." He gave a purely Romulan shrug of acceptance. "We managed a covert mission two months ago and came away from it without creating undue chaos for the Federation. We surely can manage such a mission again."

"You do realize the problems?" Uhura asked.

Ruanek tallied his answer off on his fingers. "One, a chance of starting a war. Two, a chance of killing innocent people—including the very man we need to save. Three, a chance of courts-martial for all Starfleet participants—and no, I'm not being facetious about any of this. But we all know that a covert mission really is the only way to rescue Pavel Chekov. And we can do it."

"Optimism is an emotion," Spock commented.

"Indeed it is," Ruanek agreed, but made no apology for his own. "Indeed it is."

And illogical or not, Spock thought, *it is an emotion that I share with you, Ruanek.*

FIVE

MEMORY

Karatek's empty cup fell to the deck, the ancient stone shattering with a strangely musical clatter. Behind him, T'Partha, diplomatic even in extremity, was forcing out hasty apologies. Then, Streon and T'Via flanking them, they were out the door, abandoning decorum and running toward the shuttlebay.

The unaccustomed effort and fear pushed up Karatek's heart rate. He might be warm for the first time since the great ships had voted to go on envirosave, but he could hardly be grateful for the sensation. Fire was warm, but fire, in this desert of stars, meant death.

All the mastery of his emotions that Karatek had so painstakingly studied since the moment Surak had appeared out of the desert and laid deft hands on his future vanished. What had pushed up his heart rate was not so much exertion as it was fear, worse than he had felt even when Vulcan Station was destroyed, and the exile began. He could remember the fires in the sky as the station exploded, then fire all around him.

It was happening again. Everything he loved would burn: T'Vysse, the children who remained to him and the one yet unborn; friends, associates, even antagonists like N'Keth. And *Shavokh* itself, the immensely precious, fragile metal shell that carried what was left of Karatek's entire world from one planet toward whatever refuge they might one day find.

"Could you get any information on what . . . ?" The ship's officer running near him next to his own guards, warding off the curious, might easily be fifty years younger than he. But he had to strain to keep up as Karatek tossed the words over his shoulder each time he drew breath.

The guard shook his head, sweat running down a face flushed olive with effort. His denial could mean no word had come or it wasn't safe to speak of it in this corridor.

The man flung up a hand. "This way."

They turned and dashed into a lift, which descended with such apparent slowness that Karatek wanted to line up the ship's engineers, shout at them, and never even think of the illogic and discourtesy of his action. Finally, the lift's doors parted, and they were out and running down the corridor that led to the main docking bay. Karatek got a glimpse of Streon's face before he hurled himself into the shuttle. *Someone,* at least, had received a full briefing, and the news was bad.

Karatek paused. He dropped his head, fighting to draw more breath in the ship's air, thin even for a Vulcan, and decided that that would have to suffice as a bow of courtesy.

"Leave first; talk later," T'Partha gasped. She flung herself into the shuttle before him, strapped down, and closed her eyes, trying for the rhythmic breathing that would help her restore her composure. She was too old to run races.

Logically, Karatek knew it took only 3.2 minutes for the shuttle to be turned on its landing cradle and released to return to *Sha-vokh*. It seemed to take far longer, forever, and no, you fool, this was no time to ponder relativistic time!

The shuttle hurtled out of the launch bay before it was fully un-sealed. Karatek unstrapped. Securing himself by gripping each seat as he passed, he struggled toward the copilot's seat.

"Give me the controls!" he demanded.

Who better than a propulsion engineer would know how to push the shuttle's engines past the green line that signaled danger? And he could at least grant himself this small relief: he could fly.

Screens lit beneath his fingers: all systems operational. No, better than that: nominal. At least something was going right on this day of remembrance.

"Tell me what you know!" he ordered.

"You're needed," the pilot said. "Something about the te-Vikram, about the one who is—"

"N'Veyan, yes," T'Partha, listening intently from her seat, in-terrupted. "Night and day, man, we haven't time for talking around the Fires! I am a grandmother three times over. Do you think I remember nothing of the Fires?"

So, the problem was N'Veyan. N'Veyan, whose kinsmen had re-quested the use of a shuttle so that he could meet his betrothed at the appointed place. N'Veyan, whom Karatek had seen, guarded by kinsmen. The longer the Fires burned, the less rational their vic-tim became. N'Veyan's actions, his reasoning, his life processes themselves, would become more and more erratic until he entered the *Plak-tow,* or blood fever. And if that were not assuaged, con-vulsions and madness would burn him out from within, assuming his warrior's conditioning made him so supremely unfortunate that his heart did not give way before his mind.

"I know that one, sir," the pilot said. "Used to stand and just watch the shuttles. After a while, he started to ask questions. I think he'd gotten himself some training too."

Karatek clasped his hand over his eyes so hard that green and blue flames leapt in them from the pressure.

"You think he stole a shuttle?" T'Partha's voice was calm.

"I think he tried," Karatek said. Streon nodded agreement.

Logic would have told anyone that for a shuttle pilot to leave a much larger ship traveling at near-relativistic speed, then match velocities and courses with another ship took rigorous training and composure. To say nothing of courage.

Well, N'Veyan had courage. Perhaps he still had a shred of sanity left too. The best Karatek could hope for was that he had holed up in the shuttlebay and was refusing to speak to anyone while his kinsmen tried to restrain him.

"I'm trying to reach *Shavokh* communications," the pilot said. "Wait! *Shavokh* com, this is Shuttle Four, returning as ordered. Give me ship's status."

"We have a situation in the main shuttlebay."

All Karatek's life, officialdom termed every alert, every warning, hells, every attack a "situation." What *kind* of situation? As he had his life long, Karatek managed not to ask.

"There is nothing to gain from haste but error." Surak's *Second Analects.*

Logic be burned.

"N'Veyan . . ." *Shavokh* com this shift was a woman trying to sound dispassionate and succeeding—the last logical portion of Karatek's brain told him—admirably.

"How far gone is he?" T'Partha had thrust herself into ops and leaned over the console, one hand clutching the back of the pilot's chair.

Women, Karatek knew from overhearing conversations in his own household, were often disastrously frank in speaking to one another, especially about the Fires. The tips of his ears heated.

But, was that an indrawn breath of relief he heard across the immense distance that separated him from his ship?

"After you left, word came that N'Veyan grew increasingly agitated," communications said. *"Even though we told him that as soon as you returned, the shuttle would be available."*

"Plak-tow?"

"We think so. Of course, his kinsmen shielded him. The healers say it's hard to know how long the cycles last out here; something about the time shifts. But N'Veyan grew worse. And then all the te-Vikram—well, you know how the fever sometimes makes a man's attendants behave almost as if they too . . . Sorry, sir."

The pilot Karatek had replaced shot him an almost shamed glance. They were both adult males. They knew how the Fires burned, how overpowering the longing and the physical need for the mates to whose minds they had been attuned in childhood became. They knew the stories of miraculous feats of strength, desert crossings, nighttime raids. And madness, followed by violent death.

Karatek thought back to his own marriage. The 2.23 hours he had had to wait before the guards and *systra*s had finally, finally arrived to lead him to the appointed place had seemed as endless as this journey back to *Shavokh*. He remembered how time, suffused with flame, seemed to stop. He did not remember, until he was told, that he had wept and slammed his fists against the walls until they bled.

And then he had seen T'Vysse, accompanied by a healer priestess. Seen her, taken her hand, sipped blessedly cool water, and touched his mate, in mind and, much too long afterward, in body . . .

The next morning, she had bandaged his hands herself, kissing them with her fingertips.

And now T'Vysse was in deadly danger.

Karatek drew a ragged breath and knew that the pilot, too, struggled for composure. It was not only the male and his attendants who grew erratic in these situations.

Meanwhile, T'Partha was interrogating the communications officer.

It wasn't that the te-Vikram had gotten tired of waiting. They had become afraid. N'Veyan had had his first convulsions. If he had entered the final stage of the Fires, the madness, they were out of time.

Drugs existed to slow the decline in emergencies, although they were held to represent weakness of character. There was even stasis. But the te-Vikram's customs called medical intervention during the Fires an abomination.

"It would have seemed logical to me simply to direct N'Veyan and his attendants to one of the other shuttles rather than wait," T'Partha observed. She turned to Karatek and the young pilot, then snapped, "Are you two fit to fly this shuttle, or must I?"

T'Partha was no pilot, and they all knew it. She would probably crash into *Shavokh,* if she didn't miss it altogether. But her tart question restored their self-command.

"Maintenance schedules." Communications's voice was low, ashamed. *"More: none of the men in the shuttlebay are qualified pilots. The shuttle would have been lost."*

"Along with the men in it!" Karatek interrupted.

"It was feared that if the shuttle were lost, the te-Vikram might . . ."

Karatek shut his eyes. He could just imagine the discussion, the debate between generosity and cruelty. Why waste a journey on one te-Vikram warrior? What was the loss of one te-Vikram, a potential troublemaker at that, against the loss of a valuable shuttle? It wasn't as if the te-Vikram had wanted to leave Vulcan. The only reason there were any te-Vikram on board was that they had attacked just at the moment of another, greater attack. Karatek had never known whether they had followed the exiles on board the shuttles to continue to fight or to save their own lives.

He doubted if the te-Vikram remembered either.

So. Karatek thought he could reproduce the thinking among some of *Shavokh*'s council. There were te-Vikram in the shuttlebay, almost incapacitated by blood fever. There was little harm they could do if they were sealed in. If worst came to worst, they could be vented into space. Sound the alarm, and order Karatek back from *Rea's Helm* to deal with it. He might fail. And if he did, the ship would fall into other, far more ambitious hands. Worthier hands, as they calculated.

Karatek felt his lips peel back into a snarl.

"To the Fires with that," he swore.

As delicately as he had touched T'Vysse's face with his battered hands that first morning after he woke, blessedly sane again, to find her watching him, without fear and with considerable tenderness, Karatek touched the controls, coaxing more speed from the ship. He did not at all like the vibration he felt from the deck, but they would reach *Shavokh* soon, or it would not matter.

"No!" communications cried. *"They can't! Tell them . . ."*

"What is it?" T'Partha shouted, as if sheer volume could keep the people on board *Shavokh* focused.

"Patch me through to the shuttlebay," Karatek ordered. "Main bay, what is your status?"

The language of technology, of control came so naturally to him that he was shocked to hear the shrill cry of *systras* in response.

"We can wait no longer!" The reply came in a husky, deep-desert accent. Karatek didn't know the voice, or, more likely, couldn't identify it.

"Is N'Keth there?" Karatek demanded. N'Keth and Solor had always enjoyed a rapport that Karatek had, at first, considered highly illogical. Over the years, however, he himself had become acquainted with N'Keth and developed a wary but respectful relationship.

"The old man? He tried to stop us. We challenged, and he fell . . ."

Dead, then? Karatek realized that he would grieve for the te-Vikram elder, not just because he had been a voice of restraint among the te-Vikram males, but because he had proved himself to be worthy of respect.

"We would not have his blood on our hands. We left him outside. It is no matter if you speak to him. He is useless."

"Main bay, listen to me. Do you have a pilot there?"

A long pause.

"There was a female. At first, we thought . . . no. She said she belonged to another. We follow all our laws despite temptation. So, before we sealed the bay, we put her out."

"Out of the bay or . . ." T'Partha could not bring herself to express her worst fears, that they might have spaced the woman.

"Here is no place for her!"

The proper place for a pilot, male or female, was in a shuttle.

"T'Rya's young," said their own shuttle pilot. "Not three years bonded."

That answered that question. A bonded woman. Tempting, but not available to serve N'Veyan's need, even if he could accept her.

The te-Vikram were violent, but, by their own standards, rigidly moral. Far more moral, they thought, than other Vulcans. And that skewed morality held, even when one of their own convulsed in *Plak-tow.*

"Can't you let another pilot in there?" Karatek demanded.

"You fool, we sealed the bay," came the voice. *"Welded it shut. By the time . . ."* A long pause, with the sounds of screaming in the background.

"We're out of time. He's shaking. . . . Don't let him bite his tongue!"

"Shuttlebay." T'Partha leaned over Karatek, shouting. "Hold on! We're coming in!" she cried. "Our pilot can take you to the other ship. Or"—she drew a deep, shaky breath—"if there is no other female . . ."

Karatek set a hand on her shoulder, shutting his eyes almost in awe. Back on Vulcan, the unbonded tended to be very young, their health and sanity a priority of the Seleyan order of healers. T'Partha was no priestess of the unbonded, but she was offering herself.

T'Partha was in late middle age, while N'Veyan, even weakened by the Fires, was a young man with as much warrior training as the te-Vikram could manage in envirosave. If her offer were accepted, she might not survive it.

The needs of the one, Karatek thought.

But *which* one? His old friend and colleague, or a young man who might live to help build a new world?

The choice was not his, but T'Partha's. And she had made it.

"How long?" he whispered to the pilot.

"Six-point-four minutes," the other said, hands flattened on auxiliary controls as if he could soothe the strain in the engines, the growing vibrations in the hull that threatened to tear the shuttle apart.

"Hold on!" Karatek cried out into space toward *Shavokh*.

He didn't need magnification to see the ship now.

A scream answered him.

"We can't hold him!" he heard, followed by other screams.

"He's going to . . ."

"Nooooo!"

A rush of sound, like the winds blowing across Mount Seleya, only magnified, tremendously magnified, blasted across the communications system.

Fire and debris erupted from what had been *Shavokh*'s main shuttlebay. Panels of the ship's hull peeled back, twisted by the blast as the shuttle, piloted by a dying madman, crashed into it.

The choice had not been T'Partha's, after all.

N'Veyan would never meet his mate at the appointed place now.

At least, *Shavokh* survived.

"Stay back, stand off!" A scream of near panic erupted from *Shavokh*'s control system and matched the scream of the shuttle's engines, of the small craft itself, as it bucked and lurched, struck by fragments.

Murmuring invocations under his breath, his eyes wide, Streon helped Karatek evade the worst of the debris. It took both of them to keep the shuttle from tumbling out of control.

When the shockwave subsided, the younger man slumped forward until his brow rested on the control panel. Karatek set a hand on his shoulder. T'Partha slipped off her cloak, spread it over the pilot's trembling shoulders, and went to find water.

Karatek looked out at *Shavokh*. Its damaged panels, still glowing from the explosion, peeled back and curled up, almost in the shape of a *kylin'the* blossom, but one that brought only death, not healing. If Karatek hadn't persuaded the council to reinforce the hull after the last mining expedition, they would be turning back to *Rea's Helm* for refuge, assuming that they could find the heart to go on.

"Shuttle . . . calling Shuttle One! Karatek, are you alive in there?"

"The ship!" T'Partha said.

Streon lifted his head. The veils flickered across his eyes, then drew back, leaving them quite calm.

"We came through." Karatek leaned over the pilot. "Streon's skill was . . ." In the *Analects,* Surak had always said there was no higher praise than "satisfactory." Surak, however, could be wrong. "He saved us."

Right now, though, Streon was suffering from shock and reaction. Karatek opened his mouth to continue when the man pushed him gently aside.

"*Shavokh* control, this is Streon, pilot and security officer for *T'Kehr* Karatek and *T'sai* T'Partha. Is the auxiliary bay prepared to receive us? We are coming home."

"We shall be with you shortly," T'Partha called into communications.

"Three-point-eight minutes," corrected Streon.

"Thank you," T'Partha said. "And please tell the te-Vikram, 'I grieve with thee.'"

As they made their final approach, they saw suited figures, tiny crafts, and even the rudimentary 'bots that the technocrats were testing, issuing from their injured ship, to begin repairs.

Almost before the shuttle quivered to a stop in the nearest of *Shavokh*'s auxiliary bays, Karatek was struggling out of his harness. Then he was up and making for the hatch. Alarms shrieked in the embattled ship's thin air, their pitch rising and falling until it took real restraint for him not to clasp his hands over his ears.

A guard ran up to him, the elegant upcurve of her own ears hidden by a protective headset. She thrust another such set at Karatek, along with a radiation badge. "You need to come to decontamination," she ordered.

"T'Partha, you go," he replied. "There's something else . . ."

"Logic requires we monitor any radiation exposure you incurred when the shockwave hit," said the guard.

Logic be damned, Karatek wanted to tell her, but shock silenced him. Shock, like anger and grief, was an emotion, he realized. Either he would have to confront those emotions in meditation—and soon—or he would have to revisit the entire subject of emotional control. The day Surak had walked out of the desert and become Karatek's guest-friend, he had worn a radiation badge too. It was not a phase of his life he wished to relive.

"Not now!" he repeated. He brushed the guard's hand away from his arm. She was younger than he and quicker: if she decided to make him accompany her, she probably could. But he was counting on the Vulcan respect for elders to forestall her.

He was right. But the guard was a stubborn guard and knew her job. "I want your word of honor that you will receive medical assistance as soon as possible," she told him. "Or I will carry you to the healers now myself."

Inclining his head in a tacit promise, he raced down the corridor. The deck underfoot still trembled, like a gong struck in the *Kal-if-fee.* That mating could never take place now. On board one of the other ships, another would probably die today, a woman deprived of her betrothed.

He ran toward the bulkheads that sealed off the hull breach that had once been a shuttlebay, fighting the wave of Vulcans who were evacuating the area as technical, construction, and security specialists poured in.

Burnt metal, ozone, and the reek of scorched cables within the bulkheads assaulted his nostrils, not to mention a sort of sharp, stinging sensation that hovered just beyond his awareness and made his instincts scream danger. He would be very, very fortunate if, at his age, the radiation treatments did not leave him sickly for the rest of his life.

Thick billows of acrid smoke still filled the area. The ventilation systems panted like wounded *sehlat*s to suck it back into the air ducts built into the bulkheads to be purified and released, traces of poison still probably in it.

Karatek coughed, then coughed again into an upheld hand that came away from his mouth flecked with dark green.

He rounded a corner, all but staggering as he stumbled into masked security and medical workers who knelt at . . .

"N'Keth!" Karatek cried. It made him cough again, bringing up more blood.

The te-Vikram warrior—warrior-by-courtesy, Karatek supposed—lay propped against the bulkhead. He was coughing feebly, dark green blood trickling out of his mouth. His face was bruised, and his garments sodden with blood. One leg, bent at an impossible angle, was thrust out before him. Before Karatek glanced away in a combination of courtesy and nausea, he thought he saw bone piercing the bared flesh.

A weaker man would have been unconscious. N'Keth was waving away the healer who knelt at his side, offering him painkillers since, obviously, meditations on the theme of "there is no pain" would not serve a man who served the priest-kings now parsecs behind them on Vulcan.

To Karatek's astonishment, his son Solor knelt on N'Keth's other side. He probably knew as much about the te-Vikram as anyone not blood of their blood, or sealed thus to them. What an irony. N'Keth had sought a youth to train in the te-Vikram's ways. To some extent, he had actually succeeded.

"Father!" Solor said. He bent over N'Keth. "I told you there was a 93.4 percent probability that my father would come directly here from the shuttle."

N'Keth muttered something Karatek interpreted as "logic be damned." Well, Karatek could hardly criticize the man's reasoning. He was injured; pain weakened one's judgment. And Karatek had thought the same thing not five minutes earlier.

Instead, he dropped to his knee and edged over beside the te-Vikram. N'Keth reached out and clasped his wrist, a warrior's gesture of respect.

"You must leave," he ordered.

"I just got here!" Karatek protested. He looked over at his son. Solor was young and would wish to have children: he was the one who ought to leave before he took additional radiation damage.

The healer inclined her head, lowering her eyes. Karatek recalled this one: T'Olryn. She was very young, trained during the journey to be especially aware of its hazards.

"I want you to take your son away," N'Keth said. His voice was fainter. More blood trickled out of the left side of his mouth.

Internal injuries?

One wondered that the healer had not yet ordered him sedated and carried out.

"I won't go," Solor said. Not his most courteous voice, but Solor had always been stubborn, especially when Sarissa was not present to glare him into cooperation.

He heard a painful chuckle from N'Keth. "And so you challenge again? I regret I must . . . must yield."

A long pause. N'Keth closed his eyes, as if summoning reserves of strength.

"I told him that even if we removed him to emergency facilities . . ." Healer T'Olryn's voice remained clinical as her long, delicate fingers touched her instruments as if she played a music that only she could hear.

"My choice!" N'Keth told her. "And you, what are you doing here . . . courting damage . . . better that some warrior court . . . court you! Leave us, woman!" he ordered.

T'Olryn lifted slanted eyebrows and awarded him a haughty glance. She was tiny, with masses of dark braids piled up on a proudly carried head.

"The day I cannot appreciate a little beauty like you . . ." N'Keth choked out. Wiping at the blood, more of it this time, that trickled from his mouth, T'Olryn pressed the cloth to his lips, hushing him.

"He has the right to refuse treatment, T'Olryn," Solor told her.

As the healer met his eyes, he inclined his head, respect that he turned into a bow.

And was that a chuckle, or a gurgle of blood Karatek heard from N'Keth?

He forced himself to scrutinize the wounded . . . no, the dying . . . te-Vikram. He remembered young Varen, dying in the desert in Surak's grasp. Varen's lips too had been stained with blood. He too had fought for breath and composure. And he had looked at Sarissa with the same kind of admiration.

Karatek lowered his head.

The healer reached out, her paired fingers extended to seek out the *katra* that struggled within its damaged prison of flesh.

N'Keth flinched away violently, then slumped and lay panting. Finally, he spoke again. "Always . . . I wondered how, when I was too old . . . They challenged. Those damned *le-matya* cubs . . ." He laughed, a rasping sound that hurt Karatek's ears and made Solor flinch. "I never expected . . ." He paused. "Good for them! When I told them to wait, that the shuttle would return, that a proper pilot, not some young girl, would take N'Veyan—may his *katra* return to the Womb of Fire and be reborn—to the appointed place . . . they told me that no Fires burned in my blood, and hadn't, not since exile. They . . . told me that I was useless, and they thrust me aside."

"That wasn't all they did!" Solor said. He reached down and pried N'Keth's free hand away from the gaping wound in his chest.

Never mind the fumes the man had inhaled. It was a wonder he had survived at all with a chest wound like that, Karatek thought.

N'Keth's face grew even more pinched, and Karatek knew the end was very near.

"Let him go," Solor told the healer. "You know they regard a warrior's death as a matter for warriors."

"Leave me, woman," N'Keth commanded the healer again.

T'Olryn's eyes blazed. At the illogic, at the loss of a patient, or at the criminal waste?

"Yield to the logic of the situation, T'Olryn." Again, Solor tried to persuade her. He held out a hand to help her rise.

Pushing his hand away, she drew herself up, a swift movement of upright, outraged dignity. She pulled her robes aside and stalked away through the security officers and construction crews. They parted, allowing her to pass, bowing respect as if to a senior priestess.

Karatek would have been surprised if they had not.

"Someone turn that racket down!" Karatek ordered. If N'Keth had last words for him, he needed to be able to hear them. And it was only respectful to let the man die in a decent quiet.

A guard gestured, and the whoops and shrieks of the alarms subsided.

"I . . ." He looked up at Karatek. "I don't envy you. Things are . . . You know matters are only going to get worse. The old ways, the old world . . . gone now. I will be glad to rest."

"You didn't have to get yourself killed to tell me that!" snapped Karatek. He looked down at his radiation badge, suppressing a snarl at what it told him.

Again, N'Keth chuckled. He tried to speak again. Instead, he yawned deeply, drifting away as his blood flow ebbed in a deep green tide.

"Look . . . you look after them," he said. "I was the last of our men trained in the old ways."

"Ways change," said Solor.

"But you, you will remember?" For one as sure, as arrogant as N'Keth had been every time Karatek had seen him, the uncertainty in the dying man's voice pierced Karatek's heart.

"I will remember. Commissioner T'Partha told me to say, 'I grieve for thee.'"

"Stubborn woman," said N'Keth. "Like the pilot they sent outside. They did right. I was indeed old, useless. . . . But that young healer, she is a rare one, is she not?" He tilted his head at Solor.

To Karatek's surprise, his son glanced down and sideways. He had not known that N'Keth enjoyed that much of Solor's confidence. He had had to be so busy with *Shavokh*'s affairs, he pleaded inwardly, but not so busy that he neglected his family or lost his son's confidence. Solor should have been bonded years ago.

"You," he told Solor. "Both of you. Go now before the radiation drains you like the Eater of Souls. But, before you do . . . a gift. A blade to match the weapon you stole from me so long ago!"

"No," Solor whispered. "Surely, some other kinsman remains."

"The last of my sons died today," N'Keth said. "I do not wish to wait, to die on a pallet in the bright lights of what you call a medical ward, exposed to . . . to the shameless likes of that healer whom you follow with your eyes the way a nursing *sehlat* watches his dam. I shall go now."

He pulled his hand out from beneath Karatek's and let it drop to his belt. For a moment he lay panting, visibly fighting to summon his last strength. And then he pulled out a dagger, its hilt studded with gems and heavy with the sigils of whatever House a te-Vikram might claim.

"You . . . you were my first defeat," he told Solor. "When I am gone . . . take it from my body!"

"No!" Karatek whispered, echoing his son's protest.

"He does not understand . . . explain!"

"N'Keth can no longer fight," Solor told Karatek. "If we were back on Vulcan, he would walk out into the desert and die there, preserving his honor for his clan. But, as you see, he cannot walk. So, instead, he will claim Final Honor."

"This is barbarous!" Karatek protested. The illogical waste and cruelty—and to think how, long ago, he had watched old men limp out alone into the desert without racing after them. . . .

"I am only thankful he has the strength and will to claim it for himself," Solor told him. "Otherwise, Final Honor is the duty of his closest male kin. And you heard him call me 'son.'"

Karatek shut his eyes, hoping that N'Keth would die now, right now, from the blood loss, and not subject them all to this atavism he called honor.

A thin wail of chanted Old High Vulcan came from N'Keth's lips, as the trickle of blood down his chin grew thicker. Solor joined him in the chant, his voice rising and falling in the inflections of the deep desert, gaining strength as N'Keth's voice faltered. There was no emotion in Solor's voice; the pain Karatek heard came from the tones of the chant itself.

N'Keth gasped and fell silent. "One more thing," he told Karatek. "You. You and the man who is son to me, as well as to you. Remember my true name. I am Azeraik. May the Womb of Fire grant me swift rebirth!"

As Solor supported him, Azeraik, called N'Keth, thrust the dagger into the wound in his chest, widening it, so the blood ran freely over the barren, violated deckplates. And, as he died, he laughed.

Solor lowered his head, his lips moving. Karatek stayed near his son, waiting. Finally, Solor rose. Taking the dagger from N'Keth's limp hand, he cleaned it on a dry patch of the dead warrior's tunic, then thrust it into his belt.

"Let's go," he said.

SIX

NOW

EARTH
STARDATE 54104.3

The *U.S.S. Alliance* was a sleek, elegant ship, an *Excelsior*-class Starfleet science vessel—one, though, that had served as a military ship during the Dominion War, and also in the unofficial encounters with the Watraii.

Its captain, Saavik, who was also wife to Spock, sat in her command chair like the perfect image of a Starfleet officer in her neat uniform.

Saavik also looked, she knew from years of careful practice, the perfect image of Vulcan calm and cool. Not like a half-Romulan who still, even now, had to fight down fits of hot temper. Not like a Starfleet officer who had nearly thrown away her whole career to help Spock defeat the Watraii, no matter how temporarily.

We did what was both logically necessary and humane. And if it caused trouble with the bureaucrats, so be it.

That last part of the thought had been purely Romulan.

The bridge of Saavik's ship was a clean and elegant blend of Starfleet and Vulcan tastes, appealing to the mind and eye alike, absolutely logical in its layout, with nothing out of place.

Yes, the ship might look tranquil, Saavik thought wryly, but her image of calm wasn't completely honest. Her crew was normally made up of a mix of experienced humans, Bolians, and Vulcans, a crew with whom she'd worked for quite some time and whom she knew she could trust to be efficient and effective even in an emergency. They had volunteered to go with her on that mission against the Watraii without hesitation. But Starfleet's latest experiment in accelerating the training of newer recruits—they'd tried a dozen such methods after the end of the Dominion War and the realization of how shorthanded they'd been caught—had been an order that new crew members be assigned to several ships. That meant, of course, that some of the more experienced crew members had to be transferred away to make room for the newcomers.

Bureaucracy is bureaucracy, regardless of species or culture, Saavik thought philosophically. *As Spock might say, you cannot fight it; simply accept it.*

As if he'd heard her thoughts, one ensign gave her a quick, awed glance. This was a human, Ensign Edwin Del, a Terran from a Hispanic background and one of those newly assigned to this ship— no, he would be new to any ship—who looked on Starfleet as something almost divine. Another new ensign was Nalia, a pretty Bolian young woman with skin that was a clear, light turquoise and who looked too young, in fact, to be in any service. Nalia happened to look her way and then actually blushed in confusion.

Children.

But for all their newness and occasional awkwardness, they do seem quite competent, under normal circumstances.

I only trust that we don't run into any abnormal circumstances.

That was particularly true since they were currently entering orbit of Earth—a world many of the young people aboard knew primarily as the home of Starfleet Academy and more abstractly as the seat of the Federation government. Thinking of the shore leave possible in San Francisco alone, Saavik told herself that she would need to be sure the young things were kept on leads like so many frisky *kitiki.*

The fact that she would, unless the Romulans had called off the entire meeting, also have her own brief shore leave with Spock . . .

Maybe, she thought dryly, *I should put a leash on myself as well.*

At that precise moment, with what she knew humans would have called a prime example of Murphy's Law, Lieutenant Suhur, a dark-skinned young Vulcan man at communications said, "A message is coming in from Earth for you, Captain Saavik. It's encrypted, double security, ma'am."

Saavik got to her feet. There was a logical 93.552 percent chance that the message was from Spock. Something clearly had happened, either at the Romulan–Federation conference or— But guessing was not logical. "I'll take it in my ready room. Mr. Harex, you have the bridge."

Saavik's voice, Spock thought, sounded most upset—no, to be more accurate, it held a mixture of surprise, alarm, and annoyance. *"I did not know,"* she said. *"I didn't think it possible for him to have survived. But yes, of course Admiral Chekov must be rescued. And of course I will be part of your team. After all, it was from my ship that the admiral . . . disappeared."*

"And yet . . . ?" Spock prodded.

"And yet the issue that is standing in the way is that I have several very new crew members aboard, husband. I cannot risk their lives and careers—and I do not trust their new skills on such an unusual and unpredictable mission."

"There is a choice," Spock told her. "You can offer them a shuttlecraft, an honorable chance to leave."

Only her husband could have read the barely controlled frustration in Saavik's voice. *"Yes, husband, I will do just that—though they are just young enough to be foolishly courageous."* She gave the softest sigh. *"Still, you need have no concern on the matter. I will, as I say, be part of this team. Saavik out."*

She broke the connection, and Spock allowed himself a split second of longing for his wife, from whom their careers separated him far too often—emotional thinking though that might be—and then joined Uhura and Ruanek as they continued their clandestine enlistment mission. Uhura, being who and what she was, already knew perfectly well who she had in mind. As before, the majority of the team whom they reached were those people, human or not, who had been on the first mission, many of them those surviving members of the several *Enterprises* who were available.

But then Ruanek came suddenly alert. To Spock's bemusement, Ruanek watched Uhura and the person on the viewscreen with intense curiosity.

Uhura, of course, was aware of it, but ignored it. "Ah, Lieutenant Commander Data. A pleasure to speak with you again."

"And with you, Admiral Uhura. I do understand the mission, and I shall be honored to be included."

"Data, you know that my offer still stands. You would make an excellent SI operative."

"Again, Admiral, I am honored, but I fear I cannot accept."

Uhura smiled. "I understand, and believe me, I'm not offended. You will do far more good as an officer on our flagship."

Ruanek's curiosity finally got the better of him. "No insult meant, Lieutenant Commander, but are you not an android?"

"Indeed I am, sir, though I am now equipped with an emotion chip that enables me to feel what a human would feel."

"Thank you, Commander Data, I'll transmit your new orders shortly. Uhura out."

Spock glanced sideways. "Ruanek?"

"Data's commanding officer is Jean-Luc Picard, am I correct?"

"Yes."

"Ah, well, you wouldn't remember it, Spock, since you were, well, not in your right mind at the time," Ruanek said, delicately sidestepping the fact that Spock had been deep in the madness of *Pon farr* back then, "but Captain Picard and I go back quite a bit. When you and I were escaping from Romulus, he was the one who rescued us from deep space—though he never did learn who you were—and he and I . . . let us say that we eliminated Dralath together."

"Ah." Spock carefully refrained from saying that only Ruanek could ever have managed to be both an honorable Romulan commander and a Federation warrior at the same time.

"Yes, and when I was your father's aide on Earth," Ruanek continued, "Picard and I almost literally ran into each other, and I had a good deal of evasive explaining to do."

As I can well imagine. "It is unlikely that there will be another such encounter in the near future," Spock said solemnly.

"No," Ruanek agreed just as solemnly. "Under the circumstances, I can't see Captain Picard being able to aid us just now." He shook his head. "An android lieutenant commander. Now that certainly has to be our most unusual volunteer."

"Ah, excuse me, gentlemen," Uhura cut in, suddenly alert, "but there is an incoming message. Encrypted."

"Shall I leave?" Ruanek asked.

Uhura shook her head. "You're already part of this. I recognize the style of the encryption." She glanced at Spock. "You have already puzzled out, I'm sure, that in these unsettled times it has been . . . only logical for me and my Romulan counterpart to be in frequent, if unofficial, touch."

"Indeed." Charvanek would hardly have been less logical than Uhura about it, and would be just as hungry for useful data from the other side.

Charvanek was Spock's oldest and closest not-quite-enemy. She was known to him since his days on Kirk's *Enterprise*—she who had once been a fleet commander and then the consort of the late Praetor Narviat, and was now the head of Romulan Security. That Charvanek and Uhura were acting without Starfleet knowledge or permission was certain, but it was also certain that the issue would not truly bother either of them. "The needs of the many . . ." was a Romulan adage too.

"I am not alone," Uhura said to her Romulan counterpart. "Spock and Ruanek are here as well."

"Spock," Charvanek said dryly. *"That hardly surprises me. Events do seem to keep throwing us together."*

Her voice was controlled, revealing little of her thoughts. But after the incident of the Watraii attack and rebuff, Spock thought, she surely had to trust him, at least as much as she trusted any non-Romulan. He said to her, "You did not contact this office merely to jest. Charvanek, if you have been contacting the admiral before this, you surely know that this office is as secure as anything devised by the Tal Shiar."

"I am well aware of that. Very well, I will say this and be as

blunt as a Vulcan: I have grown disgusted with Ambassador T'Kala's tantrums and other childishness and with what I believe humans call 'tiptoeing around the truth.'"

"And that truth is . . . ?"

There was the briefest pause. Then Charvanek said, with cold anger behind the mask of calm, *"Romulus has undergone another attack. And yes, it was from the Watraii. This time they managed to destroy a base before retreating. Wait, though, don't interrupt. There is worse than an unwarranted and cowardly attack. Not only have those dishonorable* tetcharik"—Ruanek, overhearing, raised a startled eyebrow at that obscenity—*"destroyed that base, they also managed to capture . . ."* After an awkward pause, she continued, *"Akkh, let us call it an artifact."*

"An . . . artifact," Spock echoed cautiously.

"Yes." The word was knife-edged. *"An artifact that is so politically and historically important that it might as well be considered sacred."*

"I understand. All cultures have such items. But what is this particular artifact?"

"That," Charvanek said, just as sharply, *"I refuse to say."*

If it is a relic of Romulan history and honor, why are you so reluctant to speak about it? "Or else, perhaps," Spock returned carefully, "you are simply not sure about its true nature."

"I said that I refuse to say! Spock, that should suffice."

Ah, then you are in doubt about what it truly is. "I meant no insult."

She gave a fierce little gust of a sigh. *"I know that. You never were malicious. But I also know how sly your words can be, Spock, you who have tricked me more than once. Yet what I do or do not know is not the issue. I will say only that it is essential for the sake of all the Romulans and the stability of the Romulan Star Empire that the artifact be returned."*

Spock raised an eyebrow, considering. Anything that was so very important . . . Romulans, he knew, might revere relics of the past, but did not hold them as so close to sacred. And yet . . .

Testing, he began, "I must wonder if what we are discussing might not be more than some merely historic relic, even one that might date from the time of the Sundering."

"Stop your prying!"

"Charvanek, if you wish us to help you, we must have honesty from you. Does this mysterious artifact not also contain some vital data as well?"

"Spock, you are too cunning for your own well-being."

And you, Charvanek, have by your very evasiveness just given me the information that I suspected.

There was only one piece of data that could possibly be so important. "Charvanek, I am not trying to be cunning, nor do I wish harm to the Romulan people. You, of all, should know that by now. But I can only deduce by your very refusal to give me any facts that the artifact contains very valuable data indeed—possibly nothing less than the proof or, for that matter, the falsehood behind the Watraii claims."

She said nothing, neither confirming nor denying.

"Therefore," Spock continued into the tense silence, "I agree that it must be retrieved before there is outright war. We must also retrieve it before the Watraii can decipher whatever data it contains."

After another few seconds of silence, Charvanek volunteered warily, *"I doubt that decryption will be that easy. While we do suspect it contains . . . what you suggested, no one, to the best of my knowledge, has ever found out what it contains."* Then she added with a touch of frustration, *"I cannot leave my post, not with the situation as it is. And you, Vulcan though you are, are the most efficient, honest being I know. Spock, in the name of peace, I urge you to retrieve the artifact."*

"Mind if I cut in?" Uhura asked. "Charvanek, I have a gamble to make with you."

"I am listening." The Romulan's voice was Vulcan-cool.

"Who would you rather have retrieve the artifact—the Federation, which will use it as a bargaining chip to assure Romulan cooperation—and I will, of course, deny having said that—or these people whom you know you can trust?"

"You presume much, my counterpart," Charvanek said dryly. *"But what do you want in exchange?"*

"One of our own is a Watraii captive."

A pause. *"Very well, what do you want of me?"*

"We both have the coordinates of the Watraii homeworld. Starfleet does not. Not . . . exactly."

"Ah. I know how that game is played. They have received partial information to get them into the region but not to the exact world. And I will gamble that you want me to reveal only partial information as well."

Uhura leaned forward. "If Starfleet goes there in full force, you know as well as I what will happen."

"Fighting," Charvanek said flatly. *"And your hostage will no doubt be slain in the middle of it . . . and the artifact will be at risk as well. A problem. Uhura, understand this: I cannot withhold the truth for long. I can give you a lead of . . . akkh, realistically not more than two shipboard days."*

"That will do," Spock said. He did not add what he was thinking: *If it takes longer, Chekov will already be dead.*

"If anyone can work wonders," Charvanek said, her voice fairly dripping with irony, *"it will be you, Spock. Very well, you will have two days. Charvanek out."*

With that, she broke the connection.

For a moment, no one in the office spoke. The mission, Spock thought, had just gotten doubly complex. *Now we must not only penetrate Watraii space, we must rescue Chekov and we must re-cover the Romulan artifact. As Dr. McCoy once said, "No one ever said life was fair."* Illogical or not, that statement did seem to fit the situation.

"Well," Ruanek finally said. "At least now we know why the Romulans broke off negotiations in such a hurry."

Uhura nodded. "There's a good cover for our original mission: the recovery of a historic Romulan artifact. It means, though, that we'll need a Romulan on the mission to verify that we get the right artifact."

She gave Ruanek a speculative glance.

Ruanek frowned slightly at her. "I don't think that I like where this is heading."

Uhura gave him her most dazzling smile, the smile that had melted the enmity of men of several species. "Why, it's only logical. You *are* the only Romulan we know who is definitely on our side."

Ruanek sighed. "I cannot argue with logic. And never mind the fact that I have been living as a Vulcan of Vulcan for all these years. I know, like it or not, that there is no one else."

"Well, then!"

"But—akkh, I also know that this isn't a logical statement—but T'Selis is going to kill me for risking my life. Again."

Spock, wisely, said nothing.

SEVEN

MEMORY

His dream made Karatek a boy again. That dawn, he had scratched off another day with an obsidian flake on a vein of exposed rock along the Forge. He had spent hours digging for food. Hunger had sharpened his focus, but weakened his time sense. Now, harsh rays of ruddy light slanted across the Forge, lower and lower as the day died in flames. If he could not outrace the falling night, he would be isolated in the desert without shelter. And he was so close, too, to completing his trial!

He dashed across the Forge till his side was one long, throbbing ache from the speed of his heartbeat. There! He found the heap of rocks he had sheltered in for two nights now. When he had left it, only that dawn, it had been free of predators.

He only hoped his heart and lungs and strength could make the best possible use of the last embers of red light on the red sand. He kept his eyes hyperfocused on the terrain, his feet feeling out the scarps of obsidian, like shards of bone jutting from the sand.

If he stumbled now, he could die, of a severed artery if he hit a sharp obsidian edge, or of a broken bone, which would immobilize him, leaving him prey to denizens of the Forge, whose night eyes and ability to sense heat would detect him once night fell. Even if no predators came, as wind rushed down from the peaks, hammering the Forge, the temperature would plummet. To be caught unarmed and barely clothed on the Forge at night was to die. Unless Karatek could reach shelter, it would not matter whether he was two days, two hours, or two minutes from the end of his ordeal: he would not see another dawn.

But there were predators other than those who hunted on four feet. As Karatek raced across the last smooth expanse of sand toward his refuge, his weight set off a *s'gagerat,* which had extended its long tendrils beneath the sand. Instantly, they snapped up around the deadly plant's central core, big enough and fast enough to stop a full-grown *sehlat* running flat out.

Small for his age, Karatek managed to slip through. But one forked strand lashed out, its thorns out to inject the powerful soporific that let the night-hunting plant trap its prey and drag it down for slow digestion.

It struck only a glancing blow. Karatek managed to stagger free, reaching the safety of his piled rocks. When he had looked back, he had seen what few Vulcans ever lived to see: a *s'gagerat* engaged in the hunt, its tendrils fully extended, seeking its quarry. He vowed to come back and burn it out. Then, he collapsed into a drugged sleep that was more than half hallucination.

In his dream, Karatek again saw a *s'gagerat* reach for its prey. This one was big enough to engulf the Mother World.

Burn it! The thing exploded into a deadly blossom. He had time only for an instant of guilt—the bloom was beautiful—before he was running again, this time, one man lost in a crowd of Vulcans racing toward the shuttles that would take them offworld to the great ships.

It was dark. It was cold. He had found no refuge.

There was no refuge anywhere.

Karatek woke, gasping. He lay motionless, breathing deeply until his biocontrol soothed his heart to its normal resting rate below two hundred.

He put out his hand, but instantly knew better. T'Vysse had left their bed to attend their youngest child, T'Lysia, their second born during the exile. What if the control of Surak's disciplines was not what the child truly needed? He knew T'Vysse longed to hold this latest daughter against the fears of night, but that was not Surak's way. Was his way, then, a gift worth giving? The question was irrelevant: they had little else they had to give. She would be the last child T'Vysse would bear, T'Vysse who had never failed him or their people. They needed every healthy child to survive whatever *kahs-wan* ordeal old Rovalat could still create, here in the great ships of their exile.

Where is your own control? Karatek asked himself. He invoked it, steadying his breathing. He wished he could touch T'Vysse's sleek hair, as black as the desert rock, and feel her warmth. She would dispel the terror of his dream by helping him recall there was no logic in it, even though Healer T'Olryn, whom his son had married after a long and highly argumentative courtship, said otherwise.

At the very least, Karatek should work in perfecting his own control. It was not, these days, as if he had that much else to do.

When Karatek had requested leave 1.1 years ago from his duties as head of *Shavokh*'s council, he had expected many things. The ship's command structure provided for an orderly rotation of duties: he had been tired; it was logical to put in for leave, especially if he wished to adapt for propulsion the crystals that continued to fascinate him.

He had not expected to regret that he was now left out of decisions that he once would have taken the lead in making. Of course, he knew how illogical it was to wish that S'lovan, sent by his kinsman S'task to run *Shavokh* and—as Karatek suspected— to try to ensure that its overall management owed more to S'task and less to Surak, was not a superb officer. He had to admit that S'task had chosen well. But Karatek could not help wishing that he felt as necessary now as he had in the exhausting days when he had led, not just observed and remembered.

He was growing weak, he thought. They all were. If they did not find a *Minshara*-class planet soon, the lighter gravity of the ships, their thinner air, with its pervasive traces of chemicals and radiation, and the constant sapping cold would produce only a sickly new generation. And whether there would be a generation after that, whether a generation after that would even be viable were both questions he had fought not to ask himself.

Karatek rose. The ship's cold seeped out from beneath the heavy tapestries that insulated him from cold blasts of recycled air. Through the thin rug, cabled and woven in a black and ochre te-Vikram pattern, the deck's cold metal made his feet recoil. Once or twice, he had even seen frost on the deck, which could tear the flesh if one stepped unwisely. But he avoided it with practiced skill, and barely shivered at all now.

His time sense told him it was the last watch before *Shavokh*'s "dawn," while a glance at his radiation badge told him he had 3.2 days before his next treatment, and almost no time at all before T'Olryn reminded him.

He knew that his life—and worse yet, the lives of his children, especially those born in space—would be shortened. No control that Surak had ever taught could tell him there was no pain in that.

He knew he could not meditate, but another task remained. Stepping into the alcove he reserved for meditation, he took the coronet from a box that, in defiance of all custom, he kept locked. He set the coronet on his head. Its filaments pierced his temples like microscopic thorns. He had grown used to that, too.

"It is the third watch. As I make this record, ship's crew has ventured out onto Shavokh's *hull for the first time since Technician T'Evoryn took a radiation burst and her body was consigned to space, even her* katra *lost.*

"Two hundred and thirty-five days ago, we paused to mine an asteroid our scanners indicated was rich in rare metal ores. It is now our goal to reinforce the ship's hull still further and to create a barrier from behind which we will direct robotic arms to upgrade the reactor with components that should push our maximum speed up three-hundredths more toward light speed. Dissenters in ship's council criticize the gain as too small to be worth the risk. Because of my prior role in helping to lead Shavokh, *my knowledge of ships' engines is no longer state-of-the-art."*

S'lovan's efficient leadership had freed Karatek to study astrophysics once more. He worked again in the propulsion laboratories to learn the developments made in the years of their exile—or journey—and knew he was of considerable use in speeding the ship.

"I have been endeavoring to compensate and made some small progress, including this last, disputed upgrade. After all, we approach light speed in increments; nevertheless, we approach it.

"The High Command, I know, has said that the speed of light cannot be exceeded in normal space. But the High Command is back on Vulcan, and there is much we have done already that the High Command would say was not possible.

"A disturbing accompaniment to this latest discovery of metals

*is an unprecedented alliance in council between the last of the Se-
leyan adepts and the politicians who, back on Vulcan, we would
have called technocrats. I remember them from my days in the
Vulcan Space Institute: they are wily, intelligent, and very patient.
It is these last two qualities—which I must consider virtues even
in a technocrat—that may have earned them the adepts' cooperation. Last year, when pirates attacked our fleet's rear guard, we
were boarded, but two adepts, working in concert, projected a
fear at the intruders. I do not know what they saw: the underpriest
to whom I spoke said it was their version of the Eater of Souls. We
might have sustained even greater damage except that* Rea's
Helm *was able to turn and, using the weapons systems that had
already received intermediate improvements, rout our enemies.
We had to halt engines to make repairs. We must now make up that
lost time."*

When the priestess on Seleya had given the coronet to Surak, she
had intended that someone who had not taken the oaths that gov-
erned her life and the lives of the order at Gol might study what had
been, at the time, a blasphemous fusion of psionics and technology.
As much as anyone could, while retaining independence from the
machine, Karatek understood the device he used to make what was
probably the most enduring history he had ever heard of. At least,
he understood it enough to keep records of the Exile without becoming drained by or addicted to the device. Like the *s'gagerat's*
thorns, its neural filaments carried their own endorphins. But
Karatek had learned to pace himself: when he thought "pause," he
could pause. And he could take the thing off and walk away.

One day, he realized, he would have to do so. Permanently.

The question was: Whom should he choose to inherit the coronet and the responsibilities of fleet memory and conscience that
it entailed?

Should another of the elders receive it, for whatever time remained? Or should it go to T'Vysse? She was already exhausted. What about one of Karatek's children? All were worthy. One of the pilots in the fight against the pirates had been Karatek's own son, Solor, while his elder son, Lovar, and daughter Sarissa had formed part of the tactical team.

It was illogical to be proud of his children for satisfactory performance of their tasks, he told himself. But then, it was illogical for him to scold himself for behaviors he planned to repeat.

Best to turn back to the task at hand.

"We have diverted 11.5 percent of the hull scanning emplacements to seek potential adversaries' ion trails and, having extrapolated from the pirates' trajectories, altered course to avoid what might well be their home star systems. This is regrettable; had our attackers been people with whom we might have waged peace, we might have learned of habitable planets. Now, however, some of the ship's complement tends to regard any outsider at all as a potential enemy. Consensus leans toward avoiding any star system that contains inhabited planets, further restricting our search.

"Because of the loss to our gene pool from the pirate attack, the adepts and the technocrats have agreed to cooperate on a study of weapons techniques. I have agreed that augmenting ships' weapons systems is logical. However, I think that the adepts would do better to focus on training our most recent generations than on seeking technological means of enhancing their mental focus. There are, they say, too few of them to work in concert and train the next generation. Although I deplore their priorities, I was voted down, and now I no longer lead. But the technocrats are not the only individuals on board Shavokh *who can exercise patience to achieve their goals."*

Karatek paused again. His nightmare still weighed heavily

upon him even if his undermind had already begun to process it. Dreams had been easier to contend with in the days before Surak. One went to Seleya or some other shrine; one spent the night in the temple, sleeping, meditating, or a combination of the two; and, at dawn, one went to one of the priests or priestesses and had the dream interpreted.

Now, however, a dream represented not a question that must be answered, but a puzzle that must be solved or dismissed.

Logically speaking, Karatek could not oppose the goals of the adepts on board *Shavokh* without opening himself to charges of inconsistency at the least and hypocrisy at the worst: moral qualms were not a subject much discussed these days. Not in council, where he had no voice beyond that of any citizen.

Should they be? Back on the Mother World, the arts of the mind had always been the products of long study at Gol or Seleya. Before Karatek had followed Surak to Seleya, the limits of his experience with those arts was the time when the visiting priestess had reached out and allowed his mind to brush that of T'Vysse during their betrothal and the times when a healer officiated at the birth of those of their children born on Vulcan, enabling T'Vysse to reassure them during labor.

As the adepts that were born on Vulcan grew old and died, it was only logical that they would wish to pass on the arts of the mind. But that they chose to use technology to do so— *No,* Karatek thought. *No.* He knew from his use of the coronet that a technological application of the mental arts was possible. For example, concerned with the decline in the ships' populations and attempting to ensure that their knowledge did not die with them, ships' engineers had created ways of automating the ships' systems in case some illness wiped out much of their complements, so the survivors could run them themselves. This said nothing about the viability of the gene pool that survived, but a good deal about the engineers' skill.

During the recent battle, they had become impressed, for the first time, with the skill of the adepts who had repelled boarders. If this new-fledged partnership with the adepts succeeded even in preliminary attempts to turn the arts of the mind into science, or at least, technology . . .

Karatek had reservations that he now realized were severe. Without the lengthy period of apprenticeship, which carried with it training in ethics and history as well as psionics, Karatek was concerned that, in the wrong hands—or minds—any device such as the one he had kept as a nearly sacred trust could be used for coercion, not the extension of knowledge.

"I understand now that my logic failed when I remained silent when accused of hypocrisy," Karatek allowed himself to record. *"It is my duty to serve, and to serve what logic tells me is the truth. And I have known from the moment when this artifact was presented to Surak that it was as much a two-edged sword as it was a memory device. Let me go on record here, before I speak at council, to say I oppose the mass production of any device that substitutes technology for the arts of the mind or that can be adapted for coercion."*

"My husband?"

T'Vysse waited outside the tiny meditation alcove, preserving the illusion, at least, of privacy with years of skill.

Karatek shuddered, bringing himself out of the deep concentration required to use the coronet, and removed it. Over the years, he had learned how to seal off the capillaries as the filaments withdrew. Over the years, T'Vysse had learned to glance away.

Once the coronet was set back in its storage case, Karatek reached out to touch his wife's hand.

"The child sleeps?"

"Now, she does," T'Vysse replied.

Would she have left the baby's side otherwise? A rhetorical question. Neither of them had been scheduled to report to their own workstations before the end of this watch. They would have time, Karatek thought contentedly, alone together. And they could share each other's warmth.

But T'Vysse was shaking her head as she led Karatek out of the meditation alcove, beyond the tempting warmth of bedcoverings, into their quarters' living area.

"Sarissa sits with her sister," she said. "She came in and told me that you were wanted. She will join us shortly."

A child might intrude on its parents' privacy; an adult daughter studying her choice of potential mates was more reticent. Especially if the daughter was Sarissa, who Karatek knew had been on duty during the last watch. Karatek remembered how she had acted as a mother to Solor. And now, though she was of an age to have children of her own, she lavished the same dedication on her newest siblings.

"Why did Sarissa leave her post?" Karatek asked. The last watch had 2.6 hours remaining. He might not be on active duty, but he remembered schedules.

"We were both dismissed," Solor said. He had been eating with more rapidity than decorum. Seeing his father, he set down his bowl and rose with old-fashioned courtesy. "Messages have arrived from *Firestorm*, asking us to scan for one of the shuttles that went missing during its prospecting expedition."

Karatek walked past the brazier, savoring the instant of warmth, toward the small heating element in which tea was steeping. Solor had added the savory leaves he favored, especially when he wished to be alert. The familiar scent both refreshed and invigorated him. Forestalling him, T'Vysse poured tea for all three of them into the delicate stone cups she had always prized.

"The other message came from the shuttle itself," Solor told him. "Sarissa heard it first."

Sarissa had served as *Shavokh*'s communications officer for a hundred-day rotation, part of ship's officers' training here, so far away from the Mother World. She found communications "most absorbing," she had told Karatek. It was a way of ensuring that she heard everything, on and off *Shavokh*. It gave her a power that, he realized, the child she had been, lost in the ruins of her home, her birth parents and betrothed slaughtered, she must crave.

"She says the message came from the shuttle's crew. From its surviving crew," Solor corrected himself. "Father, they carried new communications devices that were designed to show geological formations to the ship's chief scientists. When I saw . . ." He drained his tea and set down the cup with none of the ceremony he ordinarily knew better than to omit. "Father, they used these hand-helds to send images. There's trouble, sir. Our people are being used as hostages or slaves. And they're being forced to fight."

Sarissa then slipped into the room, half closing the door behind her and nodding to her parents. Karatek sat upright with a feeling akin to excitement. That too was illogical: boredom meant no accidents, no impending catastrophes—but no home found, either.

"Thee is late," Solor told her.

"I stopped to look in on our sister," Sarissa said. If Karatek could take leave from his duties, he supposed his daughter could spend a few quiet minutes watching T'Alaro, her sister. Her sense of kinship with the child was all the stronger because the little girl was named after her betrothed, who had died so many years ago on the Forge.

But had Karatek set her a good example?

She seated herself and drew the folds of the tabard she wore about herself off duty for warmth over her shipsuit.

"I was dismissed to come and find you," she said. "The council told me to tell you there will be a meeting when the watch changes and to request your presence."

"Solor came to tell me too," Karatek said.

She expects trouble. And if the council had recalled him from retirement, they too must be concerned.

"We should launch a shuttle to rescue our people!" Solor broke the silence.

Karatek turned to her and steepled his fingers. "The entire story, my daughter."

"Since the beginning of my rotation as ship's communications officer, I have received transmissions that turned out to be from *Firestorm.*"

"Excellent!" said Karatek.

"As communications officer, I was responsible for decrypting these communications and bringing them up to a speed at which they are comprehensible."

Given the distance that had grown among the ships, of course, the transmissions suffered time lag. "The first transmissions spoke of a mining expedition that took a shuttle to an uninhabited plane-toid. It was not *Minshara*-class, but an initial scanning assay revealed lodes of pergium that were judged economic to exploit. When the shuttle landed, it discovered what its science officers and engineers believed to be some sort of technical installation. From all indications, it had been abandoned for many years."

"Why were we not told of this?" Karatek demanded. Meaning, of course, *Why was I not told of this?*

The answer was self-evident and a reproach to his judgment.

Sarissa looked down. "The word came from *Rea's Helm.* I had not the authority. More: since it would take us approximately 3.2 years to reach the ship's apparent position, there seemed no possibility of a face-to-face confrontation with that ship's crew. Finally, I became . . . curious. When I checked ship's records, I found several communications entries encoded, concealed from ship's officers. I said nothing to anyone else, but it has taken me this long to decrypt them and bring these data to you. Here is what I have been able to learn: When the shuttle crew entered the installation, they disappeared. Instantly. That was when transmission broke off."

Karatek pushed himself forward in his chair. T'Vysse met Karatek's eyes and shook her head minutely. He took three deep breaths.

Perhaps the sleeplessness that was the logical result of having an infant in their quarters once again had eroded his control. Sarissa knew her duties as well as she knew her own mind. And she had been able, since childhood, to keep her own counsel.

His eldest daughter raised an ironic eyebrow. "It was only ten days ago that we learned *Firestorm* attempted to locate its missing crew. The shuttle remained on the planetoid. So they dispatched two people in a scoutship. One of them flew the shuttle back with what rock and technical samples its crew had been able to assemble before it . . . disappeared. Then, *Firestorm* reported, at the farthest limits of its scans, a trail of ionization. It led to . . ."

She handed Karatek a data crystal that he plugged into a monitor. Before he could activate it, Sarissa held up a hand to stop him.

"We are approximately 2.3 hours away," he said. "So *Firestorm* sent a distress call to *Shavokh*?"

Sarissa shook her head. "No."

"Get to the point," Solor ordered her.

"Calmly," she replied. "As I have always told you, it is only logical to present the information in an orderly fashion from start to finish. This message came from Evoras, an associate of Avarin, on board *Firestorm* to Avarak. You may recall he had been communications officer until the system of job rotation began. There is no way that *Firestorm*'s command crew, much less its passengers, could have known that."

"Avarak?" asked T'Vysse.

"Son of Raelyek and T'Lyrae. Cross-cousin to Evoras and Avarin."

Karatek inclined his head. "I knew the family," he said.

Solor's mouth tightened, remembering earlier difficulties. Avarak had considered himself a suitor of T'Olryn; had he not been a technocrat, disdainful of what he called anachronisms like the *Kal-if-fee,* blood might have stained the marriage ceremony. However, since their marriage, both Solor and T'Olryn had sometimes found their schedules disarranged, their housing shifted to less desirable quarters. It would have been coincidence if it had not happened quite so frequently.

T'Vysse looked down.

They had both known Raelyek, who had studied weapons systems back on Vulcan with Varekat, from the Vulcan Space Institute. In bringing Surak to speak at the VSI, Karatek had been responsible for introducing the weapons scientist to Surak. After listening to the advocate of peace, Varekat had reconsidered his life's work and concluded that it meant a life wasted. So he had resigned his position, destroyed his notes, and suicided in a blast that took ShiKahr's major weapons plant with him.

Karatek always believed Raelyek had chosen to go into exile because he had nowhere else to go. Attempts to speak with him, to counsel him had drawn only the enraged response, "Do you have to take this from me, too?"

After Raelyek had lost his mentor, his livelihood, and most of his faith, exile had taken the only other thing he had prized: his family. Raelyek's consort, T'Lyrae, had not merely refused to accompany her husband and young son Avarak into exile; she had annulled their bonding and retreated to Gol.

After the ships left Vulcan's system, Raelyek had gone very silent. He had done his work, raised a son almost as silent as he, and died attempting to bring weapons to bear on pirates. After Raelyek's death, it seemed as if his son kept his political allegiances to the technocrats.

"Once I understood that, I brought it to council. You do recall that S'task sent Commander S'lovan over from *Rea's Helm* when you retired? He has been a most satisfactory officer," Sarissa said.

Her dispassionate observation stung, as she had no doubt intended.

"The commander ordered me to keep silent, while monitoring the situation. This last watch, the following message came through unencrypted and in real time. The entire command crew watched. Before Solor could display how spectacularly he could lose control"—Sarissa's eyes flashed at her brother— "Commander S'lovan personally dispatched us to find you, brief you, and bring you to council as soon as you received the information. The commander wants you there, at least as institutional memory, although I think he would wish you to rejoin the council."

She reached out and touched Karatek's wrist in a rare gesture of affection. Then she activated the recorder.

A brief flurry of static gave way to an image of five young Vulcans, three males and two females, clustered beside a low bench on one side of what looked like the sort of miniature arena in which Karatek and, indeed, every young Vulcan had trained in the physical components of the disciplines as well as hand-to-hand combat. But where the arenas of Karatek's early training were round and filled with sand to make it easier for combatants to fall, this one was badge-shaped and paved. In the center of the arena was a symbol he had never seen before, a three-pronged emblem that filled the entire pavement. The triskele's prongs, as well as its core, were a virulent yellow.

"I know some of those people," he murmured. "Isn't that Refas, who was in your *kahs-wan* class?" he asked Solor.

"Yes, and Aloran as well. You may recall that after he failed to return, Rovalat went out in search and brought him back. I don't know the third man, but Sarissa says he is Seyhan, a mining engineer. The women are T'Sala and T'Ruhi."

The males were all roughly of Solor's age. The twin sisters were younger, and were very tall. Even after what they had endured, their hair was long and lustrous, their skin deep-toned and shining with health. Not pretty, but beautiful and infinitely valuable to Vulcan in Exile.

In the early stages of their flight from Vulcan, when the ships had flown in close formation, relatively speaking, Karatek had heard of those two. Unusual among Vulcans, they came from a single birth. Both taller and stronger than the norm, they had gravitated logically not just to the martial arts, but to the military.

All five Vulcans wore torn and bloodied shipsuits. T'Ruhi's face was marred by a livid bruise, while Seyhan's arm appeared to be bound up in a piece of his shipsuit's sleeve. And all five also wore what looked like a kind of fighting harness and, around their necks, metal rings studded with glowing badges, too unsightly and too uniform to be anything but . . .

"Now you see," said Solor. "Slaves' collars." His voice was chill with disgust.

"There is more," Sarissa said.

"Can anyone hear me?"

"My drill thrall won't stay unconscious all rest period," whispered T'Sala. *"I'll keep watch. Hurry!"*

Karatek watched the young woman leave the group and flatten herself against a gray wall, eavesdropping.

"I am Seyhan, a mining engineer from Vulcan transport Vaisehlat, *once of* Firestorm. *We were bound through this sector on a peaceful mission. Can anyone hear us?"*

He broke off, turning toward one of his companions. *"Before he died in the last pairs contest, Seroni said he thought his last modifications would extend our range. But there's no way to tell. Quiet! There isn't much time!"*

Seyhan's name indicated that he had chosen to follow Surak, but impatience, even fear, quivered in his voice.

"We have to get you out of here," said T'Sala. *"With one arm injured, I estimate you would last 3.2 minutes, if that, in the next free-for-all. I found a place where we can hide you, bring you food . . . Please, Seyhan . . ."*

"The needs of the many are more important." Seyhan waved her off. *"Please, any of the great ships—if you're in range, move off! We had taken a shuttle, with an initial survey team of twenty, plus ship's crew, down to an uninhabited planetoid, prospecting for pergium, but we found . . ."*

"Seyhan!" T'Ruhi hissed, in response to a gesture from her twin.

"My colleagues and I have been taken prisoner, transported via a technology that we have not been able to explain. When we tried to fight, our weapons were deactivated, and we were overcome."

"Hurry!" T'Ruhi whispered. *"You two, pretend to be working out. Perhaps that will buy us some time."*

Refas and Aloran moved into the center of the arena and took up a fighting crouch, each on a separate arm of the triskele.

"Do you recognize the forms they practice, Father?" Sarissa's voice almost trembled. "Do you?"

He recognized the emotion in her voice as outrage. It would have been illogical to correct it.

The two prisoners were beginning the katas of *Ke-tarya-yatar.* It was one of the most difficult forms of Vulcan martial arts. And one of the deadliest.

"They're training us to fight!" Seyhan said. *"I greeted them and said, 'We come to serve,' but they fitted us with these collars. Those who refused to fight died first.*

"Like this!" He held up another recorder. On its tiny screen, minute figures stood, struggled, fell, and died.

Karatek magnified the image. Yes, there was a Vulcan in late middle age—T'Lera, by the very sands of Gol. As the weird creature—the alien, all scales with a crest and dorsal ridges that looked very sharp—advanced on her, she raised her hand in the gesture of peace.

The alien cut her down.

A young Vulcan stood on one arm of the triskele, his eyes flickering back and forth at his opponents. One had a net, the other a spear. He gave a good account of himself before he died.

"You see," Seyhan whispered into space. *"You see. We have lost six."* He took a deep breath, restoring his self-command. *"So many dead. Killed senselessly. Not just us, but so many others, fellow beings from a wealth of planets. And more are dying, every hour."*

His voice barely shook. Even Surak would have pronounced his control beyond satisfactory. Soon, he would die.

And Karatek spoke of time for himself, a leave to enable himself to rest and to think clearly once more? He had never made a less logical choice.

"The Master Thrall is coming!" came T'Sala's whisper. *"Hurry! We have to hide you!"*

"The rest of us . . ."

The badge flared red. Seyhan started to double up in pain. He fought it, whispering, *"There is no pain,"* then fought to speak as his face contorted. Green blood trickled from a corner of his mouth where he had bitten his lip in a vain attempt to control it.

Again he gasped, finally forcing out the words. *"They use us as fighters in this arena. They wager on . . ."* His voice choked off before he tumbled down beside the bench.

"It's the Master Thrall," cried T'Ruhi. *"I won't let you take him!"* Her voice arched up into a scream as Karatek heard her topple to the ground.

"Four hundred quatloos on the two females. Once the one who has been punished wakes up." A new voice rang out.

"That voice is amplified, but I haven't been able to locate its source," Sarissa whispered.

"Five hundred!"

Karatek watched T'Sala's hand. It was trembling, both with the agony induced by the torque and the trauma of knowing she would be forced to fight her sister, most likely to the death. It covered Seyhan's image transmitter, then went limp.

"Stay away!" she whispered.

The message ceased.

"They were abandoned," Sarissa told her parents. "I discovered three additional messages from personnel on board *Firestorm* to some of the technocrats on board *Shavokh*. Clearly, our prior communications officer's loyalties were not so much suspect as divided. At the very least, we can call this a conflict of interest."

"From where does this transmission originate?" Karatek asked.

Sarissa repeated the coordinates. Karatek translated the numbers into a location approximately 2.8 hours away by a shuttle traveling at maximum speed, 3.9 hours if the shuttle was heavily armed and carrying a full complement.

"We have to go after them," Solor said.

Did they? Could they? The prisoners were *Firestorm*'s crew, not *Shavokh*'s, some might argue: the same people who sent and received messages in secret, whose loyalties were more to their political party or ethnic identity than to Vulcan in Exile. The needs of the many, they would argue, outweighed the needs of the few. Or the one. Karatek could already hear their deliberative, reasonable tones. It was imprudent, illogical, even to go up against a culture that could, somehow, transport people instantaneously from one location to another light-years distant.

Karatek could imagine the relish with which N'Ereon, one of the younger and most hostile of the te-Vikram who had been elected to council, would plant that barb. He would tell N'Ereon, he decided, that it was honorable. Assuming the council would listen to him at all.

It made no sense to wish the honored dead to return, but for a moment, Karatek wished N'Keth were alive to roar at N'Ereon about honor and desperate battles. He only hoped that Solor wasn't remembering that, too.

"I agree with my brother," Sarissa said. "And I think the commander is much of the same mind. Otherwise, why would he send me to brief you in advance?"

"Simple equity: that I should have the same advantage as the technocrats apparently enjoy, of secret messages?"

The Vulcans were becoming increasingly politicized, increasingly fragmented. Karatek suspected that the only reason that S'task had permitted his resignation was so that he could install S'lovan in his place. He could not imagine the man as a spy, but then, he would not have imagined that he himself could shirk his duty, as he had apparently done, in the name of logic.

We did not leave Vulcan so we could replicate its worst flaws, Karatek told himself. He had been idle for too long. And if S'lovan didn't like it, he could just go back to *Rea's Helm.*

Of the Vulcans trapped and forced to fight, there were no te-Vikram, and those surviving all bore either names that denoted followers of Surak or origins on the mainland, origins close to Karatek's own.

Did we make a mistake when we allowed people to remember that they were technocrats or te-Vikram or anything other than Vulcans, and exiled Vulcans at that?

Could we have stopped them from remembering?

They could hardly have stopped them from remembering that, or anything else, Karatek told himself. He certainly was a case in point.

We cannot remember that these people called to us for help and we too abandoned them, he realized. Not if they wished to retain any shred of ethical behavior. Perhaps, too, for one ship to rescue crew from another, or at least try to, might make them one people again—at least for a little while.

He removed the data crystal from the recorder. Its facets captured the light from the firepot, drawing his attention for a moment more. This too must be committed to memory.

"I concur," said Karatek. "But you will let me be the one to speak. And you will be guided by *Shavokh's* commander. No more secret messages. Or plans for secret missions. The fleet has lost enough already. Are we agreed?"

Sarissa inclined her head, the model of docility, but Karatek saw the fire in her eyes.

"Then let us go. I need to announce to the council that, like it or not, I am back from my leave of absence. And then, I shall help S'lovan make the council see reason."

EIGHT

NOW

EARTH
STARDATE 54104.3

"There is one more who will be joining you." Even as Uhura said the words, the door chime to her office rang out. Smiling, she added, "And here he is now. Come in."

At the keyword, the door slid aside to reveal a stocky, rather overweight but still-familiar figure striding into her office. "Welcome, Scotty."

"The pleasure's mine, lassie—*Admiral* Lassie, I should say." He beamed a full Montgomery Scott smile at her, and Uhura smiled back. "Ah, and Ambassador Spock," Scotty continued warmly. "'Tis good to see you again, as well."

"I too find it quite agreeable. Ruanek, this is Captain Montgomery Scott, with whom I served on the *Enterprise* captained by James T. Kirk."

Ruanek bowed politely, but Spock caught a glint of wonder in his eyes: another of Spock's old shipmates!

Even though time—and the strange out-of-time period that Scotty had spent in a transporter loop—had indeed added weight to the once-slender figure, his eyes were as bright and clever as ever. "I've taken on a new job," he told Spock. "I'm running things over at the Starfleet Corps of Engineers."

"And it's the perfect job for him," Uhura added. "The S.C.E. is running more smoothly than it has in years. Still, Scotty, we could use your expertise on this mission. You understand that we will need the use of Romulan cloaking technology."

"Aye, of course. And I'm the closest that you have to an expert."

"*I'm* certainly not," Ruanek muttered.

"You do understand the situation," Spock said. "You will be risking your new job and indeed your entire career if you join this mission."

"Spock, you know me better than that. If you think I'm going to turn down the chance to help rescue an old friend and colleague just for a *job*—well, you have another thought coming!"

Spock raised an eyebrow. "I never doubted you."

As always, Spock felt a little thrill of approval at the sight of the *U.S.S. Alliance,* which was by any standards a sleek, almost elegant ship. Any scars that it had acquired during the Dominion War had been smoothed away, and the ship gleamed in the reflected Earthlight like a new vessel.

The young man who greeted Spock, Ruanek, and Scotty as they came aboard had that "fresh from Starfleet Academy" look to him, complete down to the as-yet uncreased and just too perfectly clean uniform. His eyes were perhaps a little too wide, with a little too much wonder in them, too. But his voice was properly steady as he said without a moment's hesitation, "Welcome aboard, gentlemen. Captain Saavik asks you to meet her in her ready room. I shall escort you there, sirs."

"Excellent," said Spock.

The thrill that he'd felt at the sight of the ship heightened into something much warmer at the sight of his wife. She was seated at the ready room's desk, studying the image on a console screen, a tranquil figure in a tranquil room with walls of calming pale blue. Saavik, Spock thought with a touch of what he knew was illogical but very real pride, was a trim, slender figure, standing out against the soft blue of the walls with her black hair and deep red–and–black–and–gray captain's uniform. She was, he thought as well, the very image of a Starfleet officer.

Saavik looked up as Spock, Ruanek, and Scotty entered—and for a bare instant, her attention was all for her husband. She got to her feet.

"Spock." Only another Vulcan could have read the world of warmth hidden behind the name.

"Saavik. It is agreeable to see you again." The words were formal, as was proper in such surroundings, but he knew that she would read the same warmth in his voice.

He stepped forward and they touched hands briefly and, touch telepaths that Vulcans were, shared a moment of private joy. But in the next instant, Spock took the barest half-step back again. They both knew and accepted that Saavik was the captain right now, not the wife.

"Ruanek," she said. "Welcome. It is agreeable to see you, too. Ah, and Captain Scott, too."

"Captain," Scotty returned with a polite bow. "You're looking quite well."

"I assume, Captain Scott, that you are here to assist with the rescue."

"Aye, 'tis true—and I think after all these years, lass, you can call me Scotty."

Saavik dipped her head in acknowledgment. After all, the two of them had known each other since her early days training on the *Enterprise.* "It is well that you have joined the mission." Saavik's glance took in all three of them. "I have a feeling, illogical though such things as feelings might be, that we are going to need all the help that we can get."

As their captain and her three visitors returned to the bridge, Saavik's crew couldn't quite hide their surprise, but they were all too well-schooled to say anything untoward. The seasoned veterans accepted the visitors without much reaction. But Spock could almost feel the younger ones' awed thoughts, *That's Ambassador Spock!* or *That's Montgomery Scott!*

Scotty felt it, too. "At least no one's said, 'I read about you in the history books,'" he murmured wryly.

"Captain," Lieutenant Suhur, the dark-skinned Vulcan at communications said, "a general message is coming in from Starfleet."

"Let us see it," Saavik ordered. "On-screen. Decode if necessary."

"Yes, Captain."

"Ah, here comes the official smokescreen," Ruanek said in Spock's ear.

He'd said that in Standard since there was no equivalent word for "smokescreen" in Vulcan. Spock raised a brow at him. "You learned a great deal while in service on Earth."

"Indeed I did," Ruanek retorted, absolutely without expression.

The man delivering the message was, rather to Spock's surprise, Admiral William Ross, who had been in command of military operations during the Dominion War. Although some of the lines of stress had faded during the time of peace, he still looked grimly determined. He was not, Spock thought, very happy about what he was doing now. And the wording of the official Starfleet message he delivered was, as Ruanek had predicted, both precise and very careful:

"On Stardate 54104.2, we received information from reliable sources that the Romulan Star Empire has suffered the loss of a valuable and historic artifact. In the interests of mutual appreciation and cooperation, this will be a joint Starfleet–Romulan mission to recover that stolen artifact."

"Which translates as," Ruanek murmured, "'Maybe this will help the Romulans trust the Federation.' But no wonder no one knew at first just why the Romulans left Earth in such haste—it took some time for the news to reach Starfleet."

Admiral Ross continued. *"Understand that the artifact is irreplaceable and extremely valuable—not in the monetary sense, but in the sense that we may not have another chance for such cooperation. All care must be taken, repeat, must be taken, to ensure the artifact's safety. This will be a recovery of incredibly important historical data. Ross out."*

This time Ruanek said nothing. But Spock and he both knew that this statement, too, had both a covert and an overt face: The entire Federation would know by now that the artifact might well hold proof of real atrocities committed by the Romulans against the Watraii.

At least Uhura had managed to keep the rescue of Chekov out of the official Starfleet order. Nor did that order include any command about landing—or not landing—on the Watraii homeworld.

Small blessings, as the humans might say, Spock thought.

The official word from the Klingon High Council came in soon after the Federation announcement, predictably announcing that they could not spare any Klingon Defense Force vessels. In the aftermath not only of the Dominion War but of continued conflicts both internal and external to the Empire in the year since, Chancellor Martok simply did not have the ships to spare—especially not to send in aid of their ancient enemies, the Romulans.

"Open a shipwide channel," Saavik ordered. "This is your captain speaking. As of this moment, shore leave has been canceled. Unfortunate, yes, but that is the way of things. But now I have a more important message for all who serve aboard this ship.

"Most of you were with me when we fought back the Watraii—without Starfleet permission. You know without my having to say it how close we came to court-martial then. Now I must ask you—not order you, ask you—to risk your careers yet again."

Quickly and clearly Saavik summed up the situation and the need to rescue both Pavel Chekov and the Romulan artifact as swiftly as possible, and without involving Starfleet. "You do see the reason why we must move in swiftly and privately, I assume. And I understand that some of you may not wish to take the risk. There are, after all, those of you who are only beginning your professional careers. If any of you wish to leave, you will be free to do so, without penalty or fault. I ask only that you keep silent about our mission."

She waited, apparently calm, not stirring so much as a strand of her dark hair, although Spock could almost feel the force of his wife's tension. The younger crew members were, indeed, the most risky aspect of this mission, being the least predictable. Indeed, some of the newer members of the crew here on the bridge were glancing uneasily at each other. The minutes ticked by . . .

But no one spoke up, either on the bridge or over the open channel.

Saavik let out her breath ever so slightly. "Thank you," was all she said.

This time, unlike their last clandestine mission, there would be no coalition of vessels; there must not be a large fleet to alarm the Watraii and endanger Chekov any further. Only Uhura would know the whole story.

It was, Spock thought with a carefully buried touch of wry humor, yet another case of "If things go wrong, Starfleet and the Federation never heard of this mission."

And these members of Starfleet are, as Saavik warned, risking court-martial. Again.

Yes, and Ruanek risks worse, should we need to land on Romulus and he is recognized. The sentence of death still hangs over him. We were fortunate to get him away from the Romulan Star Empire that time during the war, after he avenged the emperor's murder.

But worry, of course, was illogical.

Ruanek strode grimly down a ship corridor, just barely keeping himself to a walk. He had excused himself from the bridge rather than risk displaying an unpleasant and very non-Vulcan example of emotion.

T'Selis had sent him a message. It had been terse and not at all reassuring, saying only, *"Do what you must."*

Now, what had that meant? Oh, Ruanek had hardly expected any passionate outburst from his Vulcan wife, not even a declaration of love. You just didn't send such private emotions if you were a Vulcan, no matter what you might say in private. But even so—

"Do what you must"?

That sounded almost, well, indifferent. Or—illogical idea or not—angry.

Ruanek knew very well by now that just because Vulcans controlled their anger, it didn't mean that they weren't capable of it. They felt anger and all the other emotions, all of them nicely packaged there beneath the calm exterior.

Trust me, Ruanek thought. *T'Selis, just . . . just trust me.*

Not at all satisfying. But he—

He sprang back. He and another being had almost collided. Ruanek was no longer a Romulan warrior hair-triggered to attack instantly, but he still had to fight the urge to snarl a challenge.

Instead, he heard himself exclaim with almost childish wonder, "You are the android!"

"Indeed I am, sir. Lieutenant Commander Data at your service." The android tipped his head slightly to one side, studying Ruanek. "And you, I understand, are Ruanek of Vulcan."

"Yes." Ruanek paused, trying not to stare. "Ah . . . forgive me for greeting you in such a childish way."

"Oh, I am not insulted."

"Good," Ruanek said. "Tell me, Mr. Data. That emotion chip you mentioned before, does it allow you to feel the concept of honor?"

"Yes." Data's light voice darkened slightly. "I assure you, sir, I would not lightly risk my career."

"And I wouldn't lightly risk my marriage, either." Ruanek paused, bemusedly studying that strange pale golden skin and those eyes that seemed so very alive. If not *quite* human. His curiosity roused, despite his best efforts to quell it. "I admit it," Ruanek said after an awkward second, "I am not familiar with android beings."

"And you would like to ask me some questions."

"Would I be intruding if I did?"

"Not at all. Indeed, I would like to ask you some questions as well." The android actually . . . smiled, and it was a very convincing smile. "I find it quite fascinating that you were raised on Romulus yet now live on Vulcan."

"So does everyone else," Ruanek muttered, then shrugged. "I have no pressing mission yet."

"Neither do I. Shall we sit together and talk?"

It might take his mind off T'Selis and that too-curt message. "That seems . . . most logical," Ruanek said. "I believe we can find a peaceful corner of the mess hall."

"Assuming, of course, that we can actually *find* the mess hall."

Ruanek stopped short. "That was a joke. That was actually a joke. You have a sense of humor."

"That," Data said, almost wistfully, "has been a matter of discussion for some time."

A wide-eyed young human who'd introduced himself as Ensign Del showed them to the mess hall and almost worshipfully withdrew.

"I am not exactly used to being an idol," Ruanek said, watching the young man leave.

"Nor am I," Data added.

The *Alliance*'s mess hall was a cheerful place with good lighting and yellow and orange overtones, clearly designed to keep the mixed crew at their ease when off duty. Ruanek and Data found a corner table and settled down to talk.

". . . and so," Data summarized after a time, "you could, were you to be fanciful about it, say that my 'father' was Dr. Noonien Soong."

Ruanek stared at the android in wonder. "And you were, uh, designed by him to be an independent entity, to constantly evolve and learn."

"Precisely. I admit that I do still find humanity both puzzling and fascinating."

Ruanek snorted. "You sound like Spock."

"Perhaps. But it is true enough. That is why I attended Starfleet Academy—I wished to learn more and to go further."

Ruanek shook his head. "And I—I wanted to learn, but until I came to Vulcan, I wasn't permitted to do so."

Data blinked. "The Romulan Empire does not educate its warriors?"

"Only in how to best defend their patrons."

"Interesting."

"That's one way of putting it." Ruanek forced a smile, not wanting to dwell on this subject. "But at least I never had to prove I was a sentient being."

"That was not a pleasant time," Data agreed. "But I did win the case, with the help of Captain Picard."

Ruanek nodded. "Of course."

Data's head tilted. "Do you know Captain Picard?"

"In a manner of speaking." Ruanek sat back as a flash of memory overtook him: the escape from Romulus with Spock, who was lost in the blood fever, the rescue by the *U.S.S. Stargazer,* captained by a younger, not yet bald Picard . . . A good deal of those memories were lost or confused since Ruanek had been injured and on the verge of utter exhaustion at the time. But he and Picard had actually worked together.

"Ruanek?"

"Never mind. Captain Picard might or might not remember me, but I certainly do remember him." Ruanek leaned forward. "Now, would you please tell me what it's like serving aboard the *Enterprise*? Spock has told me about the old one, James T. Kirk's ship, of course, and that sounded like an amazing vessel.

But I know this is a different series, a much more advanced ship."

"So it is." Data hesitated. "I scarcely know where to begin . . ."

Scotty, of course, had almost immediately gone off on a tour of the *Alliance*'s engineering section, practically rubbing his hands together in glee and anticipation. By the time he returned to the bridge, the *Alliance* was well under way toward the Watraii home-world.

"Scotty?" Spock asked.

Scotty shook his head. "My, what a frustrating situation that was."

Saavik glanced up over her shoulder at him from her chair. "I beg your pardon?"

"Why, everything was in perfect running order! Not a blessed thing needed my tinkering."

There were barely stifled chuckles from the bridge personnel, except, of course, for the Vulcans, who still managed to give the impression of being pleased. "Coming from you, Scotty," Saavik returned, "that is high praise."

"Och, 'tis only the truth!"

Lieutenant Abrams, a stern-faced, solidly built human woman who was the Alliance's chief tactical officer, suddenly announced, "Two ships, Captain Saavik, bearings 836.5 by 2362. Closing fast."

Saavik leaned forward in her chair. "Identify them," she ordered. "And get the image on-screen."

"They're Klingons, Captain."

"Interesting. Apparently Chancellor Martok has decided that he can spare us two ships after all."

"I don't think that's the case, Captain," Abrams said grimly. "They have weapons at the ready."

NINE

MEMORY

Never mind justifications by Surak's disciples that "the needs of the many outweigh the needs of the few" or Commander S'lovan's belief that intervening was for "the good of the fleet," for the first time since they left Vulcan, the exiles were united and going to war.

Perhaps not wholly united: they had seen how some of the technocrats not only could try to circumvent the council, but could adorn the council's decision to go to war with terms like "get at the effective cause," "rescue party," and—Karatek's favorite, if he wanted to choose among equally distasteful descriptors—"achieve a logical and efficient resolution."

Perhaps they should recruit aid from the ships that flew in consort with *Shavokh*. That had been T'Partha's suggestion, vigorously backed, in private, by T'Vysse. Much to Karatek's dismay, not only had Solor opposed that, but Sarissa, on whom he had counted as a voice of cool logic, had shaken her head.

"On *Firestorm,* they circumvented main communications. If I contacted the other ships within timely communications—and if I could count on hearing the truth, there is an 89.88 percent chance that I would uncover similar deceptions."

"We don't have that time," Solor interrupted. He had come to council as a guest to see Karatek take back his position and watched with what Karatek privately considered too much satisfaction.

At a glance from the ship's commander, he inclined his head. "I ask forgiveness."

"Whether *Firestorm* abandoned its shuttle willingly or not," Commander S'lovan said, "we have a duty to try to preserve life." He inclined his head at Karatek, who nodded approval.

"Will you arm us?" Solor demanded.

Avarak raised his head, fires starting to glow in his eyes. Karatek hoped that any alliance between him and his son would be brief. He looked down at the screen built into his place at the conference table. Today's meeting was an open council; any member of *Shavokh*'s complement who chose to do so could monitor it and respond. Numbers appeared and began to grow rapidly as viewers indicated their opinion, favoring weapons.

"No weapons," said the commander.

Sarissa rose, quick as a blade drawn from its sheath.

"You would send our people down there unarmed, unprotected?" she demanded. Apparently, she had extended her mantle of protection, at least, her verbal protection, from her brother to the young men and women whom Karatek could see in the viewers' gallery above the council table. They had not been content to watch from elsewhere in the ship.

"What is the use?" asked the commander. "We have all heard Seyhan's transmissions. If the . . . the entities who snatched our people from a deserted asteroid and carried them more than eleven light-years away almost instantaneously chose, I think we can—to borrow a word you seem overly fond of—logically assume that they could vaporize this ship with equal speed. Which is why I have given navigation the order to hold off."

The numbers rose, signifying assent. A paradox: consensus had approved of the idea of armed conflict only 3.2 minutes ago. How quickly it could change, Karatek mused. He needed T'Partha's skills now to shift it.

"No," said the commander. "I cannot justify issuing you weapons." He stared at the bulkhead across from him, decorated with the mosaic *shavokh*.

Did Vulcan survive? Karatek wondered briefly. Or had their lost brothers and sisters reduced it to rubble like the asteroid on which Seyhan and his mining expedition found an enemy with even greater destructive force than Vulcan's emotions?

Focus, Karatek, he told himself. If he were to help lead again, he must keep to the matter at hand.

"I say that the ship holds off. But I agree," said the commander, "that we must intervene. After all, did Surak not say that the spear in the other's heart is the spear in our own? How much more should we care for the well-being of those from the other ships?"

"Even if they deceived us?" The representative who spoke was known to Karatek: Telas, once a farmer, from one of the northernmost provinces by Vulcan's last sea. Before his constituents had chosen exile, they had lived in daily sight of depredations on their land by other Vulcans. Over the years he had learned, gradually, to trust. It seemed that he had to learn that lesson once again. Karatek marked that down as another grievance against the technocrats.

"Especially so," Karatek found himself speaking out. "If they lie, our job is to provide them an example of right, logical conduct. Surak spoke of waging peace. Commander S'lovan may no longer be one of us, but he understands."

"So, you say . . ." T'Partha encouraged him to continue. She only did that when whatever subliminal analysis she used indicated to her that the consensus flows had reached a point where they could be identified and channeled into productive use.

"I agree with the commander," Karatek said. "The entities that have taken our people as fighting slaves have weapons beyond our power to duplicate. Or, perhaps, envision. They use primitive combat as entertainment. We cannot fight them."

"This is the time to see if your people can succeed in waging peace," said the commander. Although S'task had never trusted that skill, S'lovan might be more flexible, especially if T'Partha could work on him.

"How many people are on that shuttle?" Telas demanded. It was time and past time that Karatek forgot those outmoded designations, he told himself yet again. But now. Now, he must pay attention. Of course, the man invoked the "needs of the many" axiom.

"What the needs of the many require," Sarissa interrupted, "is not cowardice, but obedience to the code of ethics that led some of us to make this journey! What made *you* choose to come?"

The numbers rose on Karatek's monitor so fast that the screen blurred.

Karatek caught his daughter's eye. Was it ethics, he wanted to ask her, that made her willing to risk the lives of her brother and his closest associates? Seeing how her eyes flashed, how Solor's head went up and his back stiffened, Karatek feared it was something more emotional and more seductive: honor. The old-fashioned, deadly honor Solor had learned from N'Keth before he died.

Leaning over, Karatek whispered to his son. "No weapons, remember. Not even the blade you took from N'Keth."

Solor flushed like a boy barely past his *kahs-wan*.

"One thing more," the commander told Solor, who rose from his chair and stood at a posture of military attention that Karatek had not seen on board *Shavokh* in years. Except, of course, on Commander S'lovan himself.

"You will go unarmed. You will wage peace against these entities and seek to expand our frame of reference. If these creatures are as technologically advanced as the evidence indicates, it may be that they know of habitable worlds."

Such worlds would not be safe, Karatek thought. They would be within range of these entities. They had not brought Vulcans this far out into the long night to serve as fodder for strangers' deadly games!

"Because it is vital to add to our knowledge base by any ethical means whatsoever, you will go to the planet bearing communications gear such as Seyhan wore. A record will be made and maintained. Karatek, are you prepared to do that? Are you able?"

Karatek knew what that meant. He might see his son and his son's comrades die, then have to relive the experience while under the coronet, remembering for all time. But he had no choice, no honorable choice. So he yielded to the logic of the situation and inclined his head, then focused, once more, on the mosaic behind the commander's chair, how the light gleamed on the *shavokh*'s pinions, glinted off its beak.

"I anticipated this conclusion," the commander admitted. "The shuttle has been prepared. You will leave before we move so far out of range that its fuel capacity will not suffice to intercept us when you return."

In other words, Solor and his crew must not only go up against the alien entities and the slaves they controlled, including fellow exiles, but must confront the cold equations of the shuttle's top speed, its maximum load, including passengers, and its fuel capacity. No matter how successful the mission was in waging peace, it would never succeed in liberating everyone.

One hand on his son's shoulder, Karatek walked Solor and his crew—brilliant, irreplaceable members of *Shavokh*'s discouragingly small younger generation—down the shuttlebay and off to their war. It had been many years since he had seen anything in this bay except gears and cold metal. Now the battered but still gleaming metal bulkheads held all the colors of his never-forgotten home. Although the temperature remained constant— and consistently lower than in the ship's living quarters and laboratories—it felt paradoxically warm, homelike now that his son was leaving.

Speaking in low, urgent tones, Karatek urged Solor to remember to control anger, cast out violence, and employ only reason. Superfluous advice: he had had many years to raise the man now at his side. If the job had been poorly done, speaking now would not amend it.

Sarissa stayed behind, speaking in equally low, urgent tones to the men and women not chosen for the mission, consoling them, attempting to persuade them, if Karatek knew her, and not to lash out at people whom they believed had lied to them.

Even if they had.

Those two were developing a cult of personality, Karatek realized. It was only logical that fiery younger people, denied full play for their talents, attempt to do so. It showed initiative. It showed passion and ability. But it was dangerous. Who knew that better than Karatek? At the behest of Karatek's own superiors, he had traveled Vulcan with Surak. And from the standpoint of a cult of personality, no more dangerous man had ever been born on Vulcan or on whatever homeworld that Vulcan in Exile might find.

Sarissa turned away from her friends and followers to T'Vysse, standing nearby, her face as greenish white as the terrible day when she had seen Turak, her eldest son, and his family torn from her side. It was a breach of control, but Sarissa put her arm around her mother and stood with her, watching in uncharacteristic silence.

Karatek and his son walked together down the shuttlebay to the waiting craft. Their boots tapped out a rhythm that reminded Karatek of war. In the 6.7 minutes it took the shuttle's ramps to extend and its crew to board, Karatek's recorder showed a free-for-all on the planet. Thus far, two people had died and one, bleeding green from a gash on his weakened arm, held off two others with what looked like a *lirpa* as wagers by the three voices he had heard before mounted into the thousands of quatloos.

Even as the ramp retracted, another Vulcan fell, her head falling back like a *kylin'the* blossom snapped from its stalk by a careless hand.

How would the shuttle's crew reach these people?

Easy enough, Solor had said with the confidence Karatek no longer could attribute to youth. They would go down to the surface of the planet, find an installation that resembled the one Seyhan had described, and be transported off the surface.

Then, they would face the greater task of trying to reach their captors both intellectually and morally. Not just trying: for the good of the many, as well as the few, they must succeed.

The shuttle withdrew its ramps and turned on the landing circle. As the warning sirens rang out, Karatek turned and walked back to his family. The shuttlebay doors slid shut like the rock gates of an ancient tomb. The ship's primary docking port gaped open into eternal night.

Even after the alarms in the main bay ceased, confusion continued. After hearing reports of covert messages passed between ships, S'lovan had reversed his earlier decision. Now, armed security guards ran into the secondary bay. A defense against revolt?

S'lovan had even ordered out a dagger, a tiny, vicious craft that had proved useful back on Vulcan for surgical strikes. At the time of exile, each ship carried twelve to twenty of them. They had largely been ignored as long as shuttles were in good supply and working order. But ever since S'task had taken command of *Rea's Helm* himself so that S'lovan could join *Shavokh,* S'lovan had had engineers working double and triple shifts to boost the speed of *Shavokh's* daggers so they, rather than the bigger, more valuable shuttles, could be used as couriers.

The guards rushed a position near the waiting dagger, then saw Karatek. One started to salute, then, unsure of his current status, broke off.

"*T'Kehr* Karatek?"

"Yes, N'Vea?" he asked. This guard had studied propulsion with him before deciding her physical strength and endurance could be put to more immediate use in security. The child of one of the few successful intermarriages between a te-Vikram and a city dweller, N'Vea was a tall woman whose spare frame and darker skin—not to mention her honesty—revealed her desert blood. He remembered her as one of the younger generation on the periphery of Solor's circle of friends.

Beneath the shining helm she wore, he could see consternation on her face. Her hands on her prisoner's shoulders were gentle as she turned him to face Karatek and the other guards.

"Rovalat!" Karatek exclaimed.

Night and day, the man who had guided his sons, and the sons of most of his closest associates back on Vulcan, must have been pushing three hundred. Karatek had heard that he was very ill of a disease that made it hard for his blood to carry oxygen, a disease exacerbated, the healers said, by a random mutation induced by conditions on board *Shavokh*.

Seeing Rovalat in the light, Karatek realized that the old explorer wasn't just ill. He was dying. On Vulcan, a man like Rovalat would have walked out onto the Forge, assuming that there he would finally meet his match. Here, he had waited—until now.

Now, he drew himself up. Pale, almost livid, he might be, but as he summoned his strength, Karatek could almost think he had been mistaken. After all, the lights in the docking bays could be misleading. Suited up, clearly ready and willing to fly, the old teacher's upright posture reminded him of the trim, formidable man capable of keeping pace with a howling *sehlat* as they ran out into the desert to bring out lost children, or of pounding the head of a trained warrior a third his age into a bulkhead in sheer rage.

Rovalat had never even tried to follow Surak's disciplines, but he had accepted exile as a fitting punishment for the loss of a third of what proved to be his last *kahs-wan* class back on Vulcan. Only reluctantly had he accepted the charge of leading the next generation, but he had resigned that position, too, 3.1 years ago and withdrawn from much of the ship's life.

In fact, Rovalat's resignation had given Karatek the idea to offer his own. The decision had been, he decided, spectacularly bad judgment on both their parts.

"What do you think you're doing?" the commander shouted over the com.

"Let me go," Rovalat asked. "You can see my most recent medical reports. The healers tell me I have, at most, two years and possibly less. Let me . . ." He started to cough and fought against spasms that would have bent him double and caused security to carry him off right then to the healers.

Redeem my old fault, Karatek knew the man wanted to say.

"Those are my boys down there," Rovalat said. "My last class on Vulcan. Let me . . ." He had never gotten over the loss of those boys, and now some of them were bleeding their lives out in the arenas toward which Solor led his crew.

"You are ill," T'Vysse said. "Here, let me help bring you to the healers."

She reached out to take his arm, guide him away, but he shook her off with a vigor that belied his age and illness.

"Your response is emotional," T'Vysse tried again, a measured rebuke.

Rovalat laughed. "I thought you'd say that. Yes, I am being emotional. Loyalty is an emotion. Duty is an emotion. Therefore, I should think you would consider them, to borrow a word you're fond of—and that's another emotion right there—extremely logical. I taught those boys. Therefore, if they allowed themselves to be captured, it is my responsibility to bring them home. Again. Or die trying. Night and day, what does it matter? I'm practically dead already."

The commander tried a frontal assault. *"You are too old to fight! If you go in, you'll cost us the element of surprise!"*

"Too old?" asked Rovalat. "Would you care to borrow a phrase from our enemies below and place a small bet? I will wager I can hold you off long enough to make it to that ship and start the take-off cycle. You will have no choice then, logically, but to evacuate the launch bay." He flashed the other man a twisted smile. "And don't tell me we can spare the metal to repair the hull again, because I know better. Some of the engineers were my students too!"

His eyes sought out Karatek's and held them.

"You have a plan, don't you?" Karatek asked.

Rovalat nodded. "I remember your son Solor. He's a smart lad, resourceful, but he's up against an enemy too big for him. He'll go in there, attempting to deal peace, and they'll take them, take them all, and throw their lives away in those damnable arenas."

"You're saying he's unarmed? Solor is armed with the greatest weapon of all, the truth!" T'Vysse said.

Rovalat bowed. "We are making history, lady, not studying it. Please. There isn't much time. Let me explain this to your husband and, if he's not convinced, I will be content to go with you to the healers."

Willing, Karatek thought, *but not content.* Not for what short time he had remaining. And he wasn't even certain he believed the old man.

Was it so very terrible to allow the old man to seek his own end, like the crippled warriors he had seen at ShiKahr's gates, going out fully armed into the desert to make the pilgrimage toward Seleya, but never reaching it? Or *T'Kehr* Torin firing into the crowd to give the last shuttles time to escape Vulcan, for all the worlds as if he stood again, as the hero of Arakahr?

Rovalat was being logical, at least according to his own standards. He was crafty, experienced, and desperate. They could use any help he could give them.

Karatek glanced over at S'lovan's face on the viewscreen. The commander shrugged as if to say "You know these people better than I." How hard it must have been for him to come over from *Rea's Helm* and try to command another ship as a stranger, an outlander in this desert of stars, trying to claim leadership of a clan.

"Frontal assault won't win our people what they want," Rovalat said. "You all know that. But you're bound by these ethics of Surak's, which have already cost you more than enough. I'm not. Let me go."

"What do you have in mind?" asked the commander.

S'lovan eyed Rovalat over the viewscreen and visibly relaxed. It was only logical for him to conclude that Rovalat was no physical match for the security forces present. Perhaps.

Rovalat's body was deteriorating, but there was nothing wrong with his mind. It had been wily enough to outwit the *le-matya* in its den and deal with the desert on its own terms. It had made generations of children fit to wander the Forge alone.

Karatek looked over at Sarissa. She glanced quickly down. Oh, he knew his daughter: that was not a glance of modesty, but of pure guile. She had concealed it quickly, but not so quickly that he had not seen it.

She had chosen to *let* him know.

He allowed his gaze to travel over to the corridor that he knew led to the arms locker. Sarissa moved over to stand beside him.

"The needs of the few, or the one, are important. He needs to be of use," she murmured. "So I have helped him." She handed him an image caster, one of only a few prototypes. Karatek had no doubt she had provided Rovalat with one as well.

If Commander S'lovan did not begrudge Rovalat the use of a dagger ship, surely no one else would object. What was an image caster compared with a ship? And such was Rovalat's reputation that it was entirely possible that he might bring the dagger, the image caster, *and* the captives back in triumph.

Rovalat looked at the commander's visage on the screen. "Let me go, sir. While the young ones on board that shuttle attract those creatures' attention, one man, operating alone and quickly, might gain access. . . . A pincers movement is more logical than a direct assault, don't you agree? If you've done your work right, that dagger can overtake the shuttle. If I catch up with it, I'll travel in with it, concealed by its mass. But I have to go now. If the shuttle gets too big a start on me, there'll be two separate signatures."

If Karatek could see the flaws in Rovalat's argument, S'lovan surely could. The beings that had turned Vulcans into fighting slaves would probably see right through Rovalat's proposed ruse. But it was the best strategy they had: they owed the shuttle's crew at least a fighting chance.

"I have a duty," the commander said, *"and responsibilities to protect this ship."*

"Then let me brief Karatek in your place," Rovalat begged. "Please."

Tears, so rare for a Vulcan, had begun to well in the man's eyes, almost hidden in the deep creases formed by years peering into distant places in fierce sunlight.

Walking over to N'Vea, Karatek detached her hand from Rovalat's arm. Like Sarissa, N'Vea was letting him lead. With her native strength and training, she could have broken his arm in seconds.

Taking charge of the elder, Karatek walked with him to a secluded portion of the deck as Rovalat spoke quickly, earnestly.

I am going to agree, Karatek realized. *I may regret this for the rest of my life, but it is Rovalat's choice to make, and it is my son's life, and the lives of his companions.*

He had not realized he had already agreed until he found himself kneeling, as if taking leave of a Head of House. Rovalat reached out to touch his brow. It was farewell. It was blessing.

And when he felt the stirring of unfamiliar thoughts inside his mind, Karatek realized it was also Rovalat's *katra.*

TEN

NOW

As the Klingon ships raced toward them, Saavik crisply ordered, "Go to yellow alert." This was hardly the time to wonder why Klingons would suddenly be attacking a Federation ship. Granted, Martok had until this moment proven himself a staunch ally of the Federation. But anything was possible in the unstable and ever-changing universe that was interplanetary politics. To the bridge crew, Saavik ordered, "On-screen."

But almost at the same instant that the image stabilized into two fierce-looking vessels, one of them standard Klingon rust-red, the other a startling stark white, Lieutenant Abrams amended, frowning, "Their weapons have just gone off-line, Captain."

Saavik sat forward in her seat, studying the screen. "We know those Klingons." Not surprising that they'd have taken their weapons off-line. "Cancel yellow alert. Lieutenant Suhur, open hailing frequencies."

"Hailing frequencies open," he replied almost at once. "It would appear that they are eager to speak with us, Captain."

"Yes," Saavik commented to no one in particular, "I thought that they might be." Since Klingons didn't begin conversations with what they considered needless courtesies, she simply declared brusquely, "You out there, you both know who I am: Captain Saavik of the Federation *Starship Alliance.* And I recognize you, too, both of you captains."

The first Klingon commander to appear on-screen was a huge, muscular warrior. *"As before, I am Captain Tor'Ka* sutai *Triquetra, captain of the* Demon Justice, *ship of the Demon Fleet of the Klingon Assault Group."*

Spock raised an eyebrow. He remembered these two well. These two captains and their crews were privateers, possibly licensed by the Klingon government, though of course not officially acknowledged. It was equally possible that they were acting on their own, since as privateers they had the right to do just that. But this may well have been the Klingon government's way of helping without appearing to be helping.

That these two ships were privateers also explained why they had first approached with weapons online: privateers had to be ready for anything. Only when they had assured themselves that this was, indeed, the *Alliance* and not some snare that had been set for them had they stood down. People such as they would always need to be both wary of and well acquainted with deception.

The commander of the second ship, which was that startling and most unusual white, was an older Klingon warrior, with the flaming red hair that sometimes appeared in the noble Houses. *"And I, as before, am JuB-Chal, captain of the* Dragon's Wrath."

His white ship, Spock remembered, was a *K'Vort*-class bird-of-prey. Its color, as its captain had told the *Alliance* crew with a laugh, had lured some enemies into thinking that it was nothing but a harmless hospital ship, then learning too late that it was not. Spock had never learned if that coloring had been a deliberate deceit by JuB-Chal or merely a convenient coincidence: Klingons seldom made use of the color white, as far as he knew, but it might conceivably have some significance to the captain's House.

Then again, Spock thought, *white may simply be JuB-Chal's favorite color.*

"Why are you following us?" Saavik asked the Klingons coolly. "We are a science vessel."

The Klingons on both ships let out roars of appreciative laughter. *"Of course you are,"* Captain Tor'Ka said in a mock-conspiratorial tone.

Captain JuB-Chal added, *"Indeed you are. Just as my nice, white* Dragon's Wrath *is nothing more than a harmless hospital ship."* He grinned, showing an array of fierce-looking jagged teeth. *"No need to use deception with us, Captain Saavik. Remember that we know you. We followed you the last time into a glorious battle."*

Only Klingons, Spock thought, *could have called that bizarre chess game of a combat, when Federation, allies, and Romulans had ranged themselves against the Watraii and tried not to kill anyone, a glorious battle.* It had, he considered, been more of a three-dimensional stalemate with occasional wild melees than a genuine battle.

"I suspect that we could make good use of them," Spock murmured in Saavik's ear.

"Mm?"

"As a distraction if nothing else."

"Exactly what I was thinking," she agreed just as softly, never taking her gaze from the viewscreen. To the Klingons, Saavik warned, "Understand that this is not a sanctioned Starfleet mission."

Both commanders burst into another explosion of fierce Klingon laughter. *"Captain Saavik, we do not mock you,"* Captain JuB-Chal said, *"but remember what we are!"*

Captain Tor'Ka continued, with his own jagged-toothed grin. *"Klingons, especially Klingon privateers, do not worry about such petty things as sanctioned missions."*

"Very well," Saavik said as though surrendering to their logic. "If you wish to join us, we gladly accept your company."

There was a thunder of shouted approval from both Klingon ships. Tor'Ka exclaimed, *"You are as wise as ever, Captain Saavik! Now we, captains and crews together, will join you on this new mission for honor, glory—and blood."*

They cut off communication. The viewscreen went dark.

"Fascinating," Spock said into the sudden silence.

Soon after their unexpected allies had joined them, Spock excused himself from the bridge. As he and Saavik had previously arranged through a moment of touch telepathy, he went straight to her ready room and keyed himself inside, then made certain that the door had sealed securely behind him once more. Seated at Saavik's table and console, Spock entered a series of specific and intricate codes, and then sent the carefully encrypted message.

Then he sat back to wait, fingers steepled in the habit that he'd had since before his days on Kirk's *Enterprise*.

What would you think of what we do, Jim? Spock wondered, allowing himself a moment of self-admittedly illogical fancy. *Would you approve of all this—or would you think us all gone mad?*

I can hear you now on the subject of our making any alliances with Klingons, let alone with Klingon privateers. But the universe has changed, Jim, since the days of our Starfleet service together, and alliances have changed with it.

Spock sat forward suddenly, all his illogical fancy gone as swiftly as though it had never occurred. An image was forming on the screen, and the opening series of coded numbers that raced across the bottom of the screen told him this was a Romulan response.

Of course the face that appeared on-screen wasn't that of Charvanek back on Romulus. There was no need for her to send so distant—and so risky—a message, not when there were trusted underlings in smaller vessels that were legitimately not quite so far away. The Romulan who stared resolutely back at Spock was a heavy-jawed captain, young for his rank but with cold dark eyes and a determinedly expressionless face.

"I am Sub-Commander Sarval," he said without preamble. *"I know who you are. And the one who gave me this mission beneath a mission sends you this word as an assurance: 'horses.'"*

That word, which had no Romulan or Vulcan equivalent, was said in Standard. Had Spock been human, he would have let out a startled burst of laughter. As it was, it took all of his Vulcan self-control not to show anything of his surprise and involuntary amusement on his face. It was the last word he would have expected to hear from a Romulan—which was almost certainly precisely why Charvanek had chosen it. Not only was Charvanek now the only person left on Romulus who would even know that the word "horses" existed, she would also be the only one on Romulus who would know its significance. Thanks to one Dr. Leonard McCoy, Ruanek had, long before coming to live on Vulcan, back in the days when he was merely a Romulan centurion, developed a fascination for those Earth animals.

And indeed he still has it, Spock thought, remembering that Ruanek was a very long distance part-owner of a breeding farm on Earth. Charvanek always did have a most unlikely and unexpected sense of humor.

"Understood," Spock replied, as calmly as though hearing a Romulan say "horses" was an ordinary occurrence. "Is the item ready for transport to this ship?"

"It is."

"Excellent." Opening a private com link, Spock informed the transporter chief, "Be ready for a package to be beamed aboard."

"A . . . package, sir?" She sounded doubtful, but willing to please.

"Precisely." The fewer aboard who knew that they were taking on Romulan equipment, the better. And the more secrecy, the safer Charvanek would be. She could hardly be seen to be giving Romulan technology to a Federation ship. After the mission would be time enough for revelations. "It will not strain your transporter's capabilities." Spock gave the puzzled but politely co-operative chief the approximate weight and dimensions, and then sent a message directly to Scotty: "The item is in transit."

"Uh, we got it, Mr. Ambassador," the transporter chief cut in. *"Whatever it is."*

"Heard and understood," Sarval said, and broke contact. The Romulan ship sped away and was soon out of range.

"I'm on my way," Scotty said en route to the transporter room, and Spock sat back in satisfaction. If anyone could do this job quickly, efficiently, and correctly, Scotty could.

The *Alliance,* flanked by the two Klingon ships, headed on toward Watraii space—and all the while the *Alliance's* engineering crew, under the command of one Montgomery Scott, worked swiftly and feverishly.

"Systems up and running, Captain Saavik," Scotty sent in triumph.

"Excellent."

The *Alliance* now was cloaked, thanks to Romulan permission—even if that permission hadn't exactly come from open or official channels.

Cloaking is very necessary, Spock thought.

Without cloaking, the Starfleet intruders would almost certainly be detected before getting close enough. The Watraii would not only attack them, quite justifiably, they would almost certainly destroy both the artifact and the intruders—and with them, Pavel Chekov.

Now, though, Romulan cloaking had given them a chance for success.

ELEVEN

MEMORY

ROVALAT'S STORY

Rovalat hurled the dagger ship out of the docking bay into the barren field of stars toward his enemy. So what if he had never been this far from the ship alone? There was no point in looking back. There never had been. What was space, after all, but the vastest desert he had ever traveled?

Wastelands had fascinated him since his *kahs-wan*. As a young man, he had wandered the Forge, explored the northern salt waste up as far as the sea, ventured onto the lava plains to stand looking up into the eyes of the Colossi, weathered the worst electrical storm anyone could recall, and been the first man to cross the Great Erg in the southern continent.

He had climbed past the shrines on Mount Seleya and ventured into the eternal snows near its preternaturally sharp peaks. At the peak of his world, the sky grew dark even at noon, the air was so thin he had to fight to breathe, and the cold was greater than anything he had ever endured, but he had mastered it. Better yet, he had mastered himself.

Seleya's upper peak loomed within his reach, but he had considered it impious to ascend. Instead, Rovalat had gazed out across the Forge, then down into the chasm between the two peaks, measuring the distance. When he finally raised his eyes again, he saw a sundweller far below him, glittering iridescent green and metallic white and amber, its wings fully extended to catch the thermals and bask in the sun's warmth. The sight made him forget the stabbing pain in his side as his heart raced and he struggled for each breath.

He had descended, returned to his family's home, and taken up his life's work: preparing and testing generations of boys to come. Except for that last, disastrous *kahs-wan,* it had been a good life, but all things must come to an end. Sooner or later, even this exile would end, and his adopted sons must be alive to see it.

To feel the heat of Vulcan's star, beating down upon the Forge again. To gaze out across the desert that had molded him one last time . . .

Since the day Rovalat had failed to save children he treasured, he had created a desert of silence and shame. *Time to atone and forgive myself,* he thought. *Just let me save the children.*

If Karatek had not understood, he would not have allowed Rovalat to depart. There could be no better heir for his *katra;* it would only bewilder the others.

Around him, below him, above him, glittered stars as relentless as his will as Rovalat forced the dagger past its maximum safe speed toward the shuttle, then coaxed it to a protective course right above his children.

Over the dagger's com, he heard the voices of others he had known from their childhoods, protesting to Karatek and urging Rovalat to return home to *Shavokh*. He laughed to himself. *Shavokh* was only a ship. The waste was his home.

Besides, there was no point in arguing. In catching up to the shuttle, Rovalat had expended much of the fuel he would have needed to return. Perhaps he might find room on the shuttle's return trip. . . . No, if all went well, the shuttle would be filled with his children, rescued and rescuers.

No room for him.

If only he could save his children, he would ask nothing more. It was not, after all, as if he expected to live long and prosper.

There! Rovalat saw the shuttle touch down on what was as barren and unprepossessing a planetoid as any they had passed. He followed its crew out, tracking them across the plain, then waiting with an old hunter's patience for their enemy to show itself.

In the end, things happened as Rovalat had expected, although more quickly than he would have believed possible. As his children extended their hands in peace, burly aliens emerged and responded with violence. His children fell.

So much for logic, Rovalat thought. It had always cost his people more than they could afford. Ironic, was it not? Young Karatek had tried to serve logic and make it serve him. But in the end, it had been the guile and passion of his children that had prevailed, that must prevail if these last remnants of the Mother World were to live on some as-yet-undiscovered world.

Peering out of hiding, Rovalat saw that he had gauged his risks correctly. The aliens were so intent on "processing" his children that they had no time to notice an aged man with just enough strength in him for one last hunt. Years of desert stillness, years of isolation on board ship had taught him a kind of invisibility.

The healers had once told him it was a side effect of his mental gifts. They had wished to send him to Seleya for further study. He had refused. He had the desert, and he had his children. He had never needed, nor wanted, more.

Now, he needed only one more thing, and he would find it. He scanned the area, his eyes dropping, from time to time, to the image caster young Sarissa had given him. He would use it to consult with the man holding its counterpart on *Shavokh,* so far away. If Karatek had helped design the engines of the great ships, it logically followed that this wilderness of conduits and passages was his kind of desert.

"Do you see?" he whispered.

"Yes," Karatek whispered back.

There! Those panels with their pulsing lights looked as if the conduits beneath might carry some form of life support. Rovalat reached out to touch them, to remove the panels, disable the control mechanisms. The vibration of the corridors altered. In some places, it ceased. Hearing a whine, then ringing, as if some distress signal had gone off, he made what speed he could to the next intersection of corridors and control panels, where he wreaked still further damage. He only hoped he could weaken this installation sufficiently for its masters to focus on it rather than wager on his children's deaths in an arena.

Heavy rock and the static of deep space overhead might degrade transmission, but Rovalat's voice never faltered as he told his story to the man who would advise him on this last adventure, then remember it for all time.

He damaged six more conduits, then decided that the gradual approach just was not working. Even if it ultimately did succeed, it would take so long that a fully loaded shuttle could never reach

Shavokh, which dared not turn to retrieve it. His hands grew chill, and his vision blurred, though he told himself that those were only side effects of the illness that was killing him even more slowly. But he knew the truth: he was afraid.

"Despair is counterproductive," Karatek whispered. *"You are lost in the desert. The sand is blowing; you cannot see the stars. How would you orient yourself?"*

"I would go to ground," Rovalat said. And indeed he had.

His composure returned. A hissing told him he had reached an air supply. Best not disable that. But other, glowing tubes beckoned.

No sooner seen than smashed.

And then Rovalat was elsewhere, in a doorless room with gray walls, lacking all furniture but three low platforms, each surmounted by a dome of force. Beneath each shimmering dome pulsed a living, glowing brain, one yellow, one green, and one orange.

An alarm sounded and, over it, shouted words that Rovalat suspected meant "intruder alert."

These . . . these things had scanned him. They had known he was here all along.

Why?

Even as his mind formed the thought, the answer came.

"Diversion."

Whatever these things were, they were bored. Even with the killing of Rovalat's children.

He did not need Surak to understand the illogic, the criminal waste of their boredom. Bored? With a wealth of beings to study and all space lying before them, given their abilities? It was not just illogical, it was frivolous and capricious. Beings who felt boredom as they bet on captives' death might welcome a novelty. But they would turn on it the instant they found something even newer.

"What are you?" he demanded.

"We are the Providers." He had heard that voice on Seyhan's recordings.

Rovalat's lip curled in disgust.

Provider? What did these creatures provide, apart from death?

Rovalat felt his blood heat. He drew three deep breaths. Control. That was the way of Surak's students, was it not? He had given the disciplines some study, earlier in his life. He'd even had a reason. Control was useful for creating stillness; stillness was useful in approaching animals more closely; and approaching wild creatures that might be deadly—and on Vulcan, probably were—could mean life.

Be patient. Be the desert. Wait, and then strike.

Rovalat put Seyhan out of his thoughts and emotions. He had not had the privilege of training him, but Seyhan had been a credit to those who had enjoyed that honor.

"Why do you steal my children?" Rovalat demanded.

Karatek's face, tiny on the tiny screen, looked so pained, despite all his fine logical control, that Rovalat wanted to laugh. Yes, he knew he had asked a rhetorical question. But it was a way of starting. When you met a wild creature, how you acted was far more important than what you said, if you used words at all. And threat display was vital.

"You steal my children for diversion?" he asked.

The brains—the Providers—pulsed. Rovalat took it for a "yes."

Again, he suppressed his rage long enough to look around. It was not, he told himself, as if these Providers were entirely discarnate intelligence, creatures of pure force. Only the *katra* was disembodied and immortal, until it decided otherwise. That provided some reassurance.

142

So, if the Providers' consciousness resided in these brains, something had to be nourishing them. Set into the silvery walls, panels of lights ebbed and flowed, reflected by the panels embedded into the platforms that held the brains.

Assumption: some form of nutrient flowed into those things, in response to some energy measurement that indicated when nutrition or waste extraction was necessary. It was just like the desert or even *Shavokh:* a fragile, closed ecostructure.

All his life, Rovalat had never damaged desert or ship. That was about to change.

Seyhan had said that his team's weapons had not worked. This close to the Providers' central installation, perhaps they could not afford to nullify all energies. Pulling out a sidearm, he aimed at a glowing section of a wall and fired.

Just as he thought. So confident were these Providers in their native habitat that they forgot to take the simplest precautions!

Part of the panel melted. The rest shattered with a satisfying crash, scattering pale shards across the room. Hot blood flowed down his left temple from a stinging cut.

"What are you doing?" the mad, worthless minds asked.

"Diverting you," Rovalat said, grinning like a *le-matya* about to pounce. In all his years on board *Shavokh,* he could count the times he had been able to grin on the fingers of one hand.

"Hurry." Karatek whispered, reminding Rovalat that time was passing. With each instant, the planetoid and *Shavokh* were moving away from each other, and people in the arenas on this wasteland of a world were fighting and dying.

He fired again. The lights in the room flickered, then flared as secondary systems kicked in. Karatek would know better.

"Are you sufficiently diverted to answer me?" he demanded.

"What do you want?"

"You have my children," he said. "I want them back."

Simple enough. He had never needed fancy phrases in the desert.

Again the lights altered. So, the contempt in Rovalat's voice had gotten through. He fired again, taking care not to aim directly at the disembodied brain. For one thing, he didn't think his sidearm could penetrate the force shields. For another, he suspected that they would produce a deadly ricochet. It was illogical to expend one's life for no purpose.

"Are you diverted? Do the impulses that pass for emotions in your brain please you? Are the neurons firing? Are you getting the nutrition you need? Are you still bored?" Rovalat demanded.

He raised the sidearm to fire again, this time closer to the yellow brain.

"Stop!"

"Why? My children came down here in good faith, and you made them slaves. My other children sought only metals to help them on their journey, and you stole them. Why should I not destroy your habitat? You are depopulating mine!"

Time was passing. The chamber seemed doorless, but these Providers might be able to bring in guards and stop him. That Rovalat could be so close, yet still fail in his quest drove him as close to panic as he had ever been. That included the time a cave he had decided to spend the night in turned out to attract a *lematya* seeking only a refuge in which to bear her kits.

That time, Rovalat had thrust fire at her, and escaped. This time, he pulled out what Sarissa had helped him take from the armory.

A fusion grenade.

"Maybe you are as far above me as I am above the creatures that creep upon the land," he told the Providers. "My sidearm can only damage your environment. But this," he brandished the grenade, "might destroy you."

The lights flickered all about him. Soon, they would bring in rescuers, warriors stronger than he had ever been. He must strike this bargain and strike it soon.

"Does that divert you? Can you still know fear? Can you still grasp the thrill of pitting your wits against a wild beast?"

Again, he thrust the grenade at them. If they had materialized him here, they could send him out into the chill of space before he freed his children. The thought made his hand tremble. He made it look as if he was brandishing his weapon.

"Shall I blow you to the Womb of Fire?" he asked. "You may be powerful, but do you want to risk an end to all your wonderful diversions? Wouldn't even boredom be preferable?"

He edged in even closer.

Agitated cascades of lights lit the room.

"Name your terms," the Providers said.

"I want all of them freed," Rovalat declared.

"They cannot all be your children."

The orange brain seemed to throb with what sounded like indignation. He had heard children whine like that. Many had not survived their *kahs-wan*. They had not been fit.

"They are someone's children, even if they are not mine." Again, he feinted with the grenade.

"And will you claim our Master Thrall as well?" Rovalat could not have imagined the satisfaction in the brains' mental voices.

The creature that materialized in the chamber was a biped, but that was where the resemblance between Vulcan and Master Thrall ceased. It was distinctly saurian, with what looked like bone plates on its crest and its spine. The harness and torque were all it wore because it was armored in bronze-green scales.

Although its forearms were disproportionately short, they ended in three-digit hands that bore very powerful claws at least twice as long as the fangs that projected beyond its snout.

Rovalat raised his sidearm and fired. The Master Thrall advanced. He fired again and again until the creature fell. The stench of burned tissue and chemicals nearly brought Rovalat to his knees, but he mastered his nausea. He had seen, he told himself, worse. He had seen his children die.

"Have you been sufficiently entertained?" he demanded. "Will you release my children now?"

It was the green brain's turn to light up and to speak. *"They can go. You will remain. That is our best offer."*

"Done," said Rovalat. Deliberately, he ignored Karatek's appalled protest. The man would have to meditate for at least a year to work off those emotions.

The lights pulsed all at once. For a moment, the chamber went dark. When it lit again, he could see the brains lying on their platforms as if whatever effort they had expended had exhausted them.

"I'm getting a signal. They're taking off!" Karatek's voice, reduced to a whisper audible only to sharp Vulcan ears, came over the 'caster. *"Getting signal . . . They can make it!"*

Don't let them hear you sound that excited, Rovalat wished at the faraway scientist wryly, *or you'll never get done meditating.*

"Get out!" Karatek ordered. *"Get out now! It's still not too late."*

Rovalat laughed, briefly and mirthlessly. "Yes, it is," he told Karatek, no longer bothering to whisper. "Even if I hadn't used up most of my fuel, I traded myself for these creatures, and I've never broken my word. You have all that I was. Remember me."

The lights came back on. Was it Rovalat's imagination, or did they have a fevered tinge, as if even these superior, disembodied intelligences could know fear and rage?

Figures formed in the chamber once again. They stepped over the body of the Master Thrall. He should have known that not all of the prisoners would be released. Still, they had released his children. That was all he had ever wanted.

"This ceases," he told them. "Right now!"

Only the *le-matya* killed wantonly. He backed into the part of the room farthest away from these new enemies.

"Retreat, and you won't be harmed," he told the advancing thralls. "Remember, you gave your word!" he reproached the Providers. Expecting them to keep it was about as useful as trying to persuade a *le-matya* not to kill. Well, he had at least tried.

The thralls advanced a step further, then, to Rovalat's surprise, disappeared.

"We have kept our word," the green Provider told him. *"Now, what diversion will you show us?"*

"This," Rovalat said, and let the fusion grenade fall from his hand.

The screen turned a violent white that drove the nictitating veil down across Karatek's eyelids. He staggered and fell, aftereffects of the final separation between Rovalat and his *katra*.

When Karatek regained consciousness, he grabbed for the image caster, ignoring the people, the voices, the hands that attempted to make him lie back, rest, tell them what was happening, and obey all their instructions at once.

His eyes still blurred, but he made himself focus. The chamber was empty of all but three platforms, three energy domes, and three glowing brains.

Karatek suppressed what wanted to be a shout of rage that all

Rovalat's courage, all his self-sacrifice, should receive no better reward than a violent death. The veils flicked over his eyes, preserving their moisture as he blinked out at the brilliant stars. Rovalat's sacrifice could hardly be considered a failure: it had bought time for the other Vulcans to escape. The ship's children were coming home.

TWELVE

NOW

U.S.S. ALLIANCE
STARDATE 54105.5

The bridge crew of the *Alliance* stared in silence at the dull gray, cloud-shrouded world appearing on the viewscreen.

"That," Scotty announced in deliberate understatement, "is not exactly the most promising sight I've seen."

He'd summed it up for all of them, Spock thought.

Of course they were still at quite a distance from the planet, not yet quite within Watraii space. As a result, the image they were receiving was not at optimum clarity.

Even so, it was clear enough for Scotty to be able to say with some certainty, "Storms, storms, and more storms, and what look like almost nonstop lightning strikes—" He shook his head wryly. "That must make life a wee bit difficult for the Watraii."

"Indeed it must," Data agreed. "Weather conditions on the Watraii homeworld appear severe enough to make the Galorndon Core's electrical storms seem mild by comparison."

"Lieutenant Suhur," Saavik said, "I understand that accurate scans are difficult at this range, and with the atmospheric distortion they are unlikely to give us too much information, but give us as much data as possible, please."

After a few moments of intense silence, save for the faint beeping of the lieutenant's console, Suhur looked up from the screen. "Scans are as complete as possible, Captain Saavik. I shall put them on-screen." As the images formed, he explained, "The Watraii homeworld appears to be a relatively young world, geologically speaking, perhaps only a billion or possibly even fewer standard years. Much of the terrain is mountainous, with approximately 42.5 percent containing ground water, but with no true seas. The planet's gravity is slightly lighter than standard, approximately 98.01 percent of that of Earth, and it has an atmosphere only 2 percent thinner than standard."

That made the atmosphere only slightly lighter than that of Earth or Vulcan, Spock mused, or, for that matter, of Romulus. Excellent. They would not need any special breathing equipment. And Chekov would at least be able to breathe comfortably. The slightly lighter gravity would be making him a little more comfortable, too.

Whether or not he might be in any condition to appreciate it was speculation unworthy of a Vulcan.

"Life-forms?" Saavik asked.

After a short analysis, Suhur reported, "It is impossible to tell, Captain. As we suspected, the storms are distorting the scans."

"Understood." Saavik glanced at Spock. "So much for our being able to locate either Chekov or the artifact from out here."

"However," Spock countered, "we do have a useful clue, at

least as far as the artifact is concerned. We have the evidence of prior analysis of downed Watraii vessels."

"Continue, Spock."

"They were composed primarily of amalgams of light metals. We can logically extrapolate, therefore, that the Watraii home-world is poor in heavier metals—although it is also undeniably rich in electrical energy."

Saavik raised an eyebrow. "Interesting."

Spock nodded. Charvanek had claimed to know very little about the Romulan artifact, but she had at least known that it was made of a very dense heavy metal, one that would not occur naturally on the Watraii homeworld, and their scans of Watraii ships showed that they had no alloys remotely similar. "The artifact should certainly show up on scans."

"True enough, Spock. But the proof will have to wait—always assuming, of course, that someone can get close enough to it for something so small to actually register."

Scotty straightened. "We can take a shuttlecraft. Now, granted, it's a challenge to outfit something that small with effective cloaking technology, but I could do it. And 'twould be no work at all to modify its fields so it could survive all that electricity."

A corner of Saavik's mouth almost hinted at a smile. "And that is precisely why it is on board," she said. "And, of course, Scotty, why you are, as well."

Spock was there in Saavik's ready room for a quick consultation. Saavik sat on one side of him, Scotty on the other, and Ruanek and Data were seated across the table from them, the Klingon captains on the com screen. *A strange conference,* Spock thought, *human, Vulcan, Romulan, and android.*

"You must understand," Saavik began, glancing about at the

others, "that the allowable time for this mission is extremely limited. We have precisely two shipboard days before we must leave or be trapped between the Watraii and the oncoming Federation fleet. Our primary mission is to rescue Admiral Chekov. Should it be possible to rescue the artifact as well, excellent. But Chekov has priority."

"We understand," Spock assured her.

"So we are not to make a direct attack," Tor'Ka said with a Klingon's lack of dissembling. He sounded rather disappointed.

"We cannot do so," Saavik replied as reasonably as though that truly had been an option. "I trust that you understand our reason."

"We do see the reason why," JuB-Chal admitted reluctantly. *"And of course, rescuing a comrade is an honorable action. However—"*

"Don't worry," Ruanek said sharply. "There still may be blood enough for you."

"There may, indeed," Spock cut in before either Ruanek or the Klingons could continue. Even after all his years on Vulcan and Earth, Ruanek's ingrained Romulan mistrust of Klingons still surfaced at odd moments. "But first we wish to rescue our comrade." *And the artifact.*

"Understood," Tor'Ka said curtly. *"So it shall be. You and we shall do almost nothing, as though we are no more than a group of clumsy* khaQpu'*."*

"Privateers must surely be familiar with the need for evasive tactics," Data commented. "This ship and yours will act as decoys, hopefully drawing Watraii attention aside so that our smaller craft may slip undetected through Watraii defenses."

"And if they attack us," Tor'Ka shot back, *"then there is an end to this decoy nonsense, and we shall fight!"*

"We shall fight!" Jub-Chal echoed.

"Captain," Lieutenant Abrams interrupted over the com link, *"we are now at coordinates 29.456 by 646.4 by 254.5, as you commanded, on the, ah, edge of Watraii space."*

"If space had edges," Saavik said, getting to her feet. "Captains, we shall do our part, and I know you shall do yours. As for us, gentlebeings, we have work to do."

The shuttle berthed in the *Alliance*'s hangar bay was as trim and clean as everything else on board, but:

"'Small' is definitely the right description for it," Ruanek commented. He absently rubbed a hand over his shoulder where he, like the other three on this mission, had just been fitted with a sub-cutaneous transponder, then shouldered his pack. "It holds . . . what? Three? Four?"

"Six," Saavik corrected.

"Six," Ruanek echoed flatly.

"Albeit not in comfort," Spock added. "Should such a non-essential fact as comfort actually be an issue."

Ruanek gave the slightest of shrugs. "Believe me, Spock, I've ridden in worse." He glanced sideways at Spock. "And at least this time I know that I can trust the maintenance."

"Don't you have the slightest qualm about trusting the mainte-nance," Scotty cut in cheerfully. "I went over it myself, top to bot-tom, and believe me, this bairn is now as up-to-date as I could make it, with the latest equipment and full cloaking capability. As much cloaking capacity as you can have with a craft this size, of course."

"Well done, Scotty," Saavik told him.

He beamed at her. "Thank you. Now all the brave bairn needs is a name, something more official than *Shuttle Three*. Will you do the honor?"

"If you feel the need to do so." After a moment's thought, Saavik put a hand on the ship's side and exclaimed, "I hereby dub you *Alexander Nevsky*. That," she added to the others, who were staring at her, "is the name of an ancient human hero who triumphed over great odds."

How she had come to know that bit of old Earth history . . . Spock reminded himself with a touch of wry humor that he had learned years ago never to underestimate his wife.

"May it prove a propitious name," Data said simply.

THIRTEEN

MEMORY

"Surak's disciples in the fleet maintain that the most recent part of our long, long journey illustrates his statement in his Third Analects: *'Disciplines that can be abandoned in times of hardship when disciplines are most needed are no disciplines at all.'*

"It would be illogical to deny that these are times of hardship. It is equally illogical to refuse to listen to all voices. Some of us maintain Surak's teachings; some opposed them, but found themselves in exile nonetheless; while others, having abandoned the disciplines, argue that this proves they were of no validity in the first place.

"The dispute would be fascinating were we back at the Vulcan Space Institute or the Vulcan Science Academy.

"An example: Surak ate no meat and urged his students to wage peace, not war. We have found that this principle is simpler to live up to when one lives on a planet or sees no planet on which one might live, than when ships' scanners find a Minshara-class

world that could well allow us to establish a home, if only it were not already inhabited by intelligent beings.

"Yes, we could wage peace with those whose neighbors some of us earnestly wish to become. But we had neighbors back on Vulcan, and the battles we fought with them endangered the Mother World's survival. It is illogical to assume we would behave any better as guests on another species' world.

"Thus, we have had to set aside ambitions to land on two worlds thus far. Right now, Shavokh *has more immediate concerns: we have had difficulty in adjusting our ramscoops, and we have had to decelerate near a binary system. The worlds circling one star are covered either in molten rock or liquid methane. The second star, however, is orbited by six planets. And one of them is not just* Minshara-*class, but a world that matches Vulcan in climate almost exactly, although it is richer in metals and has never been despoiled by war. It is, in fact, pristine. Although the evidence appears incontrovertible, after so many years it is difficult to believe that our journey may end here.*

"Two ships have already achieved parking orbits around the planet. They have sent shuttles down to collect plant and mineral samples and perform studies of the planet's climate and composition. In this circumstance, hope appears highly logical."

Karatek lifted the coronet from his head. A message informed him that repairs to *Shavokh's* engines were complete. It was time to go to the command center; he wanted to record the exact moment when the two ships exploring the world below them formally notified the rest that they had found a new home.

Peacefully, he left his quarters, drawing his fingers along the cold clear tiles of the mosaic that now occupied one entire long bulkhead all the way to the lifts. Red and gold tiles gave way to the indigo and black tesserae representing the Eridani-Trianguli spaces, lit only by the colors of the stars, the planets circling them, with delicate traceries of bloodmetal and gold for the nebulae they had seen. Once they had established a settlement, this mosaic, along with every other example of the art created during the long journey, should be preserved in . . .

What would they call it? The New Vulcan Science Academy? Perhaps Karatek would be permitted to name it.

"T'Kehr *Karatek, report, please!"* came the ship commander's voice from the speakers set into the ceiling. Interesting: the man's voice was almost shaking.

Three men and two women pushed past Karatek, barely stopping to recognize him with a nod of the head.

Karatek raised an eyebrow. What had happened to the fleet's hopes? When he had begun his meditations, morale was high. Now, however . . .

In this context, "Now what?" was not a rhetorical question.

He quickened his pace, entering the command center to find navigators and a gathering of ship's scientists clustered before the main viewing screens.

They had moved in closer to the world. How beautiful it was, glowing there in the darkness. He would encourage the artists who created the mosaic to finish it by adding this world and, indeed, the binary system with all of its worlds. And, perhaps, small jewels could be set into the tiles to mark the last orbits that the great ships would make.

"T'Kehr, what do you make of this?" Commander S'lovan demanded. "I'm getting a transmission from *Sunheart* ordering us to withdraw. Ordering us! I cannot believe they want the entire planet for themselves."

"One ship alone cannot colonize a world," said Karatek. "Please turn up the volume."

"Stay clear!" came the tiny recorded voice from *Sunheart.* *"Reverse course, break off approach! Everyone evacuate this system now!"*

"Why is the transmission so degraded?" Karatek asked. "The distance between the planet and *Shavokh* cannot account for this degree of breakup."

"Communications is trying to filter out the static," said one of the science officers, R'mor, a tall, lanky man with kin-ties to S'lovan. "There's a kind of energy . . . I don't know, *T'Kehr,* but the last time I saw this sort of pattern was when I visited the healers for headaches so severe I could barely lift my head."

"As we neared the planet, we noticed that our sister ships' ion trails just stopped. We tried to raise them, but contact was broken off, and . . . night and day, the ships are . . . they're . . ." The science officer broke off as if the person standing next to him had elbowed him.

"Magnify!" Commander S'lovan said. The viewscreen blurred, then resolved on its highest magnification, just in time to show the two ships in orbit plummet down into the planet's atmosphere.

"Energy signatures," said S'lovan. "Those ships didn't crash; they were pulled in by some sort of energy beam."

Karatek felt his hands chill. *Shavokh's* engineers had been trying to develop a prototype for a tractor beam, but with little success yet.

The great ships could not operate in atmosphere. He had just seen two of them die.

"Get out!" *Sunheart's* commander abandoned all pretense of a decent, measured control. His ship, along with the ion trails of his two consorts, described extravagant hyperbolas as they fled.

"Commander, we're starting to feel an energy surge coming from the planet . . ."

"Reverse course!" Karatek and S'lovan shouted in unison, and Karatek lunged for controls.

Shavokh's engines whined and labored to break free.

"It's building up!" he heard an engineer scream.

"Augment engines!" Karatek ordered. "Hook in the test generators. Make sure the crystals are aligned, or we'll have an explosion."

Maybe an explosion here in space would be better than being trapped, tugged down to a planet for which they had had the greatest hopes.

"Do it!" Karatek shouted.

"Do it now!" S'lovan backed him up.

With a shudder, the test engine came online. Control boards shorted out, and the entire ship lurched as *Shavokh* struggled free.

Ship-to-ship receiver in one ear, Commander S'lovan tensed as he listened to *Sunheart*.

"Yes," he barked. "We've lost track of *Vengeance* and *Firestorm,* too. Let's go now!"

Ending transmission, S'lovan turned to his crew. "I want an estimate of how soon you can get those fires out and damage repaired," he said. "When I say 'move,' I want us to be able to put as much distance between us and that world as we can, as fast as we can."

"Sir, why not accelerate now?"

"Sunheart's commander believes we are now out of range. The operative word is 'believes.' He wants to consult in person, and the other ships—those that survived"—the man visibly fought to retain his control—"are out of range. He estimates a 35.666 percent chance that both escaped whatever caused the other two to crash."

"So much for our new homeworld," came a whisper from T'Velar, an associate of Avarak. "R'mor said the only place he'd seen energy like that was when he visited the healers. What if it's not physical but mental?"

"This isn't the time for metaphysics!" the senior science officer rebuked her.

Her speculation was unlikely to the point of absurdity, but it was all they had. And it looked likely to prompt a shouting match.

"*Kroykah!*" ordered Commander S'lovan. "I want a senior healer to attend me at the shuttlebay. *Sunheart's* commander is bringing over an adept for a consultation."

"It will be interesting to hear the adept's views," Karatek observed.

"What views?" the commander asked as he rose. "She's the last of *Sunheart's* telepaths who was initiated to the rank of adept. Apparently she had an old teacher on board one of those . . . one of the ships we lost. They were close enough to communicate. She's catatonic now. If our healers can rouse her, it may be that we can learn what happened."

Karatek ran after S'lovan toward the shuttlebay. Pushing through a crowded corridor, Karatek remembered a saying he had heard in his earliest days at the Vulcan Space Institute: *The one thing we know that can travel faster than the speed of light is rumor.* He could rationalize and call it intelligence, but there was nothing intelligent about a frightened ship.

Karatek pushed past people whose rage and fear he could sense. What if they broke through? But security was there, forming a barrier. An even more effective remedy came with the approach of the chief healer, whose presence made them fall back somewhat. She had T'Olryn with her, and his daughter-in-law swept the shuttlebay with a glare worthy of Sarissa herself. Both healers wore the red and white robes of priestesses. T'Olryn's robes failed to hide her pregnancy.

Shouts echoed off the cold, high bulkheads.

"We should go back!"

"What about that planet you wouldn't let us even land on?"

"Admit it, we've lost too many ships . . . "

"We'll die here in space!"

Karatek gestured the commander to proceed. He himself turned. He should speak to the crowd before the hotheads among them turned fear into anger. He had not thought so many on board had abandoned Surak's disciplines. Nevertheless, it was his duty to try to wage peace.

"We have the opportunity to serve," Karatek said.

A yell of outrage from someone who stood far in back.

"We also have the opportunity to gain more information," he added. "Please let the healers through."

T'Olryn caught Karatek by the arm and pulled him through after her toward the sealed doors of the shuttlebay. What ordinarily would have been a severe breach of protocol brought him a flicker of awareness: *concern/cold/repressed fear.*

Karatek had always been pleased by T'Olryn's concern for Solor's family. Her own mother had not made it onto the great ships, and her father's system had proved unable to withstand the hardships of exile.

She had meant him to feel her emotions. That was her way of reminding Karatek that he was past combat age, out of training, and that his duties did not include a warrior's duty to put himself in harm's way if the crowd turned hostile.

This launch bay hadn't just been repaired since the time N'Veyan had crashed a stolen shuttle in a suicidal attempt to reach his pledged mate, it had been upgraded. Hardened, the engineers assured the council. But, unfortunately, if the new bay was safer, it was also 10.5 percent slower to seal, depressurize, allow a shuttle or dagger to dock, then repressurize so people could enter. The procedure felt even slower, which was subjective, therefore illogical—unless, of course, one assumed relativistic effects were involved.

Think, don't babble, Karatek told himself. He really would have to spend less time remembering and more time in formal meditation.

As controls darkened toward the green of safety, Karatek forced himself to stand as quietly as the healers while the shuttlebay repressurized and the hatches released.

Now, finally, he could push into the echoing shuttlebay with its bronzed bulkheads. He ran after the healers and the other senior members of the ship's crew and council, their footsteps echoing on the cold decks, as *Sunheart*'s vessel, frozen vapor drifting from its battered hull, turned on its landing circle and extended its ramp with painful slowness.

Sunheart's commander emerged before the ramp was fully extended. In his arms, he cradled his ship's last healer. Now, that was a breach of propriety that could be explained only by his apparent unwillingness to risk additional passengers, or by the strong family resemblance between healer and Commander Sevennin. Both were tall and thin, even for a race that ran to ectomorphs. Both were pale from the many years of imprisonment within *Sunheart.*

Since departing Vulcan, *Sunheart*'s commander had never left his ship, always sending a deputy to council and delegating even the most important missions to mining sites or potential homeworlds. He had never been in physical danger. It was illogical for him to blame himself for that, but he probably would, anyway.

The healer lay limp in her father's arms, not so much pallid as livid, except for the trickles of blood from the corners of her eyes.

Formal greetings were bypassed: in any event, *Sunheart*'s commander didn't have a free hand to raise.

T'Olryn hissed, then looked down in apology before she stepped forward. Taking off her outer robe, she laid it on the deck, then helped her superior ease the woman down onto it.

Karatek stepped forward and laid his own cloak over his daughter-in-law's shoulders. *There is no cold,* he told himself.

The healers knelt. Each extended a long-fingered hand, curiously similar. The elder's hand was old, somewhat gnarled, while T'Olryn's was tiny, well-kept, and bore the heavy bloodstone ring, shimmering with lines of deep crimson, that had been in Karatek's House for generations.

Very gently, T'Olryn brushed away the trickles of blood from the catatonic woman's face. Her fingers lingered near the *katra* points, the nerve plexuses touched during a meld. More blood trickled down. Under the shuttlebay's harsh lighting, its deep green seemed even more shocking. Bleeding from the nose, even from the mouth were things Karatek understood, had seen—but bleeding from the *eyes?*

T'Olryn's face went grave. If an adept-level healer hadn't the minimal biocontrol necessary to stop such a tiny flow of blood, the damage was indeed great. She turned toward her superior, who moved in, touching the other side of the woman's face. Gradually, the bleeding ceased.

Sunheart's commander turned his face away. Healers, like other adepts, worked in concert only when the need was very great.

"My mind to your mind," the healer whispered.

"My thoughts to your thoughts," whispered T'Olryn.

The woman struggled against the touch. Her mouth writhed. Only a whimper came out. Karatek had never heard such pain.

Karatek wanted to leap forward and snatch the battered healer away. How could the healers violate a mind like that?

T'Olryn raised her head. "This is surgical pain," she spoke over her patient's head to her father-in-law.

163

"There is no pain," said Sevennin, as if reminding himself.

Given the speed of rumor on board *Shavokh,* there would be whispers that it was the father, not the commander, who had broken his own rule of never leaving his ship in an attempt to save his child. The commander met those accusing gazes with composure.

"I would have taken her *katra,* if I could, and freed her," he confessed. "But my daughter knows what happened to our other ships. She *has* to know. Perhaps *Shavokh*'s healers can obtain that knowledge. She would want me to try. . . ."

Karatek looked away.

"It may even be that they can heal her," he offered.

The other man's eyes went bleak.

"Thy hope belies logic."

The clamor outside the shuttlebay grew so loud that it could be heard even with the hatches sealed. The healers' faces grew as drawn as the face of the adept lying on the deck. Her eyes had begun to weep blood again.

"You know that memory scanner we've been developing?" asked T'Veran. "It might help."

Commander Sevennin's gaze grew terrible. "I did not bring my last child here so you could ravage what remains of her mind but to help save our people," he told her. Their eyes locked, and it was T'Veran who looked away.

"Hunger!" cried T'Olryn. *"So much hunger, years of . . . Bring me food!"*

Night and day, the healers had made contact. Her sensitivity heightened by pregnancy, T'Olryn had gone to the deepest levels, relying on the immense strength and experience of her teacher to bring her back safely.

"Lure it . . . lure it to us . . . ahhhh . . ."

For a moment, both healers' faces ignited with a fierce greed.

They sighed, their features relaxing into satiation that made Karatek feel unclean. Commander Sevennin turned away. His shoulders quivered once, then became motionless.

"More . . . on the way . . . good . . ." T'Olryn purred with satisfaction. Karatek vowed that he would *never* tell his son about the look, half lust, half starvation, that contorted his wife's lovely face.

The noise outside the shuttlebay rose. *Shavokh's* commander murmured, and armed guards poured in. It was, he supposed, logical, but he regretted it. Those who boarded the ships never had been a unified people. As the years went by, they had become increasingly fragmented.

Vulcan would draw on Vulcan again. One day, war would break out, and all their journey, all the sacrifice, suffering, and toll of years would have been for nothing.

"Have you learned nothing?" A voice like that of a *shavokh,* belling in triumph after a hunt, ripped across the shuttlebay. *"No caution, no control . . . warn off, warn off . . ."*

The voice arched up in a raw scream that echoed off the high bay until all below flinched.

"They've broken the lock code!" one of the guards shouted. "Commander, shall we fire?"

"No!" Karatek shouted.

"More food!" came another cry from the woman lying on the deck.

As the shouting, frightened crowd poured into the shuttlebay, the injured healer had struggled to sit up. *Shavokh's* healers pressed close, supporting her as she wavered. Slowly, the woman's eyes opened. They were so dilated that pupil and iris alike were drowned in green.

"Would you see?" she demanded in that terrible voice. *"Well, would you see? Behold the Eater of Souls!"*

She opened her mind and projected hunger, intelligent and ancient past their comprehension. The hunger raved like a *le-matya*, like an entire planet of *le-matya*s with kits to feed. But this was a hunger glutted by living minds and spirits. Whatever possessed *Sunheart's* dying healer had fed on the Vulcans on board those ships. Then, before torpor followed satiation, they had . . . night and day, they had cleaned up after themselves. A flick of those supernally powerful intellects had brought the ships down into . . . Why, the world they had circled had not been a paradise, after all, but a methane bath. They had manipulated ships' instruments as well as minds.

All shouting ceased. So, blessedly, did those anguished screams.

The strength went out of the dying adept. Eyelids bleached almost white with her agony dropped over those blood-filled eyes for the last time. The healers eased her back onto the deck.

Sevennin took off his own cloak and covered his daughter's face.

For a moment, Karatek's eyes dazzled.

"I grieve with thee," said Commander S'lovan.

"We have all lost kin," Sevennin bowed away the ritual words.

He knelt, pulling his daughter into his arms again, then rising.

"We will return to the ship now," he said. "I have been too long away."

Karatek stepped to the commander's side.

"May we offer thee fire, water . . . ?" he asked. His words were inadequate, but they were all he had.

The elder healer started forward, her hands outstretched. There was more knowledge yet to be gained from an examination of the dead woman's mind.

How could the woman even consider asking permission to do an autopsy now? T'Olryn started forward, but her knees buckled, and Karatek caught her.

"How much more does your sister adept owe you?" *Sunheart's* commander asked. "You have her *katra,* all that she was, damaged as it is. I shall give the rest of her to a star." He started toward the shuttle. "But not this one."

He strode up the ramp into the shuttle. Supporting T'Olryn, Karatek led the others beyond the barrier as the small craft retracted its ramp. The shuttle turned on its launch circle, then darted back out into the night.

Let me guide her, came the whisper within Karatek's consciousness: Rovalat's *katra,* protective past death.

FOURTEEN

NOW

WATRAII HOMEWORLD
STARDATE 54107.1

The newly dubbed *Alexander Nevsky* with its crew of four slipped smoothly from space into the Watraii atmosphere—and was instantly converted from a smoothly operating flying instrument into one that was tossed roughly about like a toy in a child's unsteady hands. Data, at the controls, fought with the savage winds to at least keep the shuttle upright.

"Good thing . . . we have full . . . shoulder and chest . . . harnesses," Scotty managed to gasp out as the ship lurched and shuddered and lurched again, fighting its way down through the storm clouds and wild gusts of wind. "Trip's giving . . . whole new meaning . . . to the word 'turbulent.'"

Data said, "I do not believe that such a word needed to be given a new meaning. Surely the original definition suffices."

Scotty gave a choked laugh. "As if Vulcans . . . weren't literal-minded enough . . . now we have a third member . . . of the Logic Brigade!"

Data frowned slightly. "Ruanek, Spock, and I obviously cannot be related. I do not see why—"

The ship lurched again, more violently than before, and blue-white crackles of electricity shot around and through it.

"Lightning strike," Data said succinctly, fingers racing over the controls in a blur of speed. "Main systems off-line." As the ship lurched and shuddered, he added, never taking his gaze from the controls, "I have manual control of secondary systems." The wild lurching steadied ever so slightly. As the ship seemed to hesitate for a moment, then drop, he added, "I cannot guarantee a smoother trip."

"He did that once before," Ruanek murmured to Spock. "While he was serving on the *Enterprise*-D. He told me about that."

Spock, clenching the armrests just to stay seated, the safety harness cutting into him as the ship struggled, raised an eyebrow. Being what he was, Ruanek was clearly enjoying the rough ride, lips peeled back from teeth in an unabashedly fierce Romulan grin. That Ruanek and Data should have shared stories of their various adventures seemed no more unusual than anything else about this mission.

"Damn!" That came from Scotty, who suddenly had his hands full with the uneasy interface between the ship and its cloaking device. The wild jolting about wasn't helping him, since it was jerking his hands away from the controls. Scotty muttered to himself and in language he would have been embarrassed to know the others could hear, cursing over a system that first of all was Romulan and second of all, as he had warned, was not operating particularly well on a ship this small. "And this thrice-damned weather that won't let a man work!"

Refusing to let himself be distracted by the others, Spock returned his full attention to the small tricorder he held, holding it steady as best he could, and continued refining the scans that the *Alliance* had made from space. Ground readings were not affected by how the ship was being tossed about. Life-forms were finally showing up on these new scans . . . not as clearly as he would have liked, not enough to let him locate one human among the Watraii.

Odd. There did not seem to be anything on the planet in the way of true cities. In fact, there seemed to be only one major installation on the entire planet. But then, if the climate was perpetually this violent, that wasn't so surprising. Presumably, the Watraii lived underground in facilities that were as yet unscannable.

Or else . . . the other possibility *was* a surprising one, and that was that their population was abnormally small.

Fascinating.

As Data continued to nurse the shuddering, jolting ship down through the layers of cloud and frenzied winds, Spock said suddenly, "I have an accurate fix on the artifact."

Ruanek glanced sharply at him. "You're sure about it."

"Yes." He gave Data the precise coordinates.

"I will *try* to set the ship down as close to the site as possible," the android told them as the ship fought him. "I cannot guarantee it. In fact," he added as they finally broke through the last of the cloud layers, "I cannot at this time guarantee a safe landing."

Below them lay the planet's surface: a wild jumble of jagged gray mountains.

"Main systems have finally recovered from the lightning strike," Data commented, "and are coming back online. But there seem to be few surfaces that are flat enough for a safe landing."

Lightning flashed about them, striking the mountains, sending rocks tumbling. The ship lurched and dropped its way down, Data reading off the descent as they went. "Twenty kilometers . . . fifteen-point-five kilometers . . . ten kilometers—"

The ship's nose was suddenly thrust up, and Data broke off to concentrate on getting back under control.

"Old Earth saying," Ruanek muttered. "'Any landing that you can walk away from is a good landing.'"

"A true statement," Data agreed. "Two-point-five kilometers . . . Please be sure you are all securely belted in. This is as flat a surface as I can find."

They hit with bone-jarring force. The ship slewed alarmingly sideways as Data fought with the controls, then came to a full stop so suddenly that only their safety harnesses kept them in their seat.

There was a moment of silence, except for the endless shrilling of wind buffeting the ship.

"Is everyone all right?" Data asked.

"Yes," Spock said.

"Yes," Scotty said. "I've got bruises in places that shouldn't be bruised, but I'm all right."

"Did we land," Ruanek questioned wryly, "or were we shot down? And yes, I know that's an old joke."

Spock asked, "Is the cloaking device still functioning?"

"Amazingly enough," Scotty said after a few moments of checking, "we still have full cloaking."

"And this does appear to be a relatively secure spot," Data added. "We seem to have landed on the top of a butte."

"Landing right side up is good enough for me." Scotty unfastened his safety harness and got to his feet, stretching gingerly. "And landing up here on a flat surface is going to make it almost impossible for anyone below to spot us. Anyone above . . ."

"Saavik will keep them from getting within range," Spock said, unfastening his harness. "Scotty, as we agreed, you will—"

"'Hold the fort'?" Scotty suggested.

"Precisely."

Scotty glared suddenly down at his console and stabbed a finger at a control. "Oh, no, you don't. Behave yourself, you miserable piece of—" He glanced up again, slightly flushed at having just been caught talking to the machinery. "And I'll be busy keeping this blasted cloaking device operational, too."

"Of course you will," Spock agreed, expression carefully bland. "I would expect nothing less." He gathered up his small pack of supplies, as did Ruanek and Data. "Meanwhile Ruanek, Data, and I shall steal back the Romulan artifact and Chekov as well."

"And that's all?" Scotty asked dryly.

"It is what needs to be done."

"Spock, my lad, you never change."

"Not changing over the years is hardly possible, or logical."

Scotty threw up his hands. "I rest my case."

Spock ignored that unseemly emotional outburst. "Judging from the lack of settlements I scanned," he said, "it is possible that Admiral Chekov is being held in the same installation as is the artifact, or at least nearby."

"Amen to that!"

Spock continued. "I have calibrated the differences between the planetary day and the *Alliance*'s shipboard standard. A day here is two hours and fifteen minutes shorter than shipboard standard. We have arrived in the planetary morning."

"Not that you could tell," Ruanek muttered. "Gray sky, gray land. It looks almost like the Terran moon, were the Terran moon to have acquired an atmosphere. A vicious one," he added, as a new gust of wind shook the ship.

"The atmosphere is not the issue just now," Spock said. "Understand this, Scotty. If we have not returned within twenty-four shipboard standard hours, you are to leave us and—"

"And return to the *Alliance*. I may've been out of the game for seventy-five years, Spock, but I'm hardly a bairn fresh out of the Academy. You think I haven't learned that line about 'the needs of the many outweigh the needs of the few' by now? Get on with you, lad, and rescue poor Pavel."

It took a great deal of Vulcan self-control not to smile. Spock dipped his head to Scotty, and with that, he and the others left the relative security of the cloaked ship.

The storm winds hit them with a force that made them stagger back against the ship, struggling for balance, and the bitter tang of ozone was sharp in the air.

Spock and Ruanek glanced at each other: *We can do this.*

Heads down against the force of the gale, Data and they struck out over the edge of the butte and down toward the installation.

FIFTEEN

MEMORY

Sunheart and *Shavokh* fled the system where the fleet had seen two ships devoured. They dared not stop to mourn together, or even decelerate to make repairs. With the loss of even more adepts able to boost the ships' engines, any speed they could achieve would have to be maintained for as long as they could.

There would be no more exploration and no further expeditions to mine for resources they were coming, more and more urgently, to need. Any ship that fell behind would have to follow as best it could.

"Each of us is alone now," Karatek told the coronet. *"Yes, that is illogical: we are born alone and, except for times when we can join our minds with someone else, we live alone. Our solitude leaves us vulnerable to irrational fears. In ancient times, we of Vulcan believed in curses and monsters. And now that we have encountered creatures that suck the soul from living beings, some are mistaking belief for proof."*

"Firestorm *and* Vengeance, *in escaping the mind-eaters, have outrun our sensors and are still missing. As a scientist, I can run diagnostics on our equipment. I can attribute the absence of our sister ships to navigational failure, interference from dark matter, any one of a number of things apart from destruction. They may even have found a potential home. We simply do not know. But that hardly constitutes a curse.*

"With spare parts running low, we will have to learn to do without some of the amenities—such as they are—on which we have come to rely. And we are hearing now that some ships are encountering food shortages.

"We are learning that blight has struck some ships' hydroponics. True, we have stores: dried foods, emergency rations, even frozen genetic material from animals that could be grown, in time, for food. But the fact remains: right now, on some ships, there is famine and, almost as bad, suspicions of sabotage. These suspicions trouble me more than I am prepared to admit."

As always when Karatek removed the coronet and returned himself to what he regarded as the "waking" world, he shivered. He drew his newest robe about him. Constructed as it was of outworn insulating blankets, carefully pieced together, it might be bulky, especially at the shoulders, but it was warm.

No sooner did he step outside his tiny meditation chamber than his consort T'Vysse ran to him. Uncharacteristically, she hurled herself into his arms. She was trembling.

Karatek closed his arms around her, sharing a warmth that was almost more emotional than physical. For 15.8 seconds, he allowed himself to savor it before stepping back. When T'Vysse too stepped away, looking politely aside, he experienced an additional minute's irrational disappointment, replaced by concern.

"Thee is ill?" he asked. In addition to keeping extensive written records that would serve as a history of the exile, T'Vysse shared care of their youngest children, taught on board, stood watch where she was needed, and worked with the healers. Had there been enough of them surviving for a complete circle, they would have sought to initiate her. That was the only reason Karatek had for not regretting the shortage of adepts: T'Vysse already worked hard enough.

His consort extended her fingertips and touched his hand, projecting reassurance.

"I ask pardon for showing emotion," she said. "It was . . . Word has come from Command that *Firestorm* has been sighted. The ship has altered course back toward us, and navigation projects practicable face-to-face communications range within three months."

"Any word of *Vengeance*?"

"Some very distant, very garbled chatter at the edge of range," she replied. "Nothing useful. Nothing yet."

Firestorm's survival was good news. The news it might bring was cause to hope.

Karatek's reclaimed position as a ship's elder earned him a seat in the command center as *Firestorm*'s first messages to *Shavokh* and *Sunheart* came through. The communications officer split the screen so that those on board *Shavokh* could see people from any other ships within communications range. With characteristic generosity, S'task had ceded the privilege of this initial contact to others. Karatek regretted the weakness that would have made a sight of the exile's leader reassuring.

The face of *Firestorm*'s commander, T'Ranneha, fine-drawn, intelligent, and still bearing traces of what had apparently once been remarkable esthetic appeal, formed on-screen. It glowed tantalizingly before them until her words could be discerned.

Karatek activated his recorder along with, he was certain, at least 95.3 percent of the people capable of doing so on board *Shavokh.*

"We greet you, Shavokh, Sunheart," she said. *"This is a great day for us. We had feared we were all alone in the dark."*

Karatek felt his eyebrow go up. From the emotionalism of her words, T'Ranneha was another of those who had not studied Surak's disciplines. At least, not so that it showed.

Be fair, he rebuked himself. T'Ranneha's provocation was great. And for one who bore the solitary burden of ship command, the relief of finding companions must be even greater.

"We are pleased to see you," Karatek replied.

Ship's company waited as the message traveled toward *Firestorm,* as T'Ranneha and her crew processed it, then, for a reply. It was a good thing their exile had taught them to be patient, or the time lag would have strained their composure even further.

Understanding chased irritation—*Is that the best welcome you can give us?*—from T'Ranneha's face.

"Data stream coming through," said *Shavokh's* communications officer.

Like the others in the command center, Karatek tensed with hope.

But T'Ranneha was shaking her head. *"No habitable worlds,"* she said. *"And none that could be made habitable within the outer limit of ships' viability, given current resources."*

The screens flickered and went dark. Distorted voices from *Firestorm's* command center warned of disruptions in ship's communications. T'Ranneha's image reformed on-screen.

"Interference . . . an ion storm . . . we will endeavor . . ."

"A force-six ion storm," communications reported. "My counterpart on *Firestorm* is highly skilled to have penetrated that at all."

Force six, Karatek thought. *Firestorm* had only a 54.66 percent chance of surviving that. If the ship was already coming about, why hadn't it taken the extra time to go around?

Because, logically, T'Ranneha wished to spend no more time out of communications range of others of the great ships than she had to.

"What do you recommend, Commander?" S'lovan raised his voice as if shouting could do any good. He visibly collected himself, gave a minute shake of his head, and gestured to communications to seek to boost the signal.

"Ask if they require assistance," Karatek formed the words without sound, to preserve as much as possible the chain of command.

But *Rea's Helm* was already asking. In fact, that was S'task himself on-screen now, his eyes blazing.

"We will . . . we will try to communicate . . . later . . ."

No news of *Vengeance.* No sighting of a habitable world. No new hope.

But one ship more than they had had.

Was it enough? As the ships broke communications to save power, Karatek knew that they were in accord, at least for now. He admitted to a weakness in not attempting to calculate how long this new unity might continue.

SIXTEEN

NOW

WATRAII HOMEWORLD
STARDATE 54107.2

Spock stopped short on the side of the cliff, struggling to catch his breath and keep his balance, the endless blasts of wind beating at him. About him, the gale screamed with undying frenzy, the sound almost deafening to keen Vulcan hearing. If it were not too illogically fanciful, he could almost think of it as being savage as a living foe trying to hurl the invaders to their deaths.

But staying in one place for long was not safe, either. Lightning blazed all about them, striking the rocks at random, sending sharp shards flying, filling the air with a stench mixed of ozone and scorched earth. The mind wanted thunder, rain, the normalcy of a Terran storm, but that relief never came. There was only the wind and the random blazes of lightning.

Ruanek, his eyes fierce as those of the warrior he'd been,

reached out a steadying hand to him, but Spock shook his head and started grimly forward again. He could manage. There were storms almost as savage as this on Vulcan, the rare, fierce thunderstorms of the brief Vulcan spring that let the deserts bloom in one quick and frantic blaze of beauty. He had even been caught on Mount Seleya once by one of those storms, and still remembered the awe he had felt at the sheer force and fierce will to survive of Vulcan nature. There were also the primal volcanic fury and the savage electrical storms of the Forge.

Yes, but the storm on Mount Seleya was forty years ago, he reminded himself with blunt honesty. *And you haven't crossed the Forge on foot since boyhood.*

Ah, and humans were so much more frail than Vulcans. If he was having a rough time, then how were they going to get Pavel Chekov up here?

But then Spock answered himself with cool logic, *If need be, Data can carry him.*

Of the three of them, the android was the only one who was clearly unfazed by the wildness about him, presumably able to shut down part of his aural system to keep it from being overloaded, his positronic brain unaffected by the electricity about him, and his body clearly designed for greater than human stability and agility.

At least there is this, Spock thought. *It is highly improbable that the Watraii will be able to track us accurately—not so small a target, not through this much distortion.*

The steep descent did slowly level out, finally putting them below the range of the worst of the endless storm. Spock, Ruanek, and Data wove their way down through a wilderness of knife-edged rocks that were not yet blunted by time, boulders that had been brought down relatively recently by the savagery of the lightning strikes.

A dangerous zone for us.

Even as he thought this, Spock heard a near-deafening crack and under it, the unmistakable grinding roar of rock torn loose—

"Watch out!" he cried.

He and Ruanek threw themselves frantically to one side as a huge mass of rock came thundering down to a final landing athwart two smaller boulders. They were engulfed in a choking cloud of dust and tiny pebbles.

At last the dust settled. The fallen rock seemed stable.

Ruanek gasped, "Are you all right?"

"Yes," Spock began. "Are you?"

"Yes, yes, I'm fine." Ruanek got to his feet and offered Spock a hand up. Brushing himself off, Ruanek looked about fiercely. "Data? Data! Where is he?"

"Here," answered a muffled but unperturbed voice. A mound of rocks shook, then clattered aside in mini-avalanches as Data emerged from under them. He shook himself, sending pebbles flying. "I am undamaged. But I do believe that we need to remove ourselves from this region as quickly as possible."

"No, really?" Ruanek muttered.

Sarcasm, Spock thought, was hardly logical. But under the circumstances, it was also quite understandable.

Scotty stood at the entrance to the *Alexander Nevsky,* refusing to acknowledge the way his heart was pounding with anxiety. This was a fine vantage point. It gave him a perfect view of kilometer after kilometer of, well, nothing much. Rock, more rock, still more rock, and stretches of flat gray desert. Ruanek was right, it did look like Earth's moon, precolonization, with the addition of a very hostile atmosphere.

Godspeed, you three, Scotty thought. *Get Pavel out of there, get that damned artifact, whatever it is, and get back here in time. I don't want to even think about having to leave you here.*

Dammit, I hate ultimatums.

The wind was just too savage for him to stay out here much longer. Shivering, Scotty went back inside the ship and sealed the entrance. Nothing to do now but wait and keep an eye on that blasted cloaking device. Fortunately for his mental well-being, he had thought to download a good number of S.C.E. reports from the past few months into the system. As head of the organization, he kept up with the material as regularly as he could. Hmm, here was an interesting-looking report from the *U.S.S. da Vinci* about a species that put their planet into a box. Now, how did the S.C.E. crew on that ship figure out how to open that box and release the planet?

With a sigh, Scotty settled down to read . . .

Fortunately, Spock thought, the land never grew level enough to be considered a true plain. It remained a rocky plain strewn with boulders and smaller rocks. Even though that made the footing treacherous, it provided them with shelter that would at least help to hide them from Watraii sensors.

The ground was almost completely covered with a thick coating of gravel that crunched underfoot. What vegetation there was hugged the rocks in this world's analogy of lichen or sheltered in niches between the rocks.

The vegetation all seems to be relatively primitive species, Spock mused. *Either this is a very young planet, indeed, or one with so perpetually harsh a climate that nothing more complex is able to evolve.*

Which begs the question of how likely it is that any species as complex as the Watraii are here. It implies that they are not native to this world. But why would they settle on so inhospitable a planet?

One possible hypothesis came instantly to mind, but Spock warned himself that it was only a hypothesis. He could draw no truly logical conclusions without further information.

"Odd," Data murmured to Spock and Ruanek. "As we surmised from space, there really do not appear to be that many Watraii."

Spock was busy with the tiny tricorder he carried—one that was too tiny, he hoped, to register on Watraii systems. "No," he said after a moment, looking up at Data and Ruanek, "indeed there do not."

Ruanek frowned slightly. "That doesn't really make sense. If they are a dwindling or even dying species"—his not-quite-controlled tone hinted that he would approve of the latter situation—"they either are being killed off by this hostile environment or simply aren't very fertile." He held up a hand in a questioning gesture. "Yet they're using what have to be rare resources not to build transport ships and get their people out of here, but to build warships. Where's the logic in that?"

"There is none," Spock agreed. "Unless," he continued carefully, "they are not originally from this world."

"Are you saying that they may be refugees? Come now, Spock, that doesn't seem likely. They have working ships. And since they have ships, why would they take refuge *here?*"

"That is precisely what I wondered. But I can only theorize, Ruanek. Point one: What if they never actually planned to settle here permanently? Point two: What if they look at this world as merely a temporary staging point or training ground? And point three: What if they really do have a valid claim—"

"To what?" Ruanek snapped before Spock could finish. "To the Romulan homeworlds? No, I will not believe that."

Spock did not even try to remind Ruanek that the Romulans in turn were not native to Romulus and Remus, either. "Without proof, we cannot—"

A blast of green fire shot past him, narrowly missing him. Ruanek pulled Spock down to safety with him behind a low ridge of rocks, and Data dove behind another. The Watraii must have spotted them after all. They were under attack!

"Captain Saavik," Lieutenant Suhur said abruptly. "We have finally received clear evidence that the *Alexander Nevsky* did arrive safely on the planet's surface. Unfortunately, further information beyond that basic fact is being blocked by the planetary weather conditions."

"Understood." Saavik managed to make her sigh of relief seem like nothing more than a slightly deeper than normal breath. *So far, as the humans say, so good.*

To her crew, she broadcast, since they had a right to know what was going on, "The *Alexander Nevsky* has arrived on the planet's surface. You may resume your normal duties."

And of course the newcomers among you will be speculating until you drive your more seasoned shipmates half mad. And of course forbidding speculation will only make the situation worse.

To her Klingon allies, since they had the right to know what was going on, Saavik sent the message that yes, the shuttle had safely landed. Predictably, she got back two fierce and identical replies: "Qapla'!"

Well-put, Saavik thought dryly.

She truly wished more complete data about what the away team was doing. But that was impossible. And, she reminded herself sternly, it was illogical to speculate without any data at all.

Qapla', *indeed,* she thought.

*   *   *

The attack continued without ceasing. Spock, Ruanek, and Data stayed pinned down behind their rocky shelter as green flashes split the air. However, Spock realized that many of those flashes came nowhere near them, and indeed nothing more—no accelerating of the attack—seemed to be happening in their immediate vicinity.

"They're not firing at *us*," Ruanek commented with a professional's knowledge. "The angle of the beams is wrong for even the worst of aims." He risked a wary peek over the edge of the rocks, and then ducked back down. "Aha. I'm right."

"A battle between factions?" Data volunteered.

"I don't think so." Ruanek risked another look, and then ducked back down again. "I'm right. It's not a war, it's just war games. Four teams of Watraii, with the first color I've seen on this cursed world: stripes of red, blue, yellow, green. All masked as usual, by the way."

Then a new green bolt shot past them—and this time hit a nearby rock and sent sharp splinters flying in all directions.

"Those are live weapons!" Ruanek hissed. "Those idiots are using live weapons on their own troops!"

Spock took his own careful look around the rocks, and then stared in disbelief. Ruanek was right. There was already a casualty on the yellow team, lying limply across a rock. But to his relief, the others moved with such precise skill that no one else seemed to have been hit.

The blast of a shrill whistle cut the air. A second later, the war game maneuvers ended. Without the troops wasting any time, the dead Watraii was vaporized by blasts from the others' weapons, one Watraii scooped up the fallen one's weapon—and with that, the troops simply marched off and were lost among the rocks, all without a word.

"That," Data said, staring after them, "was a singularly vicious form of training."

"Make that a vicious *and* illogical one," Ruanek added in sharp disapproval. "No matter how sternly you want to train your warriors, you don't kill them. Especially if you're already working with a reduced population base. Truly illogical."

"Perhaps," Spock mused. "Or perhaps what we have just witnessed were the actions of a people who are so close to the edge that they can think of only one thing."

Ruanek snorted. "It's obviously not anything as practical as species survival."

"No," Spock continued, "not the practicality of survival but the illogic of a people who have become utterly obsessed with turning themselves into a military machine."

"To go after the Romulans," Ruanek finished grimly. "That, I assure you, will be a fatal mistake."

For which people? Spock wondered.

For neither, he answered himself. *For every problem there is a solution. There is one for this. I . . . merely have to discover it.*

SEVENTEEN

MEMORY

"I will keep this entry brief," Karatek thought. *"Regaining contact with* Vengeance *3.6 months after* Firestorm *found us should, logically, have improved morale, but it has not done so. T'Vysse thinks we need to remember who we are and what we fight for. She has therefore decided that our family, at least, will celebrate the Sanctification of the Hearth. In anticipating tonight's ritual, I find myself almost illogically excited."*

For the past 38.6 ship's days, T'Vysse had been helping her children shift watch schedules. She had traded additional work hours for foods Karatek had not seen for years so that she could assemble her family to watch as she blessed their hearth and invoked their House's gods.

She had even lit the brazier in their living quarters for the occasion. Incense that smelled like their lost desert itself poured from between the verdigrised fangs of the winged bronze *le-matya,* an heirloom of his House.

For a moment, Karatek enjoyed a great and treasurable illusion of homecoming. But the brazier's light picked out details on tapestries that warmed the chill off the ship's bulkheads, not old stone. The image of the desert that occupied one wall was a projection, not an actual view from beyond his House's walls. Still, his sons Solor and Lovar and their wives and children sat with Sarissa. Young children clung to T'Vysse's legs. It might not be the hearth he remembered, but it was all the home they had. In this moment, too, it was enough.

He looked down at T'Alaro. His daughter had graduated from creeping to unsteady steps. How fast the time had gone! The veils flicked over his eyes, concealing impermissible emotion. Surak had had no children. Perhaps he would not have understood how instinctive the urge was to smile at one's young children.

But who could be so unspeakably rude as to pound on the door when he and T'Vysse had taken pains to tell their coworkers that this night shift, of all others, they were re-creating his family's shrine?

By custom, it was the eldest son's duty to guard the gates. Lovar rose and cracked the hatch slightly to prevent the room's warmth from escaping. T'Partha pushed past him, her eyes flicking from Sarissa to T'Vysse to Karatek himself before she collapsed, gasping for breath.

"I ask pardon for this unpardonable intrusion," T'Partha gasped, drawing formality about her like a tattered ceremonial cloak. "We are in danger."

Healer T'Olryn rose to attend T'Partha as Solor and Sarissa ushered the children into the nearest sleeping cubicle. T'Vysse came to her side with one of the translucent cups carved from petrified wood that she had smuggled on board wrapped in a nightshift. In all these years, she had never broken a single one.

"Welcome to our hearth," T'Vysse said. "The danger must wait until thee has refreshed thyself."

T'Partha gulped the water down. T'Vysse nodded, tacit permission for their guest to return to ship's business.

"They're taking the ship hostage," she told Karatek. "Already, they control hydroponics and the docking bay, and they're moving toward central control."

"Who is?" Karatek asked.

"Eater of Souls take them!" Sarissa erupted, then nodded apology at the incense-breathing winged creature in the brazier. "Some of the techs like T'Velan and Avarak here, Avarin and his associates on the other ships, plus the te-Vikram, have been working on the spaceborn, trying to persuade them they'd be better off if we all went back to Ankaa, the last *Minshara*-class world we found, the one that had preindustrialized sapients. This would divide the fleet!"

The sons and daughters born during the exile knew no other life but on board ship. Some of them found the idea of being nomads in a desert of stars, much as their ancestors had traveled the Forge before settling in cities like ShiKahr and ShanaiKahr, much to their liking.

"The creatures at Ankaa are primitives," T'Vysse said. "Our xenobiologists say we would eradicate them in 39.2 years."

Solor shook his head. "You think the techs care? They probably bought the te-Vikram with an offer of all the wilderness on the planet!"

Sarissa looked down. "This could be the end of all that we are."

"Why was I not told?" Karatek demanded. If only the returning ships' reports had contained better news. "So many stars ahead, and not one, not one star suitable for us. . . ." He lamented.

"They lied!" T'Partha said. "The techs took over astrocartography long since. Those reports have mostly been falsehoods. And conspiracies, so they could help plan this mutiny!"

A buzz sounded, repeated, paused, then sounded again.

Sarissa flung herself at a particularly attractive tapestry depicting Mount Seleya at dawn, tugged it aside, and whispered into the com set into the bulkhead.

"They're going to try to take engineering," she reported. "They've got the area locked down, but Serevan hears signs of a break-in. He thinks they'll threaten the engines so we can't decelerate. And not on this ship alone."

"Madness," Karatek said. "Don't the spaceborn realize that these ships cannot last forever?"

"Rhetorical question," T'Vysse said as crisply as if she brought a class of children back on track.

"Engineering's going to need reinforcements," Sarissa said. "I'll go. I remember what to do from my rotation there."

"We need a plan!" Karatek said. "Sarissa, do you have any idea what you're doing?"

"We have a plan," his daughter said.

She pulled down another tapestry that they had hung over a ventilation duct just for the evening. Dragging over a worktable, she clambered up and began to unfasten the duct cover. As the grid fell free, she set it aside.

"T'Olryn," Sarissa's eyes met those of her sister-in-law and held. "You need to get to sickbay and release the gas. Go now. The masks . . . you know where they are. And the weapons."

"I have told you: I will not arm myself," said T'Olryn, and when Sarissa looked as if she would protest, "I am safer unarmed. Healers have always been neutral."

"Not this time, if they catch you. Please, reconsider."

"No."

Solor boosted T'Olryn up into the shaft and removed his hands from her waist reluctantly.

The healer reached paired fingers down to brush her mate's temple in farewell and blessing, then disappeared without a backward glance.

"When I heard about this plot," Sarissa continued, "I called it disloyal and illogical. I ask pardon. Because my words were immoderate, they cost me the rebels' confidence, so I learned no more. But I told Commissioner T'Partha about the threat to engineering after Serevan"—she looked down and away—"told me."

"So, there are no secrets between you and this engineer, but in the family, you keep secrets?" Karatek asked.

"For this, too, I ask forgiveness," she replied instantly. "Logically, you were too prominent to be involved in any conspiracy. It was easier for us to remain out of sight, to pretend ignorance. But you? If you knew, your behavior might betray it. Or you would have tried to wage peace, just like . . ."

"Just like T'Partha."

"I did try to persuade them of the criminal illogic of their course," T'Partha admitted. "I failed. I was standing watch when I heard footsteps and assumed they were coming for me. So I ran here to alert your children." T'Partha rose, clasping her hands together. "I have put you all in danger. I will go. You can say you did not see me. The occasion warrants the lie."

"That's no good!" Sarissa almost snarled. "They have that prototype memory sifter!"

The technology, Karatek knew, derived from the same basis as his coronet. S'task had actually authorized the venture. It was the one trait S'task had retained from his years of study with Surak: he ascribed the best motivations to people who sought knowledge.

"If they capture me, I think I can withstand it for some time, provided T'Olryn gets to sickbay quickly and you succeed in reinforcing Serevan," T'Partha said.

Sarissa swung herself up into the ventilation shaft and disappeared.

"You could claim sanctuary at our hearth," T'Vysse offered.

The bronze *le-matya* had never glowed more brightly, or the room seemed so comfortable.

"Thank you, but I'm needed. I will warn the rest of our colleagues," said T'Partha. "Karatek, monitor the ship. As soon as people collapse, get to central command, drag the rebels out, then seal yourself in until one of us signals."

"What happens if you and the others fail?" Karatek asked. Worst-case analysis always gave them something against which to strive.

T'Partha drew herself up. "Then, my old friend, you must still get to central command. But in that case, it will be your task to protect us from the dishonor of mutiny and potential genocide. You must activate the self-destruct."

She raised her hand in the old, split-fingered greeting, then lowered it, staring for a moment at her fingers. The gesture was tainted now. Karatek knew none of them would ever use it again.

Instead, she nodded respect at the hearth. Smoke rose in a fragrant cloud as if in response.

Then she was gone.

"Your pardon, Father, Mother," said Lovar. "I believe the commissioner has forgotten her mask. I have a spare. And," he added, "she may need protection. She is not as young as she used to be."

He too was gone before either of his parents could protest.

T'Vysse muffled her hand in a fold of her robe and slid shut the flanges in the brazier, extinguishing its fire. "My daughter-in-law and I will take the children to the shelters," she said.

"But the gas . . ." Karatek protested.

"We must trust in T'Olryn's healer's oath," T'Vysse said. "Besides, the te-Vikram will not harm children they could adopt, or fertile women." Politely, she looked away. "Furthermore, I calculate odds of 93.05 percent that they would turn on anyone who attempted to."

"Those odds aren't high enough!" Karatek protested.

"Now, who is thinking with his emotions?" T'Vysse said. She bent over him and touched his fingers with her own. "We all have our tasks. At least my children and I will have a night's uninterrupted sleep."

Then she was gone, T'Alaro clinging to one hand, the infant T'Lysia in her arms.

Karatek tucked the coronet into his robe. Then, from the box beneath its storage place, he pulled out a weapon very like the one he had once borrowed from *T'Kehr* Torin. He too had had his secrets.

Karatek would have to trust that T'Olryn would reach sickbay and Sarissa would reinforce engineering. Note to himself: Should they all survive, he must make inquiries into this man Serevan.

From the emergency supplies in every set of quarters, he drew out a thin mask to protect himself against the sleeping gas that would flood the ship. Adjusting the mask over mouth and nose and setting his old weapon on his lap, Karatek settled in front of the monitors, hoping to see people—and their mutiny—begin to collapse.

"Years ago, on the Forge, I killed raiders to protect my comrades and avenge young Varen. After all these years of struggle, of endurance, to think I may be forced to kill again!"

It was harder to wait than to fight. And harder yet to know that

Karatek's own family was out there, while he sat watching as the corridors seethed with frightened passengers. And with mutineers. He drew deep, rhythmic breaths to help him conquer the need to plunge out into the revolt and kill anyone who even looked at his family.

He was a coward.

No: he was a man under orders.

Someone pounded on his door. He did not answer. The noise built up, then seemed to sink lower and lower on the door, as if someone collapsed, still pounding, outside. Their first apparent success: T'Olryn had released the sleeping gas.

When no jolts in course, no groans of outraged, overstressed metal, no explosions came, he concluded that Sarissa had reached engineering.

Now, he must cast out fear for T'Partha. She was neither young nor well. She had already sacrificed her family to the exile. What more could be asked of her?

Nothing short of everything.

The thought made him want to rage. To kill. And T'Vysse was not present to absolve him.

True to T'Partha's charge, Karatek watched. On the screens were images, shipwide, of people sinking to the decks as T'Olryn's sleeping gas circulated. She had always been as efficient as she was determined.

On some decks, however, squads of mutineers, wearing the drab quilted tunics that provided warmth and some protection against edged weapons while making the wearer look bigger and more imposing, rushed out. Their eyes were wild over their breath masks.

The te-Vikram held gemmed blades, while the technocrats had energy weapons and what looked like memory sifters fastened to their studded belts. They fought until there was no one left standing, and the decks and bulkheads that had been so carefully adorned and maintained since leaving the Mother World were stained with green blood.

The com flashed.

Karatek eyed it. It could be one of his family. Or it could be that the mutineers had won and were looking for him. In that case, he knew he should get to central command. There was risk either way.

He touched the light.

"Father?" Sarissa's voice had not sounded so uncertain since the night he had found her in the desert.

"Are you well?"

"No, Father. But I live. We secured engineering. Serevan and I are going to the command center. We need you to meet us there." And then, on a long, unsteady breath: *"Please?"*

She must not have been able to reach T'Vysse or any of the rest of the family. His own heart pounded in his side, but he forced composure into his voice. "I will see you there, my child."

He edged into the corridor, holding his weapon in front of him. He heard a rush of air, as if someone sought to flush *Shavokh's* life support of the sleeping gas that had incapacitated so many people on board, giving them . . . giving *him* a chance to protect what was theirs, Karatek thought with a rush of passion that embarrassed him.

T'Vysse, he thought, who had calmly walked into what could have been a slaughterhouse.

T'Partha, who assessed the needs of the many and placed them above the needs of the one.

T'Olryn, who would soon come out to tend the wounded and bless the dying.

Lovar, gone to protect their old friend. He was eldest son: it was his task, after all, to guard the gates.

Night and day, he thought, where were they?

But the plan required him to meet Sarissa and this engineer of hers at central command. If the worst had happened, he would not cheapen the sacrifice by disobedience.

He called a lift. It contained three people, slumped on the deck and breathing unevenly. People were already fighting off the effects of the sleeping gas, he realized. Karatek went up three decks and emerged into a corridor like the ones he had seen on-screen. Blood darkened where it coated the deck and spattered the bulkheads. While some of the people who slumped against the bulkheads fought for breath, most would never rise again.

From intersecting corridors and the lifts came healers, unarmed and in formal robes. Still wearing their masks, they knelt beside those bodies that still moved, that fought for breath, that struggled not to cry, and set about their work.

Blood chilling in his veins, Karatek raced down the corridor toward central command. The last few steps were crowded with the bodies of mutineers.

"T'Olryn!" he cried, seeing Solor's wife at last. "Is the commander . . . ?"

She looked up, her delicate features suddenly decades older.

"I grieve with thee," she whispered.

She was kneeling over a man's body. Carefully, slowly, she finished turning it over. This man did not wear the padded tunic of the rebels, but a robe— Night and day! Karatek knew that robe and the sigils sewn onto it even though he could no longer recognize the face of Lovar, his eldest son.

He shut his eyes before reaching out and felt T'Olryn clasping his hand. "It was an energy weapon," she said softly. "No eyes remain to be closed."

Karatek's eyes stung as if they too felt the fire.

For long, long moments, he knelt there. Then he gained the courage to open his eyes again and saw what his son had died fighting to protect: T'Partha.

Lovar had succeeded, but only partially. The rebels had used that damnable memory sifter upon T'Partha. Her eyes were open, fixed on vacancy, until he moved into her field of vision. He put out a hand to brush her hair from what appeared to be two livid, coin-sized bruises, seeping blood.

T'Partha's eyes focused, ever so slowly, upon him.

"I told you I could hold out," she whispered.

"I always said you could wear out anyone until consensus was achieved," he told her. Stupid, illogical, meaningless words, and yet, what else was there?

One thing more. He reached out with joined fingers to touch T'Partha's temple.

"Thee consents?" he asked.

The woman nodded feebly. If he had found her two minutes later, all that she was would have been lost.

"Remember," she whispered, and the breath went out of her.

That was how T'Vysse, stumbling as she fought off the sleeping gas in her haste to reach her dead son, found Karatek: holding the woman who had been colleague and sparring partner since they had left Vulcan and—logic be damned to the Womb of Fire—weeping.

Control thyself! Thy wife deserves better, scolded T'Partha's acerbic thought in his consciousness. He would have to deal with her *katra,* too, in the days that followed. He suspected that would be quite a task.

For now, however, he could only be grateful for the reminder.

He straightened T'Partha's tumbled limbs, then rose and held out his hand to his wife. Together, they walked toward the command center. The door opened. Weapons confronted them, then came down as he was recognized.

"We are in communication with *Rea's Helm*," said Commander S'lovan, bruised and bloodstained. He coughed, then held a mask to his face with the arm that was not broken. He drew three deep, deep breaths before he could speak again. Even so, he had to steady himself against a chair.

"Forty-seven of the rebels wish to leave *Shavokh*," he said. "I have agreed to give them a shuttle. All of the ships will."

"A shuttle? Where will they go?" Karatek asked. "Will *Rea's Helm* take them in?"

Waste of a shuttle, T'Partha's *katra* whispered into his thoughts.

"Personally," S'lovan replied, "I'd send them straight to the Eater of Souls for what they've done. Not just on *Shavokh* but all over the fleet! But I won't diminish our friends' deaths by murder."

Karatek struggled not to show how moved he was by the commander's sorrow.

"Don't look at me like that, Karatek!" he snarled. "I know you studied with Surak, but I had to watch while your son died, while they tortured T'Partha, and I ask you, man, which is a more fitting punishment: a quick execution or sending those *veruul*—your pardon, please—off in a shuttle that will probably break down?"

Does logic require me to plead for the lives of the people who killed my son, my friend, my shipmates? Karatek asked himself. He drew breath to begin.

"I've managed to restore communications with *Rea's Helm*," the communications officer announced. It was not T'Velan.

Karatek awarded the younger officer full marks for precise timing of that interruption.

Karatek looked at the list of mutineers who had chosen exile from *Shavokh*. T'Velan, who had always been one to erupt, was on it, but Avarak was not. Interesting. And predictable.

"I concur." The voice that came over the ship-to-ship link was so hoarse that Karatek had difficulty recognizing it as belonging to S'task. He suppressed his dismay at the sight of the fleet's commander. S'task looked fifty years older, hunching over, with his hand to his side as if the pressure relieved a greater pain. His breathing was labored, his color livid.

"T'Kehr S'task!" Karatek cried. "Are you . . . ?"

"I apologize for the show of . . . of discomfort. My condition is satisfactory."

In the viewscreen, he could be seen to wave off a man wearing a shabby healer's robe over an insulated shipsuit that strained it at the shoulders.

"No, it isn't!" the healer interrupted. *"He has an infection of the simulpericardium. In a man his age, it could be fatal. . . ."*

S'task thrust the healer away from the screen, then doubled over.

"I ask you to agree with S'lovan. Let the rebels go." S'task struggled up and met Karatek's eyes.

"But that shuttle is inadequate to its task," Karatek began. "The odds of—"

"I have calculated the odds!" S'task snarled. *"Our history has taught us what the punishment for treason must be. And once more, we see why!"*

Karatek looked at Commander S'lovan, then away. He needed neither T'Partha's caustic presence in his thoughts, nor T'Vysse's sorrow, nor his own pain to interpret what he now heard. S'task had, in essence, decreed the fleet's first capital punishments.

Because S'task collapsed in his command chair, to be carried away by his healers, he did not hear S'lovan give the command to launch the mutineers' shuttle. Karatek did. He saw grief replace anger in the commander's eyes, to be followed by a confusion he shared.

How, he wondered, had they gone so wrong?

EIGHTEEN

NOW

WATRAII HOMEWORLD
STARDATE 54107.2

Spock, Ruanek, and Data waited where they were with the cautious patience of three people who were very well aware of the passing of precious time.

The Watraii did not return.

At last, still wary, they came out from hiding.

Data frowned slightly. "It would appear that the Watraii war games are over, at least for today."

Ruanek nodded. "From what I know about them—war games, that is, not the Watraii—you don't just stop war games, withdraw for a breather and a nice cold drink, and then return to the field for a second bout within the same day."

Spock dipped his head to Ruanek, acknowledging his greater military knowledge. "Then let us, by all means, carry on."

They continued their wary way across the rock desert of the Watraii planet, heading toward the one installation that their scan had revealed. Even accepting that the warriors were gone, they kept a cautious watch for other Watraii as they went.

"I don't see anyone," Ruanek said.

"I am not detecting any life-forms," Data added, peering down at his own tricorder.

There was not much else to see, for that matter, just an unchanging, featureless panorama of rock and dust that went swirling up in the endless winds.

"It is not surprising that no one but us is about." Spock pulled the hood of his cloak farther forward, trying to shield his eyes from the blowing dust. "The climate hardly encourages any unnecessary surface activity."

"Now, that is an understatement if ever there was one." Ruanek shook a cloud of gray grit out of his hair, running an impatient hand through the tangled black strands, and then pulled his own hood back up. "This has got to be the most incredibly barren world of any inhabited planet that was ever reported in any of the Federation or Romulan accounts."

"And that, you must agree, Ruanek, is a sweeping overstatement," Spock retorted.

"True. But, Spock, you have to admit that, logical or illogical thought though it may be, this world does lend itself to unpleasant superlatives."

"A world, by definition, cannot lend itself to anything."

"Metaphors are logically a part of speech."

Data noted, "There is, I must comment, an almost alarming lack of flora and fauna on this world. I do not even sense any form of insect life, and that lack is truly unusual. If there is lichen, there should be at least some form of primitive insect life."

"In addition," Spock added, "surface water does seem alarmingly rare. So far, we have found only that one stream of brackish water. One assumes that there is subsurface water, and that, given the poor soil and rough weather, the Watraii grow their food in belowground vats."

"Of course they do," Ruanek muttered. "They would. Fungus for breakfast, lunch, and dinner."

"Or maybe they survive on their equivalent of emergency rations," Data suggested.

"How wonderful for them," Ruanek said without expression. "No place to go, nothing to do but constantly train for war. No wonder they're shooting at each other with live weapons. I suspect that I'd rather get shot than have to live here if I were one of them—and let me add that I am truly grateful that I am not one of them—"

He broke off sharply. "Akhh, here comes another troop after all. Take cover!"

As the three of them dropped down behind a pile of broken rocks, a small troop of the Watraii marched past. Spock counted forty of them in all. Every one was fully armed with the Watraii version of rifles and sidearms. Their dull black boots crunched with perfect precision on the gravelly surface. Indeed, all of them moved as one in what was an almost alarmingly faultless military formation.

"That is truly impressive," Data murmured. "Even Jem'Hadar patrols are not often that precise. I have not seen such exactitude since the Borg."

"Unlike the Borg, the Watraii are not a hive organism," Spock retorted softly. "Both on the individual level and in battle, they have already proven that to be so."

The Watraii might be individuals, but the figures in the troop looked utterly alike in their dark gray uniforms of hooded tunics and trousers. The uniforms were so poorly fitting, however, that they hid any clues as to gender. The only differences that Spock could determine were in the slight variations in the various figures' heights and weights, though none of them could accurately be called anything but slender, possibly even gaunt. Their faces were completely hidden by their ritual masks, each mask exactly like the next. At least, Spock mused, the zigzag ornamentation on those masks was now explained. Those could only be representations of stylized lightning bolts.

But with the adults marched a group of smaller figures. . . . Could those be children?

Yes, Spock thought with the smallest, quickly repressed prickle of uneasiness.

Those were definitely Watraii children, although they were dressed in smaller versions of the dark uniforms, making them look identical to the adults save for size. They kept up that same absolutely perfect military discipline as they marched.

Perfect, yes. They were simply . . . *too* perfect, Spock thought. Even the best-trained of Vulcan children of that age would have broken control now and again with a small fidget, a shove or two, or a curious glance about—yes, and have been forgiven for it by the adults because of their youth. These children by comparison remained absolutely, eerily resolute, never showing the slightest hint of individuality or any sign of childishness, never even glancing at each other or their surroundings, moving in that precise order.

"Like so many little machines," Ruanek murmured. "But isn't this interesting? Apparently Watraii children aren't considered old enough to wear masks."

"Or perhaps they have to earn them," Data said.

"Maybe," Ruanek said. There wasn't much interest in Watraii sociology in his voice. "But what do you know? We finally get a look at Watraii faces."

It seemed almost an anticlimax to Spock after all the mystery to realize that there weren't any astonishing surprises. Watraii faces followed the basic humanoid pattern: two eyes, one mouth, one nasal passageway. The Watraii children's faces, though, for all their undeniable youth, were cold, pale, and expressionless. Humanoid faces, yes, but far more narrow, gaunt, and sharp than those of the average human or Vulcan, with little of the immature softness that humans called baby fat. The adult faces, Spock extrapolated, would prove even more gaunt and more sharply cut.

Each child's face had ice-blue eyes, as did the adults. Disconcertingly, the children's faces were all almost alike.

Almost. After a few moments of careful study, Spock could tell one from the other, and could safely assume that the children were not actually clones—a thought that gained prominence in Spock's mind when Data compared the Watraii to the genetically engineered Jem'Hadar of the Dominion. No, there must simply be too narrow a gene pool here to support a species' normal amount of variation.

That lack of variation is hardly a healthy situation for any species. The Watraii must surely be aware of that.

Yes, and judging from what they were seeing, there was another issue. It would seem that the Watraii brought their children up almost as a military resource, possibly in crèches, certainly without anything in the way of parental warmth or affection.

That is hardly a healthy sign, either, Spock mused.

Children of all healthy sentient species shared a need for affection and for play if they were to grow to be normal adult examples of their species.

Odd. A species that was advanced enough to build warships surely must also be advanced enough to correct any flaws in its own genome. Granted, the Federation's ban on genetic engineering, in place since the Eugenics Wars, proved that there could be such restrictions. But even so, exceptions could be made under carefully monitored conditions if the future of a species was in danger. Unless, perhaps, Spock postulated, the Watraii had some societal ban against making such corrections? Societal or cultural bans could be quite illogical, although quite thoroughly ingrained. Or perhaps the problem was that their scientific knowledge was amazingly limited in its scope, focused solely on militaristic technology.

"Fascinating," Spock murmured. "Were the Watraii always this cold, this vindictive?"

"Why," Ruanek murmured back, "do you care?"

Spock raised an eyebrow. "I wish to understand them in the hope, one day, of making peace with them."

Ruanek glanced at him sharply, as though about to tell Spock just what a Romulan-in-exile thought of that idea, but then remembered where he was and merely shrugged.

"Some manner of ceremony appears to be about to take place," Data commented.

"Data?" Ruanek asked. "What do you— Oh. I see."

"Indeed," Spock said, keeping his voice expressionless. "I believe that we are about to watch a Watraii execution."

There was nothing to be done but watch, not when the odds were three against forty. From their new hiding places behind more of the endless rocks, they saw the children line up in perfectly straight ranks and the adults line up across from them in their own equally straight ranks.

Down the space left between the two ranks came five more adult Watraii. Four of them were wearing the first unmarked masks—all four a stark, sterile white—that the watchers had seen.

Are these Watraii priests? Spock wondered. *Or are they perhaps a form of ritual police?*

The fifth figure was clearly the prisoner—or was that, perhaps, the criminal? His arms were held fast in metal restraints. He stopped when the white-masked Watraii did and stood rigidly still, either holding himself in such complete self-control that it rivaled a Vulcan's, or that he was under the effect of some powerful drug.

No one spoke. Moving with almost mechanical precision, the four white-masked Watraii swiftly stripped the prisoner of his insignia and his mask, revealing a dead-white, blank-eyed face. What made the proceedings utterly eerie was the complete lack of any sound other than the howling of the wind and the occasional faint crunching of gravel underfoot.

Then, as the prisoner continued to stand resolutely silent, his pale face still emotionless, the white-masked Watraii caught him by the restraints and forced him forward to where a metal pole rose out of the rocks. Now at last he began to struggle, but it was too late. Before he could break free, the four had fastened his restraints to the pole. He struggled against the pole, then gave up and stood in resigned silence. The four white-masked Watraii turned away from him as one and strode away.

As soon as the four white-masked Watraii had moved, all the Watraii stepped back from the prisoner as well—quite a way back and with more than a little unmilitary haste, Spock noted.

Metal pole, he realized. *Metal restraints.* The means of execution was suddenly all too obvious.

We cannot intervene, Spock reminded himself grimly. *There are simply too many Watraii.*

Several tense moments of total silence slid by.

Then lightning suddenly shot down from the stormy sky in one thick, blinding blue-white bolt. It struck the metal pole with a sizzling *crack*. Surrounded by light, the savage energy shooting around and through him, the prisoner convulsed again and again in violent agony, mouth open in a silent scream, skin blackening, smoke swirling up from his body.

At last, mercifully, it was over. The prisoner slumped limply, lifelessly, in the restraints. As the white-masked Watraii moved forward to examine the corpse, the sickeningly sweet stench of burned flesh roiled into the air toward Spock, and he fought not to retch.

The sudden death and stench were more than Ruanek's already tight Romulan nerves could endure. "Are *these* the people you want to befriend?" he snapped at Spock.

It was said with Ruanek's not-quite-suppressed impulsiveness—and just a touch too loudly.

Ruanek bit back an oath as he realized what he'd just done. "Sorry about that, but here they come. Too many to fight . . ." He glanced wryly at Spock. "Looks as though we get to meet the Watraii here and now."

"Necessity decides for us," Spock told Ruanek and Data, "and it does so quickly and logically. Let them take me. It is the best way for me to get to Chekov."

"Spock—"

"No. You and Data are the strongest and swiftest. You have the better chance to make the final assault on the site where the artifact is kept. There is no time to argue," he added sharply. "Now, go!"

Not waiting to see if Ruanek and Data had listened to him, Spock stepped out of hiding, one hand raised in the Vulcan salute, the other held out from his body to show he hid no weapons.

"Greetings," he said to the oncoming Watraii. "I come in peace."

NINETEEN

MEMORY

The lunglock fever that had scythed through *Shavokh*'s population had spared Karatek, but it left him susceptible to the least discomfort, including the wires that linked him to the coronet. He flinched now at the brief pain.

"We maintain course. Those of us who can remotely be considered fit for duty are serving, at the minimum, double shifts. With the death of Commander S'lovan—

"I must acknowledge the military and technical assistance of—" He could feel himself tiring. Rather than form mental "words," he allowed faces to form in his memory. The coronet would preserve them. What he had to say next, however, required careful thought.

"Of the total ship's complement, fifty-five percent have already perished of lunglock fever. Of the fifteen percent who remain disabled, approximately eight percent are projected to suffer various degrees of disability. My staff is planning a memorial service, at which time those katras *we did manage to preserve will be released.*

"An online fleetwide council has been called to discuss whether we should continue on our present heading or choose some other option."

Sending the mutineers off in a shuttle had done no good. The old quarrel had surfaced again.

Whether or not anyone had a clear set of options, however, a fleet council was a positive development. It meant that on each ship, at least one communications specialist and one backup survived to make and maintain contact as the fleet hurtled through space.

Karatek sighed and shifted position. Vertigo struck. He reeled and flung out a hand. The change of position made him cough until spots danced before his eyes as he fought to control his breathing. When the spasms finally subsided, and he wiped his lips, his hand came away streaked with green. He had been assured that, if he had survived for this long, his lungs would strengthen. Eventually.

Once again, he was alone in his mind. During the worst of his own bout with the fever, T'Partha's *katra* had decided that it was weakening him and released itself. Karatek missed T'Partha's presence in his thoughts.

He did not know whether it was fortunate or not, but it appeared that he was going to survive. So was *Shavokh,* although at the height of the epidemic, Karatek gathered that he had raved about how it would become a ship of the dead, hurtling through space until it ran into a meteor, disintegrated, or the universe perished in fire, as Vulcan's oldest tales prophesied.

"I have not the strength to calculate the odds of all of the great ships' populations falling ill within 1.3 years of one another," he told the coronet.

In what one of the technocrats had described as a mathematical monstrosity, the fleet had fallen afoul of coincidence. No sooner had S'task collapsed of the infectious pericarditis that had killed more than half of the people on board *Rea's Helm* than *Shavokh* was struck by a lunglock fever epidemic of its own.

Back on Vulcan, modern medicine—plus the Mother World's heat and distinct lack of humidity—had reduced lunglock to an unpleasant few days of antibiotics and bed rest at worst. But in early Vulcan history, it had rampaged through cities and decimated the northwestern continent.

Shavokh, however, was cold and, despite the best efforts of its maintenance staff to reclaim all free moisture, much damper than the Vulcan norm. Lunglock tended to worsen at night: the relative scarcity of full-spectrum light on board only made it worse. Besides, years of radiation exposure within a sealed environment had weakened everyone's resistance.

A secret sorrow was that the lunglock fever might well have been exacerbated by the gas that T'Olryn had released throughout the ship. But as soon as the worst of the contagion was over, T'Olryn had resigned her post as healer and retreated to her quarters. Her meditations had been so rigorous that when she had emerged—only after the chief healer had threatened to put her in sickbay and keep her there—the tiny, imperious woman had been thin, silent, and so humble that Solor had to fight down horrified rage.

Karatek could not tell his daughter-in-law it was illogical to blame herself. T'Olryn had done what she considered necessary. All else followed. If the healers had not been so necessary, they would have been disgraced. As it was, their casualties were far greater than those of any other population segment on board, not because of guilt, but because, even as they too fell ill, they had sought to reach out with their minds to the people under their care. Their duty had been their expiation.

"I grieve," Karatek continued. Then he stopped and removed the coronet. His daughter-in-law had lost her way, but she was, at the core, a logical being; she would recover. Especially with Solor to help her.

Not so his eldest surviving biological child. T'Alaro, first of the daughters born to him and T'Vysse during the long journey, had been one of the first to fall ill. T'Vysse had nursed her until she collapsed, and then Sarissa had taken over. If sheer force of will could have kept that tiny heart beating, Sarissa would have succeeded. But the little girl died and was thrust out into the sanctity of the Great Dark with a rough-cut gemstone, which Sarissa had treasured since her betrothed had died, tucked into her best robes. Then she had devoted herself to helping the remaining healers restore T'Vysse to health.

Karatek knew he would find T'Vysse in their cabin, wrapped in the robe she had to be coaxed to change, sitting where she always sat these endless days, looking out at the stars.

Sarissa would be seated with her, her usual fire muted with grief. After the death of her betrothed back on the Forge, she had refused all suitors, not that there had ever been many. Karatek had always considered that illogical. Sarissa was beautiful in a fierce sort of way, highly intelligent, and not just fertile, but healthy. He would have thought she was a highly desirable mate.

It appeared now, however, that that problem was solved. Serevan was seated in their living space, outside T'Vysse's private quarters. As Karatek entered, he rose.

"When Sarissa's duty shift ended, she wanted to come back to her quarters and sit with her mother," Serevan explained. "I asked leave to escort her. I apologize for my intrusion, and will take my leave."

Serevan was tall, broad of shoulder, dark of hair and eyes. Like

Sarissa, he had passed through the epidemic unscathed. Builder of ships, miner of planetoids, if Serevan survived to make planetfall, he was the sort of man who could be a builder of worlds. Where he stood, he would put down roots. He was earth to Sarissa's fire.

If Sarissa had brought this man into a house of mourning, she might already have pledged herself.

"Don't go," Karatek said in a voice he tried to make sound healthy, vigorous.

Although Serevan looked down and away with perfect courtesy, he was so much taller than Karatek that their eyes still met. "Your son Lovar was my agemate. I had wished to pay my respects before, but you were ill. I grieve with thee."

Karatek inclined his head, not wanting Serevan to see the sorrow in his eyes.

"Sir, I want you to know, I respect your daughter's character. Her strength."

"Worry not. Life calls to life." Karatek quoted a maxim from the *Third Analects*. "We will speak of this later," he added. "Know now, however, that I do not disapprove."

Serevan looked down and aside, but not before Karatek saw how his eyes warmed. It was logical to be . . . pleased that life called to life, that Sarissa had made her choice, and that she had chosen well.

As had Karatek himself. As he entered the tiny cabin, his eyes went instantly to the viewscreen that showed the distant star field, tinged with blue from the speed at which *Shavokh* flew. In the shadow beside the viewscreen, T'Vysse huddled in her usual chair.

Sarissa rose somewhat uncertainly. "Father," she began.

Karatek raised a hand. "We will speak with you later about your bonding, your mother and I. After the council meeting."

He gestured for her to go to him.

A flash of Sarissa's eyes told Karatek that she was indeed eager to join Serevan. She bowed, then slipped out. The door whispered shut behind her without sticking, which led Karatek to deduce his daughter had, at some point, asked Serevan to repair it.

Alone with T'Vysse at last, Karatek knelt beside her chair. With paired fingers, he touched her hand, then her face. Abandoning control, Karatek drew his wife into his arms. He wrapped his overrobe about them both to warm her. T'Vysse shivered once, then clung to him.

Warmth seeped through Karatek's shipsuit as T'Vysse at last succumbed to the release of tears. The scent of salt mingled with the herbal fragrance that, even now, rose from his wife's hair. He had not realized just how much silver shone in the simple coil into which Sarissa's capable hands had braided it.

"T'Alaro never got to see the desert," T'Vysse whispered. "Never touched minds with a boy we chose for her. Never had a real life."

Very tenderly, Karatek raised his wife's chin in his fingers. Her skin was too soft, almost papery from ill health and sorrow.

"Thy logic is at fault," he replied, letting his eyes warm as he looked into hers. "Our child was cared for. She knew that. Her life was of great value. It was only too short. It is for us to give it meaning."

The question was, how? Out of answers at last, Karatek simply knelt in shadows and starlight, holding his wife.

After a time, he raised his head and looked into her eyes again. Although he tried to keep his glance steadfast, she knew him too well for him to be able to keep up the pretense of courage and resolve. She had to know what the loss of their children had cost him. She had to know, too, how the period of her isolation had left him abandoned. His own mourning had been profound. If she had left him without anchor, she must have wandered so far in spirit that she might never have returned.

"I have failed thee," she whispered.

"Never," he told her.

Absolved, she was able, from some recess of her spirit, to offer him strength.

"I must do my share again. What has been happening?" she asked.

"There is a fleet council today, my wife," he said. Still weary from the aftereffects of lunglock, he could not immediately calculate how long it had been since he had been able to discuss fleet business with her.

"Indeed?" T'Vysse tilted her head. "And what shall thee say?"

He answered with the truth. "I have no idea."

Her eyes flashed. "Now *thy* logic is at fault. You yourself told me it was our duty to give our child's short life meaning."

Pulling out of his hold, she shed her houserobe and reached for the gown and tabard that Sarissa had laid out on the bed just as she had every day, hoping to coax her mother into dressing, into sitting at table with the family, rejoining her world.

"What are you doing?" Karatek asked.

T'Vysse had always been a woman of great peace of spirit. Now, she seemed to have absorbed some of Sarissa's fire.

"Dressing, my husband. Then I am going to the fleet council with you. Any citizen may speak, and I intend to."

Even the short walk from Karatek's quarters to *Shavokh*'s main amphitheater consumed most of his strength. T'Vysse's support, her renewed spirits, were as gratifying as they were reassuring. He did not even criticize himself for feeling regret when she removed her hand from his arm and seated herself in the front row.

Karatek took his place at the council table. He knew himself to be moving like a man in his second century, trying not to strain muscles that might provoke a damaging paroxysm of coughing. He looked over at the communications officer, then nodded.

"Ready to transmit, *T'Kehr*," she said.

"Sir" had always been Commander S'lovan.

As each ship confirmed transmission, images formed on the viewscreens, like mirrors set in a circle. Karatek raised a hand to his temples as the reflected images dizzied him. When his head cleared, he could again discern subtle differences among the ships. That screen showed the soothing deep reds and ambers of *Sunheart*'s bulkheads; the one to the left, the display of archaic armor preserved behind the speaker's table on *Gorget;* while a third revealed the glowing crest and cheekpieces of the helm on *Rea's Helm,* its color somewhat distorted because the flagship had sped ahead of the rest of the fleet.

Full-spectrum light and heat panels rendered *Shavokh*'s auditorium pleasantly warm in an attempt to ward off relapses into lung-lock fever. In *Rea's Helm*'s principal meeting place, every healer who could rise from bed clustered around those people, swathed in silvery blankets and attached to portable cardiac monitors, who had survived.

Firestorm's amphitheater was the only one to boast a crowd. That ship had been spared the epidemics that had wiped out from fifty to seventy percent of the other ships' populations. Karatek would have to monitor *Shavokh* to learn whether people's envy and resentment remained under control.

He waited, staring out across the distances that separated the ships at flushed or livid faces. Many of the survivors were almost skeletal. Some had lost much or all of their hair, while others half lay across two seats, attached to tubes or monitors. Their survival was a tribute not just to the healers' skill, but to Vulcans' innate strength.

How long could they go on like this?

It was not a rhetorical question.

Karatek made himself listen to the whispers that shivered across the amphitheater. Was it true that Karatek would stay in command? Was it true that S'task was really dying? Was it true that the ships' engines were breaking down? Had all the frozen genetic material been destroyed in that power outage on board *Vengeance*? Had it been deliberate? Even if they reached a habitable world, would there be enough of them to create a viable community?

The whispers hissed across the room and into space, weakened by static. A tech bent to adjust the communications hookups.

For the past hundred and three days, S'task had lain ill. The only times he had spoken were to thank a healer for her expression of sorrow at the deaths of his wife and children and to demand that he be moved back to his now-empty quarters, leaving his space in *Rea's Helm*'s medical facility for a person in worse condition than he.

Since then, S'task had not been seen in the command center or anywhere else.

What must it be like to lose one's entire family? Karatek refused to think about it. Nevertheless, S'task had duties. He might have broken from Surak, but he too knew that the needs of the many outweighed the needs of the few. Or the one. Now that "few" was all that remained fleetwide, Karatek thought S'task would have made the effort to join this critical meeting. He had hoped.

The whispers grew louder, turning disappointed as the navigator from *Rea's Helm* slipped into the central chair. At least, however, each ship was represented by one or more members of what had been its council.

Karatek nodded for order to be called. *Systra*s rang out, the tiny bells painfully shrill in the thin, chill air.

He glanced down at the screen set into the table. Online fleet councils were infrequent, meaning that long agendas built up. They might be here for hours.

"T'Kehr!" came a cry from the highest row of the amphitheater. The tall man who stood, demanding recognition, was big-boned but not heavy.

"N'Rayek," Karatek recognized one of the te-Vikram. He suppressed a brief instant of frustration that N'Rayek had been first on his feet. These days, any te-Vikram looked like a potential rebel, no matter how Solor reassured him about how subdued the te-Vikram were, these days. The lunglock had hit them hardest of any group on board.

"T'Kehr, may I suggest we wait to discuss . . . all this . . . this trash. Instead, I think we should focus on the most important question that faces us: Shall we go on at all? Back on the Mother World, when a warrior grew old, or was too sorely wounded to fight, rather than prove a charge upon his clan, he could choose to walk into the desert . . ."

"I never thought a warrior would talk about giving up!" came a jeer from across empty space.

Karatek braced himself for the predictable eruption of temper from the emotional members of the fleet. He had been here before: someone would erupt and be met by a stinging, logical reproof from someone else who had studied the *Analects,* but had not learned overmuch. Or a technocrat would ease in with a plausible solution that advanced only other technocrats.

T'Vysse caught his eye and shook her head minutely. Clearly, this defeatism on the part of the fiercest part of their population concerned her. And she had never guided him wrong.

"*Kroykah!*" Karatek called for order. Damn this lunglock to the Womb of Fire; there was no strength in his ordinary speaking voice. He took a deep breath and hoped his lungs would hold up long enough for one good shout.

He rose and pounded his fists on the table.

"*Kroykah!*" It came out as a strangled yell. He fell back into his chair, coughing, his mouth filling with the coppery taste of his own blood.

T'Vysse was instantly at his side, pouring water, holding it to his lips, and—by all that was illogical—glaring into the screens. She signaled, and the *systra*s rang out, their shrillness prolonged until even the people on the other ships flinched and fell silent.

She eased Karatek back into his chair, then held up her hand.

"May I reply to N'Rayek?" she asked.

Te-Vikram might not be much for allowing women to speak in council, but the fleet's law was that any citizen could speak. Whether people listened, however, was up to the logic and persuasiveness of a given speaker.

"I find your logic flawed," T'Vysse told the former warrior. "Yes, I know. I *would* say that. But consider the evidence. You speak of walking out into the desert. May I suggest that we already are in the greatest desert of all?"

Solor rose to his feet. "I concur," he told the te-Vikram. "Sir, I grew up on the Forge. During my *kahs-wan* ordeal, I met warriors. It did not seem to me that these men, even if they walked into the desert at the end of their lives, would simply sit on the nearest dune and wait for a wild *sehlat* to find them. Do your own legends not tell of the captain who lost a leg, a hand, and an eye, but who pushed on toward the Womb of Fire?"

"I know that story!" T'Vysse glanced around the room, reaching for agreement with the skill of Lady Mitrani, by now long dead back on Vulcan, or Karatek's lost friend T'Partha, painstakingly building consensus in a debate. "He was Captain of Hosts. His water ran out, and he pressed on. He fought off the *sehlat*s with his crutch. A storm built up, and as the sand threatened to strip the flesh from his bones, he continued forward until, at last, he fought through the storm and reached the desert's heart, Vorta Vor, where the water is sweet, and green plants always grow."

The man standing at the back of the amphitheater flung up a hand, the gesture of a warrior bested in a skirmish by a master teacher.

"I say we walk on," T'Vysse cried. "It may be that we walk toward our end. Or it may be that, like that Captain of Hosts, we will press on to a new beginning."

"My lady . . ." The words came from a new voice, hoarse, and long unfamiliar, but recognizable after a moment as belonging to S'task. *"I second your motion. And I recommend it be carried. With profound acclamation."*

S'task appeared in the viewscreen, with one arm flung over the shoulders of a man Karatek recognized as the flagship's chief astronomer. His other arm was grasped by a healer whose glare of outrage seemed to burn through the distance. He was so gaunt after his long illness that his heavy cloak weighed him down and made it seem natural that he could not stand alone. His temples were hollowed, the bones of cheeks and forehead alarmingly prominent, and his skin was the color of white jade. Only his eyes blazed like their lost hearthsun.

His navigator rose from the table, almost stumbling in his haste to ease S'task into his own chair.

S'task waved him away.

"We have made a discovery," he said.

His voice lost volume, and he gasped. The healer holding his arm all but pushed him into the chair held out for him.

Whispers eddied, rose, then fell into complete silence, broken only by the static of the ship-to-ship transmissions.

Regaining control, S'task gazed out into the eyes of the remaining members of his fleet with the intensity of one of the proscribed disruptor weapons that Karatek knew for a fact had been tested on a passing meteor just 18.3 days ago.

"I recognize S'rivas of Rea's Helm." With a shaking hand, S'task pointed to the chief astronomer. The man was even taller than his commanding officer, but not nearly so thin.

"We finally succeeded in refining our astrocartographic scanners," the astronomer said. *"Magnification is up 38.6 percent. Just enough"*—his eyes blazed; he tried to suppress it, but an immense grin of triumph spread over his face—*"to allow us to see . . ."*

A gesture, and S'task's face, the amphitheater on board *Rea's Helm*, all disappeared, to be replaced by the eternal, too-familiar desert of stars of which T'Vysse had spoken with such passion.

"This is what you see with normal resolution," S'rivas's voice rang out over the view of what Karatek knew was empty space and uncharted, useless stars.

"Now, with the augmented magnification, we can see this. . . ." The viewscreen shimmered, then seemed to come into focus.

"Observe," the chief astronomer said. A red light shaped like an arrow appeared on-screen. *"Look out here,"* he said. *"Past the orange binary system . . ."*

The arrow moved, edging toward what appeared to be a rosette of stars. *"Here!"* he said. *"Here, in this cluster of dwarf K-type stars."* His voice shook, as did the arrow with which he indicated stars that Karatek had never seen.

"If we had not managed to improve our scanners, we would have missed them," the astronomer went on. *"Only imagine: We would have missed them.*

"The instant I was able to study this star field closely, I went to T'Kehr *S'task. These stars—that one, over here"*—again, the arrow flickered, then homed in on a point of light—*"could possess planetary systems! I have my staff working on modifying our scanners to see if we can detect such worlds from here."*

Someone—not Karatek—coughed. It was the only sound heard on board any of the ships.

Karatek made himself breathe deeply, risking the possibility of another spasm. Not just planets, but possibly *Minshara*-class worlds.

The transmissions erupted in cheers, stampings of feet, poundings of tables. At the back, three te-Vikram shouted the warriors' cry Karatek had not heard for years. To his own barely concealed astonishment and disapproval, Solor joined them. He had his arm about T'Olryn. The former healer appeared to be weeping. Perhaps wind in her hair, sun on her face, would restore her courage. Karatek hoped so.

Meanwhile, Sarissa and Serevan joined hands and looked as if they would embrace, right out there, for all the fleet to see.

Karatek tightened his lips, preparing to disapprove, but T'Vysse shook her head at him.

"Surak," he said huskily.

"Surak never lived to see a moment like this," his consort told him serenely. "He was my guest-friend too, remember? He would have said the provocation was great." Her eyes returned to Sarissa and her chosen mate. "Think, Karatek. Their children could be born on a homeworld of their own. *Their children!*" Her dark eyes filling, she looked away until she could control herself. "I ask pardon," she whispered.

Karatek couldn't quite bring himself to laugh, not out in public. "You yourself said the provocation was great."

Then, from *Rea's Helm, systras* jangled for quiet.

"Listen to me, listen to me!" came the chief astronomer's voice. *"You have not yet heard all the data!"*

"Why does it matter?" cried a voice from *Sunheart,* young enough for optimism, old enough to know better.

"Because," the astronomer said, his voice suddenly old and heavy, *"not all the data favor us. By our calculations, it will take us ten years to accelerate, and another ten to slow sufficiently to let us enter the system."*

Serevan, looking extremely grave, had released Sarissa's hand. He appeared to be solving equations in his head. Karatek remembered a maxim from his period of compulsory service back on Vulcan. "Anything that looks too good to be true probably is."

This definitely was. He did not need the other scientist's next words to know how bad the news was, all the worse after the moment of unbridled excitement.

"Those twenty years put us outside the fleet's envelope of viability. By the time we reach there, we will all be dead."

"But we will have gotten there!" came S'task's voice.

Just for that instant, it was the voice again of the fiery young man Karatek remembered from Vulcan, the man who had inspired the building of the fleet and persuaded Vulcan's bravest and strongest—or, in some cases, least fortunate—to embark on this mission of exile.

The fleet council erupted again into a hundred conversations, speeches, and side-eddies of sheer noise.

Just as the technocrats on board *Vengeance* shouted for recognition and began to denounce *Rea's Helm* for bringing such cruel truths to light, Serevan rose to his full height.

"Why are you still talking?" he demanded. "We have work to do!"

TWENTY

NOW

WATRAII HOMEWORLD
STARDATE 54107.2

As the Watraii fanned out to surround him, Spock stood motionless, offering them absolutely no resistance, still standing with his hands open and held away from his body. The biggest danger to him just now was that one of the Watraii would take any movement on his part to be a threat and open fire. At such close range, that would be fatal.

The Watraii said nothing. One of the group might be the leader, since the others kept looking his—or possibly her—way, although he or she looked precisely like the others. At least that particular Watraii did seem to be the one the others were looking to for guidance. It was worth the attempt.

But when Spock spoke directly to that individual, beginning, "I offer no hostility," there was no reply. He bit back what would have been a facetious and most illogically useless order: *Take me to your leader.* Jim Kirk had once told him of those ancient "ess-eff" movies from twentieth-century Earth in which such words were always said by visiting aliens.

There was a certain logic to the words. Who else but a leader would a visiting alien wish to see? And in this case, there was a reasonable probability that these people actually would take him to their leader. Spock passively allowed the Watraii to fasten restraints about his wrists—although, he thought with the slightest touch of sardonic humor, if they intended to fasten him to that metal pole, he was definitely not going to remain passive about it.

But they evidently had already decided without words that he was not going to be another electrical victim. After a few murmured consultations that were too soft and muffled by the masks for even Vulcan hearing to make out, the Watraii abruptly began marching him instead toward what at first looked like nothing more than a mass of boulders.

No, Spock realized after a few moments . . . the Watraii had merely made use of the boulders as a convenient way to add a natural element of protection to their installation. It was from that installation that they would have had to come; there was, he knew, no other nearby.

Were there really no others on this planet at all? Where were the Watraii warships? This installation seemed to be mostly underground. Logic said that warships, too, would need to be sheltered from the harsh climate and fierce winds in underground bunkers.

That truly is not the issue right now. More fortunately, I believe that we were correct. This is their main installation, the one that we spotted from space—the installation in which Chekov is being held and in which the Watraii commander almost certainly resides.

As Ruanek might put it, I have just won this part of the gamble.

As Ruanek and Data hurried deeper into the wilderness of rocks, both of them moving with practiced skill, Ruanek suddenly realized that he was clenching both his teeth and his fists as he went. He fought an inner struggle with himself, trying to force himself to relax—

Akkh, useless. All those years of warrior training had made him what he was despite the intervening time on Vulcan, all those years of *never abandon a comrade, never let a comrade be taken alive by the foe*—

All at once he stopped short, overwhelmed by utter frustration. "I can't do this."

Thanks to the android's quick reflexes, Data stopped short with him, and turned to look at him quizzically, head tilted slightly to one side in surprise. "What is it, Ruanek? Are you injured or overly weary?"

"No! Data, think about what we're doing."

"What do you mean?"

"There's no honor here. We can't abandon Spock and Chekov just to save our own skins."

Data blinked. "I do not claim to fully understand the Romulan concept of honor. However, what you claim is happening—the deliberate and cowardly abandonment of comrades—is certainly not what we are doing. Of course I, too, wish to rescue them, but we both know that our primary mission right now is precisely what Ambassador Spock said: We are to recover the artifact."

"Bah."

"Ambassador Spock is no fool," Data continued. "I assure you, he knows what he is doing."

"Of course he does. I've seen him in action, Data, under circumstances that would have destroyed any lesser being, and I mean that without any melodrama. I trust him, and I trust his judgment. It's the Watraii I don't trust! They've already proved to all of us that they don't give a damn about diplomacy."

"Ruanek, please, listen to me. I know that you are not Starfleet personnel, but you did tell me that you were once a soldier on Romulus. You do understand orders."

"Yes, yes, of course I do, but—"

"We are not the only ones in this situation. Captain Scott has orders to take the *Alexander Nevsky* offworld after twenty-four ship hours if we do not return, and Captain Saavik must leave orbit soon after that."

"Do you truly believe that they will do so?" Ruanek challenged.

"I would understand if they do," Data countered.

"They will not," Ruanek said firmly. "They would not abandon us. And I will not abandon them."

"But—"

"Oh, don't worry, Data—ah, I assume that you *can* worry?"

"You may rest assured that I quite understand 'worry.'"

That had been said in what Ruanek could have sworn was a wry tone. "So, I will go on with you and recover the artifact, because, as you have so emphatically reminded me, those are our orders. And then, if you like, you can return to the *Alexander Nevsky* and take off with Captain Scott. But I will not. I will not leave this planet without saving my comrades."

"I quite agree with that," Data said. "But before we . . . worry about performing heroic and honorable acts, first we must figure out where, precisely, the artifact is being held, and how we are to recover it."

"Ah. Yes. There is that little issue." Ruanek glanced about, trying to orient himself. "I don't want to risk running a scan that might be detected now that we're so near the Watraii. I don't suppose that you can . . ."

"Locate it without using a scanner? As it happens, I have already located it with my tricorder."

"How—when—?"

"While the Watraii attention was focused upon the execution." Data paused. "I do not need very much time to absorb information. The artifact is in part of the main installation."

"You," Ruanek said in genuine appreciation, "are quite amazing."

"So I have been told," the android replied with a smile.

As he was marched into the installation, Spock warily observed every detail without giving the impression of being at all interested. The structure seemed to be made mostly of composite materials, not metal, although of course he could not be sure of that without being able to run a scan on it. But composites would be quite understandable since resources were so scarce.

And they certainly would not wish the building to suffer constant electrical strikes.

The outer doors were as heavy and as heavily guarded as Spock had expected: they were truly the entrance to a fortress. The Watraii guarding him exchanged complex codes with those inside for several minutes. Then at last one of the doors slid open just wide enough to let the Watraii and Spock enter in single file. As they passed into the installation, Spock noted that the outer wall was thick, perhaps two or three meters so, as befitted a military structure—or, for that matter, any structure that needed to remain standing in this savage environment. As the Watraii marched him forward, Spock felt the slight change of air pressure as the door slid shut again.

They were in a wide, straight corridor that sloped steadily downward. Most of the installation did, indeed, seem to have been built into the ground. The end of the corridor was hidden in shadow. There were, not surprisingly, no windows, but the yellow glow of the evenly spaced lights showed that floor and walls alike were a matte charcoal gray. That the Watraii should be using an old-fashioned electric lighting system hardly surprised Spock. Electricity would certainly be the cheapest and most easily accessible resource on this world. What did surprise him was the utter lack of any ornamentation. Even the most severe of military installations on Romulus had borne heroic murals and war trophies. Here there was nothing.

Of all the oxygen-breathing species known to the Federation, Spock thought, *only the Borg have no sense of ornamentation. In their case, the lack of any form of artistry was understandable. Yet these people may be highly organized, but they are not a hive intelligence, and the patterns on their masks show that they do, indeed, understand the concept of ornamentation.*

Then why is their installation so utterly sterile? The plainness implies a temporary facility, one on which no time need be wasted for artwork. Yet the entire structure seems to have been built to last for years. It resembles a prison more than it does a major installation . . . almost as though the Watraii are trying to turn themselves into emotionless military machines—or perhaps are punishing themselves.

It was a confusing puzzle. But without further evidence one way or another, speculation was useless. Spock could only content himself with: *Fascinating.*

The group of Watraii children was ushered away down a narrow side corridor. The little troop went obediently without so much as a curious glance back at Spock.

It truly does seem as though the Watraii don't even consider their children primarily as replacement members of the species, but first and foremost as a military resource.

He and his Watraii escort continued down the wider, absolutely straight and utterly featureless main corridor, their footsteps echoing dully on the charcoal gray floor. The air smelled faintly of antiseptic and of dust.

The corridor leveled out eventually and ended abruptly in a blank wall into which was set a smooth black door. It, like everything else that Spock had seen so far, was utterly without ornamentation, though he noted a small, lighted panel at one side. One of the Watraii tapped out a code on the panel, shielding what he did from Spock's sight.

The door slid open, creaking slightly, revealing a chamber that instantly struck Spock as the basic essence of "command central." The room was large and circular, as plain and gray as the rest of the installation, but viewscreens lined the walls, and a desk of black stone nearly hidden by a communications console was set squarely in the center of it.

At the desk sat a Watraii.

Spock needed no formal introduction to know: *Ah, they have, indeed, taken me to their leader.*

The Watraii at the desk fairly radiated authority. His dark uniform was no different from that of the others, save for a light gray slash across one sleeve, and his mask was no different from the masks of the others, either. But he carried himself with that unmistakable combination of pride and weariness that Spock knew from every captain, every admiral, everyone in charge of others whom he had ever seen.

This Watraii was the person who was, at the heart of it, responsible for everyone else.

Very good, Spock thought. *Better, in fact, than one could ever have predicted.*

"Greetings," he said, saluting the Watraii with hand raised in the split-fingered Vulcan salute, ignoring the guards standing at rigid attention to the left and right of their leader. "I am Ambassador Spock of the planet Vulcan, and I come in peace."

"Welcome," the commander replied. His voice was as chilly as the room around them, and held not a trace of emotion. "Welcome, you who have no sense of survival."

"Had I no sense of survival, I would not have come here peacefully," Spock countered, "but would have tried to attack you as an army of one."

"I do not know what game you play," the Watraii said coldly, "but I care nothing for your words—you who are one of the creatures that we have sworn to wipe from the galaxy."

Spock calmly retorted, "I mean no insult, sir, but I must make a correction. I can understand why you think me a Romulan. There is, indeed, a resemblance between those people and my own. But as I have already said, I am not a Romulan. I am of the planet Vulcan."

"Do you think we have no eyes?" There was a sudden edge of impatience in the Watraii commander's cold voice. "No intelligence? There is no distinction between you and the enemy, or so small a distinction that it matters not. You are, indeed, of the same enemy race. And your reckless invasion and attempts to trick us are not going to bring you anywhere but to your death."

"An invasion of one is hardly logical," Spock returned smoothly. "I am certain that you agree about this. Those who captured me can vouch for the fact that I was alone."

"I know that you were alone when you were taken. Whether or

not there are others hiding on the surface, others we have not yet taken prisoner, remains to be seen." The commander leaned forward ever so slightly. "But never mind that. Let us accept your claim for the moment. Let us assume that you really are here alone. Then the question becomes simply this: Why are you here?"

"Believe me," Spock countered, "I wish no harm to you or your people."

"Why are you here?"

"I am here because I wish only the truth."

"The truth," the Watraii commander echoed flatly.

"I am aware of the claims that your people have made against the Romulans. I seek to find a peaceful solution to—"

"There can be none."

"Your pardon, but there is always a possibility for a peaceful solution to even the most—"

"There is no settlement but death. And I do not have any time to waste on this nonsense. Guards!" the Watraii commander snapped. "Prepare this intruder for interrogation."

Judging from their environment, Spock assumed that the Watraii must have turned electroshock into something nearing an art form. That was not precisely a pleasant thought.

But before anyone could move or say anything more, a new Watraii rushed into the room without waiting on ceremony. He (or she?) hastily saluted before the Watraii guards could shoot, and rattled off a series of coded statistics to the commander.

The commander instantly switched on the console at his desk. From what little Spock could see from where he stood, the crisis concerned a Watraii shuttle. Coming in for a normal landing, it had just been caught in a wind shear and had been forced to make a crash landing instead. In the process, it had apparently also done a fair amount of damage to the landing area and nearby transports.

The commander began snapping out orders into a com link and to those around him, and only then stopped short for a moment, turning to stare at Spock as if suddenly remembering him.

Interesting. You are not as blindly militaristic as the others. You consider the welfare of your people before all else, Spock thought. *That is definitely a good sign.*

"There is no time for this," the commander snapped. "Throw the creature into a cell—yes, yes, all right then, if that is the only cell with sufficient security, then make it the cell with our prior guest."

Prior guest? Spock wondered as he was marched by the Watraii down yet another featureless corridor. *Chekov?*

The Watraii unlocked and opened a door. The cell that lay beyond it was so dimly lit that Spock stopped involuntarily, trying in vain to see where he was going.

The Watraii didn't actually throw him into it. Shoved, yes, but not so roughly that he lost his footing, as though they were less interested in him than they were about getting back to deal with the shuttle crash.

Understandable.

As Spock heard the door slide shut and lock once more behind him, he blinked in the near darkness, waiting for his eyes to adjust to the faint light. Now he could vaguely make out a figure standing at the back of the cell, but he couldn't quite tell yet who or what . . .

Was that figure standing in the cell actually Chekov?

Or was it, perhaps, an enemy?

TWENTY-ONE

MEMORY

As *Shavokh* braked toward system entry, Karatek panted from the additional "weight" of the coronet he wore. Because his lungs had never recovered completely from the fever, he forced himself to breathe slowly, carefully. These days, it was a fight to breathe at all. The cold, thin air was stale now past the ability of any recycling system to make it fresh. Sometimes, when an unexpected gust from, say, hydroponics or engineering huffed out of one of the ancient vents into the battered corridors, it was all he could do not to collapse, retching, on the deck.

He and T'Vysse would sit each evening in the courtyard of their house in ShiKahr. Their fingers would touch and they would simply breathe in the sweet, wild scent of the desert night.

Even with the weakness, the heaviness, and the sickness, Karatek was hungrier than he had ever been. They all were, even with their population depleted by epidemics, accidents, or just wearing out from despair.

Life had become almost killingly austere as the exiles fought to keep their ships flying. Fewer remained alive now. Some perished in industrial accidents. Others died out working on the hulls. Whenever possible, their bodies had been retrieved to be buried when they finally reached a planet they could call their own.

For the past 19.8 years, they had tested the limits of the great ships and their own strength. First, they had accelerated to reach the star S'task's chief astronomer had seen while, simultaneously, laboring to strengthen engines and hulls against the long, long deceleration period while they decided whether it was safe to enter the system or try to struggle on to the next before the ships broke apart.

Maybe it was just as well that so few children had been born in the past 19.8 years: it meant fewer to die, fewer parents to suffer as he and T'Vysse had when their little daughter slipped out of life. These days, when a child survived to come of age, what that chiefly meant was that the new adult learned a new discipline: leave enough food so that children had a remote chance of growing up healthy.

This final period of uncertainty had been more than some of the exiles could bear. Quarrels among the various factions on board each of the ships grew worse, threatening to succeed where black holes, alien predators, epidemics, and time had failed. Vulcan's exile was ending just as it began, in politics, plots, and recriminations.

And this time, they had no Surak to unite them.

It was the death, finally, of an entire family in a suicide pact that had convinced every person of logic and goodwill on board each ship that it was time at least to try to unite once more.

Did they have one more effort in them? Though so many Vulcans had died, hope had not. Not quite.

The fleet was working for a common cause again, but the different groups on board were not united. Nor would they ever be united again, except in suspicion of one another. He knew Solor was watching the te-Vikram, while Sarissa, through her ties with the engineers, managed civil relations with the technocrats—"up to a point," she always cautioned.

But the great ships still flew. Ships' systems worked. Nobody fought. And no one died, except of natural causes. Karatek, as worn out as his ship, was content to call that a victory.

With the discipline of long practice, Karatek tried to form coherent, discrete thoughts for the coronet to store. After a time, he gave it up and just peered out into the dark, looking for that one particular star that might mean his people had a future.

There it was! How it glowed, even if it was not the brightest star in the sky or even on the main sequence. Possibly, it was not as hot as Vulcan's home sun. They could live with that. They had gotten used to being cold. But right now, the very sight of it made Karatek's eyes blur. He fought off a preposterous sense of homecoming. He had never been here. How, then, could he be coming home?

Karatek had once seen Surak yield to emotion at the death of a student. More than a hundred years away from his great teacher, Karatek remained a student, in need of guidance. But he could not play the student now. Shortly, he must take his place in the command center as *Shavokh* and her consorts made the irrevocable course change and engine burns that would take them into the star system. Even if this system proved unsatisfactory, it was likely to be the last one they would ever see. The ships' engineers calculated that any attempt to reaccelerate, let alone to near-relativistic speeds, would make the engines burn out—assuming they did not explode.

Early in the ten years' deceleration, *Shavokh* had come into sensor range of the star system. Then, the ships had received further indications that at least one of the planets that circled this star might be *Minshara*-class. But the long-range scans were inconclusive. At times, they showed a world that was habitable by Vulcan standards, if very damp; at others, they showed wild fluctuations of heat and cold.

At all times, bio-readings showed the possibility of life-forms, but there were no indications that a technological civilization existed. The systems were checked and rechecked, but always gave the same answers. Whether or not there were sapient beings on that planet, they would have to wait to find out. They would have to come closer, with no hope of ever being able to escape if they entered the system and found they were wrong.

That provoked another quarrel. Early in the exile, the fleet had refused to consider landing on a habitable world because it possessed intelligent life. But if this world had intelligence, they would have no choice but to make the best accommodation with the natives that they could. It was an ethical dilemma for which the ships' commanders were sharply criticized. But, as S'task said, gathering up a desperate consensus, it was a logical risk to take.

And so, the decision had been made. Karatek still shook his head over the wildness of the night in which *Shavokh* permitted itself to celebrate. Those on board who had not studied Surak's disciplines had screamed, laughed, wept, brought out supplies of potions brewed from things Karatek refused to imagine, and danced in the corridors and shuttlebays. A number of women even conceived, as if to contradict the fear that the fleet lacked sufficient fertile men and women to populate a new homeworld.

As far as Karatek knew, however, Sarissa and her intended

mate—at least, Karatek hoped he was still only her intended mate—would wait so that any children they might have would be born on a new homeworld.

When the hangovers subsided, the survivors of the fleet settled down to plan how they would make this new system theirs.

How beautiful the star was. How it drew Karatek's gaze. Surely no other star in this strange quadrant of space . . . But he was being illogical.

He tried to imagine standing upon the soil of a new world, looking up at it through a veil of atmosphere, of fresh, sweet air. He had his old memories.

Sunset over the Forge.

Dawn breaking behind the peaks of Mount Seleya.

Now, he would create new ones. Logically, this new homeworld would have sights he would find similarly pleasing and would love just as much, if not more.

Karatek's com buzzed, summoning him to command.

He gave the star one last look and turned away, ready to give the orders that would bring *Shavokh* to its new home.

TWENTY-TWO

NOW

WATRAII HOMEWORLD
STARDATE 54107.2

The figure stood motionless in the darkness, staring at Spock. It was quite alarming in that first instant of purely atavistic reaction, but in the next moment, Spock realized the truth of it. There wasn't a threat at all. Since he was outlined against the slightly brighter light from outside, the figure couldn't be sure of his identity, either, and was standing motionless because he or she was desperately trying to puzzle it out.

His vision adapted to the dim light in the next moment. With a rush of what he could not deny was joy, Spock saw that this was, indeed, Pavel Chekov standing there. But . . . it was not exactly the man whom he remembered from barely two months before.

Instead of the energetic, cheerful person who had gleefully defied all of Starfleet and not worried about little things such as demotion or court-martial, Spock saw a Chekov who was clad in drab gray tunic and trousers, a Chekov who—for the first time in his life—looked genuinely old, genuinely worn, and quite embittered.

But, mercifully, the man seemed still to be in one piece. There were no obvious scars or bruises, either. He had not been, at least not visibly, badly mistreated.

They could not, for safety's sake, show that they knew each other. But Spock turned slightly in the dim light so that Chekov could see him more clearly. Chekov started visibly as he recognized Spock, but said nothing. However, the sudden coldness in his eyes said volumes.

Spock moved forward as though about to challenge the other for space. As soon as he was close enough to risk a whisper, he said, "Chekov."

In the softest of murmurs, Chekov returned, "Spock." There was no warmth in his voice, either.

Spock, still pretending to be potentially hostile, moved forward a little closer, as though about to shoulder Chekov aside. Keeping his voice pitched low, he continued. "I cannot say that I am pleased to see you *here,* but I am truly pleased to see you alive."

"Are you?"

Spock turned slightly, as though simply readjusting the fall of his robes. "This is hardly the place for recriminations. They are almost certainly watching or listening to us."

"Probably." Chekov sat down heavily on the cell's one piece of furniture, a cot, glaring up at him. "What do you expect of me? Do you want me to throw myself into your brotherly embrace? I was abandoned by you, Spock. I was left to the enemy."

Spock sat beside him, still keeping his voice warily low. "We thought you were dead."

"Bah."

"The evidence was circumstantial, I admit. But at the time, in the heat of combat, there seemed no doubt to any of us aboard the *Alliance* that you had been slain in that transporter malfunction. And I assure you that we did try, but there was nothing for us to recover."

Chekov said nothing to that, but his eyes remained cold.

You cannot try to recover his friendship here and now, Spock told himself. "Chekov, I assure you that if any words of apology from me would help you, you would have them in a moment. But the past is the past. Like it or not, it cannot be changed here and now."

"Ah yes, the famous Vulcan self-control. Very useful, isn't it?"

"Not at the moment. Chekov, we must focus only on finding a way to escape."

Ah, but how? Spock got to his feet, pacing the cell as though avoiding the other prisoner but actually looking for weaknesses. Smooth floor, smooth ceiling, smooth walls . . . solid walls, some careful tapping assured him. If there was a spy cam or other security device, he could not locate it. That hardly meant that such devices weren't present.

"There *is* no way out," Chekov muttered. "I should know."

"No *obvious* way," Spock corrected thoughtfully. Even if the cell had no weaknesses, the Watraii themselves might. And if they were watching and listening, there were always possibilities for them to be tricked . . .

Again, how? It was unfortunate, Spock mused after a few moments of mental calculations, that Chekov, unlike a Vulcan, could not stop his own heart. But . . . yes, there was something else that could be done. He asked Chekov carefully, "Do you remember the time when I melded with the rest of James T. Kirk's bridge crew to protect them all from illusion?"

Chekov frowned at him, then was silent for a while, not having a Vulcan's flawless memory and clearly trying to remember back so many years.

"Yes, I do," he retorted bitterly at last. "That time, I was already dead." He stared at Spock. "Is that what you want, Spock? Do you think that after all that has happened, I would actually trust my mind to you?"

"I cannot force you to agree," Spock said. He got back to his feet and pretended to be once again studying the cell's construction, at the same time giving himself a chance to avoid any unseemly display of emotion. "I merely await a logical alternative as to how we can conceal our friends' whereabouts from the Watraii."

Behind him, he heard the faintest hiss from Chekov, but then a muttered, "You win, dammit. Go ahead."

Spock sat beside him, using the folds of his robes to hide what he was doing. Hands on Chekov's temples, he began to calm his mind, to murmur the calming words . . .

"My mind to your mind . . . "

For all his bitter words, Chekov didn't even make the smallest attempt to hold him off. It was, instead, almost a violent surrender, as though Chekov no longer really cared what happened. There were a few seconds of being only himself, then a few more confused seconds when he was no longer only Spock . . . then knew he was also . . .

Chekov . . .

He was Chekov . . .

He was . . . alone . . . utterly alone . . . abandoned . . . a terrible, terrifying wave of resentment/loss/fear . . . resentment of those who were his closest friends and who'd abandoned him, guilt about how he felt . . .

No. Spock knew this much already, and understood that guilt. He must go further . . .

Yes . . .

He was with Chekov . . . materializing in Watraii hands with the horror that had been the living Watraii caught in the transporter malfunction . . .

He was with Chekov kept locked in a brig aboard the Watraii ship . . . no one speaking to him, not even when they fed him . . .

He was with Chekov . . . landing on this planet . . . arriving at the installation . . . confronting the Watraii commander . . . He heard the questioning, the endless questioning . . . No way to tell day from night, day from day . . . questioning and loneliness . . .

No torture—Spock felt a thrill of relief so strong it nearly tore apart the link, and had to forcibly calm himself. There had been no torture because the Watraii saw in Chekov a wonder, a being who had achieved age, a rare thing among the Watraii.

And yet, they thought him an enemy . . . and questioned him . . . questioned him . . . kept him here with no way out, no change, no chance . . . alone . . . alone and abandoned . . . alone with his anger and guilt and hopelessness . . . to have come to this . . . to end like this . . . alone . . .

Enough, Spock told himself, and quietly withdrew, back into himself, into his mind. He sat still for a while, dizzy and giving his mind a chance to accept that he was himself, complete in himself, Spock, and not Chekov as well.

Beside him, he could dimly sense Chekov shuddering. The mind-meld had not been easy for either of them.

Spock opened his eyes. "I understand," he said simply.

There was nothing else that he could say just then.

Chekov said nothing. Instead, he lay down on the cot, his back turned to Spock, and soon was at least feigning sleep.

Since there was nothing else to be done at the moment, Spock sank to the floor and settled his mind into the calm coolness of meditation. He blocked any worry about the precious time ticking away, the time till Scotty took the shuttle offworld. There was no time just now . . .

But time returned with a rush as the cell door opened. It was not an inquisition. Watraii guards were there with a sleeping mat for Spock and food for the two prisoners. Spock got to his feet, but the wary Watraii stayed out of reach for the few seconds that the door was open.

So be it. There would be other chances. Spock settled down on the mat again with his share of the food. Meat? No. Some form of vegetable protein: he could eat it. The meal was little more than the equivalent of Starfleet emergency rations, but it was surprisingly nutritious. Could this possibly be the normal food for the Watraii, too? A flash of memory brought back Ruanek's sarcastic "I'd rather get shot than have to live here."

I assume from the lack of commotion that you and Data are still free and hunting the artifact. And I assure you, wherever you two are, I shall do my best not to get shot nor to remain living here.

Spock's inner clock told him that it must now be night on the Watraii world. Scotty would be forced to take off in the late morning. But there was nothing else that could be done just now. Curled up on the sleeping mat, calming his mind with Vulcan disciplines, Spock settled down for the night.

"There," Ruanek whispered to Data as they crouched behind a low natural wall of rocks in the Watraii world's dim gray version of twilight.

"I see them," Data whispered back.

"It isn't that large a group. Four . . . five . . . only six in all. We could take them out."

"Yes, I have no doubt that we could. But what good would that do us?"

Ruanek glared at the android. "You've been saying something like that about every search party we've been avoiding, Data—every cursed search party that's been driving us farther and farther away from the artifact. The answer should be obvious enough to you by now: Eliminate them, and we have fewer searchers!"

"On the contrary, Ruanek. Slay these, and it is certain that more will come looking for their missing fellows."

"Akhh." Ruanek pulled out a small pack of emergency rations and bit savagely into it.

"I know that you were trained to fight. I know that you wish to lash out like the warrior you once were. And I, too, would like to eliminate some of them, I admit it. But surely you see my point."

"Akhh," Ruanek repeated, more softly. "Unfortunately, yes, I do. And yes, I know that you're right." He shrugged impatiently, snatched another mouthful of the rations, then tucked the pack away again. "More evasive action it is, then." Glancing up, Ruanek added, "Not much more daylight left. I wonder if the Watraii can see in the dark."

"We will soon find out," Data said. "Where do we head now? Down that gully?"

Ruanek shook his head. "Good shelter, but too easy for us to be trapped."

"That ridge?"

"You really do want to get us shot, don't you?"

"I don't—"

"Run along a ridge while we're outlined by the setting sun? You can't possibly think that's a good idea. And yes, that first question of mine was a rhetorical question. Come on, Data, this way, behind these rocks. We'll keep them guessing until we learn if they really can see in the dark."

Spock had not truly slept, not while he was being held in an enemy cell, but meditation had rested him sufficiently. He heard Chekov groan and stir on the cot, and turned in time to see the human sit up, staring blurrily at him.

"Was not a dream, then," Chekov muttered. "You really are here."

"I am, indeed."

Chekov grunted. "For what good that does us."

The cell door opened without warning, and several armed Watraii entered. One of them gestured peremptorily to Spock.

He dipped his head to them. "I assume by this that you have finished cleaning up the shuttle crash site."

"Come," was all one of them said.

The reason was obvious. Yes, they had finished cleaning up the wreckage of the shuttlecraft. They were ready for the interrogation.

In the instant before the Watraii separated them, Spock told Chekov, "I have never regretted more that Jim Kirk's gifts for command were not mine. He would never have given up on you, as he did not give up on me. I ask forgiveness."

Something not quite clear flickered in Chekov's eyes. It might have been a glimmer of understanding. But, Spock knew, complete forgiveness was still a long way off.

But it will come, Spock thought. *With time. Once we are safely away from here.*

Then the Watraii took him away.

*　　*　　*

Morning, Ruanek thought, getting to his feet and brushing off layers of grit, was definitely not one of those sunny, birds chirping, blue skies brightening things on this world. Dark gray, then lighter gray in this Land of Endless Winds.

No. He lowered his head as a new gust of wind brought a new dust storm swirling about their heads. Land of Endless Winds was definitely too poetic for this world.

"Are you all right, Data?"

The android blinked, then hesitated for a second, running a swift, silent diagnostic check. "I am in perfect functioning order. Despite the continuing problem of this perpetual dust."

At least, Ruanek thought, there was an advantage in scrabbling about this desolate world with an android. Since Data didn't need to slumber in the flesh-and-blood sense of the word, Ruanek had been able to get a fair amount of real sleep without worrying about anyone sneaking up on them. No one had, either. The Watraii hadn't found them in the dark.

And you, Spock? Ruanek wondered. *How did you spend the night? Are you all right? For that matter, I hope that Captain Scott is alive and well, too. And that we all get back to him in time.*

Then Ruanek tensed. "Data, I don't know about this," he said with sudden inexplicable wariness. "Something's not right."

"I do not see anything unusual."

"It's what we *don't* see that bothers me." Ruanek frowned slightly. "Are there any Watraii about?"

"I am not sure. The ground winds are sweeping up too much grit. I suspect that they are finding it difficult to locate us as well."

"I repeat," Ruanek said, "something is definitely not right. Let's get out of this area before it's—"

He broke off as they came face-to-face with a Watraii team making its way through the stinging dust. Both sides froze in mutual surprise for a moment. Then Data pointed out, "Logically speaking, our position is hopeless."

"This isn't the time or place for logic," Ruanek snarled, and hurled himself directly at the Watraii. He hit the nearest one smack in the middle with a savage headbutt, kicked out backward at another, hearing a satisfying grunt of pain as he squarely connected with a kneecap, then whirled to stab a third Watraii in the throat with his stiffened hand. He was at the same time fully aware of Data fighting methodically and efficiently at his side—of course, efficiently, Data was an android—no, he wouldn't let his concentration lapse. But it must be shocking the Watraii that their weapons wouldn't work on Data. And Ruanek was just moving too quickly, in too close, for them to try firing at him. The violence was coming as pure relief—

And it was suddenly over. Ruanek danced in one place, letting himself come down from the warrior high, then settled down to stand panting. "Not bad. Not bad at all. We got them all."

"We did, indeed," Data said without enthusiasm, dragging the bodies one by one into hiding. "We were lucky, Ruanek."

"Luck is an illogical concept, Data. And yes, illogical or not, I know that we were lucky. If we hadn't recovered from surprise a moment before they did—but we did, and they didn't, and we won."

"And now the Watraii will be coming after us with even more enthusiasm."

"Then we will just have to put even more enthusiasm into getting that artifact, won't we?" Ruanek retorted. "I don't have to remind you that the time left before Captain Scott lifts off is running short. So let's not waste any more of that time in moralizing."

"An excellent point," Data said.

TWENTY-THREE

MEMORY

"Best estimate of arrival at a habitable world: 97.3 percent. Should the exploratory shuttle missions confirm our estimate, S'task has given instructions to plan evacuation to the planetary surface."

Karatek removed the memory device, wiped his brow, and headed for the command center to wait for *Shavokh*'s own exploratory shuttles to return home.

Not for the first time, he wished his son-in-law Serevan were present to supervise the docking.

He knew that was hardly fair. Serevan had labored day and night to assemble working shuttles from other, crippled vessels and the remnants of their spare-parts inventory since the surviving fleet entered orbit.

Serevan and Sarissa had been among the first exiles to land on the two planets in this system believed capable of sustaining Vulcan life. He could hardly be expected to be in two places in the same time.

But night and day, where were they? Where were the expeditions from the other ships? S'task had issued the recall order 2.6 hours ago. Some shuttles had already risen from the planets and headed toward their parent ships.

Some. One shuttle from *Sunheart* had crashed back onto the planet's surface, a victim of catastrophic engine failure.

Two would not return. The first had exploded when it touched down. Still another, landing close to a mountain range, had encountered wind shear. Its pilot had been Solor. He might have been unfamiliar with atmospheric conditions after all these years in space, but he had achieved a controlled crash landing remarkable in that neither he nor his crew had been killed. He had reported sufficient supplies to establish a base camp and perform their mission of surveying the terrain and collecting samples. He requested, if possible, that they be retrieved.

Karatek supposed he should have expected that his decision to send *Shavokh*'s last shuttle to bring back his son's team would prompt accusations of favoritism from his old antagonist, Avarak.

Favoritism? When Karatek had lost how many children?

In actual council, of course, Karatek had ignored the outburst. He had disregarded counterattacks that Avarak should have been cast out of *Shavokh* after the mutiny. Instead, he had reminded Avarak that Solor's crew was gathering critical data that the ships had to have. Avarak had glanced away, conceding the point—after having made his own.

Karatek was quite aware that Avarak and his colleagues were not done. A reckoning would come.

In *Shavokh*'s command center, the crew focused as intently on the data streaming in from planets and shuttles as if they were adepts working at levels of meditation that could warm a body, heal a mind, or stop a heart. Another reason for rescuing Solor's crew: there were not many adepts left, and T'Olryn, one of the few survivors of the Seleyan tradition, had accompanied her mate.

Karatek smoothed his hand down the bulkhead against which he stood, savoring the unusual warmth of the battered metal. So close to journey's end, he had ordered his engineers to heat the ship. He had increased ship's gravity to match projected gravitation on the two likeliest sites for planetfall. With S'task's concurrence, he had ordered an increase in rations until, after 56.3 years, the exiles were once again consuming optimal calories for their metabolism.

Personally, the augmented diet made Karatek feel almost ill. No matter; the younger members of the fleet, who would assume the greater share of the physical labor of building settlements, needed to be brought back to full strength.

The bulkhead quivered beneath his hand, almost like a living creature. A living, *sick* creature. Karatek was many years away now from the days of his own engineering expertise, but he recalled enough to know that if that vibration continued to build, the consequences of an extended journey would be— Speculation was pointless now, he reminded himself.

If it were not illogical, Karatek could have said he was warming himself by the light of his new sun. But what actually lured his eyes wasn't just the sun, but the worlds circling it.

The world farthest from the star circled at a forty-eight-degree angle to the ecliptic. It was tiny, a ball of frozen gas, possibly a comet attracted by the star's gravity. With resources so strained, Karatek could not countenance exploring it. Nor could he allow approach or even prolonged observation of the system's gas giants that might, perhaps, have become stars themselves. Others of the planets circled too close; in years to come, those almost airless cinders might make good forward observatories.

But it was the fourth orbit from the sun that drew Karatek's attention and kindled all his hopes. It was occupied by two planets of almost equal size, one circling the other, both circling the sun, in an immense dance. At first sight, the fleet decided to name them after one of Vulcan's oldest myths: the story of the god-brothers. One was dark, one fair. Both had blazing eyes. Sometimes quarreling, but always united, when the universe was formed, they escorted their mother, the morning star, to her home, then upheld her among the stars.

Although S'task had made no songs since leaving the Mother World, he still thought like a poet. When he had suggested those names, everyone had fallen silent: Surak's followers striving for control, the te-Vikram pausing for a moment of prayer. Even the technocrats had looked down.

One of the Two Worlds turned in a day-and-night sequence that was very welcome after so many years of ships' watches. The other world's orbit kept one face locked toward the first, with the other in perpetual darkness.

Those paired worlds were the answer to their quest and to the question of why early sensors had at times shown almost seductively *Minshara*-class readings and, at times, readings that veered between blazing heat and extreme cold.

Even the earliest scans of the dominant world on which S'task had fixed all their hopes showed it to be one of awesome beauty. It was not ruddy, like lost Vulcan, but a treasury of golds and greens, blues and whites. Viewed from orbit, the world displayed three principal landmasses, enriched with lakes and rivers that gleamed like gems set in bloodmetal. Two continents possessed extensive mountain ranges that thrust sharp peaks whose height exceeded that of Mount Seleya into the haze of atmosphere that gentled the world. Extraordinary to refugees from a desert world, this world possessed generous oceans, changeable in color from wine-dark to blood green, and whipped to frenzy by tides from four shimmering moons.

But neither oceans nor mountains were this haven's most conspicuous feature. Possibly because of tidal perturbations as well as volcanic activity, an eruption had cracked the planet's mantle so that it now possessed an immense firefalls. And that was the real reason Karatek had dispatched the rescue mission: Solor's ship had crashed close to the firefalls and could most easily survey the metals in the planet's crust and core.

"*T'Kehr,*" said Avarak, who had managed to serve as communications officer for this watch and, no doubt, as eyes and ears in the command center for Karatek's opponents, "a report is coming in from Serevan, in command of Shuttle Two, now leaving the second planet's gravity well."

From various consoles came murmurs of surprise, even from those who had long studied Surak's *Analects*. Karatek watched as his hand, resting against the warm metal of the bulkhead, trembled. If Sarissa were injured, Serevan would have said so. Wouldn't he?

But Avarak was watching. It was not just a breach of control to show emotion; it was a political liability.

"Put Serevan's report on main speakers," Karatek ordered.

Even given the limitations of his vessel's communications systems, Serevan's voice seemed to boom out over the distance between his vessel and *Shavokh.*

"Report," Karatek ordered his son-in-law.

"*First, your pardon, sir. We encountered some difficulties from zenite fumes before we instituted appropriate decontamination measures.*"

Zenite ore released fumes that turned emotional beings violent, and, apparently, controlled beings emotional.

"Continue," Karatek made himself say.

"We are transmitting deep-scan assay of the most readily accessible veins—that is, accessible beneath the ice. I would not recommend venturing sunside. Much of our equipment is not sufficiently hardened to withstand the heat, which is high enough to melt critical systems."

At Karatek's gesture, Avarak screened the initial report, which made eyebrows rise all over the command center. Half furnace, half glacier, the world locked in orbit around its brother was a virtual treasure house of minerals like duranium, pergium, uridium, and, obviously, zenite.

"We've packed the shuttle's hold with something that I think you'll be glad of—I mean, something that will relieve concerns that we have had for some time: large, high-grade dilithium crystals. At first, we thought they were ice formations . . . again, I ask forgiveness, sir."

"The reason was great," Karatek admitted. Dilithium! The crystals had grown in importance to the fleet as more and more engines were retrofitted to use it, rather than the power of adepts, to boost speed. But the great ships' supply of dilithium had been dwindling for years; *Shavokh* itself was now operating on its last truly symmetrical crystals. Karatek had postponed calculating how using the remaining flawed crystals that remained would further degrade engine performance.

"Report," Karatek ordered.

"We landed on the dark side." As Karatek heard Sarissa's voice, some, but only some, of the tension in his spine eased. *"Some minor injury from frostbite when a suit's heater failed, but we got T'Lura in before she took permanent damage."*

Sarissa was sending back images now of the dark side of the world. It was icy, pocked with frozen pools of gases. Nitrogen volcanoes jutted from the surface, spewing what looked like pallid ice grains into its atmosphere.

Karatek tightened his lips. The fleet's astronomers hypothesized that some worlds in similar locked orbits were marked by a "twilight zone," created by planetary libration, in which the climate was less extreme. What twilight zone this world possessed, however, was apparently very slight. At least, however, the world's atmosphere was sufficiently dense that it hadn't frozen or bled off into space.

"Scans are showing immense reserves of water trapped approximately three hundred kilometers beneath the surface of the ice," Sarissa reported. *"Apologies for the imprecision, but it wasn't just the zenite that made us decide to limit our exposure to this world."*

The scans also showed great veins of radioactive ore.

"I wanted to limit biohazards," Serevan said. *"Even brief exposure to mutagenic metreon radiation isn't a thing we considered prudent to risk. I recommend immediate prophylactic radiation treatment on our return."*

Once that team returned, the shuttle and *Shavokh* itself should be decontaminated. He raised his eyebrows again, seeing projections of a 38.5 percent potential here for thalaron radiation, which could build up to levels that would vaporize everything it touched. No. That number had to be inflated. The only scientist he knew who had ever tried to explore the technology to create thalaron radiation had been *T'Kehr* Varekat.

"What's that?" Serevan's voice sounded fainter. Either communications were shorting out, or he had turned away.

"Thrusters? Very well. Sir," his voice increased in strength, *"we're getting some thruster trouble that I need to look at before we try to link up with* Shavokh. *I'm hearing shouting, too. Shuttle Two out!"*

"I want to be informed the moment Shuttles Two and Three dock," Karatek ordered. "The instant their personnel have boarded, their injured have been treated, and—" He saw that Avarak was not the only person present whose face bore positively un-Vulcan expressions of curiosity and greed. "—their samples have been off-loaded, call a council meeting."

TWENTY-FOUR

NOW

U.S.S. ALLIANCE
STARDATE 54107.6

Ensign Tara Keel of Starfleet looked uncertainly about the *Alliance*'s narrow but well-stocked and spotlessly clean hydroponics bay. Then she pretended to be very interested in the row of bright blue Antevian lilies to give herself an excuse for standing there, thinking, just in case anyone else came in and saw her. She was human, young, fair-skinned and blond, and fairly new aboard the *Alliance*.

The ensign was also very worried by now. This was just not the sort of mission that Tara had expected when she'd started her Starfleet career back in . . . well, it really hadn't been so long ago, really, Tara had to admit. This was actually her first shipboard assignment.

"Tara?"

She turned with a gasp, but then relaxed again. The newcomer was just one of her fellow new ensigns, N'Kriil, covered with soft brown fur that made him look like a child's toy with neat little claws. Like Tara, he hadn't been in service very long, and like Tara, this was his first shipboard assignment. "Whatever made you come down here?"

"Probably for the same reason you did, N'Kriil. No one comes by here on this duty rotation."

"Right." They stood in awkward silence for a few moments. Then he burst out, "You don't like this, either, do you?"

She didn't have to ask what he meant. "It's not up to us to like or dislike it. We made the choice to follow our captain."

The K'taris ensign's fur ruffled up suddenly, betraying his uneasiness. As it settled back down again, he shivered once to get it all back in place, then said, "The choice we made was to actually *do* something. To help someone. To, oh, you know, 'boldly go' and all that. All we're doing is breaking Starfleet law, risking our careers, and . . . waiting."

Tara absently played with one of the lilies. "We don't really have much of an alternative."

N'Kriil sighed. "I guess not. Not at this point. We can't very well up and leave. But I can't say I'm happy about it, either."

"Do you two have latent herbicidal tendencies?" a voice drawled behind them. The ensigns whirled guiltily and came to full attention at the sight of their Bolian superior. "Lieutenant Dralan!" N'Kriil exclaimed. "Uh, sir, we uh, were just . . ."

"Or is it something personal between you and the lilies, perhaps?"

Tara looked down at her hands in dismay and found she'd uprooted three of the bulbs. Guiltily, she stuck them back into their pots and tamped down the soil. The lilies drooped sadly, and she tried with N'Kriil's help for a desperate moment to get them back upright.

The lieutenant sighed. "Ensigns, please stop torturing those plants and get back to your stations."

"Uh, yes, sir."

"Right away, sir."

Lieutenant Dralan, whose specialty was weaponry but whose hobby was horticulture, ran his slim blue finger knowledgeably up each lily's central stalk, hitting each plant's central nerve, and the revitalized plants sprang back up from their droop, returned to proper life.

If only it were so simple to revitalize our crew, he thought. *Those two children—I didn't have to ask to know what they were discussing. Bah, Starfleet never should have forced so many newcomers on us. They have neither common sense nor patience.*

But you weeded a garden only as it grew. And you couldn't weed it at all till you saw which were the weeds and which the plants worth saving.

Still, Dralan thought, absently running a hand over his bald blue head, he supposed it was another one of those unwelcome messages that would have to be passed on to the captain. Just as, he thought with a sigh, the other officers had been doing.

The *Alliance*'s engine room was a neat, tidily run place with nothing out of order and everything humming peacefully as it should. But within the engine room, one of the new techs was not paying any heed to his surroundings or to much of anything else.

Anything, that was, except for the current situation. He was a Bolian youngster named Haril, and he'd jumped at the chance of joining the crew of the *Alliance* after hearing all about its fine war service, thinking that this would be a terrific way to get his career going.

All it seemed likely to do right now was send his career zooming straight into a court-martial.

Why did I agree to this? Haril mentally berated himself. *I had a chance to get off the ship before this mission began. Why did I stay? Now my career's going to be over before it begins, and we'll probably all be court-martialed, and I won't ever be able to—*

"Ensign Haril! What the bloody hell do you think you're doing?"

To Haril's horror, he realized that was definitely Chief Engineer Atherton's voice. To his greater horror, he realized only as she knocked his hand away that he'd been about to let it rest on a panel of controls, some of which were already lit by his last careless move. Oh no, no, no, if he'd been just a little clumsier, he could have fouled up the ship's ventilation system completely.

Feeling himself blushing an embarrassing cobalt blue, he muttered, "I'm sorry, sir."

Atherton was a handsome blond human woman, tall and slim, the sort who would somehow manage to look elegantly self-possessed no matter what the situation or what she was wearing. Even in this situation, even when her blue eyes were fairly blazing with anger—

Anger at me, Haril thought miserably. *Justifiable anger.*

"Sorry!" she shouted. "You damned well should be sorry, Ensign! Tell me, were you simply bored and daydreaming, or were you deliberately trying to sabotage us?"

"I . . . don't have any excuse. My mind was wandering, Commander," Haril muttered. "It won't happen again."

"That," she said grimly, "is quite true. Because if it does, I swear you'll be spaced. Now get back to work!"

Arms folded, fists clenched, Atherton watched the young Bolian hurry back to his proper station. Only then did she allow herself the luxury of letting out her breath in a long, angry sigh.

Dammit, these youngsters were starting to get in the way of everyone. They weren't bad kids, and they were doing their best to learn on this . . . this on-the-job training session, but they hadn't been on any perilous missions before. No, most of them hadn't been on *any* missions before, let alone one like this, one that was officially unsanctioned by Starfleet.

Yet another report that will have to be made to our beleaguered captain, she thought with a touch of genuine sympathy for Saavik. *I wish that I didn't need to bother her yet again, but for the safety of the ship, she must know all about what's going on.*

As though Captain Saavik didn't already have enough to worry even the staunchest of Vulcans.

Worry, Saavik told heself, was illogical. It was also counterproductive.

Ah yes, and it is also a ridiculously difficult emotion to keep under control—particularly right now.

There wasn't much that she could do about dealing with it. Saavik could hardly go into meditation here on the bridge, or even use any mental disciplines that might reduce her worry but dull her alertness at the same time. And given their location so near to the Watraii homeworld, she could hardly leave the bridge for more than a few moments.

So be it, Saavik told herself. She wasn't a raw recruit like those youngsters on board, who couldn't yet quite master their skills or self-control. Spock had been in more difficult situations than this, and so had the other three with him. And so had she, for that matter.

Think of our time on Romulus, Saavik reminded herself. *Think of how close Spock and I both came to death. Yes, and think of how much poor Ruanek had to give up to bring Spock back to Vulcan . . . and to me.*

Data, too, had faced both danger and death during his Starfleet career, including several encounters with the Borg, and had survived both. Scotty had, as well, and had even managed, in his own clever way, to outwit death. They were hardly new to peril, any of the four. . . .

Again, not like the youngsters aboard her ship. They were beginning to concern her, since Starfleet had trained them well in every aspect of shipboard behavior except the fine art of waiting and doing nothing.

They will learn. With time.

But the reports that she was almost constantly receiving from various crew members were not precisely heartening. The youngsters were becoming, if not a definite liability, a potential danger.

We need a distraction. Something useful or absorbing for them to do. Something to occupy their uneasy young minds. . . .

"Captain," Lieutenant Abrams said suddenly. "I'm picking up incoming ships . . . three of them, heading directly toward us."

"Cloaking on," Saavik ordered.

Nothing.

"Lieutenant. Didn't you hear me?"

"Cloaking isn't . . . isn't coming up, Captain."

Wonderful. They had been given defective equipment by the Romulans. No, on second thought, she couldn't see Charvanek ever being that small.

Blame Romulan postwar budget cutbacks, Saavik thought, and ordered, "Shields up. Engineering, see what you can do about restoring cloaking. Lieutenant, put the ships on-screen, please."

As the image came up, Lieutenant Abrams added what by now was the obvious identification to everyone who'd been through this before: "They're Watraii ships, Captain, and they're on a direct course for their homeworld."

The Watraii captains and crew couldn't help but see the intruders blocking their way. Unfortunate. And they couldn't be allowed to reach the planet and spread the alarm.

"They're powering up weapons," Abrams continued.

This isn't exactly the distraction that I had in mind, Saavik thought.

"Red alert," she ordered. "Battle stations. Weapons at ready."

Saavik didn't waste any time trying to open a channel to the Watraii. What could she possibly say that would slow them down or stop them? *It's not what you think; we just coincidentally happen to be here; we just incidentally have to stop you from going home?*

"Lieutenant Suhur," she ordered, "open a channel to our Klingon allies."

"We see them," the two Klingon captains replied almost as one before Suhur could speak. JuB-Chal added, *"You have the right of first kill."*

Klingon battle courtesy. *How kind of you,* Saavik thought wryly. "We have a team on the surface. We cannot get too far away from them."

"Understood," JuB-Chal snapped.

Tor'Ka said cheerfully, *"Take out the center ship, Captain Saavik, and leave the others to us!"*

No time for more elaborate strategy than that. The nearest Watraii ship, the one the Klingons had "given" to her, was opening fire, and Saavik ordered, "Evasive action—"

Green flame shot by the *Alliance.* "Complete miss," Abrams reported tersely.

"Return fire," Saavik ordered.

I do not want to kill, she thought, as she had in every battle throughout the Dominion War, *but if I must kill, then let it be quickly and cleanly done.*

TWENTY-FIVE

MEMORY

As Solor limped into the wardroom that *Shavokh*'s council now used as a meeting place, Karatek and the other elders rose in respect. His son still wore the tattered flightsuit from his mission. He had one arm strapped across his chest. A bruise as long as one sharp cheekbone, but far wider, discolored the left side of his face.

Bowing his own respect with great care, Solor took the seat Karatek indicated right beneath where some long-dead artist had painted a mural of lost Vulcan, all reds and crystals. Leaning forward with even more caution, he inserted a glowing crystal in the council's recorder.

"Activating flight log," said Karatek's son.

Abruptly, the council chamber went dark. One wall blossomed into an image of a pale green sky, glowing golden clouds, and a horizon that seemed to ripple with long grasses below a high range of mountains. The image trembled slightly as the shuttle's ancient engines braked, failed, then tried to brake again. This time, the shuttle slowed.

Karatek willed himself to relax and to observe, only observe, the data Solor presented. His apprehension was illogical. After all, if the brakes had failed, his son would not now be seated before the council.

A range of black basalt peaks grew more formidably jagged as the shuttle descended. Beyond the mountain range glittered an immense sea, its deep blue tinged with blood green, provoking gasps of wonder.

How beautiful this new world was. Karatek found himself craning his neck, as if he actually thought it would help him see the farthest tip of the continent, where an eruption of steam marked the place where the firefalls gushed into the sea.

"It will be the study of a dozen lifetimes," whispered *Shavokh's* astronomer, "to study that world."

"A hundred lifetimes," said a bioscientist whose voice held the satisfaction of a creator, or a parent. "A dozen just to map it, the remainder to catalog and name its different forms of life."

"Although, logically, this subject requires extensive further study, we recorded no signs of what we would consider sentient life," came Solor's recorded voice.

More grounds for relief. What if they had found sapient life? Would they have voted to patch up the ships to whatever extent possible and journey back into the long night? Just as well they would not have to send that problem to council.

"Let us watch the report," said T'Vysse, seated in one of the side seats reserved for witnesses. "You can speculate in private session."

Solor's shuttle banked so fast that others gasped too, this time in shock. A shadow passed across the wall, followed by another and another. At least four council members ducked in their chairs as the shadows seemed to whirl, then resolved into closer focus. They faced immense winged creatures whose plumage glittered in all the colors of the sea so far beneath. They flew in formation, like a fleet, fanning out from a gigantic central flier whose feathers seemed silver with great age. Behind it flew creatures considerably smaller, clutching immense eggs in their talons.

"We think those are females," said Solor.

It seemed a reasonable hypothesis. The winged creatures in the center of that flock were smaller, their plumage less conspicuous. They were flanked by larger, more brilliant companions.

Again, the images wavered, spun, lurched, and tilted widely as the shuttle, almost out of control, fought for attitude, then altitude, than any sort of landing other than a crash.

"First approximation analysis." Solor's voice spoke out of the darkness. "We encountered a seasonal migration of winged creatures that we can only compare to Vulcan's *shavokh,* although larger by a factor of at least three. Trying to avoid them almost brought us down. The rapid change in attitude caused a brief power loss, and we . . . encountered wind shear."

"Prepare for emergency landing," came Solor's voice in the recording. Even then, he sounded composed. *"Activating webs. Assume crash positions."*

His voice barely rose. Karatek suppressed a sensation of justified pride at his son's skill.

"You told us you crashed without serious injuries!" Avarak leapt to his feet.

For a moment, the fascinating images of the flight recorder dimmed. "I did not lie, *T'Kehr,*" Solor said. "The injuries occurred later. The mission's bioscientist was injured attempting to close in on one of the winged creatures when it settled for the night. Healer T'Olryn, she who is my *wife*," Solor emphasized the title to his former rival, "thinks his sight can be saved or, failing that, compensated for with an appropriate prosthetic. The healer will make her report as soon as she can be spared from attending our crew."

Now, sunset covered the broken shuttle's landing site. Four different colors of moonlight illuminated the wreckage. Karatek could clearly see at the horizon the brilliant thread of fire marking where the firefalls glowed in the night and the dark cloud at its foot.

Solor stopped the flight record.

"Those of you who have the opportunity to land are well advised to take it," he said. "Salt and ionization make the air both refreshing and invigorating. Not all the smells are pleasant, but we are habituated to that. When the wind changed, we believed we could detect a hint of sulfur either from the firefalls or from much smaller vents closer to the crash site. We saw considerable evidence of vulcanism." His voice warmed. "I remember. But the world is both cooler and wetter than Vulcan: this land should be fertile. Very fertile."

He started the recording once more. "On first view, however, the new world is both aesthetically and scientifically appealing."

Karatek had last heard that note in Solor's voice after the birth of his first child.

"Never mind aesthetics. Has that world got *metal?*" demanded Vorealt. He had been born in exile, and Serevan had often heard him declare that never, never would he live on a planet.

A screen lit as Solor accessed a different part of the mission report.

"Trace elements in the soil," came the voice of T'Olryn as she entered the room, one hand out to keep her consort safely in his chair. "I believe when the vegetation is tested, we will find not only that our physiology can digest it, but that it contains trace elements that have long been absent from our diet."

Solor added, "I also believe, judging from the erratic motion patterns of some of the creatures we observed, that fermentation and brewing are quite possible. With suitable quality control, we might be able to create fine wines and ales."

"We brought back samples of the planet life." T'Olryn opened a sample case, and poured out what looked to be fruit lusher than anyone had seen on Vulcan since its polar ice caps had shrunk and the deserts crept from the equatorial realms to encroach on much of the land. The fruits glowed golden and purple and teal, and perfumed the ship's recycled air with the freshness of a new world.

"Where is T'Sanvi, your metallurgist?" asked Avarak. "Still with the healers?"

"We lost her," said T'Olryn, looking away. "I grieve with thee."

Murmurs of horror and regret rose, even from the disciples of Surak. It was not illogical to regret the loss of a young life. Karatek shook his head.

"Lesson learned," Solor addressed the council. "I regret to say that we were ill prepared for the hazards of planetfall. T'Sanvi, while studying the minerals by the shore of the pond from which we were drawing water, was attacked by a predator approximately 6.7 meters in length. We believe it to be amphibious, as it was scaled and possessed webbed claws. It dragged her into a pond whose depth we were not able to ascertain due to the vegetation with which it was clogged. We were unable to recover her body."

He lowered his head.

T'Olryn continued, her face remote as if she fought to put distance between herself and a distasteful subject. "We found eggs and much smaller specimens of the creature, one of which we sac-

rificed. Judging from its dentition, I believe these creatures se-
crete their prey beneath the water until . . ." She held up a hand.
"We have named this predator the '*veruul.*'"

"Avert!" cried a te-Vikram in the back of the room.

Veruul was the name of a monster that, in ancient legend, was
said to stalk the Womb of Fire. Any encounter with such a creature
was fatal, which explained why it was more myth than science.

"I realize the word is improper," said T'Olryn. "It was not *my*
choice."

Solor leaned over to touch his bondmate's fingers. "May we go
on?" he asked. "Because of the time we spent on the planet's surface, we were able to gather data in excess of initial mission
parameters."

Lines and equations scrolled across the wall. It lit with formu-
las and glowed with spectral lines.

"What about metal?"

"Before T'Sanvi encountered the *veruul,* her first-approximation
analysis was that the assay of such samples as she had had time to
collect was low: disappointingly so. However, she hypothesized
that the planet, like all *Minshara*-class worlds, possessed a molten
rock mantle surrounding a liquid metal outer core and a solid inner
core composed of metal crystals. We had hoped to set down nearer
the firefalls to take samples, but decided that our distance from the
falls and our recovery shuttle's pickup time made such an expedition imprudent.

"Our working hypothesis: We have two choices if we wish to
exploit the world's heavy metals. Either we dig down to the mantle, or we somehow extract them from the magma in the firefalls.
For both of those propositions, however, we need metals: metals
and a level of systems hardening for which, at least, we would
have to cannibalize at least one of the ships."

"In short, a vicious circle," said Avarak.

"An illogical image, but quite accurate," Solor replied. The two men locked glances. Neither gave way.

"Given these hazards, is this even a world we wish to populate? All the ships are sparsely populated now. We might redistribute one ship's population to facilitate mining operations, repair the remaining ships, then move on."

Karatek let the discussion ebb and flow about him. What he longed for was to see this fair new world for himself. What he would settle for was a conversation of ships' leaders, including S'task himself, immediately after this meeting.

"Before we begin," Karatek asked, "in the opinion of the exploration party, is this world worth further study?"

There was land. There was vegetation. There was even water in greater abundance than Karatek had ever heard of. In Vulcan's history, there had been times when people had killed for temporary possession of even one meager, brackish well on the Forge, let alone the wealth of water that awaited them on the planet below.

That abundance of water would remove one justification for aggression, while the scarcity of metal would restrict one means. Those were both points in favor of the new world. The start of exile had been marred by violence: it was logical to be concerned that resettlement might be corrupted too.

"I do not think that consensus will favor repair, redistribution of ships' populations, and continued travel." Karatek tried to reach for consensus. "The daily sight of so much land and water beneath us might be too great a temptation to potential deserters. Let me ask: Do we, in truth, have another option?"

"What about the companion world?"

He heard muffled protests from the te-Vikram on the council.

Even more than four hundred and fifty years, real time, after the last ship left Vulcan, it remained their pride that they, not the clans of city and hill, had wandered Vulcan's deepest deserts.

"In that case," said Karatek, "we must await the report of the mission commanded by my daughter and her consort."

"You mean they're not back yet?" warred with "We already live walled off from the universe!"

And the fight was back on.

It had been a long time since the fleet had had to wage this much peace. Karatek only hoped that they were up to it.

TWENTY-SIX

NOW

WATRAII HOMEWORLD
STARDATE 54107.8

As his Watraii guards marched him down the now-familiar dull
gray corridor, Spock calmed his mind and body with carefully
chosen Vulcan disciplines. It was his turn to be questioned by the
Watraii, and if he was to make the most of the chance, his mind
must be clear, self-controlled, and prepared.

It was, save for the fact that he was a prisoner, not very different from any other ambassadorial diplomatic meeting.

Spock was marched into the command center, and calmly took
the indicated chair before the guards could shove him into it. They
took up their posts to left, right, and behind him. The unspoken message was clear: No restraints were needed with them at the ready.

Don't be concerned, he told them silently. *I am not going anywhere, not just yet.*

Of course he was kept waiting for quite some time, sitting in utter silence. It didn't surprise him at all. This was a common tactic for almost all interrogators, Spock knew: Keep the prisoner waiting so that he might weaken himself by fear and his mind's own horrific imaginings. But that tactic meant nothing to a Vulcan, Spock thought. He was hardly liable to weaken himself in such an emotional and illogical way.

Besides, waiting was nothing new to him. Those ambassadors who became successful in their jobs soon grew used to the fine art of keeping calm while being kept waiting by this bureaucrat or that.

As Spock had expected (and, indeed, had calculated out the probability to 97.659 percent), his initial questioner was to be no one less than the Watraii commander.

Excellent.

The commander entered without any fanfare, flanked by his guards, and sat down at his desk. There was a moment of silence as he studied Spock from behind the protection of his mask, presumably hunting for any signs of weakness, any signs of fear.

He found none. Apparently utterly at ease, Spock said, "I assume that the damage from the shuttle crash has been repaired, and I grieve with you if there were any deaths."

"It is not your place to assume anything," the commander retorted. "Nor is it your right to grieve."

Spock returned, with great gentleness, "Ah, but has it not been said that the death of one weakens us all?"

"We have not been weakened. And it is not your place to question me."

"I quite understand." Spock leaned forward ever so slightly, his entire body language conveying sympathy. "You have every reason to be concerned, what with the burden of all your people on your shoulders."

"We share the burden. And you are not to turn the interrogation!"

Spock sat back again, and folded his hands in his lap. "Please, ask what you would."

Although it was, of course, impossible to see the Watraii's expression, Spock read from the set of the other's shoulders that the commander was definitely off balance. Prisoners were not expected or supposed to act like this.

"Who are you?" the commander began.

"I am, as I have said, Ambassador Spock of Vulcan."

"You are a Romulan!"

"No, sir, I am not."

"Why do you deny what I can plainly see?"

"Appearances, as we both know, can be deceptive," Spock said mildly. "I am of Vulcan, as I say. The Romulans have been sundered from us for over two thousand Vulcan years."

Spock's trained ambassadorial skills caught the slightest tensing of the commander's hands, and pressed the advantage, adding, "You are logically not from this world, either."

"How can you know that?"

"Please, sir. The evidence is obvious. This is a primitive world, with almost no flora and possibly no fauna. It is too young a world for complex organisms to have evolved. Yet you are here."

"You are too clever," the commander snapped.

"I am merely a Vulcan trained to logic. You can understand, I am sure, that Vulcan cannot be held responsible for the actions of those who left their homeworld."

"I understand that you are trying to turn this to your advantage." The commander leaned sharply forward. "Let us assume that you really are what you say, a being called a Vulcan who is merely related to the enemy. Why are you here, and where are the others?"

"I will answer the second question first. I do not know the whereabouts of any others. It is possible that the two who landed with me left the ship. More than that, I cannot tell you."

"Cannot or will not?"

"Sir, from what I have seen of your people, they can hardly be worried about the whereabouts of two individuals. And I am willing to swear by any oath you wish that I have no idea where they are. Were any dangerous weapons involved, surely your scanners would have already detected them." Spock leaned back ever so slightly, someone at his ease but friendly. "As to why I am here, it is as I've said: I wish to learn the truth."

"Why?"

"If I told you that I hated the idea of injustice, would you believe me? Yet it is so. And if I told you that I believe peace far preferable than war, would you believe that? Yet that is so, too."

"Then you wish us to forget the wrongs done us, the terrible crimes?"

"No. Not that. I wish to learn the truth, nothing more, nothing less."

"You are arrogant for a prisoner!"

"No. It is precisely because I care about living beings—all living beings—that I ask. I have seen your children. I have seen no laughter on their faces, no joy in their eyes. And I ask this: Were the Watraii always this cold, this vindictive?"

The commander froze. "Ask rather whether it was the expulsion from their former homeworld that turned them into what we are today. There is no time, no place, no room for softness in our lives."

"But why come here? Why to this harsh planet?"

"Can you not guess, clever Vulcan? When we were driven out from our home, our own worlds, we chose a world as inhospitable as possible to punish us for our loss of our former home and to forge us into a weapon fit to regain it. We spend our lives in a quest for worthiness."

The truth was in every word.

The truth, at any rate, Spock thought warily, *as the current Watraii believe it.*

Very carefully, he began, "Vulcan belongs to an interplanetary organization known as the Federation. If you brought your case before the Federation, it would be heard."

"I cannot believe that."

"Why not? Your fight is not with the Federation. Hear me out. I know that you are concerned for your people. I saw that when the shuttle crashed. I know that you ache for your children. I heard that in your voice. For the sake of your people, for the sake above all of your children, believe me. Take your quarrel to the Federation."

The commander was silent for a long while. Then, almost reluctantly he said, "Tell me more."

Chekov started as the cell door slid open, and his heart began to race. Spock . . . ?

No. It was merely a small pack of four Watraii.

"Yes, yes, I know," he said wearily. "It's time for my daily bout of exercise. Mustn't let the prisoner get flabby."

But as he walked down the corridor between them, Chekov realized with every step that he no longer felt like the tired old man he'd been ever since the Watraii took him.

Hope is an amazing thing.

Of course there was also that slightly lighter gravity, and his slightly greater bone mass helping him as well. Yes, and there was also the fact that after the mind-meld, his brain was clear again, clear enough to realize one useful little fact: The Watraii had come to take him for granted.

Your mistake, gospoda.

He groaned and staggered slightly, hand going to his chest, contorting his face in feigned agony. Did the Watraii understand heart attacks?

They understood that something was wrong. They closed in, supporting him with strong grips. "Do you require medication?" one of them asked warily.

Oh, I can just imagine what Watraii medics are like! No, thank you! "Too late . . ." Chekov moaned piteously. "I will talk . . . to the commander . . . get my mind clear . . . before I . . . before I . . ."

He slumped in the Watraii guards' arms. Ha, yes, should have been an actor because they were accepting his act as real. Far more credible than that old "nuclear vessels" routine had ever been. They were half carrying him in the direction of that central command room he'd seen so many times—good! Just what he wanted. Before they could figure out that he was faking, though, he'd better have a plan. Get himself and Spock out of here.

Really? One old man against so many warriors?

Yes?

Oh yes.

Head drooping, hiding his face, Chekov smiled ever so slightly. And, sagging in the Watraii arms as he was, he looked directly at the holster of one guard's sidearm, there within such easy reach.

"Helm!" Saavik shouted as the *Alliance* swerved out of the enemy's way. "Keep us clear. Weapons, fire at will."

Those ships must not get by us. They must not sound a warning.

She and her chosen enemy captain played a swift, deadly game, sending their ships on sharply darting, twisting evasive courses.

The Watraii ship took a direct hit that sent it slewing sideways in space. The *Alliance* followed, but the Watraii managed to get off a glancing hit that shook the *Alliance*. Saavik's breath caught in her throat. "Damage report," she ordered.

"Minor damage, deck five," came the quick reply. *"No casualties."*

"Follow the enemy—"

No need. Whatever damage they'd already done was enough. The Watraii ship suddenly tore apart in a violent burst of flame. The shock wave hit the *Alliance,* but Saavik, prepared, warned, "Hold it steady . . . steady."

Even at that moment, the Klingon ships got in two direct hits on their chosen targets, damaging two Watraii ships badly enough to start a series of explosions that ended with the Watraii ships disappearing into a white-hot cloud. The Klingons let out ear-splitting howls of triumph.

But Lieutenant Suhur warned, "Captain, I believe one ship did have just enough time to send off a message burst to the surface."

Spock, Saavik thought. *Ah, Spock.*

But there was nothing she could do to help him.

". . . and so if you are willing," Spock continued to the Watraii commander, "a Federation emissary could speak with the Watraii and—"

A sudden commotion started up near the doorway. As Spock broke off in surprise, a Watraii rushed into the room. At the commander's signal, he approached and murmured into the commander's ear. Spock's Vulcan hearing caught ". . . attack on Watraii ships . . ."

Saavik. What just happened out there?

"So," the commander all but snarled at Spock, "is this your idea of peace and truth?"

At that moment, the door flew open. To Spock's utter astonishment, Chekov burst into the room like an image out of some impossible Terran adventure vid, an old man with young eyes and armed with a Watraii sidearm in each hand.

"Everyone stay where you are! Except you, Spock. Come on, man, we're getting out of here!"

Were Spock wholly human, he might have thought, *Oh hell, not now!* Instead, he merely reminded himself that it would be illogical to regret regaining one's freedom.

Together, they hurried from the room.

TWENTY-SEVEN

MEMORY

"Sarissa and her mate have returned from surveying the second planet, a world of fire and ice. Although their mission returned with considerable information, five members of their crew were lost. Some council members have already called this expedition a disaster and are demanding a formal inquiry. I am attempting to prevent an investigation from becoming a trial.

"I find it exceedingly unlikely that my children would demonstrate that level of negligence or incompetence. I have, however, no further information. Thus far, their records are sealed, and the healers have quarantined them and their surviving crew members for additional decontamination procedures. It would be not only illogical to expect my daughter-in-law T'Olryn to break confidence, it would be unethical. Being responsible for those of us who survive, S'task has requested permission to listen to today's council session via private communications link with me."

Karatek, along with many of the crews' families, had been waiting by the main bay when, to everyone's more or less concealed surprise, it had been Sarissa who had landed the shuttle. In fact, she had been the only member of the mission to have walked away from it. Serevan had been carried out unconscious, along with the rest of the surviving crew. There were also four bodies, one sealed in the sort of bag used to store materials contaminated by radiation. And one person was missing.

Seeing the blind, pain-filled expression on Sarissa's face, Karatek had started forward. He wanted to comfort his daughter as he had the night he had found her and her brother hiding outside the ruins of their home, but the healers had intervened. Working with practiced, compassionate skill, they had separated the shuttle crews' families from the general ship's population. They attended the families of the dead to meditation chambers, and took the children of the one crew member whose body had not returned into their protective care. They handed out badges and medications against radiation sickness, even to bystanders. Engineers in protective suits moved in to decontaminate the shuttle or, if they were unable to, to put it on autopilot and jettison it.

Although T'Vysse had joined their daughter and her mate in quarantine, Karatek could not be spared. Since then, he had seen none of the shuttle crew. No one knew more than the fact that five people had died on the mission to the world of fire, shadow, and ice; and one body was missing.

The truth was bad. The rumors were worse.

Released, finally, from their isolation, Sarissa and Serevan marched in, shoulder to shoulder. From his seat behind the council table, Solor made as if to rise and join his brother and sister, but a characteristic elder-sister glance held him in his seat.

Although Karatek was certain from the way Solor held his arm that he had shed the protective sling too early, he seemed to be making a good recovery.

Sarissa looked pale. Not surprising: Karatek knew what the antiradiation drugs could do to even a healthy system.

The real damage she had taken showed in the wariness of her eyes and in her body language, as if at any moment she expected to have to fight. Serevan, head and shoulders taller than she, stood at her back as if guarding it. His eyes flicked about the room, showing him to be at least as hyperalert as his wife. He sported remarkable bruises around both eyes, as if he wore a mask. From time to time he started, as if nervous—and this from a man who had studied passion's mastery since childhood!

What had they encountered on that two-faced world, half ice, half forge?

Karatek's children reached the council table and bowed respect. They nodded refusal of the seats offered them—grudgingly, in some cases. Witnesses sat; prisoners stood. It appeared that Sarissa was indeed standing upon something: not just her dignity, but a considerable outrage.

"I offer my apologies," she spoke first, as she usually did. "We would have reported earlier, but the healers had us under observation."

"Their quarantine procedures were both appropriate and thorough," Serevan added. "On our trip back, the entire shuttle's complement was exposed to zenite fumes. They produced extremely aggressive responses, especially from those not in control of their emotions."

"We had a mutiny!" Sarissa interrupted. It was clear from the way her voice rose, high and hard, that her mastery of her own emotions was still incomplete. "We had already suffered one casualty. Teveron died when he ventured too far out onto ice before its thickness could be tested. It broke, and he plunged into a pool of liquid nitrogen. We had to leave him there.

"T'Reni was caught in a rockfall. She survived extrication after 3.2 hours, but received such severe radiation burns that she refused all but palliative care. We brought her back to her family and have taken appropriate prophylactic measures for our own radiation exposure."

A little blindly, Sarissa flung out her hand, and Serevan touched fingertips to hers. "Tell them, husband," she said.

"The other deaths were the result of exposure to zenite fumes, which cause paranoia, fear, and violence," the tall engineer took up the story. "Three of the crew tried to mutiny on the trip back to the ship." He paused, allowing the enormity of their loss to sink in. "I hold myself personally responsible."

"That is illogical," snapped Sarissa. "After Adenkar used *talshaya* on Healer Salvir, you went down there to try to restore order or at least control the damages. I sealed myself in the pilots' compartment and made maximum speed back to the ship."

"I should have succeeded," Serevan looked down out of those bruised eyes. He turned toward the council. "I did indeed control the crew. And I secured our samples. But I too was exposed to the zenite past the ability of my own meditations to control it. I should report myself unfit for duty, but I cannot see how my people can get along without my work. That is, I admit, self-centered and potentially a side effect of my own exposure to the zenite. I do not offer that as an excuse, but as data to aid the council in making its decision."

"You're calling yourself mad because you have emotions, man, and you let them loose once in how many years?" cried Evoras, who headed up bioengineering. He was a small, intense man whom no one had ever accused of mastering his passions.

Throughout the long journey, however, he had consistently turned in superb work. A pragmatist, he voted sometimes with Karatek and sometimes with the technocrats, and even, sometimes, with the te-Vikram blocs.

"Now, to borrow a word you seem fond of overusing," Evoras continued, "if you want to accuse yourself of illogic, I'd call that illogical, too. To me, it sounds as if you made the best of a very bad situation. If you hadn't gone down there and been successful beyond what anyone on board this ship had a right to expect, we'd be mourning your death. Unless, of course, you are enjoying your overreaction . . ."

Serevan turned toward Evoras, then stiffened as if, finally, he revealed just how much damage he had taken in the fight to preserve the shuttle.

"Once the surviving crew were all adequately restrained and medicated—" Karatek assumed that meant Serevan had personally beaten them unconscious, then kept them drugged. "—I succeeded in sealing the laboratory so that air circulation would not contaminate the entire ship. I suited up, vented atmosphere in the compartment, and sealed the zenite samples. About that time, one of the onboard computers failed and . . ." He paused. "I must confess that I screamed and wrecked it. When I finally succeeded in controlling my emotions, I realized I had become unreliable. So I documented my reactions, then injected myself too with my suit's tranquilizers. I am told you saw Sarissa bring the shuttle back in. My wife saved us."

"Highly satisfactory performance," whispered S'task in Karatek's ear through the tiny metal bead that transmitted the council's proceedings to *Rea's Helm.* *"No blame. Tell them. Tell them now."*

"T'Kehr S'task instructs me to say that he considers your performance highly satisfactory," Karatek repeated.

"There will, nonetheless, be a full hearing," said Avarak.

Another fault line in the accord among the ships, Karatek thought. It was one thing to question his own judgment: he had inherited responsibility for the ship, not trained for it. But to gainsay praise from S'task, who rarely spoke these days and even more rarely praised was very interesting indeed. And potentially quite dangerous.

Sarissa looked down, flushing olive. "We thank *T'Kehr* S'task for his generosity. We are honored."

She handed the record of their mission to the council.

"We have other mineral specimens as well. The planet is . . . as we hypothesized. You will receive T'Neveith's report. She remains immobilized with spinal injuries and sends her apologies, along with her observation that she has never encountered anything like the richness of the pergium deposits and duranium lodes we found less than three meters beneath the surface of the ice."

"The dilithium crystals—" Serevan reached into his belt pouch and scattered a precious handful upon the table, before producing a sealed envelope of crystals that seemed to glow. "These crystals are unprocessed. I must ask you not to open the sealed crystals. The inclusions they contain are radioactive, so you will want to check your badges at the completion of this meeting. But they should boost power production by a factor of at least 3.5."

"So, in other words," Vorealt interrupted, "we have finally found the Treasury of Erebus. I may have to admit I have found a use for planets after all, or at least this one world."

Serevan raised an eyebrow at Vorealt, but refused to take up his fellow engineer's challenge. He was tiring visibly, but he waved away the offer of a chair, even of water, now that S'task had indicated his approval. "The myth of an ice demon hiding in the perpetual snows at Mount Seleya's peak strikes me as even more illogical than most myths. This is a *Quaris*-class world, and an outlier even for such worlds in terms of mineral deposits. One expects conditions to be extreme."

S'task's whisper sounded in Karatek's ear. *"Ask about life downworld. What of biospecimens? Ask if their healer found any. Did they . . . ?"*

Had they found any specimens of life on a world that was half furnace and half ice? And did the specimens survive the attack that killed the healer and could have destroyed the shuttle?

Now, Sarissa stepped forward.

"Before coming here, Serevan and I went over the shuttle. No," she held up a hand, thinner than Karatek remembered seeing it. "We were escorted by security. But I—we—found Healer Salvir's last report. He filed it just before Adenkar struck him.

"There was life," she went on. "Nothing large: I should not like to confront a large creature that could survive in that waste. But as his report indicates, he found fossils from three separate species, which argues that there might logically be more. He found them preserved in ice. Then, he indicated he had observed at least thirty-six separate kinds of extremophiles, mostly by the volcanic vents beneath the ice."

"So life can exist on that world."

Sarissa shrugged. "Extremophiles can be found almost anywhere, even in the Womb of Fire, although I understand that the Fire Plains of Raal, at the center of Vulcan's Forge, are said to be truly barren. So this discovery is not as surprising as the creatures' rate of evolution or, as the late *T'Kehr* Salvir preferred to term it, mutation. In 9.3 days, he observed several tens of thousands of generations. Enough to see changes in their genetic makeup as well as physical transformations."

She projected creatures that resembled algae and diatoms on

one wall, then flicked through a series of images. Even with his unassisted eyes, Karatek could discern subtle differences in pigmentation, in morphology.

"I'd like to see a long-term study of this world's impact on species native to Vulcan," said Avarak.

"You would sacrifice . . . "

"You yourself constantly tell us how the needs of the many outweigh the needs of the few. In the interests of science—"

"In the interests of getting down to that hell-spawned world and pillaging it for dilithium and rare metals to repair your precious ships!" snarled N'Evran.

"Are you afraid of it?"

The te-Vikram, a physical match for Serevan himself, rose slowly from his chair. "I was born in the Womb of Fire. On Vulcan, we te-Vikram were used to living on the edge of radiation-poisoned lands. I do not fear that world. It is a place of danger, a test of strength."

"Are you volunteering to live on it?"

"That's no place to live," said T'Olryn. "I wonder if any minerals we find down there are worth the risk to our people."

"An outpost, then," said Vorealt, to approving murmurs from other men and women who had been born during the exile. "Not a home. A temporary mining colony that will enable us to rebuild our ships."

"An outpost facing constant struggle to survive down to our genetic code. It's already been weakened by the years of our journey. If we went down there to live, even temporarily, we might change. . . . Come back in five hundred years, and we might not recognize our descendants."

"Are you that fearful of change? Long before we were tricked into exile, we lived in the desert. We avoided the places where our blood ran thin, our skin blotched, and our children were born mal-formed or too weak to live. And we survived."

"Are you volunteering?"

"No," said the te-Vikram. "I prefer to be somewhere warm. Or is your logic only good for rationalizing and keeping you warm and safe?"

As the shouting began yet again, Karatek indulged himself by closing his eyes, but only briefly.

TWENTY-EIGHT

NOW

**WATRAII HOMEWORLD
STARDATE 54107.8**

Ruanek bit back a sigh of sheer frustration. By now, he thought, all this traveling basically in circles, trying to get back to the installation and at the same time avoid those cursed search parties was truly starting to get to him. And there was the lack of real food (emergency rations, no matter how supposedly nutritious, did not qualify as food as far as he was concerned, and never had), a night spent sleeping on rocks, and of course the never-ending knowledge that precious time was passing without them getting anywhere— all of it was beginning to force him to realize just how long it had been since he'd been in active Romulan military service.

And how little I'd want to return to it. Ah well, as Spock would put it, one does what one can. Not that I'll ever admit to anyone that I'm not exactly the warrior I once was.

But oh, it would be lovely to have one of those perfectly logical and so very effective Vulcan therapeutic massages right now.

Administered by T'Selis, maybe . . . no, then it wouldn't be so . . . ah . . . therapeutic. . . . Well, yes it would be, in a way, but not exactly in the way that . . .

"There," Data announced, cutting into Ruanek's thoughts and pointing (but keeping warily in the shelter of the rocks as he did so). "That is where the artifact is being kept."

A thrill of sharp excitement shot through Ruanek, but he fiercely repressed it. This was not the time to go utterly Romulan, even though it would be really easy to do so by this point. "Ah," he said, leaning over the top of one rock to get a better look. "They aren't about to make this easy for us, are they?"

Data gave a soft, very human-sounding sigh. "It would seem that they are not."

Ahead of them stood a separate building, a thick, square, ugly gray thing, without any sign of charm.

"It's metal." Ruanek shook his head in disbelief. "The cursed thing is made out of metal. One big lightning rod."

"It is a fortified one, as well," Data added.

"Redundant, aren't they? I can spot the main security installations from here," Ruanek said. "They're not exactly trying to hide them. The word is 'obvious.'"

"So are the guards patrolling the building."

"Patrolling at a safe distance." Ruanek glanced at Data. "Those, we can overcome, we both know it. But lightning is another matter. Oh, and I suspect there's even more protecting the place than the obvious." He paused. "Am I right? Is there anything else, Data?"

"Oh yes," the android said after a moment. "There are sensors placed throughout the building . . . and I do believe there is . . . yes, there is a vault lying within it."

"And the artifact's inside *that,* isn't it?" Ruanek shook his head in disgust. "It's like one of those box-within-a-box puzzles I used to get when I was a child. I didn't like those then, either."

"Really? I found such puzzles quite fascinating when I first became sentient."

"Nice to know that you had a—a childhood," Ruanek said, "and toys too—"

"Actually, they were learning devices."

"Toys, learning devices, whatever you wish to call them, it's not exactly a useful fact right now. The artifact isn't going to rescue itself."

"Then perhaps I should be the one to—"

"No!" With a surge of emotion that surprised him both by its suddenness and its sheer intensity, Ruanek exclaimed, "I demand the honor of rescuing the artifact."

Of course you do, his mind whispered to him. The artifact, whatever it might be, had, after all, been the prized possession of his . . . his former people for many centuries. *And you are still, underneath it all,* Ruanek admitted to himself, *even now, even after all this time, even after you have no intention of ever leaving Vulcan, a Romulan.*

It was more than a little disconcerting to realize that fact.

Data didn't even try to argue with him. But then, Ruanek thought, the android had spent some time on Romulus. He'd know something about the Romulan heart and soul. Besides, his emotion chip was functioning. He'd understand.

Sure enough, all Data said after a moment's silence was a matter-of-fact "I can get rid of the guards."

At Ruanek's raised eyebrow, Data gave him a "watch and see" gesture, and then calmly "threw" his voice. In the next moment, Ruanek fought back a purely Romulan grin of enjoyment. How

293

the android was doing this, Ruanek had no idea, since it seemed to be on a wider scale than human ventriloquism, but he could have sworn that not just one but several not very adept and unauthorized visitors were stumbling their way through the rocks on the far side of the stronghold.

He pointed. The guards were clearly upset, muttering to each other and looking about, trying to locate the intruders. Then one of the guards pointed, and the Watraii set off after the intruders.

But one guard stopped for a moment and Ruanek heard " . . . unauthorized personnel . . . " and a series of codes. Word had clearly just been sent to the guards' superiors.

Data and Ruanek exchanged quick glances. "How lovely," Ruanek said. "They've just given us yet another reason to hurry."

"For a Vulcan citizen, you seem rather sarcastic," Data commented.

"For a Starfleet officer, so do you," Ruanek replied. "Can you scramble the security system from here?"

"Some of it, yes. Just a minute, now . . ." Data reactivated his tricorder and started operating it at a speed so great that Ruanek could not make out the android's fingers. "There . . ." he murmured, "and . . . there. One remains functioning—I will need to deactivate that one directly. In addition, it is wise to leave one working as long as possible, so that anyone monitoring the building will not become instantly suspicious."

"Good point. Come on, then, let's see how close we can get before we get electrocuted."

They stopped short just before that one remaining functioning security system could pick them up. "Ah," Data said.

"Ah? Ah what?"

"We have a new worry."

"Now what?"

"Up this close, I realize that the vault is a timed-entry one."

"What of it?" Ruanek asked. "You can still get it open, can't you?"

"Yes," Data said after a few seconds. "But it will take me some precious time to manage the feat. And we both know that the figurative clock is ticking down to the time when, one, the Watraii come in answer to that guard's broadcast, and, two, the *Alexander Nevsky* must lift."

"Then don't waste any of that time in telling me what I already know. Go ahead, get it open."

"Very well . . . a moment more . . . yes." Data smiled in triumph. "I have just scrambled the locks. They were not very complicated machinery after all. You should be able to get in now without either getting caught or having any alarms sounding."

Ruanek ignored that uncertain "should." He gave the overcast sky one wary look, then shrugged and peered into the open vault, not at all sure what he was going to find besides darkness and the eternal gray dust and grit . . .

The artifact! It didn't look particularly Romulan, yet somehow Ruanek knew what he was seeing, knew it deep within his being, even though he had never seen even a picture of it before this moment.

The heart of Romulus, he thought, *the birth of a people . . .*

No, he chided himself in the next moment, *you aren't being logical. It's an artifact, yes, but you have no idea what it really contains.*

But whatever it was, it belonged to all Romulans. That much he did know—and that he was going to get it back for them.

At first glance, the artifact seemed to be merely sitting alone on a small table of the inevitable gray stone. Ruanek had to fight the urge to simply rush in and snatch it up.

"It can't be *that* easy," he said.

"It is not." Data pointed, there, there, and there. "The artifact is guarded by laser beams that will be triggered by the approach of any being."

Ruanek snorted. "How old-fashioned of the Watraii."

"Old-fashioned?"

"It reminds me of the security setup in the late Praetor Dralath's gardens back on Romulus. Well, they failed to save him, and these aren't going to do the Watraii any good, either, not if I have any say in this." He paused thoughtfully. "We can't just shoot out the controls. I'll wager everything that if we did, we'd be sending an alarm to the Watraii. So instead, I'll have to just weave my way through—"

"Wait."

"Now what?"

"It is not that precisely simple, either. There are also active panels that will deliver an electric shock through the floor."

"A fatal shock, of course."

"Of course."

Ruanek sighed. "There would be something along those lines. I still say, how old-fashioned of them."

"Why would they require anything that is more complicated? They would not expect any of their own people to steal it, and presumably they did not think that any intruder would get this far without detection."

"Hah."

"Do you not see my meaning, Ruanek? The real guard, of course, is simply the Watraii climate."

"Right. Only those who have to be out, like those guards, or the completely crazed, like us, would be standing out here, next to a metal building. And yes, that's my Romulan background speaking, complete with emotion, not my Vulcan training. But now, how am I to get in there and get to the artifact?"

"Ruanek," Data said slowly, "I believe that I have an idea. We should be able to use a substitute weight to replace the artifact on the pedestal."

Nodding, Ruanek said, "Weight and counterweight—yes, the counterweight part should be simple enough. There are plenty of rocks of all sizes and weights. As for the way to get me safely in and out of the vault . . ." Ruanek rummaged about in his pack, then said, "Aha," and pulled out a length of thin wire. "I think this is about five meters' worth. How about you? Do you have anything else we can use?"

"I have some wire, too, precisely 9.25 meters in length. Permit me to perform some calculations." Data was silent for a moment, clearly calculating the height of the building, the height of the table on which the artifact lay, and the length of the wire. "Excellent. We have enough wire, and the wire that we have is sufficiently strong for our purposes. And I certainly can safely support your weight while you go after the artifact."

"Now, the only question is, how do I . . . ?" Ruanek frowned thoughtfully and drew out a small emergency light from his pack. "With all those security devices, there has to be something I can use."

He shone the little light around the dark vault. No, nothing but seamless walls. He shone it up toward the top of the vault—

"Oh yes," Ruanek said. "That's just what I need. Data, see those pipes? Think they're strong enough to hold my weight?"

"I cannot do any accurate calculations under the circumstances," Data began, "but I would estimate that if they are as firmly anchored as they seem, then yes, they should be sufficient. But I fail to see how you could get up there."

Ruanek's sudden grin was purely Romulan. "With your help, Data, with your help. Tell me, how's your aim?"

Ruanek clung to the pipe with one leg and one arm, trying not to drop the stone that should—he hoped—be enough to counterbalance the artifact's weight. Data's aim had been perfect. As soon as Ruanek had stepped into Data's clasped hands, the android had catapulted him straight and true right up here. Data, in the doorway, was still holding fast to one end of the wire, and Ruanek began winding the other about his waist, carefully padding it with folds of his clothing so that the wire wouldn't cut him in two.

And let's try not to think about the fact that you're now a living lightning rod within a building that's also a lightning rod.

He tugged once on the wire, testing. Data tugged back: yes, all was well.

All right, here we go.

He tugged twice on the wire and let go of the pipe. The wire caught him about the waist, and Ruanek grunted, twisting about to lock his crossed legs about the wire, too, to ease the strain. Now he was hanging upside down, which wasn't exactly comfortable, but bearable.

Data began to play the wire out slowly, and Ruanek began descending slowly toward the artifact. So far, yes . . . As long as he didn't move too suddenly, the wire shouldn't start swinging . . .

I never was meant to be a thief.

A little farther . . . Ruanek tugged once on the wire, and Data instantly stopped.

No. He couldn't quite reach the artifact. Just a touch more . . . Ruanek tugged once more, waited half a beat, then tugged again. Data began feeding out the wire again, and Ruanek began to lower—

Too low! Ruanek curled frantically up about the wire, trying not to let any of himself come in contact with the floor or the crisscrossing red maze of laser beams.

I really wasn't meant to be a thief.

Somehow he managed to give a tug to the wire, and Data pulled up again. *Let's try that again.*

One very delicate tug; two very delicate tugs . . .

Sure enough, this time Data released just the smallest amount of wire, then stopped again.

Perfect!

Hanging upside down once more, trying not to think about not being as young as he should be for this sort of thing, Ruanek delicately reached out for the artifact. If he hit it too hard, he might knock it over or set himself swinging into one of the electrified walls or the damned laser beams.

He touched it. Missed. Bit his lip as the motion started him swinging. The cursed wire was cutting off his wind, but he had to wait till the movement stopped.

He reached out again, delicately, delicately . . .

Yes. He had the artifact, and the rock in the other hand.

One . . . two . . . three!

It worked! I made the switch! I have the artifact, and the rock's the right weight.

He twisted about in midair and tugged on the wire. Data began to pull him back up again, and Ruanek began to believe that they really were going to get away with this, they really were going to get away with this and—

Just then, lightning cracked down, racing down the metal sides of the building. Ruanek frantically unwound himself from the wire even as he felt the first blaze of fire begin to shock itself along his nerves, and hurled himself blindly toward where the door must be. If he missed, he was dead; if he hit the floor, he was dead; dead either way and it really didn't matter which way—

Then he was outside, hurtling into Data, who caught him and steadied him as behind him the entire building blazed and crackled with blue-white light.

"Close," Ruanek managed to gasp, and then caught his balance again. "Far too close."

"The artifact?"

"I have it." Ruanek looked down at what he held with genuine reverence. Yes, of course it was a vital object, part of his people's very soul. But even if it hadn't been so vitally important, it would still be a beautiful thing, like the ancient relics he'd seen in Vulcan museums, all covered with graceful swirls and engravings that held who knew what secrets.

"Oh."

The single syllable from Data made Ruanek whirl. And freeze in sudden horror.

The blast of lightning had hit the stone table, just hard enough to jar the rock. It rolled, then teetered on the edge of the table for what seemed an agonizing eternity. Ruanek, watching helplessly, found himself trying to silently tell it, *No, stay put, stay put, damn you*—

The rock dropped from the table.

"Oh, now that's just not right!" Ruanek heard himself say, and was amazed at his own foolishness.

Then the world seemed to explode into a roar of alarms going off. Ruanek glanced at Data and hastily stowed the artifact safely into his pack. And ran.

TWENTY-NINE

MEMORY

"It has taken the individual ships' councils approximately 6.2 months to process the data brought back from various exploratory missions," Karatek thought. *"During that time, the fleet has lost one hundred and five people to the hazards of planetary exploration. Lesson learned: respect for planetary hazards. We have forgotten a great deal.*

"Also during this time, only twenty-one children have been born. Of that number, eighteen survive. It takes no regression analysis to indicate that we must reach a decision speedily or population attrition will render us incapable of executing any decision we make.

"S'task has summoned us to a fleetwide council. One positive effect of the missions to the barren world: we have mined and processed sufficient metal to repair at least the shuttles. There is no more talk of leaving this system. I wonder, however, if that represents consensus or simply an acknowledgment that we are out of options."

So close to settlement, the old hostilities and ambitions had kindled and intensified.

Karatek steepled his fingers and gazed over them at the amphitheater. Once, this particular room had been used for lectures that were expected to draw only a moderate crowd. Now, it could hold *Shavokh*'s entire surviving population. It was warm, not just from their body heat but because the ship's renewed fuel supply made it possible to heat it to levels approximating the average surface temperature on the world most people were beginning to think of as their new home. With the shuttles repaired, S'task had ordered deliveries of fruits and grains from the larger world's surface. (Karatek suspected a covert trade in meat, as well, to those who had rejected Surak's teachings or never adopted them. Because no healers had complained, he had deliberately taken no notice. There were times when leaders had to be aware, yet look away.)

Only a few people were absent: one healer tending a woman in labor; the pilot; the engineer on watch. But even they linked in to the discussion, which was broadcast to each of the surviving ships.

"Now that we have demonstrated our ability to restore the ships to their original conditions," said Vorealt, serving as a delegate both from engineering and the spaceborn, "I see no reason to leave them. The fleet has decided to remain in this system? Well enough. I have spoken to the other members of my family as well as to the families of others who were born during the journey. You call these ships 'exile.' We call them home. We can trade our ability to centralize records, to maintain and operate laboratories and manufacturing processes for which physical purity is necessary— without even the potential for contamination from an organic world—for whatever foodstuffs we cannot grow for ourselves.

And for ores, metals, even finished parts. If you agree to trade, here we are, and here we remain."

He smiled sharply at the others in the compartment.

"I do not think that the rest of you will decide where you wish to be as easily," he said, then reached for a steaming cup. With power renewed, they had restored hydroponics. Once again, they could enjoy tea, not as a rare luxury, but as an amenity of civilized meetings.

"What do people think of S'task's proposal that we draw lots to allocate land on the two worlds?" Karatek asked.

"That might work well on the more hospitable world, although I would ask what happens to the clans who draw the firefalls or part of a desert?"

"We would be glad of desert lands," said N'Maret. Newly appointed elder among the te-Vikram, she was the first woman to hold that office in her own right, rather than through her sons. "It appears poor in relation to the rest of the planet, but it offers access to water such as we have never known. And," she added with a glint that made Karatek pay closer attention, "I would assume that if desert land is considered less desirable, there could be compensations. Such as a larger area, or rights-of-way to the oceans."

"And who would be willing to live in ice or fire?" asked Evoras, with his customary incisiveness. "My colleagues will, as usual, condemn my illogic, but it is a pity we cannot combine the two worlds. We could, if people would consent to establishing an outpost, say, in the narrow band between the bright side and the ice, but . . . I have been speaking to several of those who wish to remain on board the ships. They favor enlarging the tunnels that have already produced such fine ores and crystals and would offer to trade technology that, thus far, can only be produced on board the ships."

Vorealt positively grinned as he rose to back Evoras. "No doubt," he added, "we would indeed be glad enough to sell advanced computer components or medicinals to you, but, because these products are time-consuming to create, we will be unable to produce these commodities in quantities sufficient to bring down the price. That will give us an economic advantage." His smile broadened. "I can see a day when everyone who remains on board the ships could have substantial estates on the world below. Assuming we wanted them."

"But there is indeed metal downworld," Serevan reminded his colleague. "The problem is getting at it. We could develop technologies for tapping the planet's core, although I would prefer not to speculate what would happen if an accident occurred. At best, a second firefalls. At worst, we might crack the planet wide open."

T'Neithan shook her head. "Unless we break up one of the ships, we haven't the metal for it, or for evolving ceramics technology sufficient to compensate for the limited metals. Given our current level of mining technology, I project that in 108.3 years, we would face the job of either restoring the habitable world—our new home—to its pristine state or seeking another planet altogether. On ethical issues, I would oppose a society predicated on consuming worlds, then moving on. We suffered the effects of that on Vulcan. It was deforested even in our day."

There was no point in thinking what had happened to Vulcan after so many years.

"And we have already decided that we are staying in this system!" Vorealt pointed out.

T'Olryn rose. "Do you not see the blind spot in your reasoning? Even at our current technological level, and without additional resources from any offworld mining operation, my opinion is that we can live better here than we did on Vulcan. This planet may be poor in minerals, but it is rich in living resources: fruits, berries, leguminous plants, and high-protein grain. For those of you"—her face took on a look of almost imperceptible disdain—"who consent to eat meat, the seas teem with fish, and the specimens you examined do not appear to contain any biohazards—although I would not want to hypothesize what they might do to your great-grandchildren."

"And your point is?"

"Simplicity. You yourself have already described the ships as a surviving repository of technology."

"Those weren't the words I would have chosen, but, yes . . ."

"Let us reason together. If the ships are in a superior technological position, they would remain dependent on the products created on the planet and for those resources that it can supply. If an exchange is possible, and if the ships are going to mine, why need we seek a high level of technology on the planet below?"

Vorealt shouted for recognition, backed by Avarak. Healers feared no one, but T'Olryn sat down quickly, lest Solor take up her cause.

She raised her eyebrows as mutterings of agreement, even of enthusiasm, also were heard from the blocs of seats where the te-Vikram customarily gathered. Many had brought young children, and they had more young children than any other family group. They made no secret of their belief that life on board the great ships was unnatural; they were eager to settle downworld and increase the size of their families on land that could support them.

Another problem in the generations to come, Karatek thought.

Avarak leapt to his feet, visibly furious. "The people I speak for want to live as we did on Vulcan, not gather fruit and nuts and look at the great *Shavokh* in the sky! Your lecture on ethical primitivism is presumptuous. Besides which, I should think you would consider it illogical to change the subject, which is, simply, this: there are not enough minerals, let alone minerals close enough to the surface, for us to create and sustain a technological civilization or even the simpler, agrarian culture you advocate. Our supply of metal is strictly limited, because we would oppose plans to cannibalize one of the ships. Which one? Would you see *Shavokh* broken up? How about *Rea's Helm,* our flagship? Even if we did, what would happen when that metal wore out, as it will when exposed to a natural environment? We only delay the problem, not solve it."

"There is," Serevan said, "the other world."

Just because Karatek meditated every day and scrutinized every thought in the hope of expanding his mastery of his emotions, he hadn't lost them, or the ability to perceive the emotions of others. Every time anyone mentioned the two-faced world, people's faces and body language changed. Anger rose as if zenite fumes had seeped into the council meeting. But this wasn't a matter of an industrial accident; hearing Serevan, who had survived the disastrous first mission to the dark side, speak of living there as a possibility aroused two emotions: fear and greed.

"Look," Serevan said, "our initial hypothesis was to build in the twilight zone, but seismic analysis showed too many planetary stresses all along it. So, we fell back on a next-best strategy: enlarging the excavations that my—" He paused, visibly struggling to control himself. "—mission initiated. We could establish a hermetically sealed area, hardened against quakes and cave-ins. From the elements trapped in the ice, we could distill water, create a breathable atmosphere, and set up hydroponics, although I suspect any mining facility would always depend on resources from the ship and the other world. If one were resigned to the hardships, I daresay people could manage living there for a short time."

"Who would willingly live in that ice?" cried N'Maret of the te-Vikram.

"I observe for the record," began Avarak, "that Serevan has established a working hypothesis for a colony, but failed to follow it to its logical conclusion: some of us are better than others in adapting to the hardships of that environment. When the zenite fumes jeopardized that mission, did you not see what I saw? That the two people who withstood the fumes and were able to bring the shuttle back were both students of Surak's *Analects?* Not, of course, to mention part of *T'Kehr* Karatek's family."

Sarissa rose too and leaned forward on the table. "Are you implying that *T'Kehr* Karatek was guilty of favoritism in assigning my consort and me to that mission? That is absurd."

Her voice fell to the sort of hiss that Karatek had just once heard a *le-matya* make before it screamed and leapt upon its prey. And she had to have heard that Avarak had accused Karatek of nepotism when he had ordered out the mission to rescue Solor's crew.

"Sarissa," Karatek spoke softly.

"I ask forgiveness."

"Granted, but it is time to seat yourself again."

Karatek rose. "Even a child would discern your implications, but I cannot dismiss them because they are logical. Serevan, am I correct that you propose establishing an installation under the ice and having it staffed by people working for, say, however many days, then being ferried off-planet, either back to the ships or to the other world?"

"Correct, sir. That would enable us to exploit one world's natural resources without damaging the other's biosphere or subjecting one group of people to genetic damage."

Karatek nodded. Logic was good for many things, but very bad for evading responsibility when it was placed in one's path. Night and day, he did not want to go back to the bad old days of radiation badges, quakes, and constant watchfulness back on Vulcan. He had renounced Vulcan as a way of trying to save it from being slagged in thermonuclear war: he had no desire to see this pristine new world gutted by strip-mining or cracked by using half-fledged deep-mining techniques. But he had been a city-dweller; the idea of a simple, agrarian lifestyle did not appeal to him.

Some people had to settle on the cold world. Some had to settle there first. Avarak could not have given him and his family more of a challenge had he stood up at Solor's *Kal-if-fee,* struck the gong, and challenged for possession of the woman T'Olryn—as he had, indeed, once threatened to do.

"With position," Karatek forced himself to breathe more easily, "comes responsibility. I have heard imputations that my family has traded on any status I might have as a leader on board this ship. To demonstrate that this is not the case, I speak now as Head of House. Given Serevan's engineering expertise, I consider it only logical that he lead the first detachment of miners. My entire House will join him. I would urge those others who follow Surak's teachings to follow us because our control renders us most able to follow decontamination procedures and emergency drills, and least vulnerable to industrial accidents such as those that jeopardized the shuttle."

He sat down, deliberately ignoring the murmurs of awe and regret, as if someone had just volunteered to rappel down the chasm that divided the peaks of Mount Seleya and test the magma that perpetually seethed below.

Have I been maneuvered into making this offer?

That does not matter, he told himself. It was the right thing to do. Even if he longed to rest in the beauty and security of a hard-won planet.

He did not need S'task's murmur of approval through the transmitter he wore to know that. He had long passed the need for that level of approbation.

But Karatek could make that decision only for himself.

"I trust," he said, "that while my House and those allied to it labor for the benefit of all, those of you living in the open air will treat us fairly. It would be just if land were not only set aside for us, but if some of you began to improve it against our return."

Let N'Maret see that she was not the only one who was able to bargain!

THIRTY

NOW

"There," Spock said as he and Chekov struggled out of the installation. Chekov's initial wild burst of energy was long gone. By
now, he clearly couldn't hurry on any farther, and his eyes blazed
with the frustration of knowing it.

But we don't have to run, or even walk, Spock thought with a
sudden flash of relief.

He wasn't certain what type of vehicle was sitting on the gravel
ahead of them. He knew only that it had already been started and
presumably ran on electricity. Chekov, still clinging to his stolen
Watraii weapons, used them to dispatch both Watraii who'd been
staffing the vehicle with two quick blasts of fire and such casual
ease that it almost alarmed Spock. He all but threw Chekov up into
one of the seats and took what was clearly the driver's seat.

310

And then he and Chekov were speeding over the rocky landscape. The weather was growing increasingly worse, the sky darkening more than usual and the air prickling as though a major storm might be stirring, and the time allotted for the shuttle to lift off the Watraii homeworld was growing alarmingly close.

Where are Ruanek and Data? Spock wondered. *They must surely be as aware of the passing time as well. Where are they?*

All around Ruanek and Data, the whole Watraii world seemed to have gone mad with a deafening clanging and wailing of alarms.

"Do not stop now, Ruanek," Data exclaimed. "We must get away from the entire—"

"It doesn't matter."

"It does matter. Ruanek, if we do not get away from this area, right now, we are going to be—"

"Look, let's agree to something here and now."

"What?"

"All right, we have alarms going off all over the place. We have search parties coming after us. We even have the artifact in our possession." With that, Ruanek's hand shot to his pack to make sure that the artifact actually was still in his possession. "And now, the Outer Dark take it all, we have accomplished our mission and we are going to go rescue Spock and Pavel Chekov."

"Agreed," Data said without hesitation. "However, I have been unable to locate Ambassador Spock's transponder with the tricorder."

"That's all right—we know where they're being held. Besides, I have a plan."

"I . . . see." Data was clearly not particularly heartened by this news, but he said, "Go on."

"Well, this is one of the oldest tricks around, and I suspect every adventure vid on every planet with adventure vids has used it, but I doubt that the Watraii, isolated as they are, will ever have heard of it."

"Ruanek, please. Your plan."

"Remember those Watraii that we took out?"

"Of course—oh." Data blinked. "Do you truly believe that we can get away with such an ancient ruse as—"

"It's worth a gamble," Ruanek retorted. "Come on!"

He raced with Data back to the search team that they had eliminated. "Here," Ruanek said, "this one should fit you." He'd lost any squeamishness years ago as a Romulan soldier. "Ah, and this one should fit me. A mask for you, Data." He paused, studying the android. "Yes, that's perfect. You really do look like a Watraii, no insult meant." He slipped on a mask himself. Ugh, it was clammy and chill. Heavy, too, far heavier than he would have expected to look at the things. And the Watraii wore these things every day.

"Very well," Ruanek said, "let's join up with the others and hope there aren't any secret Watraii passwords or handshakes. Once we break Spock and Admiral Chekov out," Ruanek rushed on, glossing over the details of how they could do that, "we'll head for Scotty and the shuttle."

And if this gamble works, it will still be there.

If not, and they were stranded here . . . well, Ruanek thought, you couldn't win every wager.

They fell in with the first group of Watraii they found, trying to march with exactly the same precision as the others. This was surprisingly easy.

Almost too easy, Ruanek thought.

But they didn't get as far as the installation's door. Their group

312

was met by an officer—or so Ruanek assumed—who snapped, "The prisoners are missing!"

That could only be Spock and Chekov.

Too easy, indeed.

The officer was staring at him. What was it, he wondered, what made him look different from everyone else? "You," the officer snapped. "Code!"

"Ah, sorry, I don't remember. Got hit in the head—and you're not buying that, are you?"

As the Watraii closed in about them, Ruanek tore off his mask and used the heavy thing as a weapon, flailing about with it. Data followed suit. Apparently what they were doing was so against tradition it was almost sacrilegious, and the others backed off in shock—

"Come on, Data!"

They didn't have a chance of making it all the way back to the *Alexander Nevsky,* not on foot and with the Watraii in close pursuit. But dammit, Ruanek thought, they were going to do their best. And at the least, well, he'd come a long way since being Ruanek of House Minor Strevon, but at least he could still face the Last Review unafraid if it came to that.

T'Selis, I love you.

The Watraii vehicle had been designed to get over rough terrain, but the climb up to the butte was almost too much for it. The engine whined and complained, and no matter how Spock tried to increase its speed, the vehicle slowed almost to a crawl.

I can almost hear Jim's voice: "Scotty, you've got to give us just a little more power." Yes, and Scotty's voice pleading with him, "Captain, the engines willna stand the strain!"

But now he actually *could* hear Scotty. The human had come part of the way down the slope to meet them, and between Spock

313

and Scotty, they all but carried the exhausted Chekov out of the car and up to the top of the butte.

The vehicle, with complete lack of drama, simply sputtered out behind them and was silent.

"That's about the way I feel," Chekov muttered. "I see Spock dragged you into this mess as well, Mr. Scott."

"Aye, that he did. 'Tis good to see you, lad."

"'Lad'? I'm older than you now, *Captain.*"

Scotty chuckled. "That you are, Admiral, that you are. Let's be getting you onto the shuttle." As Spock and Scotty guided Chekov toward the *Alexander Nevsky,* Scotty asked, "What about the others?"

"There are others?" Chekov asked. "It wasn't just you two?"

"No," Spock said. "Admiral Uhura gave us our mission, though it is not one officially sanctioned by Starfleet Command. Captain Saavik awaits us in orbit on the *Alliance,* and Uhura also assigned us Lieutenant Commander Data of the *Enterprise* and a . . . friend named Ruanek."

"We cannot desert them," Chekov said with as much finality as his frail voice would allow.

"No, we cannot," Spock agreed. "Never again. We will retrieve them. I give you my word."

As they fastened their safety harnesses, Spock took the controls, and the shuttle lifted off. As it climbed back up through the winds and the layers of clouds, Spock told Scotty, "Locate the transponders for Data and Ruanek."

A faint voice, half hidden by static, broke through. *"Spock? . . . is . . . you . . . ?"*

"Saavik. Yes. I have Captain Scott and Admiral Chekov with me. But Ruanek and Data are still planetside."

"Understood." Another burst of static, and then, *". . . here . . . repeat, come back here . . . transport them . . . break in the weather . . ."*

"Understood," Spock said.

The trip out from the planet was hardly easy, but not nearly as rough as the trip planetside had been. Even so, Spock heard himself give a small sigh of relief as the shuttle finally passed the planet's atmospheric envelope and settled into the smoothness of space.

Scotty let out a whistle. "Would you look at that! They've been in a battle, sure enough. Poor ship, with that ugly scorch mark on its side."

Soon they were back on board the *Alliance,* being hastily briefed by Saavik.

"My science officer reports that a break is occurring in the Watraii storms. Apparently this is a rarity, but it should provide a sufficient window of opportunity for us to beam Data and Ruanek aboard—if the ship's approach is very close."

"I'm off to the transporter room," Scotty announced. "This is one beam-up that I am going to handle myself!"

On the bridge, Spock settled into his chair beside Saavik's command chair. Chekov, refusing flatly to go to sickbay, settled into the other.

Saavik's quick brush of a hand against Spock's let him know— as if he'd had any doubts—how thankful she was that he was back and in one piece.

"Helm, take us in. And yes, those are the proper coordinates. We'll be able to make only one low pass before the Watraii realize what's happening and start firing. But that should be enough time to beam up our two shipmates."

It will be, Spock told himself. *With Scotty at the transporter controls, it will be.*

"Ah, Ruanek?"

Ruanek, panting, turned, turned again, then stopped with a resigned sigh. The Watraii had them surrounded.

"Ah well," he said to Data with a Romulan grin, "it was a gallant adventure! We die with—"

But before he could say "honor," a familiar shimmering surrounded Data and him . . .

. . . and they were beamed up.

"Got them!" Scotty crowed. But then he added to Data and Ruanek, "Hang on, both of you. They're shooting at us."

"Strap in," came the shipwide warning. *"All personnel, strap in."*

On the bridge, Saavik put the *Alliance* into a steep climb, out of the edge of the atmosphere, dodging the continuing flashes of garish green ground-to-air fire and not retaliating. Once out of the atmosphere, she ordered, "Shields and cloaking up at full. I assume that we *do* have cloaking again?" she added. "Yes? Excellent."

"Watraii ships launching," Lieutenant Abrams warned.

The *Alliance* sped away for the system perimeter, the two Klingon ships with them once more and the Watraii ships in pursuit.

"We are clear," Lieutenant Abrams announced.

"Very good," Saavik said. "Go to warp three. Get us out of here. And you, Admiral Chekov, to sickbay."

Chekov started to speak, then lowered his head, his breathing labored. "I regret to say, Captain, that I do not have the strength to argue with you—which is all the more reason to report to sickbay. I don't suppose you have Dr. McCoy waiting for me down there?"

"No, simply my chief medical officer."

"Thank God for small favors," Chekov muttered as he entered the turbolift.

Once in deep space, the *Alliance* returned to sublight, waiting for the two Klingon ships to rejoin them.

"Once again, Captain Saavik," JuB-Chal announced, *"you have given us a glorious fight."*

Tor'Ka added, *"It will be joyous to join you in battle again."*

"So be it," Saavik said carefully.

Spock glanced up as the bridge door slid open. Chekov stepped onto the bridge—a Chekov looking healed of a wound he might not have even known he had.

"Don't look at me like that, Spock. The doctor has given me a clean bill of health. There is nothing that sleep, a good meal, and some vodka won't cure."

"Would you like to order the *Alliance* home, Admiral?" Saavik asked politely.

"No, Captain Saavik, that von't be necessary." With a courtly smile and the slightest of bows, Chekov added, "Consider me formally retired as of two months ago. And let me say that I will be glad to get home."

Ruanek, standing behind Spock, was all but radiating contentment: He had received a belated message from T'Selis that had come as close as a Vulcan could come to expressing her love for him.

But the problem of the artifact, and deciphering the artifact, remained.

For now, Spock thought, the artifact would surely be safest on Vulcan. Saavik had, indeed, already ordered that course change to be made.

But I would not be surprised to learn that Romulan Tal Shiar agents have noted that course change, and are already sending that news to Romulus. The near future promises to be . . . fascinating.

But at that moment, Lieutenant Abrams cut in urgently, "We're not alone. Captain, what looks like the entire Watraii fleet is coming after us."

THIRTY-ONE

MEMORY

"Three years after I took it upon myself to volunteer my House to establish a mining colony on the less hospitable of our two new worlds, we have made what progress we could without actually taking up residence. The time to move has come.

"For the past three years, the fleet has helped those of us who will be the colony's inhabitants for the first six months after it goes officially online create a habitat that is, at its worst, no colder and no more comfortless than Shavokh *during the journey. I am told that when our rotation is over, we will be able to look forward to settling on land where a prefabricated house has already been built. And I will have had the satisfaction of laying down my role here on* Shavokh, *having fulfilled all my responsibilities in accordance with the dictates of my conscience."*

Ending his last transmission on board *Shavokh*, Karatek removed the coronet, secured it in its case, and tucked it into his shipsuit. He had tested it: it would fit into his environmental suit as well.

T'Vysse and the rest of his family attended him in the living areas of their quarters. Although the rooms were stripped bare, they would take only a few personal possessions, the most useful or most cherished, with them to the mining facility. The rest, they had been assured, would be ferried to the new home being prepared for them on the northern continent, within sight of the mountains and the sea. Solor had assured him of the site's beauty as well as its richness.

After three years, Karatek would have thought himself accustomed to making the journey out of *Shavokh* down to the ice. The few shuttles that remained functioned at least adequately. The pilot touched down more smoothly than usual. On the last trip, Serevan had installed stabilizers beneath the field. They too were in satisfactory operating condition.

Sealing the helm of his environmental suit, Karatek led his family out of the battered shuttle and activated its light, which cast a deceptively warm glow over the ice and frozen gases. The outpost would retain this shuttle and two more, along with an array of smaller craft, including one dagger.

When his eyes grew accustomed to the encompassing darkness, he led the way across the landing field to the seal that opened into the tunnels beneath the ice. Most of the settlers finally had mastered the art of navigating across ice. Nevertheless, it was a long walk on deceptive and harsh terrain. He was panting before they had gone halfway.

Initially, Karatek had protested the distance between the landing site and the habitat, but he had been overruled. The shuttles were old, he had been told. Until they could be replaced with shuttles built from metal produced from the veins of ore beneath his feet, it was only prudent to put distance between the landing field and the colony's inhabitants. And as the colony grew, Serevan had argued, it would expand its system of tunnels, potentially undermining the field: hence, the need for stabilizers that would, if all went well, have to be enforced.

Karatek had yielded to the logic of necessity as well as his son-in-law's greater expertise. Nevertheless, it was a long, cold walk. Karatek watched T'Vysse turn to stare at the silvery plume erupting from a nitrogen vent. Sarissa put an arm around her mother, steadying her against the frozen ripples of ice. Their boots crunched against it, a counterpoint to the rhythm of their breathing and the rapid beating of their hearts.

Ahead of them, crew from *Shavokh* and *Gorget* finished unloading supplies that had been calculated to last them six months with ease, or eight months with austerity, in case accidents or weather conditions on the other world prevented relief. They settled the last canisters in place, then headed back toward their own shuttles.

As the bulky figures in envirosuits passed Karatek like great lumbering creatures, each with one glowing eye, he nodded greetings and thanks. They had darkened their faceplates to preserve their night sight; he could not see who hurried past. Karatek understood: the way the wind was picking up, there was likely to be a storm, with visibility dropping to zero. He picked up the pace. Serevan had gone on ahead and was already unsealing the outer entrance to the habitat that would be "home" for the next six months.

Bleak it might be, but its heat and air would be welcome after the long walk. Karatek was in the first lift down. He and his family unhelmed immediately after the pale, silvery doors slid shut and air pressure equalized.

Even before they took their personal belongings to the quarters they knew were theirs, they went to the operations center, a much smaller version of *Shavokh*'s central installation, to watch the shuttles take off, leaving steam, then pools of glittering melt that quickly froze again on the landing field.

Sarissa glanced at the screens and the readouts below them, then came to full alertness.

"Husband, their engines," she asked. "Have they failed to achieve escape velocity?"

"They're past it," Serevan said. "They're turning. They're all turning."

"Shuttle One, can you hear me?" Already, Sarissa was calling out to the shuttles.

"Do you require assistance?" That was Serevan, as if his deep voice could penetrate the rock, the ice, and the storm building up on the surface.

Then Karatek glanced over at T'Vysse. The expression on her face made his blood chill as if he stood naked on the surface of the planet as the wind lashed him.

If anyone understood the violence of Vulcan's history, it was T'Vysse. But that did not stop her from crying out in horror as the massed shuttles opened fire on the tiny colony's shuttles, exposed on the landing field so far away from any help.

To Karatek's own horror, surface scanners showed four or five suited figures—it was hard to tell, given how the wind blew ice crystals and plumes across the desolation—burst from the entrance and race toward the landing field, just as the shuttles targeted the small ships. One figure, faster than the others, was caught by the blast and sent flying. It landed hard and moved no more as the enemies with whom they had journeyed through the long night of the Sundering from Vulcan stranded them on the ice.

"So that's why they wanted the field so far away from living quarters," Sarissa murmured, her voice as cold as the storm outside. "Logical."

The landing field had been created to be a killing ground that gave their betrayers the opportunity to take out any ships before the mining colonists could get them into the air.

"Karatek?" The technocrat's face appeared on-screen, pallid and somewhat blurred thanks to the perpetual storms overhead.

"It's Shuttle One," Sarissa said.

"Karatek here, Avarak. What do you think you're doing?"

"A rhetorical question, surely. You were quick enough to take all the credit for volunteering for this colony and make certain you'd get the best of anything being distributed on our new homeworld, weren't you? Well, I simply changed the terms of the transaction."

How controlled Avarak was, as if he too had studied Surak's disciplines. And how very sure of himself, now that his ships could exploit the gravity well to menace Karatek and his people.

"Call off your shuttles!" Karatek ordered. "We have people out there!"

"Call them back, or we will blast the rest of them where they stand!" All the younger man's carefully manufactured urbanity was gone. What came through was arrogance and sheer menace.

At a wave of Avarak's hand to an unseen subordinate, their third and final shuttle exploded. A moment later, two more of the single-person ships lit smaller fires.

"Call them back, *Karatek!"*

He heard a scuffle behind him. It took little logic to conclude that Serevan was wrestling someone to the floor—Solor, Karatek assumed—to prevent him, too, from rushing outside.

Another of his people had actually gotten the dagger off the ice.

With a spectacular disregard for personal survival, the pilot aimed directly at Shuttle One, clearly with intent to ram. The dagger, too, disappeared in one blast.

"Stop!" Karatek cried, not to the shuttles overhead, but to their own people. "Get back in here."

"The landing field will have to be repaired," Avarak said. He allowed himself a sharp grin. *"In addition to fulfilling your initial mining quotas and expanding the habitat."*

"S'task," T'Vysse whispered. "He cannot know. Or can he?"

S'task was ill, aged before his time. In delegating function, he had ceded some authority and lost valuable information. Karatek would not believe that the fleet's commander could betray them.

"Does S'task know of this treachery?" Karatek demanded.

"Does it matter?" came the reply. *"We will keep him busy until he falls ill again. He may not even notice. So, pay attention to what I say now. We are about to transmit your final instructions for the next six months. You will see that we are modifying the quotas in view of repairs to the field and the need to establish your infrastructure downworld. We would not wish to be unreasonable."*

Another blast from Shuttle One knocked out their principal communications facility. Avarak's face disappeared. Karatek took a deep breath, wishing it had been he who had blotted it from existence.

"When you have assembled the ore, crystals, and processed metals specified in our orders to you, you will signal us. Our shuttles will come and pick it up in return for supplies of food, structural materials, and medical supplies. If you fall short of quotas, the amounts of supplies we will off-load will be proportionately reduced. If there is a catastrophic failure of a reactor or some natural calamity damages the habitat, you will signal us. Otherwise, you will keep silent, and you will follow the instructions I have now sent you."

"We barely have power enough to send out those signals," Serevan muttered.

Avarak and his associates had planned well. With communications so sharply restricted, this colony had no chance of appealing to S'task or more reasonable members of the exile living on their brother world.

In addition to betraying Karatek and his family, Avarak had made victims out of some exiles and accomplices out of others. In the years to come of this second exile from what should have been his home, Karatek would remember. Memory had always been his duty. And, until reparations were made, he would not forgive.

The ice overhead shuddered, a sharp quake, followed by aftershocks. Overhead raged the storm, the first of the many they must survive until they took back what was theirs.

Static hissed, disrupting communications again. Then, as reception improved, Avarak's face came back into focus, and Karatek heard his voice, assured, arrogant, and enjoying himself far too much.

"You will expand the current habitat. You will harden the landing field to receive ore transports, and you will keep yourselves fit so you can work.

"You will work, or you will die."

TO BE CONCLUDED IN
VULCAN'S SOUL, BOOK III
EPIPHANY